THE
GAME
WARDENS

THE
GAME
WARDENS

D A N   H A Y D E N

THE GAME WARDENS

iUniverse books may be ordered through booksellers or by contacting:

iUniverse
1663 Liberty Drive
Bloomington, IN 47403
www.iuniverse.com
1-800-Authors (1-800-288-4677)

ISBN: 978-1-4917-8195-1 (sc)
ISBN: 978-1-4917-8194-4 (e)

Library of Congress Control Number: 2015920090

Print information available on the last page.

iUniverse rev. date: 12/18/2015

This book is dedicated to my three sons, Danny, Chris, and Mike, for all their patience, suggestions, and footwork that helped to get the book completed.

All the technical help with computers, late night discussions regarding characters, and the workability of different scenarios were greatly appreciated.

"The probability that we may fail in the struggle ought not to deter us from the support of a cause we feel to be just."

– Abraham Lincoln

PREFACE

Most people will never get the opportunity to witness nature, our greatest gift, for its true beauty. It may be because of a result of their accepted daily routine, or what their purpose in life has led them to. It is my opinion these reasons boil down to time constraints and added responsibilities, self- imposed or otherwise.

It is the purpose of this book to bring out some of those natural gifts like beautiful sunrises and sunsets, accompanied by the associated colors and natural aromas, and the sounds that are so basic and natural but often overlooked.

Someone once said that when something is bothering you to go for a walk and the problem won't be there when you get back. This phrase has worked for me, time and again, in my personal as well as my professional career, as you may see in the following chapters. When I enter a forest and pass through the tree line, it is as if a curtain has just closed behind me and the regular world of ringing telephones, honking cars, and general dysfunctions are shut out. Only the naturalness of the forest, in all of its simplicity and quietude is there to soothe my tortured mind.

Nature has its own rules and everyone is invited to this world, no matter who they are or what title they hold in life. The same gifts are there for all. However, there are those people that choose to disrespect those rules and take these gifts for granted. When this happens our natural resources are endangered. Without some kind of regulatory effort, these resources can be lost, ruined, or become extinct. Game Wardens, Fish and Game Officers, and Conservation Officers are just some of the labels given to the keepers of such laws. Names like "Woods Cop, Duck Cop, and Fish Cop are some of the connotations given to this breed of regulator probably out of spite or malice, but a disciplinarian is never popular.

Even so, this brand of individual is there to ensure that all the wonders that encompass our natural resources is kept in its most natural state for everyone to enjoy.

The other idea is to consider the rights of the inhabitants that live in this kind of environment. What we consider "the woods" or "the river," is what some of these creatures call home. Those creatures have a right to live their lives in their natural environment as we humans do in our towns and cities.

I have been in the woods and on the river at every given hour of a twenty-four hour day, under every condition imaginable, and because of this was allowed to witness some of the most beautiful and awe inspiring events possible. It is these events that I have tried to bring out while discussing some of the scenarios that threaten nature and our natural resources.

Dan Hayden
Author, THE GAME WARDENS
August 2015

CHAPTER 1

"Come on Dad, put a worm on my hook." A little boy's father stood on the bank of the town pond and watched his five year old son swing his long bamboo pole onto the shore line. Attached to the end of the pole was a white string with a bobber, sinker and wormless hook. The father replied, "You gotta put your own worm on 'cause if the game warden sees me, I'll get pinched."

The sun was setting across the small town pond. Its orange red glow cast a serene shine upon the placid water. The little boy stood in a ditch carved into the pond's bank. His dad gave him a new worm and he baited the hook.

Soon, the boy was fishing again but in this little lad's mind, he couldn't understand what a game warden was and more than that, why would this game warden want to pinch his father's skin and hurt him. The boy's bobber went down and he pulled in a little orange pumpkinseed, beginning another fishing career.

This was the memory game warden Sam Moody envisioned as he walked his patrol around the same pond he'd fished as a child. In fact, he caught his first fish here. He paused for a moment to gaze across the pond to the place where he and his dad had fished so long ago. One of the things he liked so much about this particular place was the sunsets and how the sun cast its last futile rays across the water. Suddenly, his day dreaming was interrupted, "Uh, excuse me officer, but is it against the law for me to bait my kid's hook? I don't have a fishin' license. I'm just showin' him how to fish." Officer Sam Moody replied, "Depends. Are you really teaching him or is he just holding the pole for you?" The father said, "What do you mean?" "Well," replied Moody, "If you're really showing him how to correctly bait that hook, and how to cast that line, and what to do when the bobber begins to bob, I'd say you are teaching him…and that's not against the law. But, if you're just baiting his hook, throwing the line in and letting him hold the pole until he hooks into one, then reeling it in for him, I'd say you're breaking the law." Moody looked at the man. He was in his mid-thirties, about 5'-10", needed a shave and hadn't found his comb all day. He wore what the rest of the Fish and Game Officers referred to as a "wife beater" sweater, described as a sweat shirt worn inside out with the sleeves missing. His sneakers were old and ripped and his breath smelled of alcohol. *Now,* Sam thought, *it's not illegal to drink or dress a certain way to fish but this character is sending me a message.* Sam figured this guy was just the type that would use his kid to take some fish, but after all, he did ask.

"Okay", the father said, "I get the message." The father and son continued to fish the pond. Officer Moody gave the two-some a cursory glance now and then but never saw the father touch the kid's pole again. In fact, it appeared the father paid more attention to his son's fishing technique than before but maybe that was just his imagination. Sam's thoughts began to drift back as to how he got started in this business of Fish and Game.

Unlike most Connecticut towns, the little town of Thompson had their own Fish and Game Unit. The unit was comprised of a complement of state certified game wardens attached to the Thompson Police Department and reported directly to the Chief of Police.

Like all other Fish and Game Units, it had a complement of several officers. There was a Captain, one Lieutenant, three Sergeants, and two Corporals. The remaining officers without rank were simply Fish and Game Officers. The officers with rank all had extra duties assigned them in addition to their normal Fish and Game responsibilities. The higher the rank, the greater the responsibility. There were fifteen officers in all, each one having a special talent or character trait that made him part of this special breed of law enforcement officer.

Sam had always admired this kind of cop. They weren't like regular cops. Fish and game officers presided over every animal's welfare and the natural resources that allowed them to live their life in a natural way. It was these resources that could so easily be squandered by uncaring or unthinking sportsmen.

Thinking back, Sam remembered that he applied for a spot on the unit in February fifteen years ago. His interview with a panel of wardens came in April. Waiting for that interview was one of the most unsettling periods of his life. Interview day began as a bright day but cold. Sam was up early anticipating different questions and scenarios the wardens might present him with. He sat at the kitchen table and stared into the black coffee. The more he thought about the interview the more worried he became. Finally, it was time to go. Arrival at Police Headquarters only increased his anxiety level. The desk sergeant led Sam to a small room to wait his turn. Before leaving, the Sergeant gave him a little smile that really began to worry him. The waiting was almost unbearable. His stomach was in knots and he began to get a headache. *What if they ask me something personal? Do they expect me to answer or will they just be testing my character?* When the waiting became too much Sam realized he was beginning to psyche himself out. He told himself, *that's it. I'm just going in there and whatever happens, happens.* Just then a Sergeant came in, smiled and said, "Your turn." Sam knew he was rising out of the chair, he felt his legs taking him to the panel of wardens but it seemed like he was watching the whole thing from afar.

As he entered the interrogation room he saw a long mahogany table with four wardens in full dress uniform sitting behind it. On the other side, about fifteen feet from the table was one lonely chair. He walked up to the chair, faced the panel and the warden with the most brass, a lieutenant. He acknowledged Sam with, "Welcome, please have a seat."

The lieutenant introduced himself as Lieutenant Alban, and with him were Sergeants Hunter, Smalls, and Brainard. Sam was told to just relax and answer the questions.

As the interview continued, Sam felt that he was going into too much detail but couldn't stop himself. It was his nerves and knew the panel could probably see it. *Damn it,* he told himself, *I'm blowin' it.*

Then Lieutenant Alban asked the sixty-four dollar question. "Okay Sam, you're out on the river in the patrol boat. You stop a boat with three inebriated and belligerent people in it. The driver is obviously drunk or you wouldn't have had cause to investigate. You have a sidearm on your hip and a portable radio. What action, if any, do you take?" As the lieutenant spoke Sam could picture the whole scenario, the boat, the people, a sunny day and the registration number on the boat. Sam heard the lieutenant mention that he would be equipped with a sidearm but at this point in his life, had no experience with them. He decided to answer with something he had experience with. "Uh, excuse me Lieutenant, but do I really have to have a gun? It seems to me that if I have a radio and can read the guy's registration numbers off his hull, I can call the local police and have a cruiser waiting for him at the launching area. After all, he's got to get off the water some time." Alban looked at Sergeant Hunter. The two exchanged a small smile. Seeing this, Sam suddenly felt as if someone had just run him through with cold steel. *Aw shit*, he thought to himself, *What did I say now?* The lieutenant looked back at Sam and said, "Good answer. We don't want any cowboys out there. But to answer your question, yes, you will need a sidearm, not only for your own protection, but to put an injured animal down from time to time." Sam felt good about the fact the panel didn't consider him a cowboy. He also wanted them to know he didn't have a problem with guns either but never got the chance to explain that in an appropriate manner.

The interview continued and then Lieutenant Alban said something that Sam would find himself using for years to come, "We don't want you to carry a heavy badge out there. Your first obligation is to educate the public." Sam got sort of a chill of what that statement meant. He thought, *I want to be out there talking to these sportsmen about the best fishing holes, what their pheasant take was, what the deer population was expected to be this year. I'm not signing up for this to punish every sportsman that makes a mistake.* He decided right then and there that Alban's statement would be the basis on which he would build his Fish and Game career, if he was accepted.

The rest of April came and went. Still, no answer from the Fish and Game Unit. Sam wondered what he had said wrong. *Maybe that bit about not needing a gun finished me.* It was no use worrying now. He would just have to hope that wasn't the case.

More weeks passed. Finally, one night, in the middle of May, Sam's brother Cyrus, called to go fishing. "Come on buddy. Forget about that Fish and Game stuff for one night. I'll take you up to Paradise Pond in the State Forest for some bullhead fishing." Sam agreed to go.

The next night Cyrus came over to pick up Sam in his Jeep Cherokee. "Ready to catch some fish," was Cyrus' greeting. Sam tried to look enthusiastic, but somehow, deep inside, he knew that as soon as he left the house, Fish and Game would be calling. Cyrus was right though. He had to get out and clear his mind, and off they went.

Cyrus and Sam four-wheeled their way into a hidden pond way up in the hills. The surrounding area had been home for a Connecticut Indian tribe some 200 years ago. Sam imagined they probably fished this pond all the time. Soon the view of the pond filled the front windshield of the jeep. It was beautiful. The pond sat in a natural bowl formed by a chain of surrounding hills. The sun was low in the sky but offered an orange glow to the clouds that floated above the rounded hilltops. The deep blue sky of the day was slowly giving way to a lighter, pale blue color that seemed to meld into the top of the forest covered hills. The pond was quiet and flat with only the occasional burp of a bull frog. Cyrus parked the jeep with its back end facing the water. As the two fishermen emerged from the jeep, the smell of clean mountain air filled their nostrils. There was also the pungent scent of pine present from the surrounding forest. The two men stood and talked of fishing as they looked about the pond. Cyrus said, "Ahh', this is livin," as he handed Sam a small cigar to smoke while they fished. One thing Sam noticed was the overabundance of "peepers" in the pond. A peeper is a small lean frog that makes some of those "springtime sounds" that can be heard on a warm May evening. "Well," Sam said, "betcha' there aren't any bass in here." "Why do you say that?" asked Cyrus. "Because of the number of frogs. If there were bass in here, they'd be controlling this frog population somewhat." Cyrus replied with, "Okay, Mr. Ranger Sir. Let's get to fishing."

Sam seemed to be having one of his best nights ever. He pulled in bullhead after bullhead. Cyrus had given Sam a cigar to smoke, not to inhale, but only to ward off insects. Cyrus could be seen about fifty yards away blowing a nice puff of smoke that encircled his head. Every time Sam tried this, his eyes stung so bad he had to close them or he ended up putting out the cigar. Finally, he just let the dead cigar sit in his mouth for effect. Cyrus would like that.

The sun was down now and Cyrus told Sam, "We're supposed to be outta' here at sunset. Hope the Ranger doesn't decide to pay this place a visit tonight." He smiled wryly at Sam and continued with, "Guess I don't have to worry though. I'm with a warden." Sam, now feeling anxious and mildly upset at the same time came back with, "Not yet you're not. That's all I need. Let's get outta' here." The two left the pond in darkness.

A few miles down the road, they pulled into a hamburger joint for a late supper. Staring at Sam from out in the parking lot, was a phone booth. As the two brothers talked of the night's fishing, the need to go to the phone booth was getting worse. Finally, Sam looked at Cyrus and said, "Think I should call?" Cyrus smiled back, nodding his head, "I was wondering how long it was gonna' take you to ask that." Sam got up and called his wife, Peg.

As soon as Sam heard Peg's voice in the phone, he said, "Hi... Peg?" She replied with, "You got a phone call tonight," in a teasing sort of way. This was a kind of playful treatment both partners used on each other from time to time, especially when one of them knew the other was expecting something. "Who was it?" The question left Sam's lips more demanding than he meant it to be. Peg replied, now in a more serious tone, "A Lieutenant Alban called and asked for you." Sam's mind was racing. *This is it,* he thought. "I told him you were still out fishing." Sam replied in exasperation, "Oh no, it's after 9:00 PM...what's he gonna' think?" Not realizing the lieutenant had no idea where Sam had been fishing to begin with, a guilty conscience was still focused on the ranger in the state forest. Peg reassuringly added, "He just sort of laughed and told me to tell you that you have been accepted into the police department's Fish and Game Unit, and to tell you congratulations." She began to giggle. She knew what this meant to him. Sam felt such a rush of excitement, he couldn't contain it. He had to get back in the diner and tell Cyrus.

Sam burst through the door and rushed over to his brother's table. "Cyrus...I'm a warden! Can you believe it? I'm a warden!" Cyrus just smiled and watched his brother glow in the excitement. He had been watching Sam through the diner's window, and in the moonlight, knew the outcome as soon as he saw Sam's reaction to Peg. The two brothers ordered two more coffees and just sat and talked about being a game warden. They talked of all the adventures, all the dangers. They made jokes. It was a beautiful moment.

★ ★ ★ ★

CHAPTER 2

The kitchen phone rang. It was Friday evening and the Moody family had just finished supper. Joey, Sam's youngest son answered, "Hello?" The reply got Joey by surprise, "Hi. This is Lieutenant Alban-Thompson P.D. Can I talk to your dad?" Joey's eyes looked like saucers. He dropped the phone and yelled into the back of the house, "Dad, it's Lieutenant Alban!" Sam shot out of his easy chair and grabbed the phone from the floor. "Hi Lieutenant. Thanks for accepting me into your Fish and Game Unit." Alban replied, "No, no. You did that on your own. We're happy to have you. I just called to tell you we have a Unit meeting at police headquarters at 0900 hours Sunday morning. See you there." Alban hung up.

Sam's mind was racing, *Wait a minute*, he thought, *0900, that's 9:00 in the morning. Did he say Sunday? Yeah, Sunday. Police Headquarters? Oh shit. Where's that? What do I bring?"*

Sunday morning Sam found himself at the kitchen table again staring into a cup of black coffee. "Will you please try to relax?" Peg tried to soothe Sam's nerves. She was beginning to think he was a little too excited about this game warden stuff. *But*, she thought, *he's been waiting so long*. It wasn't the months of waiting she had been thinking about. This was his boyhood dream. After graduation from high school, Sam had secured an appointment at the Federal Ranger School in upstate New York, but his parents had decided that career was too dangerous when the academy's superintendent began to outline the responsibilities of a Forest Ranger. Like the dutiful son he was, Sam complied with his parent's wishes.

He chose a technical college and studied land surveying. Marriage came next, followed by their first son, Matt. That's when Sam's second opportunity came. The company Sam worked for began to fold and Sam was laid off. Jobs were scarce and the bills began to mount. Sam assured Peg everything would be fine. There was a new land surveyor in town and he needed some help. Sam was sure the new surveyor would take him on. Peg gave Sam that look when she saw an opportunity. "Sam," she began, "This is your chance to go to Ranger School." I'll work through my pregnancy. The superintendent said you only had one year left and then you'd be farmed out to work." Sam replied, "I appreciate it Peg, but I can't put you through that. Besides it's our first baby and all." So Sam spent the next few years at work in the forests of Connecticut, land surveying and making ends meet.

The next and last opportunity came after their third son was born. Everything seemed right. Sam's education was complete. He was still young and in good physical condition and Peg had a job of her own. The town's police department was advertising for game wardens. Peg showed Sam the advertisement and said, "This could be your last chance." That was all Sam needed to hear. He went down to the station and filled out an application the next day.

As Peg brought herself back to the moment, Sam looked at her and said, "I can't believe I'm going to my first meeting."

Peg continued busying herself about the kitchen, "You'll be fine." She threw a dishrag at him.

The drive back to police headquarters was just as tension filled as the last time, just before the panel interview. Sam thought, *At least there will be three other new guys there.* He hated to be the center of attention.

When Sam arrived at the station, it appeared the squad room was already filling up. Sam hurried in so as not to be the last one. Never the less, as he entered, all the veteran wardens were already in their places. They all turned to watch the new guy come in.

After a few moments, their curiosities satisfied, the wardens went back to their loud and obnoxious behavior. It was a behavior that Sam would find later, preceded every meeting. Nicknames were thrown around accompanied by good-natured vulgarity. In front of Sam sat Corporal Jake Farmer and Sergeant Mike Smalls. "Thanks for taking my calls for me last Wednesday night," Farmer sarcastically reminded Smalls. "Par for the course. I always cover you and you never cover me." Smalls retorted with, "I always cover your calls, you damn fuckstick." Although this seemed to be harmless enough, Sam was amazed at the level of name calling and sarcastic ridicule that filled the room, yet they all seemed to be able to laugh it off.

Lieutenant Alban brought the meeting to order. Volunteers were needed to cover river patrol on the night shift for the Fourth of July weekend coming up. The town was going to have a huge firework display and boaters from all the surrounding towns were expected at the Thompson boat launch as this was the best access to view the fireworks from the river. Alban promised it to be a real zoo if alcohol was involved.

No one came forth to offer their "holiday" time to the LT. Alban turned to the side of the room where all the new guys were seated. "Moody, James, Hanks, Stafford, ...I expect you four to meet me at the station, 1800 hours, class A uniform with no side arms. You gotta' get some experience on the river." Sam knew the new guys weren't wearing their side arms because they hadn't qualified yet. Qualification meant going to the police department's weapons range and passing a shooting test. Because of the rookies' newness on the unit, there had not yet been an opportunity. "Also, each of you new officers will be assigned a Field Training Officer for your probationary period. They're called FTOs. Everywhere he goes, you go. You are only observers in a uniform at this time."

Man, Sam thought, *six months with a partner before I can go out by myself. Seems kinda' stiff.*

It was Saturday afternoon July 4th; Sam showered and put on his class A uniform for the first time. Matt, Sam's oldest son, walked into the room followed by the rest of the family. "Wow! You look good in a uniform Dad." "Thanks, Matt. It's so hot out I feel like I need a shower again." Sam never did like dressing up or wearing fancy clothes, but these duds were part of his new career. Peg ushered Sam out of the house over to the picture tree. The picture tree was an elm on the east side of the house that Sam planted their first year there. As it grew, Peg took anyone's picture by it that might be doing something out of the ordinary. "Come on Sam, put on the Stetson. It's part of the uniform." Peg was getting insistent. "It's not something I'd normally wear, Peg." "No shit. You were never a game warden before either. Put it on." The Stetson was the stereotypical wide brimmed warden hat that reminded Sam of something a drill Sergeant would wear. He put it on and Peg snapped a picture. "Good boy. Now go catch some bad guys." Peg gave him a peck on the cheek and off he went in his truck.

Once again, the drive to the station was filled with apprehension. He was now in official uniform going on marine patrol. He would be working with some of the veterans he met at yesterday's meeting for the first time. Sam parked the truck behind the police station and entered the squad room. The other three new guys also came in to await their next instruction, from whom they didn't know, but still they waited. Presently, Sam looked out the window to see the veterans assigned to them that night were all standing by the parked patrol boat on its trailer in the parking lot, talking and laughing. Sam said, "Hey guys I think they're waiting for us out there." Just then, Marine Sergeant Mike Smalls burst through the door. He was a short man but had a temper that filled the room. "What are you guys waitin' for? My patrol starts at 1800. It's 1805. Get out there with rest of the guys and get ready to roll." The four new guys came out the door. Watching from mid parking lot were the four veteran officers assigned to them. The veterans just stood there and eyed them as Sam and his contingent walked toward them. Sam couldn't help but feel like he was being sized up. Finally, the new guys reached the parked patrol boat. Lieutenant Alban spoke first. "You guys are late! Hanks, where's your tee shirt?" "What do you mean Lieutenant?" Alban started turning red. "You are required to wear a tee shirt under your dress blouse so it comes across you're Adam's apple. Keeps you from sweatin' through too." Sergeant Smalls put in, "Want me to send him home for a change LT?" Alban said no because they were already running late and boaters were probably already starting to "put in" down at the boat launch. Before they left, Alban said, "Okay, Everyone listen up. Tonight we're checking for registrations, running lights, safe boating cards and PFDs (personal flotation devices). New guys,.. pay attention, 'cause you'll be doing it before the night's over. The four wardens with the four rookies jumped into waiting cruisers and left for the boat launch.

The boat launch was literally a parking lot of boats, trailers, jet skis and cars and trucks. People carrying coolers from the parking lot to their boats weaved in and out of impatient boaters trying to back their trailers down the boat ramp. Children ran in and out of the slowly moving vehicles, people shouted remarks at one another with respect to the other's trailer maneuvering skills. Sam never saw the place like this before, or never noticed it, anyway. He was on the other side of the fence now. The wardens quickly went into action directing traffic and corralling people so the atmosphere became that of a very organized but purposeful event. Once the ramp area was under control, Alban called all the wardens over to his vantage point by the side of the ramp. "Okay guys, now that we have everyone under control, start inspecting the vessels. Remember, tonight we're looking for registrations, running lights, safe boating cards and PFDs. Go." The veterans dispersed through the sea of vehicles and boats followed by their personal rookie. Sam's FTO was Nate Bowman. As they approached a boat and trailer about ready to be backed down the ramp, Nate turned to Sam and said, "Just watch. Don't say anything, just watch me." Sam complied. Nate approached the owner of the boat, asked for his boating certificate and inspected it. Then he asked the man to produce a life jacket for everyone that would be riding in the boat that night. The boater struggled to open long locked or stuck cabinets on the boat but finally produced the required jackets. Then Nate said, "Okay sir, turn on your running lights." "I got lights. Can't you see 'em mounted fore and aft," came the reply. "Get your lights on sir so I can see they work." Nate was getting a little impatient but remained stoic to the boater's attitude. The boater flipped on his 'Nav Lights' (navigation lights) switch and nothing happened. He jiggled a few connections and flipped the switch again. Nothing. "I'm sorry sir. Pull your boat off the ramp. I can't let you launch with no running lights." The man came across the stern of the boat like a man possessed. "What do you mean I can't launch? This here river's as much mine as anyone else's. I pay taxes in this town and I pay your salary too. You ain't tellin' me I can't put my boat in, over a couple of measly little lights... I probably know the river better'n you." The boater's outrage at Officer Bowman was loud enough to attract attention from most of the other people in the area. Everyone just stopped and watched the scenario unfold. "You fuckin' game wardens are a pain the ass. All's ya' ever do is harass people just tryin' to do their own thing."

Nate took a step back from the boat keeping his eyes on the irate boater. "Sir, pull your boat off the ramp now or I will have to cite you for obstructing a public boat launch." The other wardens had heard what was going on from their various positions around the boat launch and were calmly watching Nate and the boater. All the wardens were getting ready to step in if Nate needed it. The boater started forward toward Nate once more. Sergeant Smalls stepped forward, as he was closest to the scenario. He was behind the boater directly across from Nate. "Stay where you are sir. Turn and face me now." Smalls was ten feet from the man. The boater exploded, "What is this, an ambush?" "Okay sir, step away from the boat toward me." At Smalls' prompting, the boater wheeled around and ran headlong into Nate, driving him into Sam. Nate went to the ground and Sam struggled to regain his balance but managed to stay on his feet. Sam realized the man, was pushing himself up to a straddling position on top of Nate. Sam took one step forward, reached down and grabbed the boater's arm as he recoiled to strike Nate. Getting behind the boater, who was now straddling Nate, Sam swung around behind him, bending his arm up and behind his back to render him powerless. "Stand up Sir," said Sam. The man complied. Sam held onto the man, still by the wrist of his now incapacitated arm and by the shoulder of his other arm. Sergeant Smalls was there instantly. Smalls grabbed the man's other arm, brought it behind his back also, pulled his handcuffs from his duty belt, and cuffed the man's wrists together. "Oww, take it easy, demanded the man. Smalls gave Sam a serious glance. Sam immediately got a sinking feeling. It was a feeling that he intervened in an area he had no business or permission to be in yet. Smalls led the cuffed boater to a waiting cruiser for transport to the police station. Once the cruiser left the area, and the now ownerless boat was being towed to a place for impoundment, the Marine Sergeant turned back toward the ramp area. "Moody!" The call cut through the hot, humid air of the summer evening like a crack of lightning. "In my cruiser — Now." The veteran wardens knew what was about to happen. They'd all been there once or twice before. They just turned their backs, but knew Sam had just proven he had the stuff for this job. In the cruiser, Smalls went up one side of Sam and down the other, "You're just an observer tonight, Moody. Remember? You are not even armed. You haven't even been to the academy yet... and where did you get that fancy 'bend the arm behind the man' maneuver?" Sam quickly put in, "just reacted Sarge." Smalls with an ever reddening face bellowed "You are here to watch and learn how to check vessels. That's it! Step out of line again and we'll take you home where you can think about what you did. Do you read me Moody?" "Yes Sir", came the reply.

As dusk descended upon the quiet river, Sam tried to calm himself by watching the sun set. It was always a comforting sight from this particular point on the river. Across the river, the orange glow of the sinking sun floated down into the purple black hills that seemed to catch it like a soft pillow. The night's humidity now seemed to evaporate off with the approaching darkness and somehow everything on the river seemed peaceful and quiet.

Sam needed to be alone for a while. He slipped over to a darkened area adjacent to the boat ramp. Here he could stand in the protective shadow of the great willow trees that overhung the river. He stood embarrassed and forlorn that he had not made his debut as a warden that he had always imagined it to be. Still he found himself defending his actions against the irate boater. He couldn't stand by and watch as a fellow officer was attacked. Moody also knew the sergeant was concerned for his safety. He was, after all, still a rookie.

Waves of depression flooded Sam as he stood in the shadow of the willows. *I need to get past this,* he told himself. *Hell, it's my first night. I haven't even been to the academy yet.* Sam took a deep breath and continued, *I'm not expected to do everything right. In their eyes, I don't know anything.* Sam began to feel better about himself. *Just have to remember to watch and learn for now.* Looking at the ground he nodded his head as if in agreement with what he just thought. There was a lot to learn.

He let his thoughts drift back to the sunset. The sun had fallen below the distant hills west of the river. The last remaining rays of the day struggled up out of the valley into the darkening sky and painted the clouds a light orange, as if a red beacon was throwing its beams of light out of a deep black hole. The sky became a pale blue with a purple accent, and slowly, all the color of the day seemed to meld into only one color highlighted by shadows of different shapes and sizes. The river was dark.

It was at this point another sense took over Sam's being. Instinctively, Sam could feel his ears straining to listen to anything that allowed itself to be heard. The sound of the river, although ever so constant, became more like a steady drone. He heard the waves lapping the banks of the shoreline. A distant crack or snap from the tree line, a splash out in the black water that may have been a carp jumping for its evening meal. The murmur of human voices, although indistinguishable, could be heard in a far off conversation. A constant reminder that he was not alone. The night wind gently touched his face and readjusted his hair. The warm summer breeze felt good on his skin. Sam started to feel as one with the river as he absorbed all its natural gifts, when suddenly he was brought back to the present, "Moody?!" Where are you?" It was Nate, his FTO. Sam stepped out from under his hiding place in the willows. "Over here, Nate." Sam's tone was soft and vulnerable. Nate continued, "What're ya doin' over here, man? The LT wants everyone in the patrol boats. We're goin' up stream for marine patrol. You're in the Carolina with him and the other new guys. I'm in the Avon with Smalls." The two men walked to their waiting patrol boats as they lay beached on the sand.

The main patrol boat was a seventeen foot Carolina Skiff, flat bottomed, with a forty horse Honda engine hanging off the back. The helm and control panel comprised the center console and were located amidships. On each side of the center console were the stainless steel stanchions that supported the Bimini top and radio box positioned over the skipper's head. The light bar and twin search lights hung at each end of the Bimini top and were only used during emergencies, high speed pursuits, or missing persons searches. The radio box contained most of the boat's electronic instrumentation and also included a ship to shore radio, PA system, and back up radio. In front of the driver was a control panel with all the system's indicators for fuel, engine RPM, battery voltage and oil level. The depth sounder, one of the skipper's most useful instruments was mounted behind the steering wheel on top of the console. Next to the depth sounder was a marine compass that came in handy during a foggy morning or moonless night. At the skipper's right hip, was the engine throttle. A bench seat was positioned behind him but the nature of the console's layout was designed so the skipper was in a standing position while operating the boat. It was not only more comfortable to stand but easier to see what lay in front of the boat.

The LT took the rookie wardens with him in the Carolina, leaving the two remaining veterans to watch things at the ramp. None of the new guys had been checked out yet on the Carolina so the LT drove the boat. They weren't checked out at the first mate level yet either but Alban figured this would be a good training experience. Once Hanks, Moody, James, and Stafford were aboard, Alban nudged his throttles to reverse. First gently, then increased rpms as he powered the boat off the beach. Alban flipped his Nav Lights switch and his running lights came on fore and aft. Once out in the river's fairway he brought the throttle back to idle to wait for Smalls and Bowman in their rubber boat

"Get out of the boat until I get the bow in the water, Bowman." Smalls was an impatient skipper. "Why can't you just power it off like the LT just did? Every time I go with you in this tub, I have to get my feet wet." Bowman complained. "Why don't you lose some damn weight? You're too friggin' fat Bowman." Bowman stepped over the rubber gunnel of the inflatable boat and tripped in the sand. He tried to push against the bow while Smalls increased reverse throttle to power the rubber boat off the beach. Every time Bowman pushed against the inflated bow it was like pushing against a window curtain. The bow just collapsed inward. The boat wasn't moving. "Now, you get out of the boat Smalls." Bowman was out of breath. The beach sand that gave way under his feet and the energy he exerted on the air filled bow were beginning to get him. "Hey. I'll give the orders on this boat, Bowman. Remember you're my first mate." Smalls proceeded to get out of the boat. Suddenly, Small's radio crackled, "408 from 402." Smalls heard the radio call and realized the lieutenant was calling him personally because Fish and Game officers were assigned the 400 series for badge numbers which also served as their radio call numbers. The officer's rank determined his numerical position in the series. Lieutenant Alban waited for Smalls to acknowledge his call. Smalls came back, "On the beach." "What's the problem 408?" "Just having a little trouble getting Marine 2 wet, sir. We'll be with you in a moment." The lieutenant acknowledged with a curt, "402 Roger." Finally Smalls and Bowman literally dragged the inflatable into the water until they were both knee deep in the river. "Get in Bowman - up front." Smalls climbed over the edge right after him and keyed his radio, "Marine 2 in the water." Alban came back, "Roger 408. Come up on my stern and follow my six by 100." Alban was instructing Smalls to follow his wake directly behind the Carolina and stay 100 feet back. As Smalls swung the inflatable's bow out into the river, he switched on his running lights and made for the stern of the now departing Carolina.

The Avon, or as the wardens called it, the inflatable, or sometimes the rubber boat, was about eleven feet long and five feet wide. It was composed of several inflatable chambers that when pressurized with air gave it the shape of a rubber raft with a shallow "V" hull on the bottom. The Avon had a plywood floor and the helm was amidships on the starboard side of the craft. The driver sat on an upside down milk cart and kneeled into the starboard gunnel's inflated side. This was a wet boat. It always leaked and the V–bottom always collapsed when you approached speeds over 15 knots. On the left of the steering console was a two inch pipe that ran vertically to support a marine strobe light mounted at the top. On the right of the console was the engine throttle. Hanging about the perimeter of the work boat were throw bags and extra life jackets strapped to the life lines on the inflated gunnels. Smalls, with his right hand on the throttle eased forward and increased engine RPM. The little work boat began to pick up speed. As he neared the Carolina, he fell into patrol position on the Carolina's stern as ordered.

The Carolina headed up river. Her running lights were on and Alban put Moody up in the bow to operate the searchlight. The search light was only turned on if there was a suspicious looking vessel or shore party, otherwise the patrol boats tried to appear as any other boat on the river. Under the cover of darkness, the canopy that housed the light bar and Bimini top were usually invisible.

The Avon followed dutifully in the Carolina's wake about 100 feet astern. It was normal procedure on a night run for the boats to run at eight knots. The slow speed allowed headway against the river's current and a smoother ride for the boat's occupants to see anything out of the ordinary.

As the Carolina approached the river's ledge area the LT keyed the radio, "Marine 2 from Marine 1." Smalls came back, "Go ahead Marine 1." "Mike, keep your bow right on my stern. I'm approaching the ledge and the bottom is coming up fast." The ledge area was a plateau in the river bottom that extended across the river and upstream about one quarter mile. The only path through it was a narrow channel that was about ten feet wide and about one hundred feet off the east shoreline. In low water conditions, any boat that veered out of the channel took the risk of running aground or losing a propeller. There were, however, holes in the bedrock ledge where you could find deeper water but you had to know where they were. Alban keyed his radio microphone, otherwise known as the 'mic,' and read off the depth soundings as the Carolina made way against the oncoming current, "I've got five feet, four-eight, five, four, two, uh-oh,— "I'm tipping up stern drive now." A knob on the Carolina's throttle allowed the skipper to adjust his prop depth simply by moving it up or down. The only problem with tipping up the drive was that forward momentum was affected by the onrushing current and could cause the boat to drift to one side or the other. Right now the main focus was staying in deep water.

Back in the Avon, Smalls was getting nervous as Alban called out the water depths. The Avon had no provision for tipping up the engine. If it got too shallow, he'd have to order Bowman to physically lift the outboard up out of the water. It would be a chore for any man. The only advantage the Avon had in shallow water was that it didn't draft as much as the larger, heavier, Carolina.

"Moody, keep that beacon on the east shoreline. I need to get an idea how far we are out from shore so I can stay in the channel. It gets pretty narrow through here." The LT watched the depth sounder, then glanced at the shoreline. Suddenly, the "low water" alarm went off. "Okay, all hands to the bow. We need to get some weight forward to keep the prop out of the mud."

Smalls and Bowman were having their own problems in the Avon. "Hey Sarge, it feels like the bottom is collapsing again." "I thought we fixed that leak last week," Smalls was beginning to curse the Avon. "Well, it's wet in the back of the boat too. Better get the manual bailer going, Nate." Bowman started pumping.

The two patrol boats continued up river. As they rounded a long, sweeping dogleg to the right, the outline of a long narrow island began to emerge. The island meant they were getting close to the state line and it also meant they were at the boater's party haven. Most of the boaters that launched tonight would be camping here.

Once the patrol boats passed the last of the ledge area, each skipper opened up his throttles to "full ahead" and made a long sweeping turn in front of the island's beach area while keeping their patrol formation. The Carolina led in a pass that broke from the center of the river turning clockwise to the east. As the boats came around in a downriver run parallel to the beach, Alban keyed his radio, "Okay Marine 2, let's flash 'em a couple of times with the blue strobes and then turn 'em out." The light bars from both patrol boats came on for a three second strobe. This was only a cautionary message to the partiers on the island that Fish and Game was in the area. The beach looked quiet. Considering the low water situation, Alban decided to get the boats back to the boat ramp. He keyed his mic, "408 from 402." Smalls came back, "408 at your six o'clock." Alban began, "I'm gonna' shut down to idle. Come along the port side and raft up." "Roger 402." The lieutenant kept the Carolina at idle and Smalls brought the Avon alongside. "Mike, we're heading back downriver. Try to stay in the channel. The water is real low and I don't want anyone busting a prop. Keep an eye out for parked boats without their anchor lights on." It was Connecticut state law a boat parked in an active throughway on the water keep a white stern light on while it was anchored to avoid collisions with other boats. "Okay LT, I'm right behind you." Just then James spotted the silhouette of a "low rider" against the horizon about 200 yards downriver to the west side. No lights on. "Okay boys," the lieutenant nudged his throttle forward gently, "here we go. Mike, stay on my port side, one hundred feet out. When I come up on him, I want you to come around and approach from downriver. Stay fifty feet off my bow when I raft up to him. Everyone stay alert." "Roger LT," came the reply from Marine 2.

A "low rider" is a marine term for a typically fast boat, usually with a minimum freeboard and high horsepower engine. They're built for speed and give the appearance of being all engine. Their low profile in the water makes them especially hard to see on the horizon unless they're moving.

The Carolina slid downriver at eight knots. Alban wanted to stay in the channel as long as he could. When he got abeam of the low rider, he swung the helm over so as to cross the other vessel's bow.

This would prevent any escape if there was going to be one. Then he reached up and flipped on the blue marine patrol lights. Through the darkness, someone cursed, "Shit, Wardens. Pull the anchor." Smalls was downstream bringing the Avon around in a long sweeping arc to start his approach on the two boats. Then he too, switched on his blue lights. "Christ, there's another one", someone from the dark vessel exclaimed.

Alban was now fifteen feet from their starboard side. "Where's your anchor light?" The anchored boat remained quiet. "Hello – the boat! Alban again hailed. No answer. Alban throttled back as he spoke into the radio. "Mike, stay tight and keep them on your bow. This doesn't look good." Then he addressed his own crew, "Moody, Hanks – get on the starboard side and be ready to grab their boat. James – stay next to me with the boat hook." Stafford just held onto the port side stanchion.

Alban reached above his head and turned on the public address (PA) system. He keyed the PA's mic, "This is Thompson Fish and Game. You are anchored in a narrow fairway with no anchor light. We are coming onto your starboard side. Stand by to raft up to our vessel." Still holding the mic, he turned to one of the rookies, "James, shine that searchlight on the center of their boat – broad beam – light 'em up." The searchlight's beam was so bright it would temporarily blind the dark boat's occupants. This ensured a safer approach for the Carolina and her crew. The searchlight revealed the low rider as a nineteen foot Checkmate class with a two hundred twenty horse stern drive engine. It sat so low in the water, the stern seemed to melt right into the river. The bow had an extremely sharp cut to it and the helm seemed like it was almost a part of the vessel's aft section with room for only four bucket seats. Moody took in the lowrider, bow to stern, *That boat is built for speed!* From Sam's position in the Carolina's bow, he could see the lowrider's taut, white anchor line that seemed to disappear into the black water. *If this guy tries to get away we'll never catch him*, thought Moody as he reached for the lowrider's transom.

As the Carolina approached, Sam noticed the lowrider's driver say something to the two passengers in his boat. They rose from their seats and stood in front of him, blocking most of his body from the Carolina's view. Then the driver bent down behind his human shield, but stood back up again, like he was picking something up. *This isn't right. That guy is planning something*, Sam began to feel uncomfortable with the lowrider's crew and how they seemed to "take position" for the rafting up. Sam had reason to suspect the crew, for what Sam couldn't see was that the driver had bent down to pick up a baseball bat from under his deck chair. The Carolina was now alongside. Her starboard side rafted to the lowrider's. This made the Carolina's bow at the stern of the lowrider, a typical rafting position. Hanks was standing in the Carolina's bow and holding the two boats together, as well as apart. Moody did the same in the stern. "Good evening gentlemen," Alban's tone was flat but friendly. "What's up officers?" The lowrider's driver stood behind his helm and was mostly hidden behind the two men that stood in front of him. "You have no anchor light out." returned Alban. "I'd like to see your boat registration and safe boater card please." The driver had neither. He whispered again to the two human shields standing in front of him. "Stay put —don't move." The driver eyed the officers on the patrol boat. He was looking for any opportunity, and then he saw Hanks, the closest officer to him. Hanks wasn't watching. He had his head down and was focused on keeping the two boats together and also trying to keep the patrol boat's high gunnels from scraping the lowrider's starboard side. The lowrider's driver eyed Alban and said, "Look officer, this isn't my boat." He tightened his fingers around the bat. "Just borrowed it for the night…fireworks and all." Everyone on the Carolina could smell the sickly sweet aroma of marijuana in the air. Sam thought the boat occupants seemed overly nervous and looked a little defensive. Alban noticed the human barrier in front of the driver and suspected something was afoot. "Alright, I'll take a driver's license or any identification you may have." "Ain't got one of them neither." At that, the driver prompted his human shield. He leaned forward slightly and between the two men, and murmured, "Get ready to pull the anchor."

"Okay, I'm coming aboard." Alban stepped up onto the Carolina's port gunnel. preparing for the step down onto the lowrider's deck, when the driver yelled, "Now!" The man on the driver's right dove to the lowrider's bow to pull the anchor, while the other man threw a loose life jacket into Alban's face for a distraction. The driver lunged to the rear of his own boat, to where Hanks was bent over struggling to hold the boats together. The river's current was making it difficult and required all of Hank's attention. In one graceful leap, the driver hopped up onto his own passenger's chair, raising the bat over his head and brought it down across the back of Hanks' neck as he landed back on the lowrider's transom. Hanks immediately let go of the lowrider and fell headlong into the black current. The two boats separated at the patrol boat's bow and knocked Alban backwards into the Carolina. Alban landed on his back between the

Carolina's bench seat and the helm, his head propped at a strange angle against the port gunnel. James dropped the boat hook and dove into the black water after Hanks. The violent rocking of the Carolina ripped the lowrider's bow gunnel out of Moody's grasp and Sam stood in the Carolina's stern, shocked at the scene that was now unfolding before his eyes. Sam ran along the starboard side and stepped over the unconscious lieutenant. Blood was trailing down the LT's left temple. Moody yelled, "Stafford, tend to the LT," and took the idling Carolina's controls. The Carolina was drifting toward the two officers in the water, Sam shoved the throttle to reverse. The river's current was starting to take control of the situation. The driver dropped the bat and jumped back behind his own helm. As he did, he turned on the lowrider's huge engine. The man at the lowrider's bow yelled, "anchor's up – GO!"

Smalls, who was at idle fifty feet from the rafted vessels ordered Nate to the back of the Avon as he jammed his engine throttle full ahead. The lowrider's driver saw the Avon start ahead and shoved his throttle to full reverse while making a forty-five degree turn to the rear pointing his bow upriver. The Avon came on hard when Smalls suddenly saw his two officers dead ahead in the water. He hadn't had his searchlight on and didn't see the two officers in the water until he was upon them. Taking evasive action, Smalls swung his helm to starboard to avoid hitting the men in the water, only to be faced with the starboard bow of the Carolina directly in front of him. Moody yelled at Smalls, "Port– Port!" Smalls shoved his throttles all the way back to full reverse but it was already too late. Water is an unforgiving element and allows for little error where speed is concerned. The Avon smashed into the Carolina's starboard bow, knocking Stafford overboard on the port side. The collision opened a gash in the Avon's starboard bow chamber and the Avon began to die in the darkness.

The lowrider's driver acknowledged the confusion before him by slamming his engine throttle to "Full Ahead." A rooster tail of water spewed twenty feet into the air as the lowrider's bow pointed to the dark sky. He was escaping before their very eyes. Moody had the controls of the Carolina as he yelled to Smalls, "The LT must have hit his head – looks unconscious. What do you want me to do?" Smalls shouted back to Moody through the darkness and confusion, "Let the lowrider go. We gotta' get Hanks and Stafford out of the water. You'll have to drive the Carolina back to the ramp. I'm losing air on my starboard side." Smalls was calm but knew he was putting a lot of responsibility on the rookie.

Still in the water, James pushed Hanks listless body aboard the Avon while Bowman helped pull him aboard. Smalls gunned the engine and sped for the boat ramp with lights blazing and siren wailing. "Headquarters from 408. Two officers down, Connecticut River – North section. Request ambulance meet me at the upper boat launch. Code 1." "Roger 408, Code 1," Came Headquarters' reply. Code 1 indicated a severe situation. During a code 1, any ambulance in the area responded to the scene as if stoplights and stop signs didn't exist.

Smalls could hear the ambulance sirens in the distance as he sped downriver; his engine throttles all the way to the stops. "He's not moving Mike." Bowman's voice was soft. Smalls kept his focus and didn't answer. He only hoped Moody could get James and Stafford back aboard the Carolina, and tend to the LT. He was asking a lot from a rookie on his first patrol.

Moody stood at the Carolina's helm straddling Alban's unconscious body and scanned the black water for Stafford. "Over here Moody – port side." Sam handed Stafford the boat hook and helped him back aboard. Then he looked over the Carolina's control panel. He'd never driven this particular kind of boat before but it was basically the same as any other. Before he moved the Carolina's engine throttle, he looked over at Stafford. Stafford just stood in the bow watching the Avon's lights disappear into the night. The whir of her motor slowly fading into the darkness. There was no separation between water and sky anymore. It was just black.

"Stafford! Tend to the LT! Looks like he hit his head on the gunnel. Don't move him. Get the smelling salts from the med kit. It's in the bench seat behind me. Pull the seat cushion off and get it out. Give him a whiff of those, and when he comes to just keep him comfortable." Stafford complied. Alban began to stir, "Just stay put sir." Stafford gently held Alban down and propped his head up with a spare life jacket. "Moody's taking us back to the ramp and Sergeant Smalls must be there now with Hanks and Bowman." Alban replied dazedly, his eyes still closed, "Hanks? Where's Hanks?" He was still groggy and hadn't heard a word Stafford said. Stafford went on, "Everyone is safe sir. We're on our way back to the ramp. Just lie still." Stafford still held Alban down. Moody keyed the radio mic, "Headquarters from 419 in Marine 1." "Go ahead 419." "Marine 1 is enroute to the upper boat ramp. ETA is ten minutes. Officer is down with a head injury. Marine 2 is ahead of me by five with one other PI (Personal injury). Request ambulance and hypothermia kit." "Roger 419, help is on the way."

An ambulance and two cruisers met Smalls as he powered the Avon up onto the dark beach. The shore party Alban had left to watch the ramp grabbed the Avon as it slid to a stop in the wet sand. EMTs from the ambulance stepped into the silent Avon, "Is this the hypothermic?" Smalls replied,

Dan Hayden

"Yeah…and he's been hit across the back of the neck with a club. Be careful, he's not moving." The EMT looked up at Smalls, "He's dead sir." The Carolina's lights could now be seen as she rounded the river's dogleg. Smalls pointed toward her running lights, "The LT's in that boat. I don't know what his status is, but I know it's a head injury."

Moody could see the flashing lights on the beach and rammed his throttle forward. He knew he was in shallow water but he had to get the LT in. He fought the urge to leave the deep water of the channel and glanced down at the motionless LT. The bleeding had gotten worse. Deciding to gamble, Sam turned his helm over and cut straight for the beach. *To hell with the rocks. I'm gonna' open her up*, Sam hoped the flat bottomed Carolina would ride up onto the river's surface and plane out, drawing little water. Sam's gamble worked. In seconds, the skiff was skimming the wave tops. The ride was two bumpy to even consider checking the depth finder. Sam headed for the beach.

The boat ramp was now abeam of his boat and Moody dropped the engine throttle back to half and put the Carolina into a ninety degree turn until she was lined up on the shore line. The cruiser on shore trained their searchlights on the beach to show Sam where to land. Sam came up to the beach, dropped the throttle back to idle and let his boat's forward momentum carry the Carolina up onto the sand. EMTs and cops lifted the prone Alban onto a backboard and hurried him over to the waiting ambulance. "How is Hanks?" Alban tried to look around but the EMTs had secured his head into a neck brace. "We're gonna' slide you into the meat wagon Lieutenant. Try not to move." The ambulance driver looked at Smalls, "We called in another ambulance for Hanks. It's better to keep the two men apart right now."

The ambulance, lights flashing and siren wailing, left the boat launch with Alban straining to look out the side window. Just as they reached the parking lot exit, a second ambulance arrived for Hanks. Alban saw the second ambulance pass as his exited. Its lights weren't flashing and its siren silent. He knew.

★ ★ ★ ★

CHAPTER 3

After the funeral, Sam dropped Peg at their cabin. "I'm going to pay Alban a visit before we leave for the academy. Do you mind?" "No, go ahead. I have to change and get the boys ready. Take your time." Sam left for the hospital. It was the only hospital in the valley, small, but adequate to serve the population of Thompson.

Alban wouldn't stay in bed and was pacing the floor furiously. He had been denied the opportunity to attend Hanks' funeral. His demeanor was aggravated by the fact that he felt at least partially responsible for the rookie's death. He should have been there. Alban's right arm was broken, along with two left ribs that hit the skipper's bench seat when he fell, and he was still under observation for a serious concussion suffered after hitting his head against the Carolina's port gunnel. Moody walked through the door. "Moody, goddamn it! It's good to see one of my boys." He reached for Sam's left hand, "Right arm's useless right now but it's a hell of a lot better than it was a couple of weeks ago." "Well, I had to sneak by the nurse's station. They're still not allowing visitors. Maybe you'd better sit down LT." Sam started to pull a chair toward him. "Shit, I don't need any more sittin' down! I want out of here! I'm fine." "Look sir, I just wanted to come by before I left for the academy. I want you to know that no one blames you for what happened on the river. Not even Hanks' wife." "Thanks Sam. I appreciate that," Alban dropped into the chair that Moody had dragged over to him, "but I was senior officer on scene that night. Everything that happened was my responsibility." Being a lieutenant, Alban was not going to explain his mistakes to a rookie, but he did appreciate Sam's intention. He knew he'd be answering more than his share of questions soon enough. Alban changed the subject, "They've got me on medical leave for a whole month! If they don't let me outta' here, I'm gonna' trash the place." Moody just listened to Alban vent. *Yeah, you're gonna' trash the place with a broken arm and ribs, not to mention you can't stand for any length of time without getting dizzy.* "That will be one month shy of hunting season," Moody put in. "Give yourself another month to get back into shape and you'll be ready for all those hunters we have to watch over. Stafford, James, and I will be getting out of the academy just in time to lend a hand." Moody wanted the lieutenant to know the guys still supported him. Alban was already onto Moody, and didn't want to hear it, "Alright Sam, I'll see you at graduation. Now get outta' here." Sam left.

It was late July and the humidity of the New England summer was still at hand. The recent catastrophe on the river was still fresh in Sam's mind. The details regarding the confrontation with the lowrider, the vision of Hanks' attacker swinging the bat, the panicked shouts in the dark night air, and the collision, continued to torment Sam's consciousness. He thought about Hanks' lifeless body as they removed it from the Avon to the patiently waiting ambulance, and Hanks' young wife as she came to the hospital that night to hear the news about her husband. It all seemed to happen so long ago, yet the reality was so clear-cut and ingrained into his memory, it felt like yesterday.

Sam tried to push the nightmare from his consciousness as he drove back to the cabin to pick up Peg and the boys for the ride to the academy. He'd have to put these thoughts into proper perspective if he was going to move on. He was going to the Police Academy and he'd need to have his wits about him. If this hadn't happened so soon before training maybe he'd be able to bury some of the more terrible thoughts. Suddenly he realized he was approaching the long gravel drive that led down a treed road to his cabin. Peg and the boys were out front waiting. Peg was wearing her usual smile but the boys seemed like they were being dragged along again. They weren't too keen about Sam leaving for three months.

As they drove to the academy, the atmosphere in the van was quiet. It was the same feeling he had at funerals on the way to the cemetery, *Hell, it's only three months*, he thought. Deep down, Sam knew the boys were really thinking about something much deeper. It was that their father's friend who had just been murdered doing the very same thing their own father was making a career of. Sure, Sam knew it could have been him instead of Hanks, but he remembered one of the last things Alban said to the crew that night as they started their approach on the darkened boat, *"Everyone stay alert."* Hanks had slipped up. He wasn't watching. Yeah, he was new, but still, he should have been watching the lowrider's crew. Sam decided to let some time get behind the accident before he brought it up again. He wasn't quite sure what to say, or not to say. He'd have to let father time do it's healing.

In the distance, the great stone gates of the academy stood out against the forest wall. The academy lay beyond, hidden from view by the surrounding pine forest. The van passed through the gates and continued down a long, straight, paved road bordered by forest on each side so you had the feeling of passing through a long green corridor. Presently the corridor opened to what could only be described as part college campus and part boot camp. The obstacle courses could be seen off in the distance, academic buildings spotted the whole area, a lake bordered the east perimeter, and on the far side of that, lay the officer's dormitories.

Moody drove his van up to his assigned dorm and parked. "Well, looks like paradise to me", chided Peg. "Yeah, well just remember, it could always be worse." The dorms were old, probably 1950 vintage. The dorms were four stories in height and looked like they needed a good coat of paint, and of course there wasn't an elevator to be found, at least not in the dorms.

"Peg, I think it's best if you guys just took off. I don't like long good-byes." She gave him a smirk and agreed, "Just get through this as quick as you can. We'll be fine." She reached up, held him tight for what seemed an unusually long time, and kissed him quickly on the mouth. Then, as abruptly as she had begun, released him from her grip, turned toward the van and said, "I'm going." From the van, the boys yelled, "See ya' Dad, have fun." *Have fun*, Sam thought, *hmmn?"*

Days passed, then weeks. Back at the Thompson Police Station, memories of the rookie wardens began to fade, except from the memory of one man who couldn't avoid the natural process because of his position as Unit Commander. Lieutenant Gene Alban was busier than ever attending meetings and filling out reports regarding July's river accident. There would be hearings and maybe even a lawsuit against the town by Hanks' family. *One thing at a time*, Alban thought. It was his first day back from medical leave. Everything was taking longer to do since he was still operating with only one good arm. The other was still in a sling. If he moved around too much, his ribs began to ache. The dizziness had subsided some time ago so all he had to do now was focus on his physical condition. Alban was a big man, about six feet, two inches and tipping the scales at 240 pounds. At age 54 he still sported all his blonde hair with no grey. For his size and weight he was uncommonly strong, probably due in part to the type of work he chose as his life's career. He could see into a man's soul just by listening to him talk and always knew what the man was thinking. He could not be lied to. He was forgiving to a point, but all in all, he was the typical Unit Commander who gave all the orders and received all the complaints.

Sergeant Mike Smalls walked into Alban's office. It was the first time they saw each other since the hospital. "Hey LT, how're you feeling?" Smalls was sporting a big smile, obviously happy to see his boss back on the job. With Alban gone, Smalls, who was next in the chain of command had to pick up the slack. Alban liked Mike Smalls but only trusted him to a point. He knew Mike was an opportunist and generally lazy when it came to office work, and some of his cheerfulness was more about his lighter workload than Alban's health. Alban looked up from his desk covered with paperwork, "Good Mike, thanks for asking. Didn't you do a damn thing while I was gone?" Mike's face suddenly reddened, "Well yeah, I was doing double patrols and training the new guys." "What about all this paperwork?" Alban said as he looked at the pile of reports, memos, and public announcements. "Well, I did a little of that but didn't think you wanted me to get into that stuff. You always said that was the lieutenant's job." "Yeah, but Mike, some of these memos are a month old. Hasn't anyone been calling in as to their whereabouts?" Smalls was beat red and a little taken aback at this point. His lieutenant didn't seem happy to see him. "There are some messages on your voice mail Lieutenant." Smalls retreated to his formal mode as he always did when he knew he was in trouble. Alban looked up at Smalls, "You've been doing double patrols?" "Yes sir.

That lowrider that got Hanks is still out there and I want that bastard." Alban's face softened a bit and said, "Mike, that guy is long gone. He knows we're watching for him. He'd be stupid to show up around here again, at least any time soon. It looks to me as if you've been spending too much time on the lowrider case and not enough on the rest of your responsibilities." Alban knew he was being tough on Smalls, but Smalls was the type you couldn't cut any slack. After Alban's last comment, Smalls began to lose his patience. He straightened up and looked at Alban, "Are you through with me Lieutenant?" "Yeah. Take some of these daily service logs with you and get 'em back to me before the end of your shift. Thanks for stopping by Sergeant." Alban chuckled to himself. He knew he was burning Smalls down. Smalls started to leave when he remembered why he really came in to see Alban. He stopped and turned around. Alban looked up with a questioning glare. Smalls began, "You should know, Moody really came through for us that night on the river. He was the only rookie that managed to keep his cool and stay onboard, even after the collision. I had to leave him in charge of the Carolina and with getting the others back on board. He basically took charge of the whole situation. He's the one who brought you in." Alban's glare softened to a look of indifference and looked back down at his desk, "I know Mike. I read your report. We'll see how he does at the academy. How are James and Stafford doing?" Smalls took a step back toward Alban feeling like he just received some sort of reprieve, "The accident didn't seem to affect them from what I could tell. They're all at the academy now anyway." Alban looked back up at Smalls, nodded at the door, and said, "I got a ton of paperwork, Mike. Thanks for coming by." Smalls turned and left the room.

Time at the academy was flying by, at least for Sam. Between the daily two mile runs, calisthenics, rappelling and rescue drills, and lecture classes, Sam found just enough time to write a letter to Peg every other night, unless he fell asleep first. The class was split into three different factions, each one being highly competitive with the other two. There were the State Police officer candidates otherwise known as "Stateys", then the Municipal Police Officers or "Townies", and then the Fish and Game Officers known as "the Wardens". The Wardens were the smallest class consisting of fifteen officer candidates. Moody, James, and Stafford had every class together and were usually a team when the situation required it. The trio never talked about the river accident, although each of them thought about it daily. An inner feeling of despise and regret had started to build within the three officer candidates. There had been no time to debrief them and counsel their inner senses before they left for the academy. A cauldron began to brew within the three men that would later yield an attitude toward law breakers not conducive to an officer's tolerance level. Moody started to pick up on it during casual conversations with the men and specific training activities. Once, when they were going out as observers with academy assigned FTOs, he overheard James say to Stafford, "Time to go fight crime." "Yeah, zero tolerance is my motto," Stafford replied. Moody thought, *Christ, this is a training exercise. What's got into these guys?*

Finally the first month was over. Sam could begin to see where each warden's specialties lay. Some guys were marksmen and ballistic experts, some were naturalists headed for ranger positions in State Parks, and some excelled in rescue and first aid. Sam was good at everything but excelled in "mammal tracking." Mammal tracking was the science of following any living creature and developing an entire history of everything it did from the clues it left behind. He could identify any mammal from the prints it left. One thing most first time trackers had to learn were a set of prints developed into a pair of "tracks". He could determine how old the prints were and if the animal was running or walking, standing or sitting. Some animal straddles, which was the width of the tracks, gave information as to whether the animal was male or female, especially evident in deer. Broken sticks and freshly overturned stones indicated where a creature had passed recently and left a feather or piece of fur on an outstanding limb of a bush or tree branch. Sometimes he could tell where a deer had bedded down for the night. The flattened depression that left a dry oval of leaves in an otherwise damp area always told Sam he was in the forest's bedroom reserved especially for all of its worthy inhabitants. The other tracking tool Sam learned to use was his sense of sight and sound. The tracker looked for the slightest movement about the forest and used his sense of hearing to listen for telltale sounds that offered more clues to the tracking puzzle at hand. A keen sense of hearing was invaluable to the tracker, especially when the sun went down and the forest filled with darkness. An effective listener could decide which sounds were common to the forest environment and which were out of the ordinary. Here, a good sense of smell substituted for the loss of sight. All of these natural gifts were anyone's to use for their own well-being. Together, they could lead a starving man to food or just tell him the footsteps he heard in the darkness were that of a ground squirrel or that of a man creeping around in the darkness.

Sam had learned a lot of his tracking from a childhood friend named Lee who was a little older. They had met one day while Sam was hiking through the Scantic River section of Thompson looking for a new trout pool to fish. He noticed another young man standing in the middle of the stream fly fishing. Sam watched in wonderment as the youth tossed the invisible fly to and fro. He marveled at the gracefulness of the whole action. With hardly the slightest movement of his arm, the youth could snap the baited fly from the air to an exact spot on the other side of the stream forty feet away. He watched as the fly just kissed the water's surface with barely a ripple, and then, with hardly a gesture from its master, the fly leapt from the stream's surface to a preplanned place in the air behind the fisherman, only to return to the exact spot in the stream. The back and forth movement of the fly through the air continued for a time until suddenly the head of a trout appeared at the stream's surface to snatch the fly from the air.

It was their want for the wilderness and all of its natural gifts that bound their friendship. The boys started to talk and Lee began to guide Sam along in the ways of the forest. Together they fished, hunted, tracked animals, and camped. They owned the woods and its inhabitants. It became their playground. A strong friendship grew and stayed fast through all the years of trials and tribulations. Lee became an expert in the forest and professional hunting and fishing guide. There wasn't a lot that happened in any of Thompson's forests that Lee wasn't aware of. He made his life in the woods and eked out a living using nature's offerings, harvested by his outdoor skills. Lee became Sam's mentor, and in the years to follow, would be there to advise Sam in the way of the woods.

The final month of academy training began and all of a sudden everything seemed more difficult. Classes were longer and more detailed. Routine two mile runs turned into three mile runs and the physical training instructors, or as the candidates called them, PTs, became meaner and more demanding. Sam was counting the days to graduation. He missed Peg and the boys. Everyone was getting more than a little testy.

One night after obstacle course, the feeling among all of the candidates was that of sheer exhaustion. The PTs had been especially abusive, "How are you wardens gonna' save that lost kid on the mountain if you can't get through this simple obstacle course? I'm just glad you're not my saviors. I want to live." The PTs made the wardens do the course over and over until everyone made a time under ten minutes. They didn't care if the whole team helped each other through. Everyone had to be at the finish by the ten minute mark.

Finally the day was over. "Screw the homework." James looked at Moody in contempt, "I'm goin' to bed and don't try to make me feel guilty, Sam. Stafford, you gonna' be the good cadet and read your case histories like Sammy here?" "Nah, I'm bushed. Think I'll hit the sack too." Moody knew these guys had enough for the day. Doing any studying now was pointless. Their mental and physical limits had been compromised. "Hey guys," Moody whispered to both Stafford and James, "Let's get the Townies." Moody had that hell raising look about him. The one you couldn't talk him out of. "Not tonight, Moody. You're as tired as we are... you're even limping. What are you thinking!?" The look on Stafford's face was more pleading than anything else. Moody stood up, "No, we gotta' make what we did today worth it. We got beat on all day and I need some satisfaction. Now it's our turn. I don't like those Townie pukes so we're gonna' get 'em." Stafford and James wearily shook their heads in agreement. "Okay, after lights out, we meet in the lobby outside the Townies' suite area. Don't let anyone see you. The Townies are bunked in the basement suite. We'll meet at the bottom of the stairs outside their lobby." Stafford looked puzzled, "That's all the way across the lobby from their suite. Why there?" Moody smiled, "and what's hanging on the wall at the bottom of those stairs?" "Fire hose?" Stafford was still unsure as to where Moody was going with this. Moody answered in an approving tone, "Right...and the gate valve. I'll take the hose across the lobby to their suite door. When I open the door, you're gonna' open the gate valve – only half full. I don't want them to hear the water gushing from the nozzle. James, you're gonna' help me drag the fire hose. Stafford, since you're out in the open anyway, you're also the lookout. You see anyone coming, throw a tennis ball at the door. That will make just enough sound for us to hear it and not wake the Townies. We'll drop the hose and come running." "Sam", James advised, "Stafford is so tired, he'll never reach the door, let alone hit it. That's a fifty foot throw." Sam eyed Stafford with a confident stare, "He'll make it…if he has to." Stafford just stared at the other two men, *We don't have a chance. We're gonna' get screwed.*

It was eleven o'clock PM, 2300 hours military time. Sam quietly opened the door to his room, looked both ways down the dimly lit hallway and left to meet Stafford and James in the basement. It was quiet. The day had been hard and Sam was sure all cadets had been asleep for at least an hour. Sam approached the staircase and silently descended the five floors to where Stafford and James would be. Moody and James arrived at the same time and waited for Stafford. Presently, they heard what they hoped were his footsteps on the stairs above their heads. To their relief, a limping Stafford rounded the banister and stood on top of the last landing looking down at his two accomplices. "Let's go Stafford, I want to get this over with." James was showing impatience partly due to his fatigue from the day's activities. "Shut up. I got a cramp in my right calf you son of a bitch. You're lucky I'm even here." Then, without warning, tripped and fell down the last three stairs into Moody, who was focused on the stairwell door. The two rolled into the metal door that led into the lobby outside the Townies' suite. "See? I told ya' he was too tired for this covert shit." James crawled over and tried to untangle the two warden's twisted bodies from one another. "Get off me, Stafford. You're not even tryin." Moody was half laughing at the state of Stafford's physical condition. The two men just lie at the bottom of the stairs laughing. Their fatigue and nervousness all melded into one big laughing jag. "C'mon you bastards. Let's cut the foolin' around before we get caught." James now seemed to be the one in charge. "Aw fuck you James, I think I broke my friggin' ankle." Stafford was only half serious. "Are you shitting me?," Moody looked concerned. "Nah, it's not broke. I can stand on it. Feels like hell though." "Okay," Moody said, "take your positions." While Stafford kept watch on the hallway, James and Moody dragged the fire hose across the lobby to the closed door of the Townies' suite. Both men were in a crouch by the open side of the door. Moody looked back at Stafford who gave him the thumbs up signal. "I bet the son of a bitch forgot to bring the damn tennis ball." James told Moody. "We're not gonna' need it, Pat. Just relax." With that, Moody slowly turned the door knob and opened the suite door. No one in the living area. Just another hallway running further into the suite off of which all the candidate's rooms were attached. "We're gonna' bring this hose right up to the first door and lay it on the floor. Okay?" James nodded in agreement. Just as the two wardens started to stand, three Townies appeared at the opposite end of the hallway, "Hey, what're you guys doing," one of them shouted down the hallway. Then another yelled, "Wardens! They got a hose." Now that they had been exposed, Moody yelled to the waiting Stafford, "Turn it on...open the valve!"

Moody dove back onto the floor to grab the loose hose nozzle. Doors down the hall started to open and suddenly a swarm of Townies were headed down the hallway toward Moody and James. "Moody, let's get outta' here," James was pulling at Moody's shirt tails. "No, just help me hold the nozzle," replied Moody.

Just then the pressure in the fire hose welled up to Moody's end, and being more than one man could handle, knocked

Sam to the floor. Water was flying everywhere and the hose acted like an angry snake snapping at everything in the confines of the narrow hallway. Moody still had one hand on the handle, "Pat, help me hold this." The first three Townies were running for the wardens at full speed down the dimly lit hall. Then Sam and Pat regained control of the wildly thrashing nozzle and pointed it at the onrushing Townies. The force of the water knocked the enraged Townies to the floor. Those behind them tripped over the front three. Now the hallway swelled with Townies emerging from the rest of the rooms. "Stafford, full blast," yelled Moody. Back at the gate valve, Stafford heard the commotion, and could only imagine what was happening inside the suite. It sounded like a war. Stafford just shrugged and thought, *Okay, full blast it is.*

The new surge of water came to Moody and James instantaneously. The two wardens struggled for control of this seemingly live animal they both held within their grasp. The Townies were gaining ground on the wardens. They were crawling along the flooded tile floor holding onto doorway casings or whatever else they could grab. It was only a matter of time before Moody and James were within their grasp. "Aim for the hall lights!" Moody shouted to James. The high pressure water broke the lights and wiped their sconces from the wall. Water got into the circuits and shorted out the rest of the system. The suite and hallway went dark. "Run for it." Moody grabbed James from the slick floor and the two burst through the suite door into the lobby. Stafford was waiting right outside and shoved a door wedge under the closing door, water still spewing from the hose inside the suite. The three slipped and sloshed across the lobby to the waiting staircase. The wet tile floor made the trip difficult. Undetected, they entered the stairwell and made their escape. Their wet footprints would be dry before the Townies got their suite door free. Sam was satisfied.

Graduation day brought a chill in the air. It was early October. The leaves had begun to change color and the humid heat of summer was replaced with light winds and lower temperatures. Sam was excited about finally moving forward with his career. School was out! It was time to get back out into the woods. Back to his natural environment among all the things he loved. Academy life had been tolerable. The classes were interesting and the physical demands kept him in good condition but he missed Peg and the boys. It was going to be good to get back to a regular routine. Going to work, having supper with the family and discussing events of the day, helping the kids with their homework, talking with Peg. He couldn't wait.

Sam finished dressing for the ceremony and looked out his dorm window. There was the family van pulling into a parking space. Peg got out and seemed to be giving orders to a highly excited set of boys. They were here at last, finally. He smiled to himself, picked up his duffel bag and closed that dorm room for the last time. As Sam descended the stairwell to his waiting family, he passed the landing that led to the basement suite. He just stopped and looked down those stairs for a moment and remembered. Grinning broadly, he adjusted his duffel onto his shoulder and left the building.

Graduation had been long and laborious. The officer candidates had to "pass in review" before the expectant crowd and the Academy's Superintendent. Once all the speeches and motivational talks were over, the new officers were dismissed. Peg and the boys ran to where Sam had been sitting on the parade field. He was greeted with a group hug. "Hey Dad, you got skinny," Joey was beaming broadly. Sam looked at Peg, "Looks like you dropped a few Honey. We'll take care of that when you get home." Peg's smile was that of happiness. Not because of graduation and her new officer husband all decked out in his dress uniform, but because she had her family back. Pat James and Tom Stafford walked over to stand with Sam. Peg took a step back and pulled out her camera, "Okay let's have a picture of Thompson's finest." "What are you gonna' do Mom? There's no picture tree around here." "Uh, we'll make do Joe." Peg snapped the picture then walked back to the trio and gave Stafford and James each a hug. "Bet you boys are ready to take a vacation. Was everyone a good boy?" Peg knew that these three had to have been involved in something not academy approved during the last two months. The three looked a little sheepish, "Yup, just as I thought. We'll talk about it later." Peg gave the three a smirk. "Hey Moody!" One of the PTs assigned to the wardens came walking over. "The Townies' PT gave me this tennis ball to give you. He said that you were a lucky man and that you'd know what that meant. Anyway, here's your ball and good luck to the three of you." The PT tipped his Stetson to Peg and walked off grinning. Peg looked at Sam, her arms folded in front of her, "Sam?"

★ ★ ★ ★

CHAPTER 4

On the way home Sam saw the Thompson cemetery in the distance. As the van approached the gated entrance Sam said, "Peg, pull in here." "Sam, let's get home first." "It's okay, Peg. Just pull in," he turned and looked into Peg's eyes. He had a serious look about him. It wasn't sad or forlorn, but one which showed determination.

Peg turned into the cemetery entrance and drove by the rows of stones. Sam just looked straight ahead not saying a word. The boys assumed they were going to their grandfather's grave, so the van was quiet. "Stop here. I'll be right back." Usually, when they visited Grandpa, everyone piled out of the van. Sam wanted to do this alone. Peg watched as Sam weaved his way through the gravestones. He stopped at one stone and knelt down before the foot of the grave. *He's going to show his father his badge.* Peg felt a sudden sadness. His father had been his hero and had passed on unexpectedly two years before. As Sam knelt before the grave, he removed his shiny new badge from his left breast where the academy superintendent had placed it only two hours earlier. He placed it on his Dad's military stone that lay flat in the earth. "I did it Dad." Sam was speaking aloud. "I hope you approve. It means a lot to me, more than anyone knows." Sam knew what his Dad thought about most law enforcement types. Although, Sam's grandfather had been one of Thompson's early police officers, his Dad never put any of them on a pedestal. Sam never did get to meet his grandfather the cop, but respected him for what he did know about him. However, his Dad was his hero. There wasn't another man on the face of the planet that could ever be the man his father was. Sam just knelt there. He could feel the warmth of the sun on his face and the cool autumn breeze that brushed his face. The cemetery was quiet except for the rustle of leaves that was aggravated by the wind now and then. Sam stood up and stared down at the outline of the two year old grave. His father's grave was still covered with immature grass that faded and died every fall making the outline of the hole his father lay in more defined by the greener, more well established grass around it.

The more Sam stared into the earth the more frustrated he became. He tried to picture his father's face and remembered some of the things he used to say. Still, he couldn't be sure about his Dad's reaction to his new position. Tom Moody was a law abiding man and also a man of extreme principal. He was a man who meant what he said. It didn't matter where or when. If it needed to be said, Tom let everyone know it. He always told Sam, *The most valuable thing a man has is his word...without that he has nothing.* It was no wonder Sam had such a moral character. Sam based his entire life on his Dad's words. How he wished he could talk to this man, just one more time. "I'm sure he's watching, Sam." Peg had quietly walked up behind Sam. "He would be very proud of what you've done. I knew him well enough to know that." She put her arm around Sam's waist. Sam didn't respond. After a few minutes, Sam broke the silence. He picked up his badge from the stone and quietly said to Peg, "Let's go visit Hanks." Together, they walked to rookie Steve Hanks' grave. Sam went to the foot of the grave while Peg stood a few feet behind. She knew he needed his space. The new grave had started a new carpet of grass but had turned brown with the coming of fall. Old flower arrangements lay askew around the new stone from the force of the October winds. Sam placed his hand over Hanks' engraving. Quietly, he murmured, "You were with us at the academy the whole time, pal. Don't worry, we'll do you right." With that, Sam stepped back from the grave, turned to Peg, and said, "Let's go home."

It had been a long three months since Sam had last seen his home. He smiled as he turned off the main road onto the long gravel road that led to his cabin. It was a two-story dwelling bordered on three sides by a "farmer's porch" and log railing. The porch is where Sam liked to begin his day. He would walk onto the pine porch boards before the crack of dawn, cup of black coffee in hand, and watch the sun rise from the eastern hills. The best mornings were those when there was a bit of a nip in the air. The pines emitted their pungent scent from the darkness and shielded all but the natural sounds of the forest. Soon the 'honkers' could be heard flying overhead looking for their favorite pond to land in and socialize. As the sun started to climb out of the valley, the darkened pines started to show their emerald color and shed the shadows of the night. These were nature's gifts… natural, innocent, and free of charge.

Behind the cabin was dense Thompson forest. Several forest paths led from the Moody's backyard to the family's favorite areas in the woods. The paths could bring them to quiet ponds for fishing and swimming, or to a cliff area that overlooked the Thompson valley to watch birds of prey as they soared high above the pines. There was one path that could bring anyone who traveled it to a small pine forest that included a small clearing in its center. The deer came here to graze and bed down for the day. The forest provided a barrier from civilization that kept Sam's outdoor world safe from modern day technology.

At the end of Sam's driveway, and separate from the cabin, was a barn that sported a finished loft area, accessed by an exterior staircase and door at the top. There was an emergency exit in the loft's floor that consisted of a trap door and ladder. Sam could get to his truck or car without leaving the barn if he had to. The loft was Sam's area of refuge. It was the place he went to read, tie flies, think, and entertain good friends. It was complete with two bunk beds, a desk, and a potbellied stove. A window in the front of the loft provided the view back to civilization. It looked back up the long gravel drive to the main road. To Sam, it was a constant reminder of the way back to the serious and sometimes unfriendly modern day.

Monday morning found Sam on his way to the Thompson P.D. for his first check in as a state certified game warden. He luxuriated in the drive through the quiet hills. He was back in his white pick-up truck, hot coffee sitting in the console's holder, and his favorite radio station was playing his favorite tunes. Sam watched the rolling hills of the Thompson valley brim pass outside the truck's cab. He loved the picture he got on some of the more damp mornings. A low hanging fog that had settled into the valley's lower sections still lingered and showed white against the purple black hills. Wisps and twists of the rising fog turned colors of red and orange as they struggled to free themselves from the valley's grasp while the red-orange glow of the rising sun peeked over the hills. It seemed such a waste no one else was present to witness this special sight. A flight of Canadian geese, in perfect flying formation, honked their way toward Sam's cabin. *Right on time*, Sam thought as he watched the honkers disappear behind the pines. The view of the Connecticut River always offered the best scene. The same surface fog that had settled into the hill's nooks and crannies also floated over the river's surface. The shores on each side of the river, wooded and dark, added to the cloud effect the river gave as it twisted its way through the surrounding hills. Sam's favorite scene was that of the river fog as he passed over the bridge to Thompson's west side. The long snaking cloud above the river sometimes rose high enough to encircle the bridge's iron truss work and left what appeared to be a tunnel in the sky. The passing traffic over the bridge seemed to keep the fog from getting into the traffic lanes.

Presently, Sam turned into the Thompson P.D.'s parking lot. *Alright, here we go,* he thought. He got out of the truck in his class B uniform normally used for regular patrol activity. The Class B uniform included dark brown BDU pants stuffed into the top of shiny, high top black boots. The pants contained several large pockets to hold ticket pads, a jack-knife, a tape measure, and current game law pamphlets, – all the loose essentials a practicing game warden required when on the job. Although the boots were "issued" equipment, Sam had asked for permission to pick out his own. Being an accomplished woodsman, he knew what he was going to need in the Thompson woods. When he put them on that morning, he thought back to something Peg had said when he finally chose the pair he'd be taking. In a concerned tone she offered, "Can you run in them?" Peg had a background in law, but on the court side. She had been through some of the same training as Sam, before they married and had a good idea of what he was in for.

His dress shirt, or blouse, was light tan adorned with his silver badge over his left breast pocket, two silver pens for "paperwork," and under his badge was the EXPERT revolver pin he earned at the academy firearm qualification for shooting just under a perfect score. Over the right shirt pocket hung his silver name plate – his name prefixed by the abbreviation OFR, for officer. On each shirt lapel were circular pins that held the Connecticut law enforcement crest and the state' symbol – also silver. He wouldn't be wearing any gold hardware until he reached the rank of sergeant. Over the shirt, Sam wore his short patrol jacket, also adorned with a badge and name plate.

His pants were held up with a wide black belt covered by his duty belt. The duty belt was an extra wide leather belt, attached to his pants belt with small leather buckles called keepers. On the duty belt rode Sam's radio, folding knife and sheath, Maglite, and holster for his .357 magnum Smith and Wesson revolver. The revolver was positioned on the duty belt under his right arm. To the front of the holster were two speed loaders. Each speed loader held six .357 silver jacketed hollow point shells.

Sam was so encumbered with equipment on his person he actually felt uncomfortable. The gun caught on the truck's steering wheel as he tried to exit the vehicle and the weight of the equipment around his waist made him feel restricted. *Guess I'll get used to this stuff soon enough, he told himself,* as he walked into the police station for his first roll call.

Sam walked through the squad room door and dropped into a seat in the back of the room. Soon Pat James and Tom Stafford arrived and sat next to him. The three rookies just nodded at one another. They were nervous and not quite sure what to expect. They sat and watched the roll call begin. Sam listened to the other officers walk about the room, leather creaking and keys jangling. The shift commander walked in, "Okay, take a seat, listen up for attendance." Sam sat and waited nervously for his name to be called. Finally, he heard it, "Moody!" "Here," Sam replied. No one turned around to look at him, no one said anything. He started to relax. *These guys don't care. I'm one of them now. What am I thinking?*

After roll call monthly schedules were passed out. The schedule showed what days and times an officer was either on patrol or on call from home. On call was not scheduled duty. It was specific nights that required law enforcement coverage. If a call came in, police dispatch called the officer at home by phone. It was up to the officer on call to decide if the call required an "on site" visit" or merely a consultation by phone. Until probation was over, the rookies would have to call a veteran warden to go with them if the call required a visit by the officer.

Sam's schedule showed he was on night patrol for the entire month. On call times were scheduled night hours. *Shit, Peg's gonna' love this*, he mused. He walked over to Pat James and Tom Stafford, "What are your schedules like? I've got all nights." Stafford beamed at Sam, "Daytime – all days." James was smiling at Sam, "Me too, buddy. Looks like you got the graveyard right off the bat." *What's going on*, Sam thought. He considered the circumstances for a moment then told himself, *Aah, I was just the unlucky one this month…probably. They'll get their nights next month.* Suddenly Lieutenant Alban walked into the room, "Stafford, Moody, James. See me in my office after roll call. You have assignments."

The three rookies crowded into Alban's office. His arm was still in a sling and the black eyes from the concussion had long gone. Alban was looking down at some documents on his desk as the rookies stood before him. Finally, he looked up at the rookie wardens, allowing the hint of a faint smile. "Welcome back boys. I've been looking over your performance ratings at the academy. You guys did pretty good. Now I want you to think hard on something for the rest of the week. That was schoolin'. You are in the real world now. You make a mistake and you're dead. There is no PT to come over and tell you how to do it over the right way. You have to make quick, accurate decisions with no regrets."

The lieutenant paused a moment and looked over the three men. "There is still one month of probation left, then you're on your own. Don't let me down. Then he turned his gaze back down to the paperwork on his desk. "Stafford... you'll be riding with Bowman for the next month in the Blazer, James... you're with Smalls – river patrol." Then he looked over at Moody, who was beginning to feel like he had done something wrong. "Moody...you're on nights with Sergeant Hunter. You two have a lot in common and he ought to be able to show you some neat tricks." He looked away from Sam before he finished the sentence, ginning. Then Alban stood up, "Be safe gentlemen. Keep your eyes open and listen to your FTO." With that, he nodded at the door, "Good luck to ya', and sat down again.

Sam drove back to the cabin slowly. This time the beauty passing outside the truck's cab went unnoticed. His thoughts were immersed in what had gone wrong. It couldn't be anything he'd done at the academy. He graduated top of the warden class and earned special recognition slashes to wear on his uniform for leadership. Well, there was the fire hose incident but supposedly no one really ever identified him. That was just blowing off steam, anyway. What was going on?

Alban sat in his office grinning as he watched Moody pull out of the P.D.'s parking lot. He'd seen the look on Sam's face when he gave Sam his assignment. All night duties and assigned to a tough sergeant known for his eccentricity in the woods. Sam didn't realize it but Alban had intentionally planned Moody's training this way. He'd seen Sam's natural skills at work and knew he was the only one of the three rookies that had an inborn leadership trait. When Sam walked into a room, everyone knew he was there, and a sort of calm seemed to fill the room. His past performance showed it was a natural trait for Sam to take charge in a bad situation showing no more panic than that of a man taking his wife out for a quiet dinner. He was likeable, and arrogant when he had to be, and intelligent, but didn't flaunt it. Moody had the stuff and it was Alban's intent to mold him – his way. Alban knew the well-seasoned Sergeant Hunter would show Sam "the hot spots" around town and the ways to deal with them. Even though Hunter was a little rough around the edges, he was the best choice of veteran wardens to be able to show Moody anything. It would be up to Sam to glean out the proper methods from Hunter's influence. Sam was already a well-known and accomplished woodsman. Hunter would be the one to hone Moody's skills to the streetwise, or in this case, woods wise level.

Sam pulled the truck up to the cabin's porch. Peg was out front raking leaves. "Hey, how did it go Mr. Game Warden?" She walked over to Sam's truck smiling as he wrestled himself out of the driver's seat once more. She was leaning on the rake handle and eyed him curiously. When he turned to meet her gaze, she knew he wasn't happy about something. She had a knack for that sort of thing. "What's the matter?" she said. "Aah," Sam replied. "I'm on the night shift." Sam started around the back of the truck to where Peg stood. He pulled the tailgate down so they could sit and talk. Peg grinned unsurprisingly at Sam, "Yeah?" Peg answered in a sarcastic tone. "What did you expect – Rookie? Did you think they'd give you Alban's hours?" "No...," Sam replied sheepishly as he stared into the gravel driveway, "but they gave Stafford and James days." Peg came over and sat on the tailgate next to him. She knew what kind of man the Thompson P.D. was getting, and also there had to be a good reason for their decision to put Sam on nights. Peg paused for a moment and said, "...and when do the bad guys come out to play," she egged Sam on. "I don't think people poach during the day too much around here." She was looking up into the trees in a sort of wistful manner. "If I was the lieutenant, I'd want my best people on shift when things got rough." She continued to look into Sam's face as she waited for a reply. At times like this, Peg never gave him a straight answer. She always tried to get him to see the picture for himself. Sam liked to say she could steer him like a horse. "It doesn't bother you?" he said as he looked up into her eyes. "I'm going to be working when you guys are sleeping, and visa – versa, …and when I'm home, I'll be on call. It's just a hell of a way for my family to have to get used to my new career – that's all." Peg put her right elbow on Sam's left shoulder, like someone sharing a secret with an old friend. She looked down at the gravel too and said, "Look buddy, we're all in this together. We'll take things as they come – roll with the punches – so to speak. I think you're on nights because that's where the action is. Also, it just happened to work out that you got nights first. Stop being such a baby. This is your job now. Deal with it." Sam knew by her tone it was time to stop complaining. Whether she liked it or not, it appeared she wasn't going to complain. Peg slid off the tailgate and as she walked toward the cabin's porch, said over her shoulder, "Lunch will be ready in twenty minutes. Better get some sleep afterward, you might be up all night." Smiling to herself, she climbed the cabin's front steps, walked across the wide porch, and disappeared into the cabin. *Hmph, got a lot of sympathy there*, he thought as he slid off the tailgate and followed her into the cabin.

★ ★ ★ ★

CHAPTER 5

After lunch Sam tried to take a nap; not something he was accustomed to during mid-day. It was no use, he was too keyed up from all the distress he had just put himself through. He couldn't stop thinking about Alban's attitude and Peg's insensitivity out in the driveway. *Man, he thought, my first day at work and I get sent back home to go back to sleep so I can stay up all night.* He got up from his bed and walked out onto the porch that wrapped around the cabin's exterior. There was a sliding glass door that led out to the porch from his bedroom. He stood on the porch and looked out into the hills. *I wonder if I'll get any action tonight.* He began to pace back and forth along the wrap around porch. Once in a while, Sam would stop and glance out into the woods. He was nervous, excited and frustrated, all at the same time. Finally, he decided to go to his loft above the barn, where he could relax. He stepped off the back porch steps and walked across the gravel drive to the barn. Thoughts about that morning still flooded his consciousness. He began to climb the stairs that led to the loft over the barn, reached the top, and went inside. As he lay on one of the bunks toward the rear of the loft, he watched the sun start its descent in the western sky. He looked at his watch – *only two o'clock.* Time was running out, he'd better get some sleep soon or he was going to have a tough time staying awake tonight.

Sam began to concentrate on the autumn scene the season provided outside his loft window. The sun, low in the sky, drew a wide array of colors from the foliage in the distant hills. The leaves were beginning to turn, but still had a month or so before they would fall. Colors ranged from orange to yellow with some reds and greens, and various other color contrasts that served as a blend for the entire scenario. The autumn picture reminded him of a patchwork quilt, as it lay rumpled on an unmade bed – soft and colorful. The sun showed through his loft window and felt warm against his clothes and skin. Sam began to relax and settle into the bunk's mattress. A dog barked in the distance – he was asleep.

"Sam, it's 4:30," Peg was bent over Sam, gently shaking him awake. "C'mon Sam, get up, you're on at five o'clock." Sam started to stir, "What?" He replied slowly. His eyes were still closed and he felt very groggy. He was having some difficulty clearing his head, "What time is it?" Peg stood up from trying to shake him awake placing her hands on her hips. "I told you, it's four-thirty. You're on call in half an hour." Then, consciousness seemed to flood his brain all at once. He sat upright looking straight ahead, "Oh my God... my first night on call!" Sam began to scramble about the room trying to gather his equipment and dress at the same time. "Sam, you don't need to rush so. They'll be calling you here, if they call at all. You're only on call tonight, remember?" Sam stopped in his tracks and sat against his desk. "Oh yeah, it's only stand-by calls tonight." Feeling a little embarrassed, he looked over at Peg, "Guess I'm already at the office, huh?" She just shook her head as she stared at the floor. The mental anguish he had put himself through earlier in the day had really rung him out. This was a typical

Sam thing, she thought as she stood leaning against the bunk bed in the corner of the loft. Sam, now fully awake, walked over to his desk and realized how he had overreacted in front of his wife. *Better say something to break the ice*, he thought, "Peg, the Potbelly stove is goin', can you put a pot of coffee on?" Once again she was already one step ahead of him, "It's already perking, dear." Sam liked the old-fashioned percolator type coffee pots that sat on a hot surface and perked the coffee up to a glass bubble at the top of the pot. When he saw the color he liked, the coffee was done. He walked over to the pot belly and poured a cup, "Want some," he held the mug out to Peg. "No thanks. Gotta' go check on the boys." She left the loft. Sam listened to her descend the stairs outside. *Geez, I kinda' made a circus out of that. Wonder what she's thinking?*

He looked over at the silent phone. Dispatch had the loft's phone number and the one for the cabin, but they were instructed to call the loft's number first. He planned on taking his calls from here any time he was on stand-by duty. The loft was going to be his office when he wasn't at the station or in the cruiser. He felt it was a good way to keep his job separate from his family life. He took another gulp of black coffee; *five o'clock PM, I'm on call.*

Sam sat at his desk and watched the phone — nothing. He began to realize he could literally go through an entire night on call without the phone ever ringing if nothing happened that might require his attention. He had got himself all worked up over nothing. *I'm just on call — standing by. Just here at Thompson's service in the event anything happens that requires a game warden's attention.* He got up and walked over to the potbelly, stoked the fire, and poured himself another cup of coffee. As he took another sip of the black stuff, he gazed out the loft window into the dark woods behind the barn, *this is gonna' drive me crazy if I just sit around and wait for the phone to ring every time I'm on call.* He decided to do a little wood carving. It was one of his favorite pastimes and also tended to relax him. He pulled his Swiss Army knife out of his pocket and retrieved a block of pine from the potbelly's wood storage. Just as he sat down to start whittling; he heard footsteps coming up the stairs outside. The door opened… it was Joey, "What are you carving Dad?" He stared at the block of wood in Sam's left hand. "See this block of wood Joe? There's a little man inside and I'm gonna' bring him out of there." "I don't see any man in there," Joey studied the wood hard. "Well, he's in there. You just can't see him yet."

The phone rang. Sam glanced at the clock on the wall – six thirty. He picked up the phone with anticipation, "Hello?" The voice on the other end of the phone began, "Sam? This is Thompson Dispatch. We have a call for you."

Sam started to relax. It seemed like the worse a situation got the more relaxed he became. It was his nature. He sat down at the desk and picked up a pen. "Go ahead. What do you have?" Sam motioned Joey out of the loft as he spoke into the phone. "I'm gonna' tell Mom." That was what Sam was hoping for - sort of a private pony express. He wanted Peg back in the loft before he left for the call. Dispatch began to explain the call in a very calm and clear manner. Sam noticed the tone immediately and felt it was because they knew it was his first call. "One of our cruisers reports a car parked by the side of the road at the end of a wooded cul-de-sac. Officer reports hunting gear in the back seat and there's a 'No Hunting' sign nearby. Want to check it out for us?" Sam's heart started to pound, "Sure, I'm on it." Dispatch warned, "It's an isolated section, Sam – off Vision Drive. No houses or buildings anywhere close." "Okay, I'll give you a call when I get there." He hung up the phone and turned to get his gear. Peg was standing in the loft doorway, feet together and hands covering her mouth. Sam looked away quickly. She watched, not saying a word as he strapped on his .357 Magnum, Model 66 revolver. She had heard the entire call on the phone. He could only wonder what was going through her mind. Sam decided not to push his luck, so he said nothing. Then he heard her say, "Be careful!" Trying not to look nervous, he gave her a quick glance and a peck on the cheek, "Aah, they'll probably be gone before I even get there."

Sam was in his pick-up truck heading for a remote section of Thompson. He considered calling another four hundred unit for backup, *Aah, most of those guys are at the hunting trip meeting anyway. Besides, I'm only going to check out a car on the side of the road with some hunting gear in the back seat. I don't think this warrants me calling out the cavalry.* His decision made, Sam's thoughts went right back to his immediate situation. It was dark and he was a little vague as to where Vision Drive really was. He thought it might be one of the new roads put in last year. Sam passed a dairy farm and turned down a secluded road to the isolated area Dispatch had spoken of on the phone. "Headquarters from 419." "419," came the reply. "Can you give me a better description of the car's location?" "Roger 419. Stand by." Sam came to a fork in the road and saw a road sign, *That's gotta' be it.* He stopped the truck and turned around. In the distance, the truck's headlights revealed the back end of a dairy farm *Nope, guess not,*" he stopped the truck and turned around again. *This is embarrassing,* he thought. *A law enforcement officer on his way to a call and can't find the right road.* He drove back down the first road he had turned down earlier. *"C'mon Dispatch, get me that location.* "419 – on that location?" "Go ahead." Sam stopped the truck to listen. Turn north off Phoenix Avenue by the dairy farm. Continue straight ahead for two miles. There are no signs, so watch your odometer. There will be a glacial boulder on the west side of the road with a peace sign painted on it. Take that left – that'll be Vision. The car in question will be at the end of the cul-de sac." Sam shifted the truck back into drive, and thought, *glacial boulders, peace signs – geez*.

"Lieutenant Gene Alban stood at the front of Fish and Game's meeting room. It was located in a separate building across town from police headquarters and provided a haven reserved for 'game wardens only', to have private "get togethers", meetings, or just go and hang out. All their equipment, ammo, snares, life jackets, nets and the two patrol boats were also stored there in a garage attached to the back of the small building. The boys could come here to relax, study for an upcoming promotion, or just chat. Located across the railroad tracks from the river, the 'Warden House', as it was referred to, also provided a serene atmosphere conducive to the job these men were engaged in. A radio stood on the desk in front of Alban and crackled to life. It was Moody calling headquarters for a location of the car on Vision Drive. "Did anyone hear Moody call for back-up?" Alban was looking at half of the Fish and Game department, all veterans, seated in front of him. They were planning an upcoming hunting trip on the Canadian border. No one said a word. "Son of a bitch – these Newbies are gonna' drive me crazy. He knows he's supposed to call for back up on a night call, especially when there may be hunters involved." Alban's face started to turn red, as it always did when his blood pressure started to climb. "LT," Sergeant Hunter chimed in, "He'd be calling me because I'm his FTO. If he gets into anything, I'm there. He knows where I am." Alban replied quickly, "Well, he still hasn't called in, and that's procedure." Mike Smalls sat in the back of the room chuckling. If anyone was one to breach procedure, it was always Smalls. "Hey, LT," Bowman is still on his way here. He's gotta' go right by the section Moody is in. He never turns his damn radio off so he's probably listening to Moody right now. If I know Bowman, he'll probably stop to check up on him."

"Two miles by the odometer...and there's the boulder... and there's the road." Sam was talking out loud within the confines of his truck. Proceeding down Vision Drive, Sam noticed visibility was particularly bad. It was mid-October, the tree canopy was still up, and the night was overcast. He switched on his fog lights. Almost immediately, a car by the side of the road came into view. He reached for the radio mic when he noticed a second car parked behind the first. *Damn it*, he thought, *I thought they said one car...and they're both out of state vehicles.*

Corporal Nate Bowman was listening to Moody on the radio as he drove to the Warden House, *Shit, I'm already late for the hunting meeting and Moody's out there by himself. Wonder if I should see if he needs some company?* Bowman turned away from his intended destination and started to circle the forest Moody was in. He was just finishing his first loop of the area when he heard Moody call Dispatch, "Headquarters – 419. I have two cars out here. I'll be forty-four in two minutes." "Roger 419," replied Dispatch. Forty-four meant the officer calling in the code was about to leave his vehicle and would be on foot. Bowman started to sweat, *Ah shit, he's getting out of his truck. I'll circle the area one more time.*

Sam slowed his truck and approached the two cars from the driver's side of the vehicles. He wanted to keep the cars between him and the tree line. He pulled the truck up so his headlights were trained on the driver sides of both vehicles. If anyone were watching from behind the tree line, the high beams from his truck would blind them as to Sam's position in the cul-de-sac. The other side of the cul-de-sac offered more tree line so Sam felt he was going to be a hard target to hit if the opportunity arose.

Sam got out of the truck and walked up to the lead vehicle, *Massachusetts plates – Shit*. Pulling his portable radio from the holster, he keyed the radio mic, "Headquarters – 419. First car is a white Chevy Malibu, Mass plates 7-6-3 whiskey, zulu, sierra." He hoped he could remember the whole military alphabet. Assigned words were substituted for every letter of the alphabet since certain letter sounds could be mistaken for others during a radio transmission. Sam knew all the cops in town were listening to the rookie's transmission and he did not wish to be the brunt of their jokes for the next two weeks. Glancing at the tree line, he walked to the rear of the second car, "Second vehicle, red Pontiac Grand AM, marker plate,"…Sam stopped his transmission. Dispatch noticing the break in transmission, stopped taking down information and started their missing officer count of five seconds, "419, We didn't copy that last transmission. Come in." Sam had heard footsteps behind the tree line and stood motionless behind the roof line of the second car. The only good shot these guys would have, even if they could see Sam through the glare, was from the neck up. "419 – Do you read," Dispatch was getting nervous. Sam keyed his radio, "Roger Dispatch – I have people approaching me from the woods – I'll call you back." "Okay 419, be careful."

"Damn that Moody." Alban was furious. The scene was escalating and Alban knew it. "Why hasn't Bowman acknowledged the call?" The room of wardens just stared at the Lieutenant. "Why don't you just call him yourself sir," Smalls was starting to push Alban. It was part of their relationship. Alban glared at Smalls, "Because I want to see what Moody does – that's why, wise ass." Smalls came back, "He's pretty cool in these situations, LT." "Situations? Situations? He was in one situation…and he was lucky. I don't want another Hanks to happen here."

The footsteps on the newly fallen leaves became louder. Sam's company was getting closer. Suddenly, just as Sam thought the owners of those footfalls would emerge from the tree line, the noise stopped. It became deadly quiet. No bird sound – no crickets. Just the wind rustling through the trees. Then a discomforting thought came to Sam's mind, *They can see me checking out their license plates in the truck's light beam.* Sam knew if the would be poachers had a mind to, this would be the time they'd be taking aim at the rookie warden. The other choice would be to just stay hidden.

Sam looked at his watch. It was already one hour past sunset and any hunting should have ceased over an hour ago. Connecticut state law required deer hunters to cease their hunting activity at the sunset hour of that particular day. Today, sunset was at 6:02 PM. It was now 7:15. The law also stipulated a hunter could leave the forest with his weapon after sunset, provided the weapon was unloaded. If the hunter was a bow hunter, the arrows need to be safely tucked away in their quiver. Sam hoped for the latter case.

Sam decided not to give these people any time to think. He immediately held out his six cell police flash light, up and away from his body, at arm's length, and trained it on the tree line. He held the light away from his body in the event they shot at the light. The idea was that such a shot would only hit the supporting arm. Seconds passed and still no sound, "Come on out," Sam yelled into the trees. "I can hear you and I know where you are." Almost immediately, one pair of footsteps could be heard moving along the tree line. The person that belonged to the footsteps was careful to keep just inside the protective curtain of the darkened trees.

The steps continued on up the tree line away from the cars. Then the silhouette of a huge man emerged from the darkness. The dark form against a shaded sky revealed the shape of a very large man carrying a hunting bow. Sam stayed where he was and watched as the dark form approached. *That has to be the biggest man I've ever seen!* He thought. The approaching man was still just a black shadow, walking faster and more deliberate now. The bow hung at arm's length by the man's left side.

The hunter stepped from the narrow strip of grass that separated the street from the tree line, and onto the pavement. His angle of approach was toward Sam standing in the middle of the cul-de-sac. Sam stepped away from the side of the first car and turned to meet him. All indications were that the man carrying the bow was approaching Sam in an effort to communicate his reason for being in the woods after dark. As Sam anticipated some kind of greeting, he was surprised by the man's next action. The man just walked right by, never even giving Sam the satisfaction of a cursory glance, and said, "I have permission to hunt here." Without breaking stride, he continued to the rear of the second parked vehicle and started to open the trunk. Sam couldn't believe the arrogance of this character – to just walk by a law enforcement officer obviously interested in your vehicle, without so much as a hello. Sam became very insulted and said to himself, *I don't think so, asshole.* Sam then addressed the man for the first time since he had left the tree line, "Just a minute, Sir. Step away from the vehicle please." The man straightened up and retorted, "I told you I have permission." Sam replied, "Good, I want to see your paperwork." The man was getting impatient, "Paperwork? You mean my license?" The big man's size and demeanor began to intimidate Sam, but he was doing a good job of not letting it show. "Yes, sir – your hunting license and consent form to hunt this property." The hunter started toward Sam, then stopped and just stared at him. Sam stared back, *Man he's big – brawny too. Hope I don't' have to mix it up with him.* Sam was no puppy either. He was six feet tall and weighed 200 pounds, and held a brown belt in karate. Still this guy looked pretty intimidating. Turning to face the man from ten feet away, Sam was looking into the man's chest. Seconds passed, then Sam said to himself, *He doesn't have any papers. He's a poacher!* The man shouted at Sam, "I told ya', I got permission!" The man was getting indignant. Sam replied in an even but stern tone, "Good, let me see it then." Sam braced himself. There was another long pause. It looked like the man was trying to decide what to do. Sam kept his eyes fixed on the hunter, showing no emotion. The hunter looked down at the .357 strapped to Sam's right hip and thought, *Little bastard ain't scared of me. Think's he's Mr. Big Balls with that cannon on his belt.* An eternity seemed to pass before the two men, then the big man yelled over his right shoulder into the trees – his eyes still on Sam, "Pete, come on out here He wants to see the permission slip." The hunter stood in the darkness not moving. Sam's heart skipped a beat, *Shit, they're together! Listen for his footsteps.* He reminded himself. *I don't want him coming around behind me.* Another pause, then someone started walking from the same place in the tree line where Sam had originally shined his big six cell. A second hunter exited the woods exactly where the first came out. He also carried a hunting bow. Sam turned so he could keep an eye on the big man in the cul-de-sac and also watch the second approach from the left.

The second hunter was much smaller than the first. In fact, he was slight of build. The second man walked up to Sam, "Hi Officer, anything wrong?" Sam just looked at the guy for a minute and noticed he was shaking. Sam thought, *We sure have a couple of winners here!* His nervousness seemed to take Sam's discomfort away. "Want to see my license? I got my deer tags here too – I'll show 'em to ya." He took out his billfold and with shaking hands tried to hand it to Sam. With no emotion and very matter of factly, Sam said, "Remove the license from your wallet sir." Sam was taught that even though most of the hunting public may be aware of this, officers are not allowed to take anyone's wallet in hand to avoid any allegations that may arise. The man was so nervous he dropped the wallet spilling the entire contents on the pavement. Several credit cards and other items covered the area around Sam's feet. Sam knew that in some cases an act like this is merely a ploy to distract the officer. Sam stepped back and shined his big police flashlight on the man. "Pick 'em up – slowly," Sam said rather dryly. "Uh, sorry. No problem Officer," replied the nervous hunter. Still aware of the big man's presence to his right, Sam looked over and watched him fidget. He was looking all around the area, up into the dark sky, and stamping his feet lightly on the pavement as a little boy might do when the need to relieve himself presented itself. *This guy is just too impatient*, Sam thought. Sam addressed the big man, and ordered him in a stern tone, "Sir, put your bow and quiver down on the pavement and stand over here by your buddy." The man snarled back at Sam, "I'm not puttin' my bow down on the road. Are you nuts?" "Do it now," Sam bellowed. Sam's voice was deep and threatening. The big man complied. Sam had to get these two guys closer together, where he could see what each one was up to.

The three men stood in the dark cul-de- sac not saying a word. The only sound was that of the smaller hunter trying to collect the contents of his wallet on the ground. Finally, he stood up and produced a sheet of paper with the landowner's signature on it. The typed verbiage told the reader these two men had permission to hunt the land on this date. "Satisfied?" the big man glared at Sam. "Nope. I still haven't seen your licenses or deer tags." Sam knew he was pushing the big man's limits. Reluctantly, the men produced their licenses and deer tags. The big man handed his paperwork to the smaller man to give to Sam. Sam looked up from the paperwork at the two men, "You guys know what time it is?" "Yeah", replied the big man. Sam continued in an even tone, "Then you know it's an hour and a half after sunset. You two should have been long gone by now." The big man grinned sarcastically and looked away from Sam, "Aah, we got turned around in the woods on the way back from the tree stand. Just didn't judge the time right." Sam looked at the small man, "What are you hunting for?" "Deer," he said slowly. The big man shot his partner a cutting glare. Sam looked at the two bows as they lay on the pavement. All the arrows were quivered and there was no sign of blood on them. Sam thought, *Poaching with bow and arrow? It's quiet enough, I guess. They probably quivered those arrows when they hid from behind the tree line, but I can't prove that. All their deer tags are intact. Hmmm*. Sam looked back at the two men, "Okay, pick up your equipment and put it away."

Sam watched as the two men picked up their bows and went to the rear of the second vehicle, opened the trunk, and began loading their equipment. He positioned himself behind the two hunters so he could watch what they had in the trunk as well as what they were doing with their hunting implements. *They're staying away from the other car,* Sam thought. *Wonder why? If I ask, they can tell me it's none of my business. They've got all the required paperwork, so there is no probable cause, so I can't even ask to search it. It's just that their actions are giving me an altogether different message. I don't think these guys are legal but I can't prove it. Damn.* Sam knew these two were up to no good. They probably had a dead deer out in the woods waiting for them to pick up …or they had an illegal deer in the trunk of the first car. They were only here at the cars to drop off their equipment when they bumped into Sam. "Okay guys, look – I don't like the fact you two are still out here after sunset. There's not enough dense forest for you to be lost for that long. The sign says no hunting but you have a "typed" permission sheet, which isn't settling with me." Sam paused and the two men began to glare at him again. *Go ahead, incriminate yourselves*, he thought. Sam waited for them to say something, but neither man said a word. Sam broke the silence, "So here's the deal. I can't prove anything but it smells real bad. You guys have one minute to get in your cars and leave the area. If I see or hear of either one of your vehicles back in this area in the next week, I'm taking you in on suspicion of deer poaching." Sam paused and waited for a response. Pushing his luck, Sam added, "or we can all take a walk out to where you guys were hiding in the trees and take a look around. What's it gonna' be?" The two men separated and ran to their cars without a word. The first car spun his wheels against the dry pavement of the cul-de-sac and the other followed in hot pursuit. Sam smiled to himself, *I got 'em – bastards!*

Sam sat in his truck at the middle of the now dark and silent cul-de-sac. Another man may have been nervous to be out in such a desolate area by himself where you could hardly see your hand in front of your face. Sam just accepted situations for what they were and relaxed in the comfort of the blackness. He let his head lay back against the seat's headrest and just absorbed the black around him, the cool night air and the wind whistling through the trees. *Whew, glad that's over*, he thought, and let out a sigh of relief. He started to relax in his cover of darkness. *Think I'll just sit here in the dark for a while to see if they come back*. He stared out the truck's window and could feel his heightened senses begin to withdraw. It was at that point he realized that the permission slip the hunter had shown him was okay as additional information but anyone could have typed that. What he forgot to ask them for was a Deer and Turkey Consent Form. If the men had one, they didn't offer it. *Damn, how could I have forgotten that? That was my one chance to nail those bastards…couldn't prove anything else – shit!* Sam sat in the dark cul-de-sac for a while longer with his window open. No automobile noises, nothing but the woods and its natural sounds. Finally, he turned on the truck's cab light and started writing up the call in his service report. He signed the section closed and checked the box "advised in person." He threw the clipboard onto the passenger's seat, reached for the radio and keyed the mic, "419 clear – Vision Drive. Area and both vehicles secured." A relieved and waiting dispatcher replied, "Roger that 419. Thank you!"

Sam returned to his cabin. It was 8:00 PM. He'd been gone an hour and a half. Sam climbed the stairs to the loft and opened the door. There was Peg, standing in the same spot she was in when he had left on the call, her hands up near her face, fingers on her jaw. Carefully, she asked, "Were they armed?" "Yeah," Sam said matter-of-factly. "They had bows and arrows...I had a .357 magnum." He gave her a quick peck on the check and walked over to the lower bunk and rolled into it. The adrenalin rush had been severe. He closed his eyes and fell asleep.

★ ★ ★ ★

CHAPTER 6

Tuesday morning found Sam asleep in his bunk. His uniform was still on and a bright autumn sunbeam poured through the loft's east window pane. *What time is it*, he asked himself as he scanned the room for the clock. *Seven AM…I've been off Stand-by duty for an hour. Only that one call — unless I didn't hear the phone ring.* A sudden pang of anxiety swept over his body, then he dismissed it as he became more conscious. *That hunting call was plenty for one night.* Sam looked around the room for his boots. Peg must have removed them while he was asleep. He began to freshen up and get his things in order when the loft phone rang, "Moody here." It was Lieutenant Alban, "Sam, I want to see you in my office at 0900 — right after roll call. Be ready to report on last night's activity." "Okay, LT." Alban hung up. Sam looked at the phone, *The guy never says hello or goodbye.*

Roll call had been pretty routine. Nothing was mentioned about the hunting call from the night before although there were smirks aimed in Sam's direction accompanied by a lot of whispering. Sam just sat there and took it all in. Finally roll call was over.

Sam stood in the hall outside Alban's office. The rest of roll call was starting to spill out into the hallway. Some of the guys looked up the hallway and made quiet jokes to one another or pointed, as they watched Sam waiting for the Lieutenant. Some just looked and snickered. Sam was starting to feel uncomfortable, *Is Alban keeping me out here for punishment or what?* He looked back at the officers congregating outside the roll call room, *Assholes.*

Finally, the door opened, "Come in Sam. Have a seat." Sam walked over to a chair opposite Alban's desk and dropped into it. Alban closed the door and started toward his desk.

Down the hall, a group of wardens began to congregate. Roll call had just dismissed and everyone had seen Sam waiting outside Alban's office. Corporal Jake Farmer, a senior warden on the unit, watched Moody enter the Lieutenant's office and grinned widely, "Looks like Moody is going to get an ass kickin." Corporal Bowman, turned to look down the hall and smiled viciously, "Yeah, and he deserves everything he gets. What a dummy – going on a night hunting call with no back up. Not to mention he's still a rookie." Bowman didn't have any special allegiance to Farmer or dislike for Moody. He was a follower and always took the side he thought was safest. "Hey," Tom Stafford stepped into the circle of wardens. "Seems like you two have a lot to say about last night, don't you?" Farmer gave Tom a condescending look, "What's your problem... Rookie? Sticking up for your buddy? Now that's real sweet." Stafford could feel his blood pressure rising. He stepped right up in front of the older warden, and James followed. "I don't have a problem – you have the problem." Farmer snarled back, "Hey, back off kiddo. You on me about Moody?" "Yeah, asshole," Stafford snapped back. "You stand here putting Sam down when you don't even know what the circumstances were." Bowman interrupted, "Hey Tom, he didn't call for back up." Stafford ignored Bowman and kept his eyes fixed on Farmer. "All you guys stand here talking about what you would have done – what Moody should have done," he scanned the faces of the officers around him, "Where were you guys when Sam was out there in the dark alone last night? Huh?" Some of the officers looked at the floor as they all knew the answer. "I'll tell you where you were. You were all sitting in the Warden House, nice and comfy, listening to Sam's radio transmissions and not a one of you got off your ass to go see if he needed help. You assholes make me sick." Bowman started to step toward the tall and lean Stafford, "Why you,"…Pat James still standing behind Stafford, reached out and put one of his huge paws on Bowman's chest and warned, "Whoa' fat boy." Stafford turned and glared at Bowman, "You fuckin' coward! You drove right by those woods last night and never even stopped to see if Sam was okay." Bowman's face turned a deep red. He was being called down by a rookie in front of the guys, not to mention the fact another rookie had physically stifled him, and everyone saw it.

Bowman looked up at the six foot-four inch, 230 pound James, then looked back at Stafford. "Hey, I circled those woods twice," then looked back at James, who still had him at arm's length. "Oh yeah?" Stafford looked accusingly at Bowman, "then why didn't you go in?" Bowman was struggling for a way out of this without losing too much face, "Aah, what do you rookies know anyway." "James, get your hand off the Corporal," Farmer's temper flared. James just kept his eyes on Bowman, "Step back away from Stafford and you can have your shirt back," James grinned widely at Bowman. "Now the rest of you back away before I get feeling paranoid – NOW!" The circle of veterans grouped around James and Stafford slowly began to back away from the rookies.

The joking and name calling subsided but the tense atmosphere thickened. They could see the six foot Stafford, eyes fixed and determined, and jaw set, was too hot to deal with. He was a tall but wiry man that carried a severe look when he was angry. No one wanted any part of the foreboding James who made it clear as to what his intentions were. He had the hands of a black smith and arms to match. Unlike Stafford, James never showed emotion. He just followed through on his promises. James and Stafford stood there in the hallway, back to back, and intimidated the entire Unit. The two rookies made a good team, however they knew they just alienated the entire warden unit for the sake of Sam's reputation.

Farmer was the only veteran that didn't obey James' order. He remained in the center of the circle of wardens with James and Stafford. "Feelin' pretty tough – all academy trained graduates. And look at those shiny new silver badges. Well let me tell you something boys – you don't know shit yet. As for Moody, all he did was ruin the night for a couple of poor hunters. All because he's a cowboy." Stafford shot back, "You don't know they were just a couple of innocent hunters." "I always take the hunter's side," Farmer replied. "Especially in this case. Moody's right out of the academy, just aching for a pinch." Farmer went on, "It was the same thing during the river accident last summer. Him cuttin' across the rapids in the Carolina when he should have been in the channel. Mr. Hero – that's what he's all about."

Stafford looked at the rest of the wardens. By the looks on their faces, he realized he had put them all on the spot. He started to calm down and stepped back from Farmer. "Look, all I'm saying is - 'don't criticize the man because you knew what was going on and didn't step in to try and correct the situation. You also don't know what his reasons were." Noticing that Stafford was backing off, Farmer took advantage and stepped closer to him. The sixty year old warden's face was full of contempt for the rebellious newbies. Thirty years of field experience showed plainly on his weather-beaten and leathery face. "Look assholes – see these two stripes?" He pointed to the corporal stripes on his left arm. "I outrank both of you kids. Stay out of my way or you're gonna' get hurt. I can promise you that." The other wardens, could see the end of the confrontation was near and started to drift away into separate smaller groups of three and four. The murmur of several conversations allowed bits and pieces of different phrases like, "hot headed buddies" and "too big for their britches." Farmer, feeling victorious, pushed his way past Stafford and James, and walked toward the cruiser bay to begin his shift.

Moody sat silently in Alban's office waiting for the Lieutenant to finish reading his report on the alleged poaching incident. Finally, Alban looked up and stared into Moody's eyes. In an even, quiet tone, he calmly asked, "Sam, why didn't you call for back up last night? You had a hunting call – you know the rules." Sam, now realizing he was on the carpet replied, "The call was only to check out a parked car with hunting equipment in it. Once I got there, the situation started to escalate and I had my hands full. I handled it best I could LT." Alban looked at Sam, "The situation escalated – EXACTLY! That's why we want you to call for back up." Sam respectfully listened to his lieutenant and thought, *but you all heard me on the radio. Why didn't someone come in or at least call me?* Alban could see Moody was thinking, "Would you do it again Sam?" "No sir. I admit I underestimated the situation, but it really wasn't something I couldn't handle by myself. But I do have to ask why no one came out if it was such a big deal." Alban's temper started to flare, then he caught himself, "Would you do it again Sam?" Sam's reply was immediate, "Look LT, I don't know what the next time is going to bring. I'm not in the habit of calling out the cavalry for just anything. This wasn't as you referred to it, "a hunting call." It was a car parked by a No Hunting sign with hunting equipment in it. Dispatch asked me to check it out. So in my mind I was looking for an empty car." Alban's temper started to flare again as he leaned across his desk toward Moody, "Do it again and you're suspended. Is that clear Moody?" *He's just covering for everyone – didn't even answer my question.* "Yeah, I learned my lesson," Moody reluctantly offered. Alban looked at Moody, *He's gonna' do the same thing next time – little bastard.* Alban liked the fact Sam wasn't one to panic but he had to keep the safety aspect in Sam's face. He was still too new an officer. These game wardens had to have the confidence in themselves to make quick and accurate decisions regarding any situation that presented itself. The nature of the job was that most of the situations would be taking place in isolated places, like dark woods or out in a remote spot on the river. Alban also knew he had over reacted to the whole thing because of what happened to Hanks last summer. Sam had given him the right answer but he had to make sure Sam understood. *This guy's gonna' go up in rank fast – pure warden material,* Alban thought, although he'd never let Sam know his feelings. "Okay, Sam, you're dismissed."

Sam nodded at the lieutenant, rose from the chair and started to walk out. "Moody," Alban called after him. Sam stopped and turned around, "Off the record – good job last night. You did handle the situation, and I do think you had some real, live, bad guys out there. Just be more careful next time." Moody quietly replied, "Thanks, LT. I will." Sam turned and left Alban's office with a reddened face, *Christ, I'm always in trouble around here.*

Out in the hallway Sam noticed a group of wardens dispersing outside the roll call room. They were watching him leave Alban's office. All of them except Stafford and James, who had their backs to him. *Wonder what's going on down there? He* asked himself as he walked up to the waiting Tom Stafford and Pat James, "Hey guys. What's cookin?" Stafford turned toward Sam, "Everything okay?" "For now, Sam replied. "Let's go get a coffee." James gave Sam a friendly slap on the back, and the three rookies headed for the cafeteria.

Jake Farmer found his patrol car in the station's cruiser bay. It was an olive green blazer known as car six. Still upset about his confrontation with Stafford, he opened the door and flung his briefcase and gear bag onto the front seat. "Rookie bastards", he said to himself as he climbed up into the raised four-wheel drive vehicle. Jake slammed the door closed, started the car, and shoved the gear shift into reverse. As he pulled out of the station yard, he picked up the radio mic, "407 in service." Detecting the grisly tone in Farmer's voice, Dispatch answered, "Good morning 407 – Roger..."

Jake began his patrol through the west hills of Thompson. The area had always been his beat and he'd come to know many of the farmers and "cabin people" that lived in the hilly sections. To them, Jake was a modern day Robin Hood. He brought meat and fish to the more needy people that he smuggled from the Police Department's evidence locker, where it was stored as proof from a poacher's take for court evidence – if they could find it. Jake was accustomed to allow the same people to hunt Thompson's forests and fish the streams without the required licenses. He felt this was his donation to the underprivileged.

This one merciful act probably helped to soothe the guilt he felt from his first marriage. In his younger days, he had a wife and child that he left to circumstance. His temperament and strange working hours had made him a less than worthy father and husband, so he just never returned home one day. He knew they'd get along somehow. It was strange that Jake never felt the need to offer his estranged family any of the gifts he allowed the cabin people. That courtesy was saved for only a chosen few.

Farmer was a handsome man, considering his age. He was six feet one inch tall and a little overweight at 240 pounds. At sixty years old, he was still pretty spry and could keep up with most of the middle aged wardens. His hair was snow white and a little longer than department standards allowed. Deep wrinkles adorned the weather-scarred face that thirty years of field exposure had given him.

The years of service had also given Jake the opportunity to know the law enforcement game. He knew who the law breakers were and who the nuisance people were. In Jake's mind, - nuisance people were those lawbreakers who had no idea of the laws and didn't deserve his attention. He had developed contacts that either sold him information or could get him involved in a sure money making proposition if he so desired. The messy divorce from his first marriage had left him empty handed and his ex-wife liked to live comfortably. Jake was always "in" if there was an extra buck in it for him.

Car six passed the Thompson Bridge and took a side road that led up into the West Hills' ridge section. The washed out road was getting looser and narrower, the higher Jake climbed. As he reached down to shift into four-wheel drive, the blazer's radio crackled, "407 from Headquarters." Picking up the mic, Jake answered, "Route 129, by the bridge." "You have a possible sick skunk at the Middle School." "Not right now," Jake said aloud to himself, "Gotta' go see what Billy and the boys are up to. Friggin' skunk can wait." He picked up the radio mic and answered, "407 - received", and continued his climb up the old logging road.

An old ramshackle cabin finally appeared in the distance. It was set back, off the road, and nestled in the trees. There was no yard except for the cleared area in front of the cabin's porch that was littered with tree stumps and a huge pile of logs. The cabin's owner, Billy Jaggs, stood by one of the piles splitting wood. Billy stopped and watched Farmer's green Blazer approach, "Hey, old man." Jake pulled off the dirt road and parked on the cabin's lot between some old tree stumps. Billy walked up to Jake's window and leaned in with a grin. Jake just sat in the Blazer and scanned the entire area, "Where's the rest of the boys, Billy?" Farmer appeared a little cautious. "Not here," replied Billy. "Probably out huntin' or something." Jake was referring to the other three men Billy shared the cabin with. They were all middle aged, single guys, and worked menial labor when and if they felt like it. "Billy, what's going on up there?" Jake nodded at the wooded hills beyond the cabin. "Aww, c'mon, Jake. Don't make me start sayin' stuff you already know about." Jake got out of the Blazer and leaned against the door. "You got deer stands up there again, don't you?" Jake smiled knowingly at the woodcutter. "Hey Jake – they been there for years. You know that." Farmer looked down and scuffed the ground with his boot, "You working, Billy?" "Well, I was, but got laid off in September. I'm makin' what I can off this loggin' business I got goin'." Farmer looked at the man, "You know that area up there is an animal safe zone. That means you can't hunt it. It's a sanctuary where animals can go and not get shot. Know what I mean, Billy?" Billy just smiled at Farmer, "You tell me the same shit every year, Jake. You know I'm takin' what I can. I got no money and I gotta' eat. Woods is full of deer – more than anybody needs." Farmer looked off into the hills, "Okay, Billy. Just don't get caught." Farmer turned and faced the man and poked Billy's chest with his finger, "I never spoke to you – understand?" "Yeah, yeah," Billy slapped Farmer on the back as he turned toward the cabin, "Come on in the cabin for a coffee," then slipped twenty dollars into Farmer's hand. Jake stuffed the bill in his shirt.

★ ★ ★ ★

Chapter 7

The weeks passed and fall turned slowly to winter. The northeast winds arrived in the Thompson Valley in time to see the first snows land and the town's ponds turn to ice. There was something about this time of year that made the valley a quieter place. Perhaps it was the snow itself that absorbed the normal working sounds of the valley, or the blustery winds that came in over the North Rise. Most likely, it was the mere fact that winter had arrived in all its fury and people just stayed inside. Whatever the case, Thompson became a quiet place, but at the same time just as beautiful, covered with a blanket of white that enhanced different parts of the town the summer elements ignored.

Sam's potbelly stove was getting a lot more use and the dwindling woodpile behind the barn was proof of the declining temperatures. Winter was here, and it was time to break out the winter gear. Snowshoes and walking staffs were pulled off the loft's walls and placed in the truck box on his pickup truck. Extra hats and gloves were stuffed into every nook and cranny of the truck, and sand tubes were placed over the truck's wheel wells to give the midsize more traction on the more slippery days.

The colder temperatures also brought a decline in the number of animal nuisance calls, especially at night. Colder temperatures usually forced the valley's animals into their dwellings until they had to come out to hunt or drink. The valley seemed to slow down in every way.

It was January, and Sam accepted the fact he was going to be a night warden forever. He had to get up early today because he was still required to attend regularly scheduled roll calls every Friday at 9:00 AM. *Lucky I didn't have any calls last night. Getting up at this hour would be a lot worse. Just gonna' have to come home and go back to bed anyway,* Sam thought as he rolled out of bed to get ready for the early morning roll call.

The new month's schedule was posted outside the Shift Commander's office. A group of veteran wardens stood across the hall from the posting, laughing and making jokes. Sam thought, *Why even check it? I'm just gonna' be on nights again. Aah, Shit,* and he walked up to check the posting, not giving the other warden's playfulness a second thought.

Going down the list, Sam skipped the daytime officers, *Where the hell is my name?* He checked it again. No Sam Moody. *C'mon man wake up,* Sam started at the beginning and went down the list again. This time his mind's eye caught the name in a place it wasn't supposed to be in. "Days?" Sam said aloud. "Alright then!" *Who's he got me partnered up with?* Sam followed the line across the posting, *Corporal Jake Farmer. Okay – Haven't worked with him yet but he seems okay.* Stafford and James had never let on about the hallway incident with Farmer and Bowman – and neither had the rest of the Unit. Sam figured the "Cowboy" nickname was just a result of the bow-hunting incident and dismissed it as such. Lieutenant Alban, on the other hand, knew every detail. Alban did have his informers and once the story was out, had a habit of interrogating the messenger until all truths were bared.

Moody's assignment to daytime patrol was no accident, nor was the partnering of Moody to Farmer. Alban's managerial style was to put any two men together that might be having the slightest difficulties with one another. His motto was 'You never really get to know a man until you've pulled an eight hour shift with him in the same car. Let 'em work it out between themselves.' Every member of the Unit hated this approach to problem solving but it was one item that could not be questioned.

A few wardens stood behind Sam whispering and snickering. Sam turned to walk away and came face to face with Jake Farmer, who had been patiently waiting his turn to view the monthly schedule. "Hey partner?" Sam smiled enthusiastically and stuck his hand out to shake Farmer's. "Looks like we're partners this month." Jake just rolled his eyes and ignored Sam's outstretched hand, "Oh boy," he said sarcastically, never giving Sam the satisfaction of a glance. "Can't wait." Farmer checked the roster to confirm Sam's allegation and headed for the locker room. Somewhat surprised, Sam looked to the other wardens watching from across the hallway, "What's that all about?" "Gee, don't know Sam," one of them replied in a half serious tone, "Maybe he just doesn't like Rookies." With that the two veterans started laughing and left Sam standing in the hall by himself. Sam watched the men leave, *Well, that's his problem. Doesn't even know me yet.* He decided not to let it bother him. He was on days and that was what he cared about most right now. He'd deal with Farmer, if and when it came up.

The next morning Sam was up at five AM perking his coffee and watching the sunrise through the kitchen window. It was January, so the sun was lower in the sky than usual and seemed to take longer to rise above the pines that stood before Sam's porch. *Dark morning*, he thought, then glanced at the thermometer that hung on the porch beam just outside the window. *Fifteen degrees, Ah, Farmer is old – we'll probably spend the day in the truck.* Little did Sam know Corporal Jake Farmer had every intention of testing the new warden's capabilities.

The coffee stopped perking and Sam filled his mug with hot, black coffee. As usual, he walked out onto his porch and took it in gulps, as he absorbed the winter scene before him. The snow was deep, the air was cold, and the sky was clear. He smiled as he thought about his brother, Cyrus. Hadn't seen much of him lately, but could picture Cyrus standing by the porch rail, coffee in hand, breathing in the cool, fresh mountain air. Cyrus would take a gulp of the hot coffee, look at Sam, and utter his usual, *'Ah, this is livin.'* It was a pet phrase Cyrus used when all was right with the world. *Gotta' get him out snowshoeing or hiking*, Sam promised himself. With the academy stint and new job, there hadn't been any time for his brother and best friend. A hawk screeched overhead, diverting Sam's attention to the present moment. He drained the mug and left it on the porch rail before heading out to the barn to start the pickup truck.

The drive into the valley seemed to pass quicker than usual today. Sam didn't notice the usual country scenes he took so seriously every morning. Suddenly he realized he was turning into the Station Yard. He reasoned it was probably due to his excitement about finding out what Farmer was all about and what was going on up in the West Hills. The West Hills activities were never talked about. Everyone just figured Jake Farmer had that area for so long that everything was under control.

Sam pulled into the Station Yard and wasted no time getting to the cruiser bay. He loaded up Jake's Blazer with the Marine and Game briefcases, re-supplied the vehicle with carcass bags and rubber gloves, tidied up the traps in the back, and got the heater going. When he was done, Sam stepped back from the vehicle and looked at the Blazer, warmed up and ready to go, *That ought to start his day off right*. Farmer came through the cruiser bay's doorway, "Hey Moody! What in hell are you doing to my Blazer?" "Just getting it ready for ya' Jake." Farmer just stopped, letting the door slam behind him. He just stared at Sam for a few seconds, then said, "Hope you didn't mess anything up. I have everything situated so I know where it's at. Now I probably won't be able to find anything." Jake noticed the disappointment on Sam's face, "Okay, get in, we got a long day ahead of us." Sam climbed into the passenger side of the vehicle, *Cranky old bastard. I can see this is going to be a fun day.*

Jake and Sam started to pull out of the Yard, and in line with procedure, Jake picked up the radio mic, "407 and 419 in service." Dispatch gave a routine acknowledgement and the two wardens headed for the West Hills. "Where we headed, Jake?" Sam was enthusiastic, trying to put the last few minutes behind him. "West Hills – Got some high altitude patrolling to do. Hope you brought your snowshoes." Jake smiled to himself. He was better than most on a pair of snowshoes and had every intention on running Sam into the ground, *I'll show Mr. Showoff here what real patrolling is like.*

Jake drove. He wanted to make sure they went where he wanted to go, and more than that, when he wanted. Sam had picked up on that message early in the ride. Passing the Thompson Bridge, Jake broke the silence, "We're gonna' walk the West Ridge today. Hope you're up for some hiking." Jake had picked the West Ridge because of the irregular terrain. Sam smiled. He knew the land and was onto Jake's game. "Fine with me." *At least we'll stay warm he thought.* "The West Ridge is an animal safe zone, Jake. Shouldn't be anyone up there, except maybe some sleepy animals." Jake gave Sam a condescending glare. "You don't need to be telling me where anything is schoolboy. I want to see how you handle yourself in the high country." Sam had had enough of Farmer's attitude, "You'll know all about that when I have to carry you down, old man."

The ride to the West Ridge was a bumpy one. The logging roads to the top weren't plowed in some places so they had to be in four-wheel drive all the way. "Okay, Sam, get your snowshoes on. You are gonna' need 'em. Snow up here is two feet deep in some places." The veteran intended to push Sam's limits today. He was going to walk him through the worst terrain he knew, but with a mind to keep him away from any tree stands he knew were in the area. After all, Sam didn't know Jake's game, and Jake couldn't risk losing the hard earned advantages that took him thirty years to build because of some rookie's naiveté.

The two wardens patrolled the West Ridge all morning. They each wore small daypacks on their backs that contained a small first aid kit, a snack, dry socks, and a thermos of hot coffee. Walking would have been impossible without the snowshoes strapped to their feet. The snowshoes were specially made for law enforcement personnel and were oval in shape but much smaller in size than the conventional kind. Both Jake and Sam held ski poles in each hand to help with their balance in the deep snow. The poles were especially useful when traversing a side slope or descending a steep incline. There were many dips and rises in this set of hills and one had to remember to lead heal first when descending, otherwise the tip of the snowshoe would bite into the new powder like a shovel and send the wearer tumbling down the hill. Climbing was just the opposite. All weight was moved forward and the poles were used as an added hold to the slippery slope. An accomplished snowshoer could make good time with a minimum of effort through the woods if he knew what he was doing. The main rule was never to walk backward. This was a sure way of embarrassing yourself.

Bastard ain't lettin' up, Jake was starting to get winded. How could he have been so foolish as to think he was going to out walk a man twenty years his junior. Sam looked over at Farmer as they descended a small rise, *Son of a bitch keeps on going.' Not bad for an old crow. Can't let him see me sweating' or I'll never hear the end of it.* Farmer took a few more steps and looked up at the next rise they had to ascend. The inside of Jake's coat under his daypack was soaked with sweat. If he didn't get some dry clothing on under that coat the bitter cold could start to cause problems with hypothermia. Farmer stopped, planted his ski poles in the snow, and took off his hat. "Hey Sam, let's take a break. There's a good spot on that ledge over there. The pines above it will keep the wind off us while we take some coffee."

The ledge was situated between a pine forest and a small stream that passed through the center of the small ravine they were in. The stream continued down the mountain eventually emptying into a small pond. Sam took off his snow shoes and daypack. He could feel the dampness of his coat against his uniform shirt. *Better get that dried,* he thought. *That's all I need is for Farmer to have to save me from hypothermia.* Sam reached into his daypack and took out a heavy sweater. Then he took off his coat and replaced it with the sweater. He hung the coat from the limb of a nearby pine and let the coat flap in the breeze. "Moody, are you crazy? Its twenty degrees without the wind chill. You're gonna freeze in that sweater." Sam looked over at Farmer, "Better do the same Jake. Your coat has to be as sweat soaked as mine. You will freeze once we start walking again." Farmer smiled victoriously at Moody, "Oh you're sweating? I thought you were in shape." Sam just shook his head, *I wonder how much he weighs. It may be a long walk back.*

The ledge was situated at one end of the narrow ravine and served as a natural bench to sit on while the exposed rock reflected heat from the sun back onto the men like a natural heater. In front of them, lay the Thompson Valley. Sam pulled his thermos from the daypack and poured himself a cup of steaming coffee. Wisps of vapor rose from the cup as Sam brought it to his lips. Each man just sat on the ledge shielded from the biting wind and drank the warm liquid. No one spoke. A hawk soared over the valley hunting for prey while its mate flew high above waiting for the moment. The only sounds were that of the wind as it filtered through the pine needles above their heads and the rub of tree limbs as they moved against one another.

Sam took another sip from his coffee cup, stood up to stretch, and turned to look into the ravine that served as their place of refuge against the bitter cold. Then he saw it. Twenty yards from where the two wardens rested was a tree stand. It was in an old oak about fifteen feet off the ground. "Son of a bitch!" Sam was shocked. Jake had been watching the two hawks soar in the sky, "What?" Jake turned toward Moody. "Over there," Sam pointed to the old oak. "A tree stand in the middle of an animal safe zone. Somebody is taking deer out here." Farmer tried to look surprised, *I didn't think those boys got up this far. I better play it cool or Moody is gonna' ruin everything.*

Jake's mind was racing. He had to get Sam out of the area before he started looking around and asking questions. "Ya' know, Sam? You were right about taking the coat off, before. I am soaked through and freezing my ass off." Sam turned and looked at the Corporal in disbelief, "Jake, we got an illegal stand here!" Farmer never looked up. He just started getting his gear together, "I gotta' get back to the truck before I get a good case of hypothermia. Screw the tree stand. I'll take care of that tomorrow." Then he looked straight at Sam, "Don't bother the LT about it either. He'll just get all worked up and start hassling me about what is going on up here. Right now, I'm more important than some damn deer. Let's go."

Sam just stood in the snow, *He's not even surprised. Ten minutes ago he was hell bent on walking me into the ground, and now he wants to go home.* Sam walked over to Jake who was hurriedly putting his snowshoes back on. "You going to report this tree stand, Jake?" Jake looked up matter-of-factly, "Yeah, I told you I would, didn't I? I'm senior man here and it's my responsibility. Don't worry about it."

Sam suddenly felt very uncomfortable. He didn't like leaving such important information to another man, especially one he didn't trust. *Okay, he is a Corporal, but I'm beginning to have my doubts about this guy.* There was something wrong here but he couldn't put his finger on it. *I can't even tell anyone what we found here because it's the Corporal's responsibility – Shit.* Sam felt cheated, after all, it was his discovery and Farmer is going to take credit for it.

"Hey Jake, wait a minute. I want to check this out a little bit." Farmer rolled his eyes, "C'mon Sam, I'm freezing." Farmer was lying. He just wanted a reason to get Moody out of the area. Sam ignored Farmer and started toward the tree stand. Over his shoulder Sam yelled to Jake, "Go ahead. You start back. I'll catch up to you." Farmer stared at Moody's back and murmured, "In a pig's ass. You're leaving with me, asshole."

Jake slipped his day pack on and followed Sam over to the tree stand. Sam began to climb the tree, "What are you doing Moody? It's cold out here." "I want to get into the poacher's head. See why the stand is where it is." He got to the stand's platform and hoisted himself up. *There's only one firing position for this stand*, Sam noticed. "This guy knows his business," Sam yelled down to Farmer standing below.

Dan Hayden

"Why do you say that?" Farmer sarcastically replied as he watched Moody in the tree. Sam pointed to a deer run about twenty yards from the tree stand, "See the deer tracks in the snow over there? They come out of the pine forest where the deer are probably bedded down, come right by this tree, and over to the stream." "So what," replied Farmer. "So, the deer come out of their bedroom at dusk to get a drink and this guy nails 'em. He knows they're gonna be thirsty after sleeping all day, so he plants himself right in their daily path." He looked out into the forest from his perch on the tree stand, "Bastard!" After a moment, Sam went on, never looking down at Farmer, "He must be a rifleman. There is no room for a full draw up here and the only position that allows a clear shot is between the two trunks on my right and left. See how the main tree trunk divides into four smaller ones? The trunks behind me only allow enough room to lean against them and shoot toward the deer run. You can't swing the gun in any other direction."

Jake got a sinking feeling as he listened to Sam, *Guess I underestimated this one. The guy knows his stuff.* Farmer had to get Sam down and moving, "C'mon Sam, out of the tree – NOW. Do I have to order you down?" Sam had begun to put himself in the poacher's shoes. He was trying to get the feel of the man who put this stand up here and understand his thinking. Jake's sudden order snapped him back to reality, "What? Oh, sorry Jake. Guess I got a little carried away." Sam started climbing down from the tree stand. As he slid under the stand's metal rail he noticed the paint was flaking away and the apparatus was an older model. A heavy chain with a padlock secured the stand to the old oak. "Better bring a hack saw when you come back. It's chained and locked up here." Jake just rolled his eyes.

The walk back to the Blazer was considerably easier. Farmer's pace was faster but he made it clear they were going to follow the same trail they broke coming up here. He said it was less effort to walk on the already tramped down snow. There wasn't much conversation between the two men except for an occasional reminder from Farmer that he was in a hurry. It came up every time Sam stopped to look at something or veered off the snowshoe trail. *Seems like he doesn't want me straying too far,* Sam thought. *What's going on?* As they walked, Sam began to rethink the situation. The worst thing Farmer could have done was to leave Sam alone with his own thoughts. *This guy was all over me about who was the better snowshoer, and who's in better shape, until I saw that tree stand. It almost seemed like he couldn't get away fast enough. I wonder if he's embarrassed that I spotted an illegal stand in 'his' territory?* Meanwhile, Jake was worrying about how Moody was going to handle the situation. *What if he says something to Alban… or anybody for that matter? I'll have to call him later tonight, well after shift, and tell him I came back up here and cut it down, before he gets a chance to talk to anyone. In his mind, it'll have been taken care of. That should put it to bed. Bastard will probably still ask me about it but I shouldn't have to worry about the others.*

The two wardens trudged on, following the trail they had packed down this morning with their snowshoes. There had not been time to stop for lunch because they left the ledge so quickly. Their snacks still lay in their daypacks. When the green blazer appeared over the next rise, it was approaching two PM. Both Jake and Sam took off their daypacks and snowshoes and threw them into the back of the Blazer. Both men were cold and exhausted. Still trying to take Sam's mind off the day, Jake held out the Blazer's keys, "You drive Sam. I'm kinda' tired." Sam looked at Farmer through narrowed eyes and took the keys, *What is with this guy? He never lets anyone drive.* Seat belts on and engine running, Sam shoved the gear shift back into four wheel drive and Car 6 pounded its way back down the mountain roads into the sleepy Thompson Valley.

Sam pulled into the station's cruiser bay and Jake picked up the radio mic, "407 and 419 are 22." Twenty two was code for the station house. The code was necessary for listeners with less than honorable intentions. Law enforcement administration didn't want anyone knowing where their officers were at any time. Dispatch replied, "Out of service 407? You have three hours of shift left." Farmer keyed the mic, "Roger that. I'm still on patrol, 419 is going to remain here at 22 for paperwork." "Dispatch – Roger." Sam looked over at Jake, "What's this about, Jake?" Farmer reached over and patted Sam on the arm, "Calm down there, Cowboy. I got some business to take care of that does not require your presence. You know, boring stuff. I'd like you to clean out Car 5 and get all the gear stowed and cleaned up. After that you can head on home. Sam was visibly upset and started to leave the Blazer's cab, "Uh, Sam? Remember - keep the tree stand thing between us. I'll tend to it." Sam looked a little confused, "Whatever, Jake. See you in the morning." He grabbed his daypack from the back seat and left the cruiser bay. He was cold and tired and looked forward to the comfort of his cabin and waiting family.

Jake got back into the Blazer and backed out of the cruiser bay, *Patrol hell. I'm goin' home to take a snooze. Moody can do the grunt work at the station and if they need me, I'll hear the call on the radio. They'll never know the difference.* Farmer lived at the southern end of the valley, right by the river. His house was situated above the flood line but well below the main road. He could park the Blazer between the house and the river, out of sight from the main road.

Jake had a beer then lay down on his bed making sure to set the alarm clock for 5:30 PM, one-half hour before the end of shift. He figured he'd wake up, get back in the truck, and on the way back to the Station, call himself out of service. He lay back on the bed, and thought about Sam Moody. *This* *guy is trouble. He's too good to take any chances with. I gotta' figure out what I'm going to do with him. Bastard is…*Jake was asleep.

Three days had passed since Sam first found the tree stand in Jake's, West Ridge Territory. He hadn't said a word to Peg or any of the officers at the P.D. Jake never brought it up again – not even to let Sam know what had happened. Sam had decided to play this one out and see where the cards fell. After all, he was told it was the Corporal's responsibility. He got to the Station early this morning and went straight to the cafeteria for a cup of hot brew. A good hot cup of coffee might settle his nerves before roll call.

Sam just sat down at one of the tables when Lieutenant Alban walked in, "Hi Sam. How are you and the old crow getting along?" Sam stood up from his chair, "Morning Lieutenant. You mean Corporal Farmer?" Sam was a little embarrassed by the question. Alban didn't answer, just continued his questioning stare at Sam. "We're doing okay sir. Why?" Alban grabbed a coffee at the counter and came over to Sam's table, "May I sit down?" "Of course," Sam replied. Alban seated himself right next to Sam and spoke in a lowered tone as he leaned into Sam's space, "What do you think of the West Hills Territory?" Sam just looked at Alban for a moment, obviously confused. Alban went on, "I heard you snowshoed the West Ridge the other day." "Yes sir, we did. No action except for that empty tree stand I found, but Jake took care of that already." Alban's head snapped to attention, "Whoa, whoa, what tree stand?" *Uh oh*, Sam started to sweat and could feel his face getting red and hot, "It should have been in the daily report Farmer submitted on Monday. It's already taken care of, I guess." Alban started to raise his voice, attracting some sleepy looks from the other inhabitants of the cafeteria, then dropped to a low tone again, "What tree stand?" Sam now realized Jake had not 'taken care of it' as he said, or Alban would have read about it in his report. "Look LT, you're going to have to talk with Farmer. That's his territory and his responsibility." Alban, somewhat more composed leaned closer to Sam again, "Sam, if there was a tree stand up in those hills, it was an illegal one. It should have been reported immediately, taken down by the patrolling officers, and impounded for evidence." Sam suddenly felt like an accomplice to a crime. Alban continued, "If any of that happened, I haven't heard one word about it." Alban leaned back in his chair, looked at Sam, and thought, *It appears Sam knows something is up but doesn't know what it is yet. I think he witnessed something he wasn't supposed to, and accidentally let out the information.* The LT just sat there for another minute wondering if he should push Sam any further. Sam was already red faced and shifting in his chair. Finally, Alban decided, Think *I'll just wait awhile and see what Jake does with this.* "Alright Sam," Alban put both hands on the table as he started to stand up, "I'll talk to Jake about it." Then he leaned back down to Sam's eye level and quietly said, "You and I never talked about this – Okay?" A relieved but confused Sam Moody met the lieutenant's gaze, "Sure LT," and nodded knowingly. Alban turned and left the cafeteria. Sam just sat there for a minute, thankful the interrogation was over. He stared into his cup of black coffee and thought, *What a mess this has turned into.* He got up and went to roll call. Sam felt cheap as he entered the room and sat down next to Farmer.

★ ★ ★ ★

CHAPTER 8

Days passed, then weeks, and no further word about the tree stand ever came up again. Sam never found out what really happened and it bothered him to think that no one, not even Alban, let him know that something had, or had not been done. Sam figured he had pushed the part regarding so-called 'secret' information as far as he could without turning Jake in. He decided he would confront Jake about it man to man as soon as he could get him alone. It had been weeks since they were partners. Sam was still on days and had been on patrol with several other wardens since that day up in the West Hills Territory with Jake Farmer.

One day while off duty, Sam decided to take a hike up into the higher elevations of the East Hills. The rolling terrain was located in the mountain range behind his cabin and the access road was only a mile from his own driveway. Peg was away with the boys visiting her parents for the day and he hadn't seen his old friend Lee in quite a while. It was high time he had a talk with the man.

Once out of the driveway, Sam turned his truck east on the main road. About one-half mile later an old logging road appeared on the north side of the highway. It wasn't used very much and was not maintained very well, but it was the only way in that would get him close enough to Lee's mountain hide-away by truck. The old logging road finally ended in a small clearing strewn with stumps and misplaced boulders of all sizes. Heaps of brush piles were scattered about as old rotting logs lay thrown about one another like fallen soldiers after a fierce battle with some formidable foe, and had been left, lonely and quiet, for nature to reclaim as one of her own again. Clouds of white smoldered from the rotting piles of timber to meet the first light of day. The clearing was surrounded by tall pine trees and sunlight poured through the manmade hole in the forest ceiling. Sam called this nature's parking lot. One that could grow back to a forest and in time be cut down and used again.

Sam parked the truck and walked around to the back of the pickup to drop the tailgate. It was a two hour walk from this clearing to Lee's place in the high meadows so he had to gear up. He sat down on the tailgate and changed from sneakers to hiking boots. It was early April and the snows were gone but the trails were pretty washed out. Mountain runoff had coursed down through many of the normally dirt covered trails exposing jagged rock and tree roots. Sam took his boot knife from the truck box and pulled the blade from its nylon sheath. He ran his thumb along the blade's length to check its sharpness, then slipped it back into the sheath and stuffed it loose inside the top of his right boot, pulling the bottom of his jeans over it. He loaded his day pack with a small snack, water bottle, and dry socks. Six cigars wrapped in a red neckerchief were placed on top of the daypack's contents. Sam knew Lee used them for special occasions so he tried to bring him a few every time he visited. A pair of mini binoculars hung from Sam's neck and a compass was placed in his right vest pocket. Almost ready to leave, he stood up from the tailgate and felt for his trusty Swiss buck (jackknife) in his right vest pocket, put on his green baseball cap, and headed for the trail that would lead him to his old friend's cabin. The last thing he did was clip his belt badge to his right hip.

The trail became steeper and rougher as Sam climbed higher. There had been a lot of snow melt this year and the going was slow. Every half an hour, Sam stopped to take a drink from his water bottle and rest. He noticed the trees were starting to bud and scattered snow patches still lay about the leafless forest. The only greenery was that offered by the tall pines that accounted for about one third of the forest's tree population. Sam took another big gulp from his bottle and looked up into the cloudless sky. The air smelled clean and fresh like it had been filtered by the disappearing snow. A stiff spring breeze blew through the trees causing the only sounds in the forest. Trees rubbed against one another and fallen leaves rustled along the steep forest floor.

Finally, Sam crested a small ridge that protected a small basin tucked into the side of the mountain. He stood at its lip and looked down. The basin was primarily flat and supported a green pasture. It was what the locals referred to as High Meadow. There were no trees, only huge glacial boulders that protruded through the flat green grass. The area was probably kept that way from years of goat and sheep ranching. A small stream ran through the center of the meadow and emptied into a pond at the far end. A log cabin with a roofed porch laid half way between the stream and distant tree line. Smoke spiraled from the cabin's chimney, providing the only hint of human habitation in the meadow. Some goats grazed outside the cabin and sheep milled around on the near side of the stream. Sam started his descent into the basin, *Hope he's home after all this. If he only had a phone, I could at least let him know I was coming. Sam continued working his way down the basin wall.* Logs cut to form a crude staircase led the way into the ancient meadow and provided the only evidence of modernization. *I guess this is Lee's idea of a driveway*, Sam thought.

Sam reached the bottom of the basin wall and emerged from the tree line. Walking across the exposed meadow was a welcome experience. It was flat and open. The grass was short from the constant goat and sheep grazing, the warmth of the sun caressed Sam's face, and the stiff breeze that had been evident on the climb up, was shielded by the basin walls. The air in the meadow was still and warm. A hawk soared high overhead and shrieked, probably hunting or calling for its mate. A goat looked up with an uninterested gaze as Sam approached, then went back to his grazing. The sheep ignored the two legged creature and calmly wandered to other parts of the meadow to eat. Water gurgled from the small stream and provided a calming sound comparable to the best classical music but so suited for this place above the clouds. The only sound allowed here was what the basin walls allowed to spill over their brim. This was a mountain paradise.

Sam walked up to the cabin's porch. Still no sign of life. As he started to put his boot down on the first step, a voice came from within the cabin, "Come on in, Sam. Been waitin' for ya." It was Lee. The tall lanky man appeared at the cabin's door. He was about six foot- two inches tall, a little taller than Sam, and appeared to be about one hundred and ninety pounds. He had jet black hair that fell to his shoulders and a thin face that sported a mustache that fell to each jaw bone. His facial features were severe, set off by bright blue eyes. The mountain man just leaned against the cabin's door casing with his arms folded in front of him. He wore faded blue jeans tucked into the top of high leather boots that came to his knees and a red flannel shirt that was a little tattered around the collar. His head was cocked to one side as he smiled warmly at his old friend who stood startled on the porch step. The intoxicating aroma of freshly brewed coffee flowed from the cabin's opening.

"Saw your truck heading up the old logging road about two hours ago, so I put a fresh pot of coffee on. Seems like you're right on time." Sam glanced at his watch, *Exactly two hours. This guy doesn't miss a trick.* Sam climbed the porch stairs and walked across the roof covered porch. The two men faced each other and Sam stuck out his hand smiling, "Been a long time old buddy." Lee narrowed his eyes at Sam. "Yes it has – Officer Moody. Come on in."

The two old friends sat at a skillfully constructed kitchen table hewn from a great tree. A fire blazed in the stone fireplace across the dimly lit cabin. Even with the door open, it was comfortable inside. A pot of coffee perked on the hearth. Lee looked across the table at Moody, "Congratulations old buddy. You cut the mustard." Sam smiled sheepishly, "Thanks Lee. How did you know?" Lee rose from the table to check on the coffee, "Had to hear it in passing conversations with some of the trappers and hunters around here. Thought I might have heard it first from you though." Lee's tone was a little sarcastic. Sam knew he was just trying to make him feel guilty for not having visited in so long. Sam just nodded at the floor, "This is the first chance I got to get up here – with work and all." Lee picked up the coffee pot from the hearth and walked back to the table, "It's good to see you Sam, but I know you didn't come up here because you felt like taking a walk. What's on your mind?"

Sam told Lee what he had seen on the West Ridge in the West Hills Territory. He never mentioned any suspicions he had concerning Farmer's involvement, but the obvious was clear. Lee just sat at the table and stared into Sam's eyes as he spoke, taking in every detail. Every time Sam paused for a reaction, the mountain man remained quiet and expressionless. Sam was careful not to place suspicion on anyone or shed light on any discussions he had with Farmer or Alban.

Finally, Sam was done. He knew Lee was a listener and expected the quiet reaction he received while explaining his concerns. Sam sat back and sipped his coffee. For a few minutes the only sound in the cabin was that of the fire as it crackled in the fireplace across the room. The two men knew each other well enough that they could sit for a great length of time without speaking and still feel comfortable. Sam patiently awaited an answer from Lee while enjoying the silence of his company. Likewise, Lee was happy to be in the company of a good friend that had come for guidance. He considered Sam's story and what he would tell him. After a time, Lee raised his eyes from the table, sat back in his chair and said, "Did you happen to bring any of those cigars I like to take fishing with me?" Sam reached into his daypack and threw the rolled neckerchief to Lee. "There's six in there but they're only for fishing," Sam reminded. "Keeps the bugs away," Lee said. It's a little trick I showed your brother, Cyrus, years ago." Sam gave Lee a disgusted look, "Yeah, I know. Don't remind me."

Lee stood up and walked to the fireplace. His back was to Sam as he stoked the fire, as if buying time before he spoke. "There's been tree stands in those West Hills for the last five years, Sam. Then he turned to face Moody, "…and not a one of 'em is mine, I'll have you know." "That's not why I came up here and you know it," Sam shot back. Lee leaned against the fieldstone fireplace, "I know that ole' buddy. You're not getting sensitive on me are ya' – Officer Moody?" Lee cracked a vicious little smile.

"Okay, Lee, cut the shit. Are you going to tell me what's going on up in those hills or not?" Sam knew Lee was teasing him. Lee looked at Sam, "I see you're wearing your badge on your belt. Did you bring that just to show me or are you on official business?" Sam got up and headed for the door. Lee didn't move from the fireplace, "Sit down Sam. I'm just bustin' your balls. You don't know how proud I am to say my best friend is a State Game Warden." Lee paused and looked for a reaction on Sam's face. Sam just stood glaring back from the cabin's open door. "There, now I've said it," said Lee. "Happy?" Sam sternly replied, "I didn't come up here for that either, Lee."

Lee walked back to the table and sat down. His face became sullen and serious. "You're a warden old buddy. I'm just trying to see where you're coming from. There are people out there that will hate you just for wearing the badge." Sam turned to face Lee at the table, "What are you telling me? You think I'm different because of this badge?" Sam was getting angry. Lee sat back in his chair and put one leg up on his table. "Look, Sam. I told you that shit has been going on up there for five years now. What more do you want?" Sam came back to the table and sat down. Sam took a minute to collect himself then looked across the table at Lee, "Looks like there may be some politics going on here, Lee. I'm just a warden with no rank and I don't have an assigned district yet. I feel very restricted as to what I can do – about anything." Lee was staring into his coffee mug. "Did you ever think of asking Jake Farmer? I heard that's his district up there." Sam just stared at Lee in disbelief. *Where does he get his information?* "I could," answered Sam. He was with me the day I found the tree stand." Sam still wouldn't let on to Lee that he suspected Jake of foul play.

"Well, what did he say when you showed him the stand?" Lee let a slight smile cross his lips as he looked to the cabin floor. "He said he'd take care of it but he was wet and cold and needed to get back to the Blazer." Lee, still looking at the floor just nodded his head. Finally, Lee looked up and stared straight into Sam's eyes, "Sam – You watch yourself up in those West Hills. There are some games being played up there. The poaching up there is bringing in some good coin to those cabin people and they will kill anyone that gets in their way. You have already been tagged as a threat because someone has been letting on about your tracking skills." Lee paused for a moment hoping Sam would get the message. Sam came back with, "I'm just doing my job. There's a problem and I aim to get it fixed. I don't care what those cabin people think of me." Lee shook his head from side to side," Yeah, but you have to learn to play the game, Sam." Sam stood up quickly, knocking over the chair he was sitting in. "Lee! I never thought I'd hear you say…," Lee raised his hands in the air, "No, No, No. I don't mean the bribery –poaching game. I mean you gotta' be privy as to who is doing what. Then you'll know when it's time to strike. It's just like hunting or fishing." Sam picked up the chair and sat back down nodding his head.

Lee knew he had just driven the point home. He got up from the table and walked out onto the front porch. He took out his pipe and lit it. Sam followed him out just as he blew a puff of smoke into the cool mountain air. "I better start headin' back down to the truck. It'll be dark soon." Lee just nodded and watched Sam head for the porch steps. "Remember what I said, Sam. The West Hills Territory is tough right now. Get to know the players and where they're playing before you get in the game." Sam turned, looked back at Lee, and nodded.

"Thanks for the cigars and say hello to Peg for me." Sam turned and started down the steps, "Will do." Sam had his answer.

★ ★ ★ ★

CHAPTER 9

Sam sat in front of his own fireplace staring into a crackling fire. The warmth reached out and touched his face and arms. He could feel heat radiating onto his blue jeans and boots. As he looked deeper into the fire he found the space to think, but the fire was so uncomplicated in itself there was really nothing to think about. The soft warm colors of the flame seemed to move about at the center of the fire but then again they didn't. Several shades of yellow and orange became more distinct the longer he looked into the flame. It was peaceful and warm here. It was a state of consciousness but the flame kept enticing him to let his thoughts melt away. It was hard to think seriously about anything. He felt his eyes getting heavy and his body start to relax. The cold from the day's hike was slowly ebbing from his entire body and he could feel tired and taut muscles starting to soften.

The kids had gone to bed long ago and Peg was still milling about in the kitchen. Sam was in such a state of relaxation he didn't hear her come up behind him. "How was your visit with Lee today?" Peg started to massage the back of Sam's neck. She knew what Lee was to Sam but there must have been another reason for him to go up into the high hills on his day off. Something must be bothering him. "Okay,"

Sam said as he started to close his eyes, "He said to tell you hello." *Something is definitely not right*, thought Peg. *Where are all the wild and crazy stories he usually comes back with? He's too quiet.* "What did he have to say about you becoming a game warden?" "I think he was a little pissed that he didn't hear it from me, but I think he's okay with it." Peg looked up at the ceiling, *Okay with it? Hmmm.*

Peg tried to draw Sam out a little more. "He's probably thinking about how awkward it's going to be if you're the one that will be checking his licenses and traps. Now he's going to have to tow the mark." "Nah," Sam said, not getting the humor in Peg's comment, "you don't have to worry about Lee. He's a straight shooter." Peg just rolled her eyes. "Well, what is it then?" Sam turned to look at Peg, "I think I've uncovered something. Something big, and one of our guys is involved." *Oh, finally,* she thought. Peg came around Sam's chair and sat on the fireplace hearth. "Do you want to talk about it?" Sam just stared into the fire for a minute not saying anything. Then, as if he was thinking out loud, said, "I think Jake Farmer is part of something dirty that's going on in the West Hills Territory. I can't prove anything but I know what I saw and what I feel." Peg's questioning expression turned to that of concern, "Have you spoken to anyone about it?" "Only the situation. I haven't dropped any names yet." Peg paused hoping he would offer more information. When he didn't, she asked, "Did you ask Lee if knew of anything that might be going on?" Sam looked away from the fire and into Peg's face. He knew what she was up to and didn't want to upset her. "Yeah, that's why I went up there today. Just to see if he had heard anything about that area." Peg began to look worried, "What did he have to say? He usually knows everything that goes on in these hills." Sam had to be careful. If he told Peg what Lee had said about that being a dangerous area and the wrong people were already kicking his name around, she'd be ready to make him leave the Unit. "He just warned me about that particular area. People trying to make a few bucks by poaching the wild game up there." Peg leaned toward Sam with a desperate look. "What are you going to do?" Sam had turned back to staring at the fire, "I'm going to ask him myself – when the time is right." Peg was confused, "Ask who what?" "I'm going to ask Jake if he ever reported that tree stand. *What tree stand*, she thought. *Is he already keeping things from me?* She decided not to press Sam any further.

The next morning after roll call, the wardens began their usual migration to the cafeteria for a cup of coffee before shift started. Sam called to Jake as he started to leave the squad room, "Hey Jake! Got a minute?" Jake stopped and told the others to go on ahead. "Yeah? What's on your mind? Sam didn't quite know how to start. He looked at the floor and could feel himself start to sweat. "Well, what do want, Sam? I don't have all day." Farmer was impatient. Sam looked up and straight into Farmer's eyes, "Did you ever report that tree stand I found up on the West Ridge?" Surprised at Sam's bluntness, Jake cocked his head to the side as if he didn't understand the question. "You mean that old tree stand from back in January? The one that looks like it hasn't been used in twenty years?" Sam kept his stare on Jake's eyes. Farmer's eyes were darting all about the room and his voice betrayed a nervous humor. "Yeah," Sam said. "That one."

"That was two months ago and you're just asking now?" Sam knew Jake was playing with him. He still hadn't answered the question. Sam could feel his frustration turning to anger. He took a step closer to Jake, "Did you report it or didn't you?" Sam had a determined look. He wasn't going to let this conversation end without an answer. Farmer saw the look on Sam's face. Rather than cause a scene he decided to answer Sam. He leaned in close to Sam and spoke in a quiet tone. "No, I didn't report it. You saw how old that thing was. I figured no one has used that stand since the area had become an animal safe zone – and that was years ago." Sam's face was starting to flush. Jake could see the anger in his eyes so he tried to talk in a fatherly tone, "Look Sam, it's a dead issue." Jake turned to walk away, "Hold on Jake, I'm not done." Sam stood his ground and was prepared for anything Jake wanted to do. Farmer stopped, surprised by Sam's tone. "What do you mean – you're not done?"

Sam held Jake where he stood with an icy stare. Everyone who knew Sam called it 'the look.' It had a paralyzing effect on the part of the recipient. It didn't matter who it was. The look, made the person want to stop and consider what he was doing or saying. In simple terms, it was a caution sign. "What happened to the stand, Jake? Is it still out there?" Jake couldn't help himself. He was overwhelmed with Sam's pointed approach. There was something about this guy, Jake thought. Something in his tone and look that suddenly made him burst out with the secret he held so close for the last two months. "No. It's not there anymore. I went back and cut it down. The thing was so old I figured it was long forgotten, so I kept it for my own." Then he leaned into Sam's face with a snarl and said, "Try proving that, asshole. You'll look like a fool." Farmer turned and walked toward the group of wardens sitting across the cafeteria. Sam just watched him leave. *You played me, you sonuvabitch and I am going to take you down if it's the last thing I do.*

★ ★ ★ ★

CHAPTER 10

A few days passed and fishing season had opened. It was always the third Saturday in April. Contrary to popular belief among the fishing public, Opening Day meant that all inland bodies of water that had previously been closed for fish stocking were now open and ready to be fished. The state only stocked certain streams, lakes and ponds, so from February to April, those bodies of water remained abandoned, only to be visited by the state stocking trucks and their charges. The Connecticut River, however, was not a state stocked body of water and remained open throughout the year. This difference is what caused confusion among fishermen. Some believed that because the Connecticut remained open throughout the year, a fishing license was not necessary when fishing it. Others thought the water belonged to no one since it flowed through several states and anyone could fish there – again, without a license. Then, there were the few who figured they could sneak in over the state line, fish the river without a Connecticut license and use the excuse that they didn't realize they were in Connecticut. Every game warden was privy to all of these stories and more. The best thing a fisherman could do when confronted with one of 'Thompson's Finest' was to cooperate and be polite. Many a fishing confrontation escalated from a simple license check to a physical tussle with the warden not always on the winning side.

Sam was just returning from a nuisance animal call, as the wardens called it. A bird fell from its perch atop someone's chimney and was trapped in the firebox at the bottom end. Sam had freed the bird, ironically a chimney swift, and was on his way home when he decided to stop by the river to see how much fishing activity there was. He pulled off the main road and onto Bridge Lane, so-named for the covered bridge it hosted nearly 100 years ago. The lane headed straight for the Connecticut River and crossed a set of railroad tracks at the bottom of a long hill. Sam slowed as he approached the tracks and gently prodded his truck over the active rails. The rails or 'gauge' as railroad men referred to them, were elevated from a small dip at the base of Bridge Lane. Once atop the railroad crossing, the river lay directly ahead. The old bridge was long gone but three ancient piles that once served as footings for the bridge piers remained. To a non-resident, they were merely islands in the river and served as duck blinds during waterfowl season. To fishermen, they were a continual hazard to be wary of when going up or downstream. To any of the locals, the old footings were a proud reminder of Thompson's past. One of the first evidences of modernization that revealed an effort to reach beyond the confines of the large valley for trade and commerce.

Almost immediately after crossing the tracks, the old road bent sharply to the left, south as the crow flies, running alongside the river's edge. The river lay about sixty feet below the elevation of the road at the bottom of a sheer cliff. A natural border of trees lined the narrow strip of land between the road and cliff's edge. Several naturally formed alcoves, made larger from years of use, provided parking for cars and small trucks to pull off the road while their owners climbed down the cliffs to fish.

Cars lined both sides of the road. On the river side, would be fishermen, pulled their vehicles into any available space the trees allowed. Sam noticed an old red pickup truck with out of state plates. *Let's start with these guys*, he thought. Fishing the cliffs was an activity in itself. The climb down to the rocks below was an adventure, to say the least. This was the perfect location for someone to dip a line if they were trying to avoid a license check, or just game wardens in general. Sam, however, was not the typical game warden. Scaling these cliffs was not even a concern. He'd played all along this area as a boy and knew every inch of rock. He got out of his truck and stood at the top of the cliff and looked down one of the narrow paths that led to the cliff bottom. *I hope the poison ivy isn't too thick yet. Damn guys have to fish the worst possible places just so I won't come down to check them.*

Sam started down the path. It was extremely steep and narrow. Scrub brush and small saplings growing out the side of the cliff face prohibited any view of the water below. As Sam continued his descent he had to hold onto roots and small tree trunks, or in some cases small rock outcroppings, just to stay on the trail. He couldn't help but wonder why someone would go through all this trouble to fish without a license. Finally, the trail widened and the paths incline loosened. The roar of the river below became increasingly louder as he neared the base of the cliffs.

Sam stepped off the path onto a large slab of bedrock. The greenish brown water sped by at an alarming rate. The current's speed was faster than normal due to the large spring runoff. There had been more snow than usual this year and the snow melt severe. The river always reflected the intensity of the previous winter. The rock walls of the cliffs amplified the noise of the rapids in front of Sam. Any conversation down here would have to be accomplished in a series of shouts. Holding onto an outstretched tree root he looked up river. Two men could be seen straddling an old oil tank that had washed ashore. They looked pretty focused on their fishing and didn't seem to be going anywhere soon. *I'll check them next,* Sam thought. *Where are the other guys?*

Sam started making his way between, up, and over huge piles of bedrock slabs that lay at the foot of the cliffs. There were circular holes in some of the rocks as if they had been drilled through by a power drill. Sam knew it was indeed a drill that had done the work, but it was nature's drill. Many times the river would deposit a small pebble into one of the rock's cracks or depressions. The swirling current rushing by caused the pebble to travel around and around wearing a circular hole in the rock. It was one of the amazing forces of nature that Sam always marveled at. A musty odor filled the air. It was a reminder of rotting debris the river had thrown along the river's edge through the years. The air felt wet and damp, accompanied by an intermittent breeze that slid down the cliff wall.

Occasionally Sam stopped and scanned the area for fishermen. To do this while climbing along the rock pile was a sure way to fall. Eventually, he could see a clump of swamp elms growing straight up from a hidden beach that protruded into the river. Although the beach wasn't visible from where he stood, Sam knew it was there, as he had spent many an hour as a boy exploring and fishing the area himself. Sam just stopped and looked at the area remembering some of the precious moments he had spent down here with his brother Cyrus. The cliffs were a forbidden area for the Moody boys but he and Cyrus sometimes found the time to sneak down here to swim and play pirates. As Sam stood there among the rock and brush, the breeze carried the faint sound of human voices over the rocks. They were men's voices, although indiscernible, it was the sound of people talking over the sound of the river. Sam climbed up onto the last slab of bedrock before the beach. Two men stood fishing with their backs to him. An older man, short in height, and raggedly dressed, fished off the beach. He used a soda can pole, as the wardens called it. The soda can pole was a fishing device used by the underprivileged people that couldn't afford a regular fish pole. It consisted of an empty soda can with a line, sometimes a string, attached to the pop top. The more elaborate ones had an elastic band tied to the end of the line that secured it to the pop top to act as a sort of shock absorber. The remaining fishing line was wrapped around the can all the way to its lip. The last four feet contained the hook and heavy sinker for the river. This end the fisherman held in his other hand. When he was ready to cast, he merely swung the four foot section in a circle and let the sinker carry the line out into the water. Reeling in was accomplished by rewinding the line around the can again.

The second man was younger. He stood about twenty feet downstream of the first man and on top of one of the huge boulders. He was better dressed and used a spinning pole. Sam sat on a rock and watched the two fish for a few minutes. They were obviously together by the way they spoke to one another. They spoke Hispanic and seemed to enjoy each other's company. Sam decided it was time to say hello.

Sam's footfalls were silent as they landed on the soft beach sand. He was still making his way through the small swamp elms that sparsely populated the beach closest to the cliff bottom, then he was out in the open. Neither man had seen him yet. He approached the man on the beach first. "Good afternoon sir," Sam was smiling. "How's the fishing?" Sam kept one eye on the man standing on the boulder to his left. That man was barely paying attention to the scene on the beach. The old man turned to Sam with a surprised

111

Dan Hayden

look and replied with a nod of his head and continued
fishing. The old man seemed to be about fifty-eight to sixty
years old and was short and squatty. He looked about five
foot-five inches tall and weighed about one hundred and
seventy pounds. Sam noticed four smallmouth bass lying
at his feet, connected together with a branch that passed
through each of their gills. The fish rolled back and forth
with the movement of the lapping waves and were still
alive in the water. One end of the branch stuck firmly into
the wet beach sand. "Did you catch these fish with that
can?" Sam was trying to make conversation with the older
gentleman. He seemed a kindly sort with soft eyes and a
gentle rounded face. Once again, the old man replied with a
nod of his head to indicate that he had, and turned his back
to Sam again. _Uniform must be making the guy nervous or maybe
he doesn't understand English. I'll just check his license and get out
of here._ Sam moved around to the man's other side, "May I
see your fishing license?" The old man looked up at Sam
with puppy dog eyes, "I no got one. You gonna' take the
fish?" The man's eyes seemed to fill with water.

Sam looked at the man standing before him and saw his own
grandfather and felt sorry for him. His grandfather had been
an Italian immigrant of the early 1900s, coming to America at
the age of nine. Sam knew the hardships these people faced –
some he witnessed firsthand. The man standing before him
was clearly Hispanic and by the way he spoke could not have
been a resident of this country very long. He seemed a quiet,
gentle little man. Someone you wanted to warm up to and put
your arms around, and tell him it was going to be all right.
The years of struggle showed clearly on his wrinkled face and
calloused hands. His eyes showed desperation.

He was dressed in ragged clothes and needed a shave. He
wore a dirty old baseball cap that sat crookedly atop curly
white hair that looked like it would defy any brush. The old

112

dirty plaid shirt he wore was covered with an army surplus jacket that was stained and frayed at almost every corner. His jeans had patches at the knees and his shoes had no laces. Everything he wore looked like they came right out of the Salvation Army bin.

Sam's heart sank, and as he stared at the decrepit, used up man he thought, *Any man still using a soda can pole in his late fifties has to be fishing for his dinner. I won't take food from anyone's mouth.* Sam had to stay professional and keep his emotions from showing, keep stoic, as they called it. He couldn't just let the old man off because he'd think he could get away with it again. On the other hand, he probably didn't have the money to pay the fine either. It would have been seventy-seven dollars per fish caught, and another seventy-seven dollars for fishing without a license.

In a quiet concerned tone Sam asked the man, "Where are you from sir?" The man put his head down, "From Massachusetts," he replied, and pointed North with a bent finger. Sam paused for a minute remembering the red pickup truck parked up on the cliff. "No, I'm not going to take the fish." Sam's tone was even and monotone. The old man looked up and smiled broadly. Then Sam added, "But you have to promise me you will get a license before you fish in Connecticut again." The man enthusiastically agreed. "I will, I will." Sam added, "I'll be watching. I come here a lot." The old man just kept smiling and nodding his head. Then Sam said, "Okay, you have to pick up your fish and leave right now. Don't stop to talk or anything. Just go to your truck and go home." The old man nodded and looked to his son standing on the boulder behind Sam. "Let's a' go." The young man jumped off the rock and started toward Sam and his father. The old man picked up his fish and the two started to leave. "Just a minute," Sam said to the younger man as he walked by. "Yes sir?" The young man was well spoken and dressed in nice jeans and a fishing vest. Sam looked the young man in the eyes and gave him the same icy stare he was known for when someone did something that didn't meet his approval. "Is this your father?" "Yes sir?" The young man said questioningly. "I suppose you don't have a license either." "No sir. Sorry." Sam feeling as if he could sense the whole family scenario before him, could feel anger and despise for the man's son. He stepped into the young man's face, "How come you're fishing with the pole and your father has to use the soda can?" The young man didn't answer, but the father quickly interjected, "Hey, I like the can." Sam turned and looked at the old man and thought to himself, *Yeah, and you're the one with all the fish too.* Sam turned back to the son and whispered in his ear so the father couldn't hear, "Buy your father a fishing license. If I ever see you down here again without one, I'll pinch you without hesitation. Understand?" The young man nodded. Sam stepped back and the two men seemed to be waiting for permission to leave. Sam just waved his hand in the air and said, "Okay, now get out of here." The father and son hurriedly left the beach. Sam just shook his head, *Now for those other two on the oil can.*

After the old man and his son were out of sight, Sam left the beach and started making his way back through the rocks. Picking his way through the great slabs of bedrock he wondered how it was that these rocks had been deposited here. The scene never failed to amaze him. He continued working his way through the cliff's debris pile until he arrived at the bottom of the footpath that had brought him down here. He stood on a rock close to the path and looked upstream, *Yup, still there. Let's see if they have any licenses.* The two men he had spotted fishing off an old oil tank when he had first arrived were still consumed in their activity.

Sam walked along a narrow ledge that curved around a large rock outcropping at the base of the cliff. The walking was a little more treacherous in this area. It was the bottom of the steepest part of the cliffs and in some cases the water came right to the cliff wall. The rushing current washed right by the ledge Sam walked on, in some cases, within a foot of his outside leg. It was cold and deep, the cause of many drownings through the years. His own mother had almost perished here while picking flowers as a child. The river had no mercy, especially this time of year.

Sam's ledge started to give way to the river's height. In some places water splashed over the ledge making the path extremely slippery. Suddenly the ledge stopped. There was still about thirty feet to go before he got to the oil tank, but to his dismay, a ten foot section had relented to the current's strength and no longer existed. There was no trace that a ledge had ever been there.

Sam looked at the cold water for a moment then at the two fishermen. They hadn't seen him yet. He felt inadequate and embarrassed at the same time. To get to the men from here was impossible. He'd have to backtrack and climb back up the cliff, walk up the road about a hundred yards, and descend a second path that led to the men's position.

Sam considered the situation for a moment, *If I hail them from here and they're illegal, they can make a run for it. On the other hand, even if they run I can still beat them to the top. They'll be pretty slow trying to carry their poles and stuff.* He decided to call to the men, "Yo, over here," Sam yelled above the crashing rapids. The two men turned in his direction. "How's the fishing?" The young man furthest out on the oil tank immediately recognized the uniform and frowned.

Sam was wearing what the wardens called their goon suit. It consisted of a short jacket with Fish and Game Department patches on each shoulder, blue jeans and black combat boots.

His 357 magnum was holstered in a 'high rider' under his right arm and was visible as it came up alongside the bottom of the short jacket. A folding type hunting knife was holstered under his left arm and also stuck out from under the jacket. All topped off with a baseball type cap and sunglasses. To most people and especially lawbreakers, the uniform was intimidating. It was tough looking and to the point.

Both men seemed in their mid to late twenties and fashionably dressed. The first man to recognize Sam leaned toward his friend and said something to him. The friend smiled and turned away from Sam. Seeing this, Sam chuckled to himself, *They think I can't get out to them — yuppie bastards.* Then, both men waved to Sam in a condescending manner insinuating they couldn't hear him. Sam stepped closer to the end of the ledge, "Let me see some licenses." The man who had noticed Sam first fumbled with his vest pocket finally producing what appeared to be a fishing license. Sam couldn't see the year of issue but under the circumstances would settle for a visual. The other man just turned his back to Sam and started fishing again, as if he wasn't part of the scenario. Sam still had the attention of the man flashing him a license so he pointed at his friend. The other man turned to face Sam again but with a bothered look. He motioned that he couldn't hear what Sam wanted. Sam yelled again," Show me your license." The man on the oil tank replied this time, "It's up in the car," and pointed to the road above.

Sam was getting frustrated. It hadn't been an easy climb, the noise on the river, the broken path. It all started to tear at his threshold of patience. He stood watching the two young men smiling and playing dumb across the water from him. *Yeah right. You don't have a license. Okay, have it your way.* Sam cupped one hand around his mouth and yelled over the river's noise while pointing a finger from his other hand directly at the man, "I want to see you up on the road."

Then Sam pointed to the road above. The man yelled back, "I told you I have one. It's in the car." Sam pointed up at the road again, "Show me. You have five minutes. I'll meet you at the top." The smiles the two men had sported fell from their faces and were replaced with a forlorn expression. "Just you," he warned the second man. Sam turned and started for his climb back up the cliff.

Normally Sam wouldn't have gone to such extremes to check a license but these two guys had an attitude. They looked to be in their mid-twenties and a little cocky. One thing Sam just couldn't cotton to were what he referred to as the 'yuppie types.' These were generally well dressed young adults who wore or used only the name brands but didn't generally know what they were doing. He could have overlooked that personality trait but when they started playing dumb and patronizing him, Sam decided he was going to play out the whole deal for them.

Sam reached the top of the cliff first. Out of breath and sweating, his patience long gone, he thought, *Damn Yuppies. They wear all the fancy clothes, use all the expensive gear, but can't afford a license.* There was no way Sam was going to cut this guy any slack. Making him climb the cliffs and interrupting his fishing was only the beginning.

Sam walked over to the trail head at the cliff's edge where he expected the alleged fisherman to appear. To his surprise the man appeared within the time allotted, smiling and ready to cooperate. Sam watched him climb the last few rocks to the top, *Well, I'm impressed. He must have left when I asked him to.*

The man stepped out of the trail head. "Hi Officer. That's my car right over there," he said as he pointed to a yellow SUV parked on the opposite side of the road. Sam smiled dryly back at the man, "Okay good. Let's go get the license." He stepped aside and let the young man lead the way. The young man started across the street and abruptly stopped in the middle of the road. Sam also stopped, leaving about five feet between him and the man. The man turned and faced Sam. He looked embarrassed and his tone was apologetic, "Look Officer, I don't have a license. I lied." Sam said nothing but continued to watch the man's face. "I live in southern Connecticut and only came up here to visit my buddy for the day. We didn't decide to go fishing until I got here." The man paused looking for Sam to say something. When he didn't, the young man continued, "I didn't get a license because it was a one day thing, ya' know? I mean what were my chances of getting caught without a license one day out of the year?" Sam was listening patiently, and started to retrieve his ticket book from the thigh pocket of his BDU pants. "I'd say they were pretty good from the looks of things."

The young man looked nervous. He saw Sam pull the ticket book from his trouser pocket and threw his hands in the air. "Oh man, what's this going to cost me?" Sam looked up from his ticket book, "First things first." Sam ushered him to the side of the road where his car was parked. "Is this really your car?" "Yes sir," came the reply. "Let me see your operator's license and vehicle registration, please."

The young man produced the documents. His name was Joel Balducci. Sam called in the vehicle's marker plates and ran a check on the car. Dispatch confirmed with a positive check on both driver and vehicle. "Okay, Joel, your car checks out but I'm going to have to write you a voucher for fishing without a license." Joel threw his hands in the air again and started pacing in front of Sam, "Shit. What is this going to' run me? Oh, man!" Sam waited for Joel to calm down and stop his pacing. "This is a voucher which means you have five days to buy a license, make a copy of it, and send it to me, care of the Thompson Police Department. If you fail to do so by exactly this time five days from now, I will issue you a ticket for $77.00 through the mail. Do you understand?"

"You mean I have five days to buy a ticket?" Sam looked up from his voucher, "That's right, but if you try and fish on this voucher over the next five days, anywhere in Connecticut, without buying a license, and you get checked by a game warden, it'll be an automatic ticket for $77.00." The man's face sobered, "Okay, I get it. I'll get it to you as soon as I can."

Sam finished writing the voucher and handed the man his copy. "Remember, five days from this hour." "Okay officer. Thanks for the break." Sam looked the man in the eye and said, "No break here son. You have to pay the State $15.00 for a fishing license or pay a fine for $77.00. You're paying either way." Joel knew Sam was giving him the best way out. "Okay sir. You'll get it." As Joel started to leave, Sam said, "One more thing." "Yes sir?" "You're done for the day. If I stop down there to check later and find you fishing, I'll pinch you right on the spot. That will also cause me to check the year of issue on your buddy's license, and if it's not this year, I'll have to pinch him too." "Don't worry Sir. We're outta' here. He turned and disappeared down the trail.

Sam watched him leave and was satisfied with his decision to give Joel a voucher instead of an immediate ticket. Everyone wins in this case. The state gets their fifteen dollars, the fisherman pays only fifteen dollars instead of seventy-seven, and now he has a license if he decides to fish in Connecticut again this year. As for going back down the cliffs to check and see if Joel was fishing – he couldn't care less. It wasn't worth the aggravation. The state would get their money soon enough, one way or another.

★ ★ ★ ★

CHAPTER 11

Roll call began on time, as always. Lieutenant Alban stood at the front of the room and paced from one end to the other, reading off the latest developments, making the necessary announcements, all the usual points of business. Sam sat in the back of the room, over in the corner with his buddies, Pat James and Tom Stafford. Alban kept glancing at the trio. There didn't seem to be any reason the three could think of but it was more obvious than usual. When Alban got to the point in the meeting where he discussed department procedures, he seemed to make each point while staring at Sam. Finally, 0825 arrived, "Okay Gentlemen, get out there and stay safe. Have a good day." Alban dismissed the group.

The game wardens all started to prepare to leave and start their morning shift. Chairs were being shuffled about, the usual banter and insults filled the air, gear bags were being zipped and unzipped, the sound of Velcro tearing cut the air, and above it all Alban's voice rang out, "Moody, Stafford, James! Hold on a minute." The three yearlings had started to make their way to the cafeteria for a coffee. The tone in Alban's voice stopped them short of the door. Alban made his way over to them as soon as the room cleared of dispersing wardens. He looked the three men up and down.

"You guys doing okay? Everything going all right?" The three men looked confused as they scanned each other's faces, then nodded in a positive way back at the lieutenant. Moody was the first to speak. "What's going on LT? Why the concern?" Alban looked serious and more concerned than he should for the present moment. "Just checking on you. It's fishing season and boating season is starting. I just want to remind you guys to be careful. Make sure you have a partner before you go pinching people. Watch out for each other. Take nothing for granted."

Sam now understood what this was all about. Ever since that night on the river last July when Hanks was murdered, Alban seemed to be overly cautious with all his men, especially the new officers. It was almost as if he was afraid for them. The river accident had left some hidden scars in everyone, and no one talked about any of it. It was beginning to become obvious with Alban, although Sam had suspected it for some time. Sam tried to diffuse Alban's state of mind and made the mistake of playing it down, "What's the matter LT – don't think we can handle it?" Alban's face began to turn red as it did every time just before he blew his stack. "James, close the door." Moody continued to hold Alban's gaze in his while Stafford dropped his head and stared at the floor. James busied himself with closing the roll call room door.

"Yeah, I think you can handle it." Alban's tone started at a normal level but it was beginning to rise, "That's not the point. I don't want any of you taking unnecessary risks out there."

Stafford and James just listened. They had no idea what Alban was alluding to. "I read your patrol report yesterday, Sam. You issued a voucher down at the cliffs below Bridge Lane." Sam sat on one of the desk tops, completely relaxed. "Yes sir, I did. It went smooth, no problems." Alban looked at the floor for a moment and scratched his head. "Who did you have with you for back up?" Alban was still looking at the floor. Sam expected the question and remained calm. "No one. I was on my way back from a nuisance animal call and decided to check the cliffs. That's when I found some illegal fishermen." Alban looked up. He didn't seem angry, just concerned. "Sam, that area is dangerous enough without you going down there looking for trouble. Just the kind of people the place attracts is enough to make it dangerous." Sam smiled at the lieutenant, "Sir, I grew up down there. I know the place and the people better than most, and most of 'em know me. I didn't want to waste time with a call for back up, especially since I saw nothing that justified it." Alban started getting red again, "When you were writing that voucher the guy could've clubbed you over the head. You can't watch him and write at the same time. I don't care how good you are." Sam stood up from where he had positioned himself on the desktop, "LT, I knew what I was doing. I was watching for all that mickey mouse stuff, just like I've been trained to. If I have to wait for a 10 every time I'm going in on someone, I might as well forget about catching any lawbreakers." Alban's tone softened, "The problem with you Sam, is that you have no fear and one of these days it's going to get you. It only takes that one time for you to slip up. Look at what happened to Hanks…" he looked down for a second and paused for a moment, then continued, "Look all I'm saying is I want you guys to buddy up in the more dangerous or remote areas. Okay?" They all looked up at the lieutenant and answered at the same time, "Yes sir."

Alban's mothering attitude had made it awkward for all of them. Even Alban seemed to be uncomfortable with it but it was like something he had to do. Sam had had to bite his tongue because he knew Alban played the same game. Alban never called for backup, even when he was being shot at. Sam decided to let it go this time.

Tom Stafford sat in the P.D.'s cafeteria drinking hot coffee with Sam and Pat James. He leaned back in his chair with his two feet resting on his gear bag. "Man, oh man, Moody. You do walk a thin line. I don't know why I hang with you." The huge Pat James was stifling a laugh, "Yeah, Sammy. You're more trouble than your worth. I thought Alban was gonna' take us down with you just because we look alike." Now that the ordeal with Alban was over, the three comrades joked about what could have happened. The three were fast friends and had been through a lot together. It was obvious to them, and everyone else, they would be there for each other, no matter what the circumstance. Sam sat there and smiled as he sipped his black coffee. "C'mon Sam…admit it," Stafford continued. "You had to be a little nervous in there with Alban just now. Just the teensiest bit?" Sam looked up at Stafford, "Fuck you, he's as big a pussy as you…and you don't make me nervous." Sam continued to stare into his coffee. Stafford's face dropped wide open, "What are you…," then he saw Sam start to crack a smile. "Bastard." Sam and Pat erupted in huge laughter. Then Stafford saw the humor in it and joined his friends, laughing along with them.

The jovial mood was interrupted by the sudden appearance of Jake Farmer. He came through the cafeteria doors like a bull in a china shop. As usual, he looked unkempt. His shirttail stuck out of his BDU pants on the right side, his shirt had coffee stains of various sizes on the sleeves, and a frayed pad of papers peeked out of one of his shirt pockets. His hair was already in disarray and one pant leg of his BDU pants spilled over the top of his jungle boots. James saw the opportunity and seized the moment. Having no love for the disheveled Farmer, James yelled from across the cafeteria, "Hey, Farmer. Looks like they got the right name for you. I bet you were brought up in a barn too." Moody and Stafford started to laugh uncontrollably. Farmer stopped and looked at the six foot-four 240 pound warden seated across the room from him. James just smiled back in a defiant sort of way, as if he wanted something to come out of this. By now everyone knew about Farmer's reputation, not from Sam, but by Farmer's general behavior. The only one who had seen it first hand and could prove anything was Sam. Farmer made the wise choice and decided to let James have his way. He looked away from him and went to the counter to get a cup of hot coffee. "Who's walking the line now?" Sam chided James.

Back in his office Lieutenant Alban sat at his desk reading over Officer/Warden Sam Moody's personnel file. *The guy is definitely doing well. Hmmn, Experience level is progressing faster than most and shows an extraordinary level of leadership skills.* Alban's reading was interrupted by a knock on the door. "Come." Alban announced. Fish and Game Captain Fletcher stood in the doorway. His big frame seemed to fill the entire door space. He was a gentle looking man with short white hair separated in the middle by a patch of baldness. He looked to be in fair condition for a man in his late fifties and walked with a limp caused by a gunshot wound from a now retired poacher. Fletcher began, "You wanted to have a word Lieutenant?" Alban stood up from his desk, "Yes sir. Come on in and have a seat please." Captain Fletcher ambled over to the guest chair in front of Alban's desk. "I've been going over Sam Moody's fitness report. The guy is performing way beyond our expectations for his level. His judgment and leadership skills are well ahead of the other men, and his knowledge of the laws is unsurpassed by any other." Fletcher leaned back in his chair, crossed his right leg over his left, and pulled out his corncob pipe. He didn't say anything for a couple of minutes. He just tinkered with the pipe obviously in deep thought. Alban knew not to interrupt and calmly waited for Fletcher to reply. The Captain never gave Alban a second glance. He continued to clean his pipe ever so thoughtfully, routing it out and tapping it against his boot as it hung in the air above Alban's clean floor. Finally, as he began to light the pipe, he squinted up at Alban through a small cloud of smoke that rose from the pipe in his mouth. "Sounds like you want to promote him." Alban was sitting bolt upright in his chair. "Yes sir, but not right away." Fletcher's eyebrows rose as he listened to Alban's answer and stared into the hollow of his corncob. "Seems he's still a little green to me," Fletcher offered. He was going to make Alban explain himself. "Yes sir, he is, but he shows extraordinary skills for a game warden just starting out. The part that bothers me is that he's a cowboy. He's got no fear...just thinks he can handle anything comes his way, regardless of procedure."

Fletcher was still staring downward past the tip of his pipe. A small smile emerged from the serious Captain's face and then he looked right into Alban's eyes. "Can't have any scaredy-cats in this business Gene. He's a yearling and he's full of piss and vinegar. I want him to have the self-confidence with no second guessing. In this business a man has to make a decision fast and it has to be the right one. He's learning and he'll find the time for procedure. What I like about him is that he's thinking. He doesn't call in for back up until he thinks it's necessary...doesn't panic." Alban wasn't quite sure where the Captain was going with all this. "What are you saying, Cap?" Fletcher stood up and looked down at the confused Alban, "I'm saying it's not time to promote him. Not because of anything he's done, or not done, but because he's still in the mold. He's coming along just fine and I'm watching him too." Alban stood up, "Well I'm going to need a new Corporal soon to take Johnson's place and Moody is the only one I'd consider at this time. It's just his no fear attitude that bothers me."

Fletcher started to walk to the door. "I know you need a new Corporal, Gene but don't do Moody any injustices by promoting him before he's ready. Give him a little more time in the oven, then talk to me again." Captain Fletcher smiled as he turned away from Alban standing behind the desk, and left the office.

★ ★ ★ ★

CHAPTER 12

Memorial Day weekend was approaching fast. It was the formal start of boating season among the general public. It always seemed some people felt they had to launch their boat on that weekend even if they didn't get it wet for the rest of the season. The weekend always proved to be one of the busiest besides Fourth of July, however, this weekend was much more dangerous. Boaters that did have any boating skills were a little rusty from the long winter rest and new boaters anxious to get out on the water had yet to achieve the necessary skills required of the fast moving river. The water was still cold and high and fast due to the spring runoff. Many obstacles remained hidden under the dark swirling water of the Connecticut River as if waiting to claim an unsuspecting novice. Through the years the river had claimed many adults as well as children, mostly in the time period between mid-March to early June.

All of Thompson's wardens were called to an emergency meeting regarding the river's present strength. Alban stood at the front of the meeting room and reminded everyone about the spring rush on the river and its dangerous characteristics. The men were briefed on lifesaving methods and appropriate rescue gear, and a checklist was run on every Fish and

Game watercraft regarding the current status of lifesaving equipment. Alban then addressed Marine Sergeant Mike Smalls. "Sergeant Smalls please give the group an update on the Carolina and the Avon. I want those boats ready for launch twenty-four hours a day, seven days a week." Smalls stood up from his seat, "Boats are at the ready, LT. Equipment has been cleaned or replaced and provided for on both boats. I would like the men to get some refresher training on boat handling and river rescue practice though." Alban nodded and looked over at the Training Officer, Sergeant Tom Brainard. "See to it, Tom. I want everyone practiced up before Memorial Day weekend." "Okay, LT." Brainard looked at the group of wardens, "River rescue practice is this Saturday at 0900. Meet at the boathouse in Class D uniform. Bring your issued PFDs." He looked at Moody, Stafford and James…"and for you new guys, that means personal flotation devices…you know, life jackets." The room broke into muffled laughter. Brainard was an okay guy and liked by most of the wardens. He had a cutting, wise-ass attitude, and a devil may care spirit, but not a harmful bone in his body. The remark was meant only to liven up the group for the upcoming practice.

Class D uniforms meant jeans and department issued T-shirts, topped off with a brown baseball type cap with the Fish and Game logo on the front. A short wind breaker with no department patches was the cover. Black jungle boots were always worn. The Class D was an informal training or work uniform so the men could still be identified as Police Department personnel during such activities.

Saturday morning arrived and one by one the wardens pulled into the gated boathouse parking lot. It was a beautiful morning and the river could be seen rushing by hard and fast in the background. Sam opened the door of his truck and just sat there, slumped in his front seat as he closed his eyes and let the new spring sun warm his face. His left leg hung out of the open door and rested on the truck's running board. He was completely relaxed and the bright sun bathed his body in long awaited warmth. The winter had been long and cold and he had spent most of it in the woods. He could feel his muscles start to melt into the seat cushion as he listened to the roar of the river highlighted by the chirping of returning birds back for the summer. Occasionally, the sound of another pickup truck entering the parking lot could be heard but Sam never opened his eyes to see who it was. He just sat there in his cab held at bay by the trappings of the spring sunshine.

Suddenly Sam's euphoric and almost drunken daydreaming was interrupted, "Hey Moody, wake up! It's training time and I own you for the next four hours." Sergeant Tom Brainard approached Sam's truck from the boathouse garage. Brainard sported the broad wise ass looking smile he was known for. His behavior, although good natured, was sometimes inappropriate for the situation. Sam, surprised by Brainard's loud and boisterous greeting, jumped in his seat. The Training Officer saw Sam's startled response and thought it all the more funny. Sam collected himself and remained seated. When his heart stopped racing he turned toward the grinning Brainard who had by now reached the truck's open door. Brainard stood outside the truck waiting for a reply but Sam wasn't about to give him the satisfaction. "Gee, did I startle you?" Brainard offered in a sarcastic tone. "I'm sorry." Sam turned away from Brainard and leaned his head back against the seat's headrest and closed his eyes for effect. "Lay off, Brainard, will ya?" Brainard decided to push his point, "Let's go, Moody. Out of the truck right now…or do I have to drag you out?" Moody opened one eye, the one Brainard could see, "Tom…I have fifteen minutes before I'm scheduled to report. That means I'm off duty right now. You lay one hand on me or my truck and be prepared." Brainard realizing he had been out of line, caught Sam's meaning from the flat serious tone in his voice and the cautioned look from the one open eye. "Okay, okay. Don't get your dander up. I was just having a little fun with you." He turned to walk back to the boathouse, "See you inside in fifteen minutes." Sam didn't answer the Sergeant. As he heard Brainard turn to walk away he just smiled and said to himself, *What an asshole.* He knew Brainard would make him pay for the showdown once they got out on the water.

The wardens were all starting to congregate inside the boathouse. The building sat on the river bank surrounded by forest, about one quarter mile downstream of the public boat launching area. The building included a four bay garage, complete with a machine shop and storage locker. Both of Fish and Game's patrol boats were parked in the last two bays, closest to the river.

Outside the garage was a gas pump so the boat's fuel supplies could be kept continually topped off. Across from the garage was a small administration building where Public Works employees could have breaks and lunch and shower after a hard day on Thompson's roads. The entire compound was surrounded by an eight foot tall chain link fence that included two gates.

During an emergency, the first officer to the boathouse entered the garage by a door closest to the parking lot, next to the gas pump. He had to make his way through the next three garage bays usually crammed with Public Works equipment. In some cases, the scramble to get to the Carolina could be perilous. Sanding machines for the town's dump trucks hung from the garage rafters and the officer rushing for the boats had to duck under them to get to the next bay. Snow plows, detached from their vehicles, also proved to be a challenging obstacle. Captain Fletcher had grappled with the Public Works department several times over the years to keep their equipment out of the way. Depending on the sensitivity and tone of Fletcher's complaint resulted in how much equipment would stay in the way. It was all very petty between the two departments, a struggle for boathouse real estate, with Fish and Game usually on the short end.

Sergeant Tom Brainard stood just inside bay 4 next to the dormant Carolina. He was having a coffee with Lieutenant Alban. The two were talking about some upcoming saltwater fishing trip and were laughing as they discussed the plans. Corporal Nate Bowman was pretending to inspect the Carolina's bow storage area, a position close to where Alban stood, so he could listen for any opportunity for an invitation. Sergeant Mike Smalls busied himself with last minute preparations for both patrol boats and wasn't talking to anyone. The rest of the wardens just milled about the boats drinking their coffees or making light conversation with one another.

Sam looked at his watch. It was 8:55. *Better get in there or Brainard will be busting my ass.* He jumped down from his truck, shut the door, and started for the open garage doors. Brainard watched Moody cross the parking lot while Alban continued on about the new bluefish rig he was planning on trying this year. When Sam was almost in front of the group, he openly greeted him with, "Well, Officer Moody is here now everyone. I guess we can get started." Brainard sported the same wise-ass smile he always wore when trying to crank someone up. Alban looked up into the garage rafters and anticipated Sam's retaliation. Moody continued toward the group not saying a word. He pretended he hadn't heard Brainard's greeting and stood opposite Alban and Brainard at the opening to Bay 4.

Brainard kept his eyes on Sam. When it was obvious Sam wasn't going to play his game he said, "Sam, get the Blazer and hook her up to the Carolina's trailer. Stafford, get the white pick-up and hook onto the Avon." Brainard turned around to face the rest of the group. "Let's see how good these new guys are at backing up the trailers." Some of the men smiled but most just put their heads down or looked away.

Lieutenant Alban cringed every time Brainard used the "new guys" phrase. After all, they weren't new anymore. Moody, Stafford and James had been through the academy, and each had experience in several Fish and Game related ordeals through the last twelve months. It was obvious that ninety percent of the wardens felt the trio had earned their place on the unit. It was time to put the initiation thing to bed. "Okay, hold up a minute," Alban said as he nodded to Brainard. "Tom, can I have a word with you please?" Alban led Brainard to the rear of the Carolina's bay. "What is it, LT?" Alban looked up from the garage floor, "Cut the shit, Tom." Brainard gave Alban his confused and innocent look. Alban's expression was that of boredom, "Don't play that charade with me, buster." He stepped closer to Brainard, and in a stern tone that could only be described as a loud whisper said, "Get off that 'new guy' thing right now! We have three good men standing over there and I don't need you giving them any shit just because you feel like it." Brainard rolled his eyes and started to open his mouth but Alban cut him off, "Do you read me Sergeant?!"

Brainard's face flushed a deep red. "Geez, LT. I was just having a little fun with them." Alban was already walking away. He hadn't even stayed to hear Brainard finish his reply. He left Brainard in the back of the bay.

Once the boats were hooked up and ready for transport to the boat ramp, Sam Moody and Tom Stafford towed their respective vessels to the public boat launch. They positioned the boats and their trailers at the top of the launch's ramp and turned the truck's engines off. Training Officer Brainard was standing between the two patrol boats at the top of the ramp. He had directed the two drivers as to how to position the boats. The trailering by Moody and Stafford was flawless, yet Brainard made no mention. He walked around to the side of the Carolina and waited for the group of wardens to congregate. Now in a more serious and professional tone he began to give a rundown in the operation of each boat's control system, where specific gear was stored, and finally instructions on backing trailered vessels into the river. "Okay guys, take five. Meet back here after the break and I'll lay out today's training exercise." The wardens dispersed for a smoke or to relieve themselves in the surrounding forest. When they came back Brainard began, "Gentlemen, this is River Extraction practice. Its purpose is to simulate a drowning victim somewhere in the river. Your job is to get to him within the allotted time without damaging your boat and make the save. I will have a fireman in the water as the victim. He'll be wearing an orange immersion suit to keep him warm and dry since he has to be rescued by all fifteen of you. I'll be anchored upstream of the swimmer in a fire department boat. When I call your number on the radio, you are to launch the vessel I assign into the river with your assigned partner and come up river through the channel to make the extraction." Brainard paused for a moment and looked at the group staring back at him, "I repeat, stay in the channel. If you break a prop on the way to a rescue you are no good to the victim. Does everyone understand?" The group nodded back and shifted nervously in their ranks. They all knew the channel was hard to negotiate this time of year because of the river's dogleg right, just upstream. The high and fast water tended to push a rescue craft out of the channel to the center of the river when a skipper tried to negotiate the bend.

"No questions? Okay, here's the deal. I'll be grading you on speed of response, how well you negotiate the channel, and technique for the extraction. Scores will be from one to ten with 1 being bad. When you get to the man in the water, toss him a throw bag and pull him into your vessel." Brainard held an orange bag in the air with a bit of rope protruding from the open end. A throw bag was an orange bag full of coiled rope. When the rescuer threw the bag, one end was tied to the rescuer's wrist and the bag part went out to the victim. If the victim grabbed the rope the rescuer could pull him to safety. "Everyone know how to use one of these?" The wardens all nodded to say they did. Brainard went on, "The victim will not be helping you at all. You must treat the situation as it is really happening and the victim is helpless." Brainard stopped and looked at the group and said with a smile, "Remember, you have a current to think about out there. If you don't overshoot with the rope or your bag you have lost the victim. Good luck." Sam was watching Brainard's facial expressions, *Hmmn, I wonder if he's going to take part too.*

Brainard turned and left the group for a waiting fire department boat. The Thompson Fire Department had agreed to lend their rescue boat and crew to help in Fish and Game's river practice. The two firemen helped Brainard climb aboard and sped up river, out of sight of the waiting game wardens.

The group of wardens paced nervously about the boat ramp as they waited for Brainard's call. They had no idea who would be first, what boat they'd be in, or who their partner would be. Everyone hoped they'd get assigned to the Carolina. The Avon was hard to launch and not very maneuverable on the water.

Finally, their radios crackled to life simultaneously, "406 to Fish and Game Rescue Teams. This is a drill. We have a man in the water opposite Thompson Cemetery, 200 yards upstream of the ledge area." Brainard paused for a few seconds to give the men time to absorb the assignment, then he continued, "419 and 422, you are in Marine 2." *Aw shit*, Sam thought. *I don't mind being first, but why does it have to be the Avon.*

Tom Stafford was Sam's partner. Together they raced across the parking lot to the dry and waiting Avon while the rest of the wardens cheered and yelled expletives. It reminded Sam of a Boy Scout relay race. Stafford wasn't much of a skipper so he jumped into the pick-up truck still attached to the Avon's trailer. Sam climbed onto the trailer and crawled over the Avon's huge inflated gunnels. When Sam was in position behind the helm, he signaled Stafford to start backing the boat and trailer down the ramp. As soon as the rubber boat hit the water, Sam pointed at Stafford to stop the truck and unhook from the boat's trailer. Sam went to the stern of the Avon and lowered the propeller into the water then scrambled back to the helm to choke the motor. Meanwhile, the clanking of chains against the metal trailer rang through the still air of the launch as Stafford struggled to free the Avon from its trailer.

Both men worked independently of the other, watching the others next move as a cue for what he had to do next. It was very methodical and organized. Once the engine turned over, Sam brought the choke back to its rest position and powered the Avon off the trailer and into the river behind him. Stafford, still on shore watched the Avon clear the end of the boat trailer skids from inside the attached pickup truck and gassed the truck's engine to pull the sunken trailer from the water.

Once Sam got the Avon away from the ramp, he nudged the throttle to "Forward" and pulled the rubber boat up onto the sandy beach to pick up Stafford. The group of wardens watching the Sam and Tom show, good naturedly yelled words of encouragement or offered graphic descriptions of their impression of the launching.

Tom came sprinting across the parking lot from where he left the truck and trailer to the waiting Avon. "Dive for it, Tom. Time is running out," someone yelled. "Hey Tom, you left your lights on," said another. Everyone was clapping and laughing, except for Tom and Sam. They ignored the cat calls and kept their concentration and had worked up a sweat. Tom slid over the smooth rubber gunnels in one graceful leap and took his place in the Avon's bow.

Sam told Tom to move to the stern while he powered the rubber boat off the beach. Once they were back out in the river, Tom moved back to the bow and knelt down in the crew space. As soon as Tom was back in position, Sam rammed the engine throttle forward to the stops. A rooster tail of white water fifteen feet tall shot up into the air from behind the Avon. The scene drew cheers and laughter from the beached wardens who watched from the parking lot, "Yeah baby," someone yelled. "Go get 'em Moody," another prompted. Marine 2 was on its way to the extraction point. Sam keyed the Avon's radio mic, "Marine 2 is wet and enroute for the extraction."

Sam pointed the Avon's bow between the first and second bridge piers that extended from the Thompson shoreline. Over one hundred years old, the piers were all that remained of a turn of the century iron bridge. Now the old piers were an important landmark that marked the beginning of the river's channel. Sam passed between the ancient pillars and angled the boat over in front of the first pier. He was concentrating on hitting the channel dead center, *Now to make the approach for the channel entrance,* he thought. *Got to get my stern lined up on that first pier.*

Stafford huddled against the inflated bow. Spray from the choppy river was coming over the bow and soaking him. Sam looked down at his pathetic position and smirked. Stafford answered Sam by showing him the middle finger of his left hand. The current was strong and kept pulling the rubber boat's bow out of the channel. They were entering the river's dog leg, a long sweeping bend where the current seemed to slingshot around and cause havoc with any vessel that defied it.

The Avon was less forgiving than most boats and was usually forced out of the channel at this point. Sam struggled to keep her on course and thought to himself, *"Good thing this river is high right now or I'd be hitting some rocks for sure.* Then he decided, *If I can't hold her in the channel I'm going to have to try for the center of the river. Water is a little deeper there.*

Stafford could see the Avon was slipping out of the channel. "Sam, you're missing the channel. Get her over to starboard." Sam was physically struggling with the helm now. "Can't do it, Tom. She's not responding. Current is too strong. I have to go for the 'center river cleft.'" Sam was referring to a shallow 'V' in the river's bedrock bottom located just about centerline of river. It was the next best thing to being in the channel. Getting to it without hitting any submerged rocks could be tricky though.

Brainard stood on the bow of the fireboat watching Marine 2 move out of the channel through a set of binoculars. He keyed the radio, "419, you are 50 yards west of the channel. Get back to deeper water immediately." Sam knew Brainard was going to make this a public display but only he knew the predicament his boat was in. Not someone watching through a set of binoculars a mile away. Sam picked up the mic and replied, "Negative 406. I have deep water here. Will keep present course through the ledge area." Stafford turned around and looked at Sam with questioning look. "He's gonna' be pissed when he sees you, Sam." Sam was turning the wheel one way then another, increasing throttle, then reducing it, trying to avoid the upheavals of water that indicated there were rocks below. "Don't have a choice, Tom. I'm the skipper of this boat, not Brainard. I have to make decisions based on what I see, not what he thinks." Just then Sam swerved the Avon around a huge hydraulic, "Tom, keep an eye out for rocks and tell me which way to steer." Stafford just threw his hands into the air as if to say, *Oh well, I tried*, and turned around to watch for rocks.

Sam was right. The center river cleft, as it was called, stayed deep, and when Stafford saw the ledge fall away into the dark water beneath the hull of the Avon, he turned back to Sam, "We're clear, Sam. Ledge is away." Sam pushed the throttle to full ahead again and asked Stafford, "Do you see the swimmer yet?" Stafford scanned the river's horizon with his binoculars. He scanned from west to east, then came back to near center of river again, "Yeah, I got 'em. About a half mile dead ahead, center of river. Thompson Cemetery is to the east."

The Avon was still west of the extraction point and Sam gently angled the boat over, carefully compensating for the onrushing current. The Avon's radio crackled to life again. It was Brainard, "Marine 2, you are seven minutes into the rescue. Eight minutes remaining." Stafford keyed the mic this time as Sam was busy with the Avon's controls, "Roger 406. We have you in sight. ETA to extraction point is two minutes."

The distance between the swimmer and the Avon closed rapidly. When Sam got within fifty yards of the extraction point he began backing down on the throttle. Stafford yelled back to Sam, "Remember to overshoot the swimmer so I can get a line to him." Sam nodded in compliance.

Twenty yards now remained between the swimmer and the approaching Avon. Sam was bringing her in slow and controlled. The Fireboat was anchored just a few yards upstream of the swimmer, making an overshoot from this angle impossible. Brainard just stood watching from the bow of the Fireboat with a smug look on his face. Sam saw the situation and said to himself, *Damn Brainard, He did that on purpose.* Sam's angle for the overshoot above the swimmer was clearly compromised by the position of the Fireboat, so he crossed below the swimmer and came upstream on the swimmer's east side. Sam pulled the throttle back and slowed to just above the speed of the current. "Okay Tom, get ready!" Stafford stood in the Avon's bow ready to toss the throw bag, one knee firmly pressed into the Avon's port gunnel, the other leg straight and stiff, was locked into the crotch of the starboard gunnel and floor.

When the Avon got abeam of the swimmer Sam yelled, "Now Tom! Aim over his upstream shoulder." Stafford made a perfect toss with the throw line passing just upstream of the immerged fireman. Sam pulled the throttle back to neutral so the Avon could drift at the same speed as the current and swimmer. The swimmer wore an immersion suit that covered his entire body making his efforts to maneuver in the water difficult. He grabbed for the throw line and couldn't close his mittened hand around it. The line went underwater as the current started to carry it by him. His last chance to grab the line resulted in a fumbled reach that came up short and the elusive throw line floated by his outstretched hand by less than twelve inches.

Stafford and Moody watched helplessly as the line drifted by the thrashing swimmer. Sam realized the current had them and didn't want to lose any distance between the Avon and the person in the water, so he instinctively pushed the throttle ahead, engaging the propeller. The forward momentum knocked Stafford backward against the starboard gunnel. A surprised Stafford yelled, "Sam, what are you doing?" Brainard stood on the bow of the Fireboat grinning as the rescue began to deteriorate. He wanted Moody to fail so he could gloat. It was vengeance for the morning's confrontation.

Sam didn't answer Stafford. He just prodded the Avon back to a position abeam of the swimmer and tossed Stafford a new throwbag. Stafford was still trying to reel in the line from the first throw. "Forget about that one, Tom. Throw him another." Tom dropped the mess of tangled line and made another perfect throw over the swimmer's head. This time the swimmer grabbed the line as it lay across the top of his shoulder. "Pull him in, Tom. Nice toss."

Sam brought the boat's engine back to idle and helped Tom haul the wet fireman over the side. Brainard stood at his perch on the Fireboat's bow and clicked the stopwatch. "Twelve minutes and fifty-six seconds," Brainard yelled into the open air, as if there were spectators watching, "… and two tries." Sam repeated the last of Brainard's statement to himself as he looked up at Brainard,…*and two tries. He's gonna' give us a low mark. What an asshole!*

Brainard dropped his stopwatch, letting it fall to his chest where it had been hanging, and looked down at the Avon's crew. "Nice recovery, Sam. Good thinking. Stafford…nice throwing." The fireman slapped Tom Stafford on the back, "Thanks, pal. Looks like I'm gonna' live." Then he put one foot on the Avon's gunnel and launched himself back into the river. Brainard looked at Moody and Stafford, "Okay guys, return to the launch. You're done here. Grade is a six."

Stafford turned to Sam and mouthed the grade to him with a questioning look. Sam looked Brainard right in the eye and said to himself, *six out of ten, you bastard! That's what I get for being in a bad mood this morning.* Then he glanced at Tom Stafford, "Sorry Tom. It's my fault for missing the channel. You did your job well."

Back at the boat ramp, Alban had been listening to the extraction on his portable radio. *A six for Stafford and Moody... after that recovery?* He looked down at the ground and shook his head, *Brainard's gotta' be giving them the business 'cause I reamed his ass in the boathouse this morning. I'm going to have to have another talk with that boy.*

Sam let Stafford drive the Avon back to the launch while he untangled and repacked the spent throw bag lines and stowed them for the next team's use. No one said a word all the way back to the launch. They knew Brainard had dealt them a bad hand but there was no way to prove it. Finally, the launch area appeared from around the bend. Tom passed the old piers and drove the Avon up onto the beach and cut the engine. Bowman and James were on their way out in the Carolina. Bowman was at the helm and yelled to the Avon's crew as they passed one another, "Gee, you guys could have at least given me some competition. Six is gonna' be easy to beat." James was in the bow and consequently flipped off his skipper, then nodded to the Avon's crew as the Carolina took him out into the river. Stafford stood in the beached Avon and saluted James' gesture.

After Rescue practice, everyone met back at the boathouse for a short meeting. Brainard went over the high and low points of the training, and made sure he acknowledged the fact there had been no equipment damage.

Stafford and Moody sat in the back of the room feeling ashamed they had come out of the practice with the lowest scores of the day. "Okay guys, you're dismissed. Good luck out there next weekend." As the wardens began filing out, he looked at Moody and Stafford. "Don't worry boys. You'll have plenty of opportunity to redeem yourselves." Stafford stopped and turned to face Brainard who was grinning from ear to ear. "You can count on that, Sarge. Only next time it won't be so subjective." Brainard just laughed and watched Moody and Stafford leave the room.

When everyone had left, Lieutenant Alban stood up from his seat at the back of the room. Brainard turned around, surprised to see there was still someone there. "Oh, LT. I thought everyone had left." Alban walked to the door that led to the parked Avon in Bay 3. "Let's go," he said motioning to the door. Brainard looked confused. "What do you mean, LT? Practice is over. I have to log in everyone's scores." Alban held the door open, "It's your turn now. You're going to do it for me before you grade another soul. Move it!" Brainard headed for the stowed Avon. Smiling to himself, Alban followed the Training Officer into Bay 3 to hook up the Avon for another practice run on the river.

★ ★ ★ ★

CHAPTER 13

Sam sat in his loft above the barn waiting for the next call. It was Friday evening, the night before the start of Memorial Day weekend. He sat on the lower bunk with his back propped up against the headboard, staring through the skylight in the loft's roof. The night was partly cloudy, and windy in the higher elevations. Sam could see the dark clouds outlined by sporadic moon beams, racing across the dark sky.

The night began to drag. He glanced at his watch. It was 8:30 PM. *What a slow night,* he thought. His mind began to wander, and suddenly without reason, his thoughts turned to the Jake Farmer problem. It had been two months since anyone spoke about the mysterious things that were happening up on the West Ridge. It seemed as if Alban had dismissed the whole affair to hear-say, and it was obvious Farmer was trying to keep his distance from Sam, Tom, and Pat. *What was this guy up to,* Sam thought. *Am I making more of this than I should? The guy hates my guts as well as Stafford's and James.' But why?* Sam began to think about the day he and Farmer snowshoed the West Ridge together and spotted the tree stand, and how peculiar Jake had reacted. He thought about his conversation with Lee up in the High Meadow and what he'd said about the activities that were going on, and his warning to stay away. How was Farmer involved, and why? He was a law enforcement officer... and where did Alban stand with all this? Sam thought about the discussion he and Alban had about Farmer in the P.D.'s cafeteria early one morning, and how Alban said not to approach Jake about it. Was Alban in on it too or was he discreetly setting a trap for Farmer? The thoughts ran around and around in Sam's mind until he began to feel drowsy. His eyelids were getting heavy and the soft crackling of the fire from the potbelly stove across the room began to lull him into a semi-conscious state. He started to nod off and finally he was asleep.

"Sam, wake up! Sam!" Sam awoke with a start. He knew it was Peg but he couldn't get his eyes to focus on her. He'd been in a deep sleep and was having trouble waking up. "C'mon Sam. The Police Department is on the phone. The phone has been ringing and ringing." Sam began to collect his thoughts and swung his feet over the side of the bunk. Rubbing his eyes, he asked Peg, "What time is it?" "It's 11:50 PM and dispatch wants to talk to you." She handed him the portable phone she had brought from the house. "Hello, Moody here." "Sam, we have a boat accident in the river. There are three ashore and two missing. Get the boat." Sam's mind was suddenly crystal clear. "Okay, I'm on it. I'll call 402 and 408." "Thanks, Sam," Dispatch replied. "Call us when you're in the water. This is a code one."

Sam hung up and dialed Alban's home phone. A drowsy Lieutenant Alban answered. Sam cut him off in mid-sentence, "LT, it's Sam. We have a boat accident...Connecticut River...two people missing." Alban came to life, "Where we meeting?" "Boathouse," replied Sam. "Okay, Sam. Call Smalls. Get going." "Right LT."

Sam got Smalls out of bed and gave him the same message. As he hung up the phone he heard Alban calling in on the radio, "402 responding." Sam could feel his adrenalin begin to pump through his body. His heart started to race. He was out of the loft door and descending the exterior staircase to his truck when he heard a second radio transmission. This time it was Smalls, "408 responding – upper boat launch." Reaching the bottom step, Sam raced over to his parked truck and keyed his mic as he climbed into the truck's cab, "419 responding." Dispatch answered Sam since he was the emergency contact that night, "Roger, 419. We have three wardens en route. We'll get the patrol cars to keep the boathouse gate clear for you." Then Dispatch put out a general call to the night shift, "All units in the vicinity of the Connecticut River upper boat launch, block the south side of Prospect Street and local avenues so the wardens have a clear shot to the boat. This is a code one!"

Sam sped through the dark Thompson Hills with his red light flashing. The clouds had been whisked away by the spring winds and it was moon bright and clear. There was still a cool crispness to the night air, typical of late May weather. Sam got to the boathouse street entrance in record time and thanked God there had been little to no traffic. As he turned the corner onto Prospect Street, he could see the police cruisers blocking the road. He saw Alban's big diesel go through the open boathouse gate, red lights flashing and wigwags strobing in the dark night. Right behind him was Smalls. They had all arrived together.

The three wardens worked frantically in the dark to get the big Carolina hooked up onto Alban's truck. Smalls ran through the boathouse dodging Public Works equipment in an effort to get to the Carolina's bay door. "Come on, Smalls," Sam heard Alban mutter in the darkness as they waited for the huge bay door to rise from the ground. Suddenly the retract mechanism could be heard engaging and the door started to rise. Alban barked orders while he backed up his truck to the open bay. Just as the Carolina's trailer hitch fell onto the truck's tongue, Sergeant Brainard came barreling through the yard's open gate. He ran across the parking lot and jumped into the Carolina. "Let's go," Brainard yelled as he donned a life jacket. Sam looked up as he finished securing the wiring harness to Alban's truck. "Get out of the way, Moody. We're rolling." Sam jumped out of the way just as Alban started to pull the Carolina from its resting place. As soon as the Carolina was clear, Alban goosed the truck and sped out of the boatyard leaving a dust trail in the air. Sam ran back to his own truck thinking, *That's a hell of a note. I get here and hook everything up and Brainard takes off in the boat.* He turned his red light back on and followed the Carolina to the boat ramp.

When Sam turned into the boat launch area all he could hear was Smalls screaming at firemen. "Get those fucking trucks out of my way!" Every fire department in Thompson had responded and parked their trucks side by side across the ramp's launching area. Some firemen turned their heads at Smalls outrage but seemed confused, "Now damn it, or I'll start breaking headlights." Two firemen scrambled into their trucks and pulled the huge hook and ladders out of the way.

Alban expertly placed the Carolina and its trailer on the ramp between two huge pumper trucks with only inches to spare on each side. Within seconds the boat was in the water and Brainard had the motor running. Captain Fletcher arrived and calmly boarded the Carolina. Alban stood next to Sam and watched as the activity escalated around the launch. One of Thompson's fire chiefs yelled to Fletcher, "Hey, can my diver ride in your boat?" "Yeah, get him in here now. We're leaving," answered Fletcher. The diver scrambled aboard and the Carolina pulled away from the busy ramp disappearing into the dark night. Only her running lights showing in the blackness.

Sam looked at Alban. He knew the lieutenant wanted to be out on the river too but the extra space had to be reserved for the missing people. "Hey, LT. Let's go get the Avon," Sam was hoping. Alban looked at Sam, "You're committing yourself for the rest of the night once you put that boat in the water. You know that?" Sam just nodded in agreement.

When the Avon slid into the black river, Alban was at the helm. Sam jumped into the bow and keyed his mic, "Marine two is in the water." Dispatch came back, "Roger 419. Begin your grid at river's center and work toward the dam. Watch for other rescue craft in the area. Air one is en route with 'midnight sun.'" Sam looked at Alban who had just begun to put the Avon into its assigned grid pattern. "The state's rescue helicopter is going to be here with 'midnight sun.'" Alban nodded and replied, "It's gonna' be like daytime when he turns that thing on." The firemen had already lit up the river's banks with portable light towers creating an awful glare on the water.

Within an hour, two more fireboats had launched, making the total rescue craft in the river four. Dispatch continually reminded the boats to stay in their own grid patterns. "Marine 2. Change your grid to center–river above the dam. Fire personnel downstream have found empty lifejackets and coolers below the falls." Sam acknowledged the new pattern as Alban moved the Avon to a sweep pattern that was dangerously close to the dam. All four rescue craft paced back and forth across the river. No sign of life had yet been reported. Sam began to get a sinking feeling. It had been over an hour since the call not to mention the amount of time the missing people had spent in the water. His hopes of recovering a live soul were beginning to diminish. "419 from Dispatch. Make your pattern upstream of the two center bridge piers. Fireboat B will relieve you at the dam." "Roger Dispatch," replied Sam. The Avon headed for the

Dan Hayden

most northern end of the accident scene. By now, no one expected to see a live recovery.

The hours passed. Sam checked his watch. It was 4:30 AM. He was cold and stiff from riding in the Avon's bow. The radio broke the dreary silence of the night, "All boats, all boats. State Police Divers have one. Keep clear the east bank by the piers."

One by one the rescue boats pulled up onto the ramp's bank south of the recovery. The young man's body was found only fifteen feet from shore. The accident had happened at the river's center making it clear he had tried to make the swim. Everyone broke free of their boats and went to Site Services' portable trailer to warm up and get some coffee. They had been on the river four and a half hours and only one body had been recovered. Alban was right. It was going to be a long night.

Sam stood on the launch's sandy beach sipping a cup of hot, black coffee. He had purposely wandered away from the rest of the searchers to put the night into some kind of perspective. It was obvious anyone they recovered from the stricken vessel now would be dead. He looked out over the dark river listening to the waves lapping at the beach under his feet and tried to comprehend the feeling of loss that he had for these people whom he'd never met.

As he drank the black liquid, he felt the night wind against his face and a chill run through his entire body. The night air was damp and the two elements had seeped deeply into Sam's inner core over the past four hours. The mood started toward depression sparked by a feeling of defeat by the river. She had claimed yet another set of victims. A night of well-meaning fun had turned into an evening of disaster and sadness all because of the audacity of youth and flagrant irresponsibility.

The chatter of other searchers filled the night air but Sam didn't hear them. His mood focused on the accident and brought back memories of Hanks' accident almost a year ago. It was always the same thing. One simple mistake and it was all over. Sam turned his gaze from the river and looked down at the sand. The young man the divers had brought in was twenty-seven years old. The divers said if he had stood up instead of struggling to reach the shore he would have found he was in chest deep water, if he had stayed with the boat he'd still be alive, if he had worn his life jacket...Fate had it that he did none of these and paid with his life. No one was allowed a mistake on the Connecticut.

"You okay?" It was Alban standing behind him. He turned to see the lieutenant standing there with a concerned look on his face. He looked tired and cold too, holding a hot cup of brew with both hands. "Yeah," replied Sam. "Just trying to make sense of it all." "Well, you can stand here all night, and for the rest of the year, and it'll never make sense, Sam." Sam looked over at one of the boaters who had made it to shore. He had been forced to remove all of his clothes by the EMTs, except for his underwear to prevent hypothermia. He sat on the dark beach with a blanket draped over him, head down, and sobbing. He was the driver and owner of the swamped boat and would be facing two counts of negligent homicide due to his intoxicated condition at the time of the accident, not to mention overloading the boat. Sam spoke without looking at Alban, "I bet he's wishing he could take it all back...do it all over." Alban looked over at the poor spectacle on the beach, "The only thing he's worried about right now is what is going to happen to him next. The loss of his buddies won't hit him until tomorrow when he sobers up completely."

Sam finished off the last of his coffee. "Ready to get back to it, LT?" He was hoping Alban was ready to get back to work. Standing around in the dark was warmer than being in the boat but the minutes passed like hours. The other rescue squads were all watching each of the other four for the slightest move to get back on the river. These kinds of things always ended up in a competition between departments. Everyone wanted to be the hero. As soon as Alban boarded the Avon, and Sam pulled up the beach line, the other crews were making for their boats. The scene disgusted Sam. *Who cares who finds the body first. It's gonna' be a dead body, no matter who finds it,* Sam thought as he watched the silent competition.

Sam and the lieutenant worked their grid pattern back and forth across the dark river. Presently the faint rays of a dawning day could be seen rising in the east. *Sun up,* Sam thought. *When are they going to relieve us?* As if on cue, the radio came to life and broke the silence on the water, "All boats, all boats. Return to shore. Search is discontinued until 0900 hours this morning. Thank you and good morning." *Finally,* Sam thought. Alban headed for shore.

All the search vessels were instructed to just beach on the shore so they could resume first thing later this morning. As Sam climbed into his truck, Captain Fletcher called to him, "Moody! Where do you think you're going?" Sam looked confused, "Home, Sir. They cleared us for the night. I have to get some sleep...have to march with my kids in the parade today at 10:00." Fletcher continued to stare at Sam. "Okay, but this search is your responsibility. Keep your radio close by because they'll be calling you first." Sam's heart sunk. He was exhausted and chilled to the bone. The thought of another eight hours on the boat was incomprehensible. *And what about the kid's parade... and Mom's barbecue?* Then he stopped and put the whole thing in the back of his head. *First things, first,* he thought, and headed straight home for bed.

Sam awoke to a bright, sunny, May morning. Peg was already up getting the boys ready to march in the Memorial Day parade. He rubbed his eyes and the world before him started to come into focus. The smell of coffee brewing tugged at his nostrils and the aroma of sizzling bacon beckoned him from the bedroom. Sam got up and walked into the kitchen. Matt and Steve were in their Boy Scout uniforms and Joey was wearing his little league shirt. Steve, Sam's second oldest child, welcomed his father to the table, "Hey Dad, are you still gonna' march with us today?" "Yeah, I'll be there," Sam replied and then yawned while he stretched his knotted body into a long reach for the kitchen ceiling. Peg watched from the kitchen counter with a bemused smile, "Do you think you're really up for it, Sam? You were out on that boat all night." "I'll be fine. It's only a couple of miles walk anyhow." Steven smiled broadly with Sam's answer.

On the way to the parade, the boys talked excitedly about the parade and how many people would be there. Sam pulled the truck into the school parking lot across from where all the marching divisions were forming up. "Okay, guys, got everything?" The boys said they did as they excitedly poured out the doors in a rush to get to their own divisions. Sam just shook his head and rubbed his eyes again. He was exhausted. He looked down at the portable radio resting on the console. Reluctantly, he reached for it as if reaching for a hot poker, clipped it to his belt, and got out of the truck.

Sam started to walk over to Matt and Steven's division with Joey following close behind. "We'll get your brothers set and then look for your baseball team... okay, Joe?" "Okay Dad, but let's hurry. I don't want them to start marching without me." Sam just smiled as he got closer to the boy scouts standing around their troop flag, pushing and shoving each other, and just having a good time in general. Several troop members looked up just as Sam and Joey approached

151

their group, and Sam's portable crackled to life. "Thompson Dispatch calling, 419." Sam stopped dead in his tracks. Matt and Steven's faces lit up. The police were calling their dad in front of the whole troop. The rest of the scout troop waited in anticipation for Sam's reply. Sam keyed his radio, "Answering, Thompson Road." "Sam, County Sheriffs are down at the boat launch. They want to launch the boats." "Roger. I'll be there in fifteen." Dispatch acknowledged. The scouts were all listening to the transmission in awe. An adult from the troop yelled to Sam, "Go ahead, Sam. I'll get Joey to his division." Sam looked at his boys and apologized, then headed for his truck.

When Sam arrived at the boat launch the county sheriffs were standing on the shore by the beached boats. Obviously, they were waiting to go out on the river and assess the accident scene for themselves. The sheriffs were assigned the accident investigation because it was ruled a homicide that resulted from negligence on the part of the boat's driver. The more information they could dig up, the better. The boat's driver was already being charged with one count of negligent homicide and a second person had yet to be found. There was going to be a lot of investigative work followed by a huge paper chase.

All the sheriffs turned in Sam's direction when they heard his truck come down the access drive into the lower parking lot. Sam had called Sergeant Hunter on the way to the boat launch to help him with the boats. Hunter pulled in right behind him.

As Sam stepped from the truck's cab he heard one of the Sheriffs say, "Finally, Fish and Game shows up. Now we can start to get this investigation underway." The sheriff looked at Moody and decided to give him a piece of his mind, "Where have you been, Officer? We have been standing here for fifteen minutes." Sam just looked at the short, fat sheriff and decided not to honor his question with an answer. Instead, he just bid the whole group a good morning and set about his business of getting the Carolina ready for launch. The sheriff continued, "Hey, I'm talking to you, Mister. Where have you been?" Sam was in no mood for this guy or his attitude. He had only two hours sleep in the last two days and was feeling a little stiff from riding in the cramped quarters of the Avon the night before. Sam stopped prepping the Carolina and walked over to the man. Sergeant Hunter who had just witnessed the whole thing from his truck stayed where he was, leaned against his own truck's cab and smiled to himself, *Oh boy. Sam is going to nail him now.* The outspoken sheriff just stood there with a surprised look as Sam stopped working and watched him approach. Sam walked right up to the five sheriffs and stopped in front of them. "Look, I don't report to you or any of your buddies here. If you gentlemen are interested in going for a boat ride, I suggest you be real nice to me because if I hear one more word from you that I don't care for, I'll leave your ass on the beach. Do you understand me?" The sheriffs all looked at each other. The other four just shrugged their shoulders in embarrassment. Sam started to walk away when suddenly the outspoken sheriff blurted, "Tough guy, huh? I'm calling your captain," and started to pull out his cell phone. Sergeant Hunter seized the opportunity and walked up to the man, "Hey Sheriff, put your phone away." The sheriff turned and saw the sergeant stripes on Hunter's jacket, "Oh good, a superior. Did you hear...," Hunter cut him off, "That officer over there," pointing to Moody, "was the lead officer in last night's search effort. He's been out all night and was just pulled from his kid's parade to take you out on the river – cut him some slack."

The sheriff looked as if someone had just taken the wind from his sails and he began to turn red. One of the other sheriffs murmured, "Way to go, Jack," and led the other three away from the situation. "Uh, I didn't know. It looked like he was late, that's all. I had no idea." Hunter had started to walk away before the embarrassed sheriff could finish talking.

Once Sam had packed his sheriffs in nice and cozy and launched the Carolina, he made for the accident scene which was between the two middle piers in the river and upstream about a hundred feet. He drove the Carolina back and forth so the sheriffs could try to formulate an idea of what actually happened. In the distance, he could hear the faint sounds of the parade and tried to picture his boys as they marched down Thompson Road. He thought about how disappointed his mother would be when he didn't show up at her barbecue. *They're all just going to have to understand. This isn't my fault.*

Sam started to pull away from the spot where the first body had been recovered and asked, "Have you gentlemen seen enough? I still have another body to find." They all indicated they had, so Sam took them back to the ramp.

Hunter joined Sam in the Carolina once the last sheriff had left and together the two Fish and Game Officers resumed their search for the second body. The day passed slowly and around noon it started to rain. Sam was exhausted and was beginning to have difficulty focusing on driving. "Let me take over for a while," Hunter offered. Sam moved away from the boat's console and sat down in the bow. Meanwhile, the state police divers were still being towed back and forth across the accident scene. It was the Carolina's job to keep any stray boats off the divers. The hours passed and at 4:30 PM one of the divers signaled the Carolina. They had found the second body. Sam signaled to indicate he understood and keyed the Carolina's radio mic, "Dispatch from Marine 1."

Dispatch replied, "Go ahead, Sam." Sam continued, "The divers have number two. We'll escort them and tow the subject in. Request an officer to clear out the sightseers from around the launch area." The dispatcher came back, "We understand, 419. Thanks for your effort."

The long drawn out search was finally over. It had taken most of the weekend and ruined everyone's plans that had any involvement with Sam. He was just so tired. He'd deal with everyone else later. Hunter looked at Sam as he pulled up onto the beach. "Okay, you are done here, Sam. I'll put the boat away." Sam immediately shot back, "No, I have to help secure the boat." Hunter put the boat in neutral and shut off the engine, "Your shift is over as of this moment. Go home and get some sleep. That's an order." Sam was too tired to argue. He thanked Hunter and headed for his truck.

★ ★ ★ ★

CHAPTER 14

Another early morning roll call found Sam and the rest of the Fish and Game Unit listening to Lieutenant Alban summarize the Memorial Day weekend boating accident and tying up loose ends. Fish and Game had come through for the town of Thompson once again. They had been on scene for the entire ordeal and led all the other public service departments in the search efforts. The sheriffs were still creating, and following a paper trail in the conviction of the boat's driver, who had been charged with two counts of negligent homicide.

Sam was tired of hearing about the accident. He had more hours invested than anyone on the Unit and didn't want to hear one more detail explained again. Alban started to close the meeting and paused just before dismissing the Unit. He waited for everyone's attention then said, "Before I dismiss you, I have a promotion to recognize." All the wardens straightened up and glanced around the room. They realized it could be any one of them. Alban never let on concerning these issues. He continued, "This individual is a dedicated, hardworking individual with all the talents required for becoming a successful Fish and Game Officer. Recently he was responsible for leading a search on the Connecticut

River and made the Unit a credit to Thompson's rescue service." Alban paused a couple of seconds to let the men digest what he had just said, then looked over at Sam who sat in a rear corner of the room. "Officer Samuel Moody, front and center." Alban looked Sam in the face and smiled.

Sam sat bolt upright in his chair, *Holy shit!* He thought. *It's me. So soon?* The rest of the wardens whooped and cheered, and whistled, and gave crude opinions of the matter. But it was all in good fun. Sam had gained a lot of respect over the last year and had made many friends. They were genuinely happy for him, except for Farmer who sat across the room from Sam and just rolled his eyes over the whole thing. Sam still sat in his chair utterly surprised. Alban realized he was in shock and said, "Yeah, it's you Sam. Come on up here." Sam got up and walked to the front of the room stopping just in front of Alban and Captain Fletcher. Alban ordered the entire room to attention. The wardens became quiet at once and stood up from their seats. Alban turned to Moody and held out a pair of Corporal stripes with his left hand, "Good work, Sam. Congratulations, Corporal Moody." Sam took the stripes then shook Alban's extended hand. Alban saluted and Sam returned it. "Dismissed!" The room exploded into cheers and whoops of laughter, everyone patting Sam on the back and shaking his hand. Farmer just watched from his seat in the opposite corner of the room.

As everyone shuffled out for their daily patrols, Corporal Jake Farmer caught Sam's eye just before he left the roll call room, "Corporal Moody." Sam turned smiling, and realizing it was Jake Farmer, became more serious. Jake looked at Sam matter-of-factly, "Just remember son...I still have time in grade on you, and so doesn't Bowman. Wear those stripes in good health." Sam stood at the door not saying a word. Stafford stepped up next to Sam and said, "Don't you worry Corporal Farmer. James and I will make sure he does." Jake turned to meet Stafford's icy stare, nodded, and left the room.

After the meeting, Alban sat in his office going over some overdue reports. There was a knock at the door and Alban answered, "Come." The door opened and Captain Fletcher walked in. "Got a minute, Gene?" "Sure, Cap. Come in and have a seat." The captain seated himself in a straight back wooden chair directly in front of Alban's desk. "What's on your mind, Cap?" Fletcher had been watching Alban and now dropped his gaze to the floor as he reached for his pipe and smoking tobacco. He didn't answer as he rummaged around in his pockets or as he stoked his pipe. This was the usual routine one could expect from the quiet captain before he gave any kind of answer, especially if it was of any concern.

Fletcher blew a puff of smoke from the pipe and looked up at Alban, squinting through the white fog. "Did you see Farmer's reaction to the new Corporal a few minutes ago?" Alban had indeed witnessed Farmer's warning to Sam at the door but had brushed it off. He knew there was something between the two men, and also of Sam's concerns regarding Farmer's extracurricular activities, but had nothing he could put his finger on yet. For now, he considered the situation a conflict of personalities. Alban looked back down at his desk, "Yes sir, I heard it. Didn't think much of it though." Fletcher took another puff from his pipe and blew it gently into the air, making a soft whistling sound as he did so. He watched the smoke float toward the ceiling. "We have a problem here, Lieutenant." His voice began to grow louder. "Do you mean to sit there and tell me you know nothing is going on?" With that, Fletcher turned his gaze on the unsuspecting lieutenant. Alban's face flushed red. He thought he could keep the personnel problem out of Fletcher's hair but the situation had become obvious to everyone in the station. Alban answered, "No sir. I know something is up with those two guys but I can't prove anything yet." Fletcher stood up suddenly knocking his chair over backward. He ripped the pipe out of his mouth and looked like he was about to blow. Fletcher began bellowing at Alban, "Prove anything? What are you doing about it? You know Jake's reputation as well as I do and you have heard all the incriminating stories regarding his patrol area in the West Ridge Territory. Now he's threatening fellow officers...and one of our best up and comers too." Alban started to shift in his seat. Fletcher was kicking his ass. The Captain continued, "Did you see Stafford face off with Farmer? The damn kid came to Moody's rescue and threatened Farmer right back. We have dissension in the ranks Lieutenant, and possibly a dirty officer. Get to the bottom of it now! I want to know what this whole thing between Moody and Farmer is about and I want Farmer called on the carpet about his so-called activities on the West Ridge. If he's dirty, I'll have his badge. I want an answer one week from today."

Fletcher turned to walk out of the room and kicked the overturned chair out of the way as he headed toward the door. He grabbed the door knob with an angry twist and slammed the office door shut as he left.

Alban just stared at the closed door for a minute. He was still quite overcome with the Captain's fury. He knew he had let things go unattended longer than he should have but how could he go about this investigation without disrupting the Unit more than it was?

Fletcher had pinned him down and was waiting for an answer. He was going to have to do something but Farmer was one of his oldest friends. What if he was dirty? It would be Alban's responsibility to bring him to justice. *Damn old coot*, thought Alban. *He doesn't need the money. Why is he doing this? He knows the penalty.* Too many rumors were winding their way around the P.D. If they ever got out to the public, the reputation of the whole department would be at stake. Alban decided, *I'm going to have to call him in for a talk.*

Corporal Jake Farmer was in his patrol car heading for the West Ridge. He thought about Moody's promotion and the way the whole Unit had celebrated his achievement. He knew Moody was quickly becoming popular with the rest of the wardens. Everyone respected him and his outdoor skills. Jake knew he'd have to be more careful than ever now. Suddenly his concentration was broken by the patrol car's radio, "407 from Dispatch?" Jake picked up his mike and pressed the talk button, "Route 12 en route to the West Ridge." Officers always gave their position before speaking. "Return to Base, 407. LT wants to see you." Farmer punched the steering wheel with the palm of his hand he held the microphone in, "Aw shit! Now he's gonna' give me shit about the way I talked to Moody back there. Damn it!" Farmer keyed the mic, "Roger, 407 returning to Base."

★ ★ ★ ★

CHAPTER 15

The Moody's sat around a big oak table in their kitchen having breakfast. They had got used to eating breakfast when Sam returned from roll call so they could all eat together. The mood was jovial and excited. It was their last day home before going on vacation and the family was discussing Sam's promotion. "Wow, Dad...Corporal...cool!" Matt, Sam's oldest son was excited about the new rank. Peg smiled to herself as the family talked about the new rank. "Let me see the stripes again," asked Steven. When an opening in the conversation presented itself, Peg looked across the table at Sam, "What does this mean, Sam?" Sam took the stripes back from Steven and looked confused. "What do you mean?" Peg became more serious, "I mean in the way of responsibility. Are you going to be putting in more hours,...are you switching to days,...what?" Sam sat back in his chair and became serious. "Obviously, the promotion means more money. Wearing the stripes automatically makes me more responsible for anything the Unit is involved with, and makes me susceptible to filling in where we may be shorthanded, but I don't see any drastic changes at this rank.

Peg worried to herself. She knew about Jake Farmer and worried about how Sam would handle him. Sam was as honest as the day was long and enjoyed the simple things in life. He couldn't tolerate dishonesty or liars, and had a special dislike for poachers. If Farmer was up to something, it wouldn't be long before Sam found him out, and without a doubt, would try to correct the situation.

She had heard stories through the grapevine about Corporal Farmer and his deeds up on the Ridge. Thompson was a big place with a small population and word travelled fast, especially when it came to Thompson's biggest attribute... its wilderness beauty and everything that came with it. Some people made their living off of Thompson's abundance of natural resources by applying it to recreational use. Mountain climbing, canoe adventures or guided tours down the Connecticut River, camping areas, guided hunts and fishing trips, all provided some of the sleepy town's citizens with paying jobs. Of course, there were the small factories and stores but Thompson's greatest appeal to out-of-towners was what it could offer in the way of outdoor recreation. Jake Farmer's reputation was that of someone who threatened not only the natural gifts of the land but all of its inhabitants and their well-being.

Peg found comfort in the fact that, at least for the next week, Sam and the rest of the family would be out of reach to any of this business. Their vacation to New Jersey would take them well out of harm's way for a while. A visit to a famous theme park would also provide the needed change of pace than what the family was used to.

Corporal Jake Farmer walked into a distraught Lieutenant Alban's office. Alban was surprised by the unannounced entrance and jumped slightly when he noticed the figure standing before him. "Yeah, LT? What do ya' want?" Farmer was highly disturbed and felt highly inconvenienced by the unexpected call back to the station. Alban stood up as if threatened by Farmer's sudden appearance, "Don't you knock before entering, Corporal?" Farmer grinned, "Hey, you're the one who called me back. I'm here, okay?" Alban could feel his blood pressure rising, "You had better drop that attitude right quick, Corporal, or you will be sorry you did come back." A now enraged Farmer now shot back, "Don't threaten me, Alban. You called me back and I'm back. What's this all about anyway? You want to chew my ass about that fuck, Moody?"

Alban pointed a finger at Farmer and began in a softer tone, "Sit down, Farmer. This is your last chance." Farmer retorted, "Last chance for what?" Then seeing the fire in Alban's eyes, took hold of the back of the chair and sat down. Alban continued, "We'll talk about your insubordination later. Right now, I want to know what is going on between you and Moody." Alban stared deep into Farmer's eyes as if he could learn more from seeing inside the man than from what he said. Farmer broke the eye lock and looked down at the desk, "Look, that puke has been getting on my nerves since day one. I don't want anything to do with him, never did...and what do you do? Put him on patrol with me right from the start." Alban began to see Farmer's vulnerability and began to relax. The lieutenant leaned back in his chair, "Why do you feel Moody gets on your nerves, Jake?" Farmer was at a loss for words. He couldn't explain his answer and began to get frustrated. Alban asked again, "I asked you a question, Corporal." Farmer's anxiety was approaching a dangerous level and he felt like he wanted to throw something or at least scream at the top of his lungs. Anything to just relieve the pressure building inside of him. Suddenly Farmer stood up and bellowed at Alban, "I don't know...Okay? He's just in the way. Little bastard. Little do-gooder bastard. He's messin' with my style." Alban started to understand. He put together the concerns Sam had mentioned to him earlier in the year and all the scuttlebutt that was going on around the station. "Why do you call him a do-gooder, Jake?" Jake leaned forward suspecting he was being accused of something, "What are you saying, Alban? If you're accusing me of something you had better come out with it now." Alban remained reclined in his chair. He was getting to Farmer.

Just then two uniformed officers appeared at the open office door. "Everything okay in here, LT," asked one of the curious cops as he searched Alban's face for an answer. The other just eyed Farmer. Before Alban could answer, Farmer lashed out at the two cops in the doorway, "Get the fuck out of here... townie pukes! This is Fish and Game business." With that he raised his right hand and slammed the door shut in their faces.

Alban stood up and yelled, "Mr. Farmer get hold of yourself!" The door swung open again. This time the two cops entered, ready to pounce on the enflamed corporal. Alban glanced at the two officers, "It's okay boys...thanks. I can handle this." Slowly the two cops backed out of the room. "Close the door on your way out please."

When they were alone again, Alban, still standing said, "Sit down Jake." "Fuck you, El Tee," Farmer replied in a sarcastic tone. Alban realized there was something very deep seated here and all he was accomplishing was making Farmer angrier. The man was going to need some time to cool off. He couldn't have him out among the public ready to blow like this. Alban continued, "Okay, stand then." Farmer stood fuming and glared back at the lieutenant. Alban, in his most formal tone said, ""Corporal Jake Farmer, you are here-by suspended of all duties until further notice...without pay. Do you understand?"

"For what?!" Farmer leaned forward on Alban's desk and bellowed into the stoic lieutenant's face. Alban reached down and pushed a key on his intercom, "Sergeant, please have two officers come in here and escort Corporal Farmer out of the building." Then he looked up at Jake, "Okay, Jake. Give me your gun and badge." Farmer stood motionless, eyes fixed on Alban. Alban repeated his command, "Give me the gun and badge, Jake." The office door opened and two uniformed policemen entered. "Sir?" the first cop offered. Alban was still waiting for Jake to remove his gun and badge, his eyes locked on Farmer's. Farmer gave no indication that he was about to remove his badge or handover his gun. Without taking his eyes off Farmer, Alban said to the two wide eyed policemen nervously awaiting their instructions, "Officers, remove Corporal Farmer's gun from his gun belt." The smaller of the two cops moved in front of Jake and took his gun, while the larger officer stood behind him. The cop stepped back from Farmer and turned the .357 revolver on end, pushed open its cylinder, and emptied the shells from it. He slapped the cylinder back into place and handed the empty revolver to Alban. Showing no emotion, Alban, still staring into Farmer's eyes said, "Now remove the Corporal's badge from his blouse." The cop turned back to Farmer and reached for his badge but Farmer slapped his hand away. The larger cop from behind started forward but Alban held his hand up in a signal to hold back. Farmer turned his head in the direction of the cop who had taken his gun, "Back off, asshole. Nobody touches me." When he saw the cop wasn't going to force the issue, Jake slowly raised his own hand to his left breast and unclipped the silver badge. "Shove it up your ass, Alban," Jake said as he threw the badge against the wall behind the lieutenant. The badge hit the wall with a crack and bounced to the floor.

Alban sat down and dropped his gaze from Farmer, "Get him out of here." The two cops looked at the six foot one inch, 240 pound warden standing before them with desperation. Farmer didn't move until he was satisfied everyone in the room understood the only way he was leaving was under his own power. After an awkward minute, the cop behind Farmer offered, "Corporal?" Farmer stood his ground for another few seconds, gave Alban one last look, and left the office. The two relieved officers followed him out of the building.

Farmer left the building, slamming the door behind him. His exit attracted a lot of attention because of the reckless and boisterous manner he chose for his leaving. Other officers witnessed the slam-bam departure from open doorways and windows. That's just how Jake wanted it. He wanted everyone to know how angry he was and how tough he could be. This was his chance to make a statement.

Jake walked across the parking lot to his own pick-up truck and got in. He started the huge diesel and floored the fuel pedal leaving a trail of burnt rubber and blue smoke behind him.

Alban watched the exit from his office window. He picked up the phone and called Dispatch, "Lieutenant Alban, here. Send two cruisers after Farmer. If he continues that recklessness, pick him up and let him spend a night in the tank." The five dispatchers looked at each other in utter amazement. From their locked and sound proofed room they had no idea of what had just transpired. One dispatcher picked up the radio mic, "Roger, Lieutenant. You got it."

Alban slammed the phone back down into its cradle. He sat down, leaned forward resting his elbows on the desk, and held his head in his hands. He wondered how things had escalated out of control so quickly. He thought, *What next?*

★ ★ ★ ★

CHAPTER 16

Jake Farmer sat alone in his living room watching television. He was staring at the television but not really seeing anything. He was still fuming over the morning's ordeal with Alban and his suspension from the Unit. *How could they do this to me? He* thought. *Ungrateful bastards.* Jake stood up from his easy chair and walked across the room. The floor was littered with empty beer cans, old newspapers, and pizza boxes, some of which still contained their contents.

Even though he lived alone, Jake was accustomed to talking out loud to himself when he was in the house, "Damn Moody! He started all this. He gets promoted and I get kicked out. Fuck!" Jake threw the can of beer he held in his right hand across the room. The can struck a glass picture frame that hung near the fireplace shattering it and sending both items to the floor with a crash. Beer oozed from the fallen can and mixed with shards of glass from the broken frame. Jake ignored it and continued to focus on his dilemma.

He stared through the picture window and into the shallow forest that separated the front of his house from the road above. *What about all my cabin people on the West Ridge? Fish and Game is going to assign someone else to that area while I'm gone, and then I'm fucked.* Jake thought about Billy Jaggs and his cabin mates, *That little bastard will start talkin' as soon as someone scares him enough, or offers him money. My whole plan, the whole set-up is ruined. The cabin people will think I sold out on them and go back to the way they were. Shit!* He slammed his fist down on the window sill.

Jake's blood pressure was rising at an alarming rate. Before he knew it, he was beginning to breathe heavy, so he started pacing the floor. He couldn't help but to imagine the worst of every scenario that came to his mind. He began to predict who would betray him, who would talk, what could happen. The more he thought about it, the more upset he became. Finally, he realized he was out of breath and perspiring profusely. *I gotta' get some air*, he thought. *I'm gonna' pass out.*

Jake walked out onto the deck behind his house and grabbed the railing. He was getting dizzy and knew he had worked himself up over things that may never happen. He needed to calm down. Still holding the railing, he lowered his head and slowly settled himself into a sitting position. He felt the cool breeze off the river brush against his face. Jake closed his eyes and let the rejuvenating breeze wash over him. The dizziness was beginning to subside, and with his eyes still closed, Jake raised his face to the sky and tried to absorb the coolness of the moment. The trees shielded the noon sun from him and soon he felt his head start to clear.

He began to feel better and his strength was returning in leaps and bounds. A calmness seemed to sweep over his entire body. Slowly he opened his eyes and reached for a wicker chair nearby. He pulled it close and hoisted himself up onto it, laying his feet across the railing. *I gotta' get out of here for a while. This rinky dink operation in the West Hills is over. When the cabin people realize someone has taken over for me, they'll think I gave up on 'em, and they'll never trust me again.*

Jake stared out over the river and knew he had to leave, at least for a little while. He had to put this whole scenario behind him. He recalled the letter he wrote to Billy Jaggs when he felt Moody was beginning to suspect things in the West Hills Territory. A get away to his favorite place in New Hampshire would provide the time needed for things to settle down and get forgotten. It would also provide him the time to be out of site and out of mind, at least around the Thompson P.D. *Maybe a little vacation in New Hampshire will help,* he thought. *That little town where we went deer hunting last fall...what was it called...Pine Hill. Yeah, that's it. Pine Hill, New Hampshire! That's where I'll go. It'll give me a chance to scout the deer herd for this fall's hunt.*

Jake was all set. He'd made up his mind. He was going north to New Hampshire. Far enough away to get this place off his mind for a while. The get-away would do him good and the scouting activity would take his mind off Fish and Game. He got up from the chair and went to his bedroom to start packing some clothes.

"Fuck 'em all," Jake said aloud as he tossed the last duffel bag into the bed of his pick-up truck. "I AM OUT OF HERE!" He felt like a new man. He had a purpose and he had a destination, and best of all, no one else knew anything about it. He climbed up into the Dodge's cab, started the engine, and drove out to the main road. After a few minutes, the entrance ramp to the interstate appeared. Jake was beginning to feel excited, then he realized, *Ah shit, gotta' stop by the P.D. I might need my nine millimeter and that's still stashed in my duffel bag behind the back seat of the Blazer.* Jake thought for a moment, *Better get that letter I wrote to Billy too. Think that's in there too. Better grab that and mail it on the way so he can let my sister know where I am.* Jake turned the truck around and made a quick visit to the Police Station. Because his presence was not allowed at this point, he would have to make quick work of the exchange. He pulled through the gated entrance and scanned the area. *Good, no one around,* he thought, smiling to himself. The Blazer was still parked out front in the parking lot where he had left it. He pulled in next to the Blazer, retrieved the nine millimeter from the duffel, hung the duffel back on its hook, and exited the parking lot. The whole ordeal lasted about one minute. He left the parking lot unnoticed.

Jake accelerated as he entered the entrance ramp and onto the highway as he headed north. Feeling more satisfied than ever, he settled back into his seat and turned on some country western music. Life was good. Smiling to himself, he tried to picture the rest of the hunting party's faces next fall when he came back with a deer before they even knew the herd's whereabouts. Suddenly, it occurred to him he had forgotten to retrieve the letter to Billy Jaggs from his duffel bag. A cold chill ran up his back. Then he got hold of himself before he allowed another anxiety attack to start, *Aah, what am I thinking? I'll just write him another letter. This is only July. I'll be back by September.*

Jake knew the drive to New Hampshire would be about four hours long. He was counting on that time to think and sort things out without any distractions. As he drove down the highway, his thoughts began to drift back to all the people he had trouble with in the past year. The new guys, or rookies, as he liked to refer to them, were at the top of his list. *It's those three rookies,* he thought. *Everything was so routine until Fletcher hired them. They must think they're some new kind of game warden or something. They're so full of themselves, the bastards. One way or another, I'll make 'em pay.* He paused a moment to admire the female driver passing him on the left, then looked back at the road, *Yup, they'll pay,* he promised himself.

Hours passed and Jake could see the outline of New Hampshire's White Mountain Range looming in front of him. Soon he'd have to get off the highway and cross a small iron bridge that crossed over into New Hampshire. The scenery became more desolate and more beautiful the further he drove, although it was wasted on a man like Farmer who only noticed the land for what it could give him.

Before long the bridge appeared off to the east side of the highway and Jake took the exit. He crossed the ancient structure constructed for a generation's technology long past. The bridge's narrow lanes were a reminder of the smaller vehicles it was designed to serve. The river below sported sandy banks and foliage that never aged and probably looked the same as when the bridge was built. Only a man's construction seemed to grow old.

He knew of a little gas station and general store just over the bridge where he could get fuel, food, and some basic supplies. Once he crossed the bridge, he took a quick left and pulled into the gravel drive that served the old mom and pop store. It was a little white building with white clapboarding on its exterior, sporting two very old gas pumps just outside the front door that seemed old enough to have Esso advertised on them. A couple of old codgers loitered outside the store's entrance and eyed Jake's arrival with a suspicious eye. One man smoked a corncob pipe and the other sat on the porch stoop chewing a wad of tobacco.

Jake parked the new Dodge diesel and began to walk toward the wooden porch, the gravel crunching under his boots as he went. The two old men watched as if his unexpected presence concerned them. The noisy diesel, the crunching gravel. Their look gave him the immediate message that he was an outsider. As Jake approached the wooden steps he gave both of the elder gentlemen a nod, "Afternoon gents." Neither man answered. They just continued to survey the refugee from Connecticut. Jake walked past and continued up the old stairs. Opening the door, several bells hanging on ribbons jingled and announced his arrival. No one seemed to be in the store until an inconvenienced voice from the back room announced, "Hang on. Be with ya' in a minute."

Jake poked around the store. There was a little bit of everything from hunting ammunition to loaves of bread. Everything the locals might need in their daily lives at a moment's notice. A man of about eighty years old came hobbling out from a back room shielded by a curtain that covered its opening. He limped on his left leg and held a cane in his right hand. "What will ya' have Sonny," the old man looked squarely at Jake. "Uh, just some fuel for now, old timer. I'd like to look around a little." The storekeeper pointed his cane at Jake, "Well, don't take all day. I got lots to do 'round here." With that, he turned and limped over to the store's window and looked out at Jake's truck. "I see you're from out of town. What're you doin' up here in New Hampshire?" Jake smiled to himself, *People up here never change. Old bastard is into my business already.* "Just lookin' for a place to hunt this fall, is all," Jake said without looking up. He was more interested in which sandwich under the glass deli counter was bigger.

The old man stared at Jake again, as if he didn't believe his answer. "You're a might early, Son. You're not gonna' see nothin' in those woods this time of year. Woods is too thick." Now Jake looked up and met the man's stare, "I'll see whatever is there. Is that okay with you, Mister?" The storekeeper got Jake's message to back off and lowered his eyes with a shrug. "Okay, how much fuel you want?" "Fill it up," Jake said, "and I'll take a ham sandwich and a six pack of that beer over there."

Farmer paid for his food and drink and prepaid the fuel he was about to pump, then walked out of the little store. He threw his bag of beer and food on the passenger seat and walked over to the fuel pumps. *Man, they sure are nosy around here! These New Hampshire types don't trust anyone.* Jake pumped his own fuel under the watchful eyes of the sentinels outside the store, waved goodbye, and spun his tires in the gravel drive, leaving a dust trail back onto the roadway.

★ ★ ★ ★

CHAPTER 17

Lieutenant Gene Alban sat at his desk and stared at the clock. It was two o'clock in the afternoon. *Maybe I better give that old coot a call to see if he's okay. I was pretty hard on him this morning.* Alban dialed Farmer's number and let the phone ring and ring. *Well, he's either drunk or out joyriding. Probably for the best anyhow. He was pretty hot when he left here.* Alban hung up the phone. *I'll have to inform the rest of the Unit at roll call tomorrow morning. Someone is going to have to take Farmer's territory until he's off suspension.*

News from the morning's suspension travelled like wildfire through the Police Department. No one knew exactly what happened except that Farmer had his gun and badge taken away and was suspended indefinitely. Someone even thought Farmer had punched out the Lieutenant and was given his walking papers. Rumors and speculation flew like confetti, but no one except Alban knew for sure.

The next morning the roll call room was extraordinarily quiet. All the wardens were seated in their usual places. Two seats remained empty. Jake Farmer and Sam Moody were missing which added to the scuttlebutt. If it had been anyone but Moody, no one would have paid much attention.

The Unit sat patiently waiting to hear about Farmer. Alban took a few extra minutes before starting the early morning meeting. Finally, he stood from his desk, collected himself, and walked into the room of waiting wardens.

The entire Unit stood to greet Alban's entrance, then sat down again. The room was very still. Occasionally, creaking leather could be heard as officers shifted in their seats. Alban looked around the room and read the questioning faces. Finally, he called attendance, went through old business, then new business, keeping the big news for the end. As a final item he added, "Corporal Jake Farmer is officially on suspension I'll be needing a volunteer to take his territory until he is reinstated...if and when that happens." Alban looked up from his podium at the stunned wardens. No one in the room breathed. The West Ridge Territory was a forbidden place to everyone but Farmer, who had worked his way into the hearts of the cabin people over the years. No warden wanted any part of any dealings that might be going on up there. "No takers, eh? Okay, then I'll assign the area...and the subject is not up for discussion."

"Sergeant Hunter. You are off nights as of this moment. Starting tomorrow you will take Jake's territory." Will Hunter was the likely choice and all the wardens knew it. Next to Sam, Will was the best tracker on the unit and had the most experience with lawbreakers. That experience was due in large part from spending so many years on the night shift. He was also almost as smooth a talker as Farmer and could probably slide into Jake's role without too much trouble.

Hunter just nodded his head in affirmance while everyone else breathed a sigh of relief. Alban looked about the room, "Any questions before I dismiss the group?" One warden stood in the back of the room, "Yes, sir." It was Pat James.

"Where's Sam Moody?" Alban let the faintest hint of a smile show at one officer's concern for another, "On vacation, Pat. He's just on vacation."

Farmer was getting into the higher elevations. There were more dips and rises in the roads and the area was more forested than ever. Jake was looking for the little farming town of Pine Hill. Every time he passed an open field he thought he might be getting close but the higher he climbed the less farms he found. Jake pulled over to the side of the road to read the map. *Where the hell is that place? I know it's somewhere around here.* Jake continued to pour over the road map. After a few minutes, he was startled back to reality by a tapping noise on the driver's side window. Jake swung his head swiftly to the window while reaching under his seat for the loaded 9mm pistol he kept Velcroed to the bottom of the seat.

It was a New Hampshire State Trooper. He signaled to Jake to roll down the window. *Damn, can't shake these uniform types. Everybody's watching me. Sonovabitch!* Sporting his usual scowl, Jake complied and rolled his window halfway down. "Yeah, what can I do for you?" Jake's tone was that of inconvenience. The officer was taken aback by the abrasive greeting, "Well, good afternoon to you too," the trooper was just as sarcastic. Jake said nothing. After a few strained moments the trooper said, "I noticed you over on the shoulder here and saw the Connecticut plates. Figured you might be lost." The trooper was young, handsome, and well spoken. Jake looked over the trooper standing outside his window and thought to himself, *Another Moody. Just wearin' a different color uniform.* "Well, you figured wrong, sonny." The trooper stepped back from the truck and a little rear of Jake's window. He had noticed Jake's right hand that disappeared below the driver's seat. Detecting the abrasiveness in Jake's voice, the trooper increased his sensitivity awareness. "May I ask what your business is here, sir?" Jake could feel his blood pressure starting to rise, "No you may not!" *Damn it! I'm getting questioned by Moody and he's not even here.* "I'm on vacation and reading a damn road map. What's the problem?" Jake's voice was getting louder.

The trooper was staring Jake square in the eyes and became very serious. "Sir, please show me both hands. Slowly raise them to where I can see them." He placed his own hand on the snap of his holster. Jake suddenly realized he still had his hand on the 9mm under his seat. Immediately, Jake let go of the pistol and raised his hands into the trooper's line of sight. "Okay, now step out of the truck. Keep your right hand in the air and open the door with your left." Jake complied and opened the door with his left hand. He stepped down onto the truck step and paused, "Mind if I use my right hand to help myself down...Sonny?" "Go ahead," came the reply.

"What were you reaching for, sir," the trooper asked. Jake was getting angrier by the second, "Look, you shocked the shit out of me when you snuck up on me. I guess I was reaching for anything I could use for protection...out here in the hills and all." The trooper's voice remained stoic. "Put your hands on the rear of the truck's side while I call this in please." Jake turned back to the trooper, "Hey, come on, you don't have to call this in. I'm an officer, myself." The trooper snapped back at Jake, "Hands on the truck...Now!" Farmer stood with hands spread against the side of his truck's bed and his feet spread out beneath him. *I can't believe this. All I'm trying to do is get away from this very thing and now I have to assume the position. Me of all people.*

Jake listened as the trooper called in his marker plates and also heard him call for back up. *Shit, once they call in that marker plate, Thompson P.D. will be alerted. Damn.* It wasn't three minutes before another state cruiser pulled up in front of Jake's truck. The new trooper got out and walked up to Jake's captor, "What have we got here," careful not to mention the first officer's name. It was too late though. Jake had already made it a point to glimpse the officer's name tag pinned to his right breast. *Officer T. Simpson,* Jake burned the name into his memory. "Belligerent motorist. Says he's an officer but I haven't heard back from Dispatch. They're running his plates now." "Why is he spread across the back of his truck," asked the second trooper. Simpson replied, "He was holding something under the seat when I first stopped him. I got a bad feeling." The second trooper who obviously outranked Simpson stood behind Jake and frisked him. "Okay, go ahead and search his truck. He's clean here."

The first thing Simpson did was reach in under the seat where Jake had held the 9mm and pulled it loose from its Velcro holder. He looked at his partner with raised eyebrows then back at Jake. "Have you got a permit for this, Sir?" Jake still spread eagled against the side of the truck said that he did. "Why were you holding this when I was talking to you earlier?" Simpson was anxious to hear the reply. Jake had to answer while staring into the ground because of the position they had made him assume. "I told you that you scared me, and I knew I was all alone out here." Simpson smiled, "But you continued to hold the pistol the whole time we talked until I told you to put your hands where I could see them. Were you that nervous?"

Before Jake could answer, Trooper Simpson's radio crackled to life. "Highway Dispatch to 805. Marker plate comes back to a Jake Farmer, registered in Thompson, Connecticut. He's a State Game Warden attached to the Thompson P.D. Holds the rank of corporal. Will await your instructions."

The two troopers looked incredulously at one another. Trooper Simpson looked back at Jake, and as he spoke to his back side said, "Well, Corporal. Looks like we have a situation here."

★ ★ ★ ★

CHAPTER 18

The sun rode low in the western sky. Its hot rays were replaced by an orange glow reminiscent of a raging fire that had diminished in the cool mountain air. The peaks of New Hampshire's White Mountains began to darken and bring a quieting effect with the impending dusk.

Jake Farmer watched the end of the day come as he sat in a camp chair with his back against the side of his red pick-up truck. The scene was a calming one, even for a man like Farmer. In front of him a small camp fire crackled and around him the woods lay silent. He propped his feet up on a large boulder and finished a third can of beer. He had finally reached a peaceful plateau, one that he was unaccustomed to attaining. The beer helped, but most of his fatigue was derived from the mental stress induced by the day's events.

Jake reached down by his right side and pulled another can of beer from its plastic holder. Without taking his eyes off the sunset, he cracked open the pop-top letting beer and foam spray the ground in front of him. He took a swallow of the cool liquid, then another large gulp. Propping his head against the side of his truck, he smiled dryly to himself and closed his eyes. Memories of his encounter with the two state troopers drifted into his consciousness. Jake relaxed and let the scene unfold before his closed eyes. *They think they won, the bastards. Taking my 9 millimeter away really gave them a hard-on. Well, they just don't know who they're dealin' with.* Jake put the can of beer back on the ground and rolled up his pant leg. Inside his right boot, a small .22 caliber derringer revealed itself. It lay in a specially made holster sewn into the inside of his high top boot. *Assholes missed it. What a couple of hicks!* He pulled the small pistol from its nylon sheath and inspected it. Feeling as if he had won some kind of game, Jake slipped the tiny gun back into its sheath and rolled his pant leg back down.

Jake stood for a moment to stretch and looked about his campsite. He thought back to earlier in the day and how he came to choose this particular site. On a whim, he had followed an old logging road that bordered a huge farm. He recognized the farmhouse as the one he hunted near last fall but it was getting late and decided to camp in his truck for the night. The dense pine forest and seclusion of the area made his mind up for him. He would be safe here. Now he stood feeling good about himself and his decision. *Wonder who owns this piece of land?* He thought. *Hope they don't mind me taking advantage for a night. I'll be damned if I'm gonna' pay good money for some flea ridden motel room.* He looked about the site again and nodded his head as if to agree with the decision he had made. Finally, somewhere he'd be left alone.

The cool mountain air felt good, but as the sun disappeared behind the wall of mountains, the air temperature went with it. Jake walked over to the far side of his camp to relieve himself. When he returned he picked up another log and placed it gently on the fire, and sat down again. Leaning back against the security of his truck and gazing above the top of the pine wall that surrounded him, Jake felt secure. More than he had in a long time. He began to consider his present situation, *I kinda' like it up here. Think I'm gonna' stay awhile. Tomorrow I'm gonna' see about a room for a couple of weeks. Get to know this place. Who knows...Maybe I'll end up stayin.' Really got nothin' to go back to anyway.*

Jake leaned his head back against the side of his truck again and folded his arms in front of him. He was beginning to nod off, *Whatever happens, I just gotta' remember to pick up that 9 millimeter from the state police barracks before I head back to Connecticut.* He thought of how stupid the New Hampshire Stateys were to have let him get away with only a warning for illegally transporting a gun over state lines. Hell, he had crossed three state lines and the only other thing they did was impound his gun until he leaves the state. *Yup, the old badge came through for me again,* he thought, and laughed out loud. Suddenly, a thought occurred to him and he stopped laughing, *Alban probably knows all about it by now. Bastard probably extended my suspension too...aah, fuck him!* Jake's head began to nod and he fell asleep where he sat.

In the morning, Jake awoke stiff and cold from being exposed to the chilly mountain air. His slightly intoxicated state had attributed to his sleeping through what otherwise would have been very uncomfortable sleeping conditions. He struggled up out of his camp chair, groaning and grunting as he rose, to a standing position. Feeling a little dizzy, he walked stiffly over to the smoldering campfire and kicked out any remaining hot coals and poured the remains of his unfinished beer from the night before on them for good measure. The sun was just coming up in the east but it was still plenty dark. He wanted to get off this property before anyone spotted him trespassing. He packed up his camp chair and threw it into the bed of his truck, slamming the truck's tail gate behind it. In his haste, Jake spared no noise.

Jake got into his truck, backed out onto the old logging road, and headed back to the main road. As he neared the end, he could see lights from the old farmhouse on the adjoining property. He swung the truck left onto the main road and headed for the old house. An old mailbox, weather-beaten and lonely, stood vigil at the end of a long narrow, gravel drive. The name on the mailbox revealed the owner, Helen Woodruff, and below stenciled in black letters, Pine Hill Farm. Jake smiled and said to himself, *I'm here. Now for some breakfast and a room.*

★ ★ ★ ★

CHAPTER 19

Jake Farmer pulled up to the lonely mailbox. The old farmhouse at the end of the long gravel drive showed signs that someone was up and about. Lights in almost every room were on and once in a while a woman passed by a window. Jake looked at his watch. It was six-thirty AM. *Ahh, what the hell, I'll just go introduce myself for now.* He eased the big diesel forward. The sound of gravel crunching beneath the truck's huge tires broke the silence of the early morning as the truck slowly but steadily approached the old farmhouse. Jake parked the truck by the barn and got out making sure not to slam the door.

As Jake came around the side of the barn he noticed the same woman he'd seen in the farmhouse windows, peering out at him between drawn curtains. He looked around the old barnyard as he walked toward the big porch that surrounded the main house, *Hmmf, no sign of much activity. Just an old beat up Dodge pick-up truck parked by the side of the house.* He looked back at the window where the house's inhabitant had been peering through. She must have realized he noticed her and quickly left the window. Jake smiled to himself, *Might have a widow here.*

Jake walked up the seven steps and onto the old pine board porch. Suddenly, the porch light by the front door in front of him came on. A fragile voice from inside came through the door. "Can I help you?" Jake started across the porch and the voice came back sharply, "Please stay where you are and tell me what you want." Jake stopped and realized he was pushing his luck. It was six-thirty in the morning for Pete's sake. "Uh, sorry Ma'am. I'm scouting these woods for a deer hunt in the fall." He paused waiting for a reply. She said nothing. "I'm up here from Connecticut on vacation and don't know the area. Spent the night in my truck in those woods back there. Wonder if I could bother you for a cup of coffee?" A long pause followed Jake's last word, then the fragile voice came through the door again, only much softer now, "Who are you, I mean what is your name?" Jake's heart began to beat faster and thought to himself, *Yeah, I'm almost in.* "Jake Farmer, Ma'am I'm a State Game Warden in Connecticut. Don't worry." "You got a badge on ya," the woman asked. Jake reached into his pocket and remembered Alban had collected the badge when he suspended him. "Uh, No Ma'am. As I said, I'm on vacation, but I do have a police I.D. card. here if you want to see it." Slowly the face of a pretty, aging woman appeared subdued behind the screen door. "Okay, bring it here." Jake walked the next few feet to the door and handed her the I.D. card through the small crack the woman allowed between the door and its casing. Jake could tell she still had the chain on the door and as he peered through the dark screen, noticed she was holding a shotgun by her right side.

The woman studied the I.D. card for a few minutes glancing up at Jake once in a while. Finally, in his most soothing but needy voice said, "Sure could use a cup of hot coffee, Ma'am. There's nothing around here for miles or I wouldn't be bothering you." The woman studied Jake hard, then abruptly unhooked the chained door. "Okay, come on in, Mr. Farmer. You're in luck. I already have a pot brewing." "Thank you," Jake said as he walked through the farmhouse's front door.

The interior of the house was very neat and comfortable. Although clean, it showed years of use, probably from children now long gone, a husband, and all the activities that came with the lot. Jake followed the woman down a narrow, dimly lit hallway to the back of the house where the kitchen was. She leaned the shotgun into a corner of the room and said, "Have a seat, Mr. Farmer. Your coffee will be ready in a few minutes." In the light of the kitchen, Jake took stock of his hostess. She appeared to be in her late fifties, early sixties, and was quite good looking for a woman of her age. She was slight of build and about five foot six inches tall. Her hair was slightly grey with evidence of a brown past life. She moved about the kitchen without a word and kept her back to Jake. As she positioned the sugar pot and creamer and placed a cup in front of Jake, he noticed her hands gave evidence of a hard life. They were worn and wrinkled.

Jake decided to break the awkward silence, "May I have the pleasure of your name, Ma'am?" She turned sharply and faced Jake as if not expecting such a remark. "Uh...Oh, I'm sorry. I've invited you into my house and haven't even introduced myself. I am Helen Woodruff." Of course, Jake had already known that from the name on the mailbox but decided it was a good way to ease his way into her soul.

Jake began a long drawn out conversation about his game warden career and Helen sat down with her own cup of coffee and listened. Eventually, she began to ask a few questions and became more comfortable with the stranger from Connecticut that sat across the kitchen table from her. As Jake talked and laughed he waited for any signs of other house tenants, especially a husband. After an hour, the house still seemed to be the dwelling place of only one inhabitant. He also noticed she was starting to relax in his presence so he made a false statement about having to leave, "Well, will ya' look at the time! I guess I've imposed on you long enough,

Helen. Better be off." She stood up and went for the pot of coffee, "Oh, what's your hurry? You said you're on vacation. Have another cup of coffee before you leave." "Well, okay... if you don't mind." She smiled across the table, "No, no. Tell me more about Connecticut."

Jake could tell he was talking to someone who hadn't got out much in the past twenty years. It appeared the farm and whatever other ties she had to the place kept her pretty close to home for a long time. This was a lonely woman. Finally, he decided to ask about her husband. "So, where is Mr. Woodruff? I'd like to meet him and let him know how much I appreciate the hospitality of you New Hampshire people." Helen's eyes dropped to the table and she pursed her lips as if a hot poker had just run her through. Jake noticed the sudden change in Helen's demeanor and knew he had struck a nerve. When Helen didn't look up, Jake said, "I'm sorry. I didn't mean to pry." Helen just shook her head quickly in a side to side fashion, "That's okay. You didn't know." Jake reached across the table and took Helen's hand in his. "Know what, Helen?" Her head still bent down, she replied, "He passed away two years ago. Had a heart attack harvesting corn." Her hand lay limp inside Jake's huge paw. She made no attempt to grasp his hand or acknowledge that another was holding hers. Jake saw immediately he was way over his head and released her hand gently, slowly pulling his hand back across the table. "Oh, I'm sorry, Helen. The place is so well kept I figured you had to have help around here. I didn't mean anything." Helen stood up and walked over to the window that looked out over the empty corn fields. "He would be sixty this year. He was a good man... hardworking, and a good father." Jake just let her go on. She was voluntarily feeding him all the information he would otherwise have had to pull out of her. "He worked this farm as a boy and then another forty years after we married. He gave me four girls who are off and married with families of their own"...she paused a moment then said, "but he always had time for those girls. Yes, sir. He'd climb down off that tractor right in the middle of plowing a field to have pretend tea with them." Jake could see she was thinking back and remembering. Helen started to laugh, "Why, there was this one time, Emily, our number two daughter stood at the edge of the cornfield waving a teacup at him. He came down off the tractor, all dirty and dusty, one suspender hanging from the top of his overalls, and walked right up to her and said, 'Is it tea time yet, Miss Emily,' and right there on the edge of the field, they sat on a blanket Emily had dragged out there, and drank tea from empty tea cups, and talked like they were in some faraway place." Helen paused, "He was such a good father." Suddenly, Helen turned around to face Jake as if she realized she had forgotten she was reminiscing in front of a perfect stranger. "Oh, excuse me. Sorry for going on like that. Your question just took me off guard." Jake just smiled at the pretty widow and said, "No apologies necessary. It was a nice story."

A few minutes of awkward silence followed. Helen, leaning against the kitchen counter, staring at the floor, and Jake looking into his coffee cup. Finally, Jake said, "How do you keep the farm up? Seems a bit much for one person." Helen looked over at him, "Well, I don't grow the fields anymore. Can't afford any hired help. Once in a while one of my son-in-laws will stop by to see if anything needs fixin.' They all live too far away to be droppin' by all the time so I do what I can. Good thing I got the telephone so I can at least talk to them once in a while." Jake just watched Helen and thought, *Man, this is one lonely woman. Been dealt a pretty hard hand too, but I think there's room for me here.* When Helen finished talking, Jake looked up from his coffee, "Look, Helen, I don't mean to sound presumptuous, but I am looking for a room during my stay up here. I'd be obliged if I could rent one of your rooms...and I'd be happy to help out with the chores...

if you don't mind. I'll pay whatever you want. We'll both make out on the deal." Helen looked up as if she didn't know what to say, "Oh, I don't know, Mr. Farmer. I hardly know you." Jake came back quick but with a soft, reassuring tone, "Helen, if you were advertising to rent a room, you wouldn't know me any better, now would you?" Helen smiled, "I guess not. That's something my husband would have said."

Jake felt like she was weakening. He flashed her his most tender smile and said, "Come on, Helen. It'll work out for both of us. You'll have some cash coming in and have help with some of the work around here, and I'll get a good bed with home cooked meals." Helen looked at Jake slyly, "Wait a minute. I don't remember the home cooked meals being a part of this." Quickly, Jake put in, ""Oh, come on. Name your price, I'll do the daily chores, you provide the room and two meals a day...breakfast and supper." Helen cocked her head to one side and slowly started to think out loud, "I don't know. Never done such a thing before." Jake knew it was time to play his hand. He stood up and grabbed his hat. "Okay, Helen. You just think about it. I'll come back in a day or two and we can discuss it again. The last thing I want to do is pressure a sweet little thing like you." She looked at him confused and surprised at the same time. It had been a long time since anyone had referred to her as a sweet little anything. He grabbed his hat from the table and started for the door. "Thanks for the coffee and the good company, Ms. Woodruff." Jake was almost all the way down the hallway, and still, Helen remained speechless at the kitchen counter. Just as Jake reached for the door, Helen blurted, "Jake." He turned to see to see her staring down the hallway at him. "I'll give it some serious consideration. You come by here tomorrow night for supper. Six o'clock sharp. It'll be fried chicken and mashed potatoes. Don't be late." Jake nodded and turned back to the door as a wicked little smile started across his face, "Yes, Ma'am. I'll be here."

Without another word Jake opened the front door and exited the farmhouse. He had work to do in town if he was going to try and re-create the set up he had in Thompson, way up here in the White Mountains. Hell, he already had a place to stay, and probably a girlfriend to boot. Helen's farm looked to be about three hundred acres and was known to be a prime area for hunting game. Now all he had to do was to get to know some people he could trust. He'd have to scope out the local saloons, diners, and game clubs. Get to know the locals. He was going to need to get his finger on the pulse of this little town before he could put his plan into action.

★ ★ ★ ★

CHAPTER 20

The summer season passed without incident in the town of Thompson, Connecticut. June had been wet, breaking the rainfall record that stood for thirty years, but July and August were hot and humid as usual. It had been a quiet summer by normal standards. There was the occasional boater with a broken propeller requiring a tow or a routine fishing violation, but nothing stood out this summer season that was any different than the others. It was a welcome calm from the Hanks tragedy of last summer.

Most of the department had returned from their vacations and Thompson's Fish and Game Unit was almost back to full complement. There was one seat still vacant in the roll call room and that belonged to Corporal Jake Farmer. The Unit's brass had not seen fit to call him in from suspension yet and for the most part, Jake's absence went unnoticed in the valley. The only people that missed Jake were the cabin people in the West Hills Territory. To them, Jake meant money.

Sergeant Hunter had been patrolling Jake's territory as ordered but had yet to achieve the level of trust the cabin people had for Jake. Hunter was a good warden and a good

Dan Hayden

tracker, and the cabin people that lived in those hills knew it. They weren't about to let their guard down before a new warden. It might happen someday, but that would be years away, if it ever did.

After roll call one morning, late in September, Alban dismissed the Unit and addressed Hunter, "Will, can I see you in my office?" "Sure, LT," Hunter replied with his usual smile. Hunter followed Alban into the lieutenant's office. Alban went directly to his window that overlooked the valley with a view of the Connecticut River, and stood staring out. He waited until he heard Hunter's footsteps on his office floor and said, "Close the door, Will...and have a seat."

He heard Hunter sit down in the single chair that occupied the space in front of his desk. Without turning from the window, he asked, "How's it going up on the West Ridge?" Hunter sat uncomfortably in the wooden chair and found it difficult speaking to the lieutenant's backside. "It's going okay, LT. The cabin people seem pretty nervous every time I show up. Hell, Some of them stop what they're doing and run into the house as soon as they see my Blazer. Gives me a real warm feeling, ya' know?" Alban turned from the window and looked Hunter in the eyes, "How do you know they're nervous, Will?" Hunter began to feel as if he was being interrogated, as most people did when they sat in that chair. "Just by the way they act, Sir. They're real skittish...especially if I get out of the patrol car." Alban lowered his eyes to the floor and thought about Hunter's answer, "Any of them ask about Farmer yet?" Hunter was answering quicker now, "Yeah. A guy named Bill something...uh, Billy." Hunter struggled to remember the name, "Yeah, that's it...Billy Jaggs."

Alban stepped over to his desk and sat on the front corner facing Hunter. He folded his arms in front of him and leaned in toward the sergeant, "What did he say, Will? I want every word." Hunter shifted in his seat, "Uh, the first time he saw me he just wanted to know where Jake Farmer's been hiding." Alban's eyes narrowed, "What did you say?" Hunter's nervousness was escalating and he began to stumble over his words, "I just told him Jake was temporarily unavailable." Alban leaned back away from Hunter, "Okay, good. I don't want you telling any of those people anything. I want them to tell us. What else did he say?" Hunter paused for a moment before answering, then said, "He said something kind of strange like – 'looks like somebody finally caught onto him." Alban nodded his head and looked at the floor.

Hunter looked up at the lieutenant and after a minute asked, "Where is all this going, LT? I don't mean to pry but if something is going down, I'd like to know about it. After all, we're talking about the territory I'm assigned to."

Alban looked up from the floor. When Hunter caught Alban's gaze he asked, "I know Jake is suspended, but where is he?" Alban just stared at Hunter for a moment then said, "He's in New Hampshire, Will. I got a call from the New Hampshire State Police Barracks a couple of months ago. They apparently had a reason to run the marker plates on his truck." Hunter was confused, "So he went north to get away...so what?" Alban stood and barked at the sergeant, "So what? So he was carrying a nine millimeter Beretta under his driver's seat, and reached for it when the trooper approached his window." Hunter frowned, "C'mon, LT, we all carry concealed when we're off duty. The guy probably took Jake by surprise." Alban walked back to the window and stared back out at the river again. After a moment he said, "He kept his hand on the gun the whole time the trooper was speaking to him. He was ordered 'hands in the air' and out of the truck, and then frisked. They found the nine under his seat when they searched his truck."

Hunter remained seated and stared at the floor in front of Alban's desk. "Did they arrest him for illegal transportation over the state line?" Alban, still with his back to Hunter replied, "No, just took the gun and gave him a warning."

Hunter stood up. The conversation had been shear exasperation. "Have you heard from him, LT?" Alban paused and replied, "No, not personally. The records department got an e-mail from him a week ago informing us that when his suspension is over, he'll be taking a month's vacation. Guess he's finally putting in for all that vacation time he's stored up....and that bothers me. He's got something cooking and I don't like the smell of it."

★ ★ ★ ★

CHAPTER 21

September gave way to October along with all the other scenarios the autumn season brings with it. The early morning air was cooler with frost covering everything that lay unprotected. Rain was more frequent and the increased force of the winds that blew through the valley was noticeable. Foliage that adorned the deciduous trees slowly started to turn colors of bright orange, yellow, brown and red. It was a pretty time. It was a time for tourists to come to the valley to shop and picnic, or hike the nature trails, or visit one of the many farms that let a horse drawn wagon take you out to a quiet apple orchard, hidden away from the rest of the town's business. The time of year also perked the interest of harvest seekers not so focused on beauty and gratefulness. These people were users of the land that took all it could give them with no thought or intent to give it back. They had darker ideas for the land and everything it supported. For them, it was a time of deception, betrayal, and greed. These people were called poachers and one of the prime reasons Thompson's Fish and Game Unit existed.

Late night reports of small arms fire are not uncommon this time of year, especially in the West Hills Territory and also in Thompson's Southeast Region. The small game and deer were plentiful there and attracted all kinds of hunters.

Lieutenant Gene Alban sat at his desk and looked at the calendar on the wall, *Here we go again, poaching season. Gonna' be a lot of hours sittin' in the cold, dark woods sipping coffee and waiting for something to happen. Ahh, maybe this year will be different.*

Alban sat there and thought about some of the past poaching calls and how the Unit must go on alert because of the activity. Poachers usually strike at night under the cover of darkness, usually when there is no moon, stealth being their best ally. They are usually better armed than any of the wardens, bringing in state of the art, higher technology weapons. Alban was reassured by considering what was on the warden's side, and that was familiarity of the territory, especially over transient would-be hunters. Also, the fact that the wardens are well trained in the woods and how to survive under extreme conditions. The lieutenant stood up from his desk and closed his daily planner, *Gonna' have to prep the boys for this. Harvest moon is back.*

Alban went outside his office and posted a bulletin. It read, ***ATTENTION ALL FISH AND GAME OFFICERS* MANDATORY MEETING TONIGHT AT THE WARDEN HOUSE. THERE WILL BE AN IMPORTANT DISCUSSION REGARDING HUNTING, POACHING AND LEGAL TAKE. MEETING WILL BEGIN 1900 HRS SHARP. ALL OFFICERS ARE EXPECTED TO ATTEND. NO EXCUSES CONSIDERED. -LT**

Down the hall, Corporal Sam Moody walked into the warden's locker room and began suiting up for the morning's patrol. "Any of you guys read that bulletin that Alban posted?" Everyone was busy pulling on boots, adjusting duty belts, and loading their weapons. Corporal Bowman spoke from the back of the locker room, "Aah, it's probably another one of his 'be careful out there' announcements, because people are carrying guns. Bowman continued, "It's huntin' season–Yay." Bowman's attitude was gradually getting more sarcastic, "Give me a break! Every year he gets so worried one of us is gonna' catch a seven millimeter in our class B's. Maybe he ought to go back out on patrol once in a while and see what it's like." Moody shot Bowman a quick glance while the other wardens continued with their preparations. "Okay Bowman, that's enough. I was wondering about the posting, not your personal take on the matter." Bowman just shrugged his shoulders, finished the last of his primping, slipped his .357 magnum into its holster, and walked out of the room. Once Bowman left, Sam eased the situation by saying, "He'll probably tell us about it during roll call this morning. I'm sure it's got something to do with Opening Day for hunting season."

Lieutenant Alban stood at the front of the roll call room next to the podium he never stood behind. For once he was waiting on the unit to take their seats instead of the other way around. The wardens shuffled in one by one and sat in their usual places. Alban didn't seem to notice any particular person. He just stood and waited for the unit to assemble There were the usual coughs and clearing of throats that always seemed to accompany a room full of people before anything was spoken. When it appeared all were accounted for Alban began, "Gentlemen, before I call roll, I want everyone to pay attention to what time of year it is. We're back to hunting season and these woods are full of guns and knives. It's not something to take lightly. At least one quarter of the hunters out there are new at what they're doing, one quarter are not good at what they're doing, and barely know the rules, the third quarter are professional hunters, and the last quarter are out to take what they can get...rules or no rules. I want you all to come to the Warden House tonight for a briefing on approach and tactics. Every year the game changes a little, the guns get a little bigger, and the ammo gets a little more powerful. I expect everyone to be there." Alban stopped and looked around the room. "Any questions?" No one dared raise a hand. The question would have to wait for tonight if there were any. "Okay, good." Alban began roll call..."Beech, Bowman, Brainard...and the rest of the unit turned a deaf ear to all but their own name.

Once roll call was over and the traditional coffee slugged down, the men headed for their Blazer cruisers to take them out into Thompson's hills. Corporal Sam Moody left with Officer Frank Beech, his new partner. Beech was a happy go lucky sort, always ready with a joke. He was the type that never showed his anger, never talked about a man behind his back, and always wore a smile. Moody asked him about his calm demeanor one time and Frank said, "Look Corporal, I've been to the other side. Had a heart attack and was pronounced dead with no heartbeat. I mean, I was on my way up that lily white staircase they talk about on TV. I saw it, sir. Just couldn't get my feet to start movin' yet, and then ...wham! Some do-gooder doctor decided he hadn't burnt enough flesh off my chest yet with those fuckin' paddles they shock you with, and jerked me back to this hell we're livin' in right now. After that ride, Corporal Sir, I figured there isn't much can scare me down here anymore." Sam took in what Beech told him and filed it for information to be used at some pertinent moment but classified him as a loose cannon. There was no fear left in Beech. He'd already seen the worst, and that could be both good and bad.

Beech was a little taller than Moody, at six foot-three inches, but he was wiry. He weighed around one hundred eighty pounds with his jungle boots on. The thing Sam liked most about Frank was his marksmanship. Frank held the certification of Master Revolver Marksman, and had achieved it several times. With his cool nature and deadeye, Sam knew he had back up wherever and whenever he might need it. Beech was also a little older than Sam but had the eyes of an eagle. It was no wonder why Sam personally selected Frank as his partner.

Beech and Moody climbed into their Blazer, Car 6, and headed for the Southeast Territory. As soon as they turned out of the P.D.'s driveway a call crackled over the radio, "Headquarters to 419. Shots fired in the Southeast Territory by Town Farm Road. Too close to residential homes. Report is of a heavy gauge weapon. Expedite!" Sam picked up the radio mic, "Roger, en route." Sam stepped on the gas and headed for the rolling hills of the Southeast Territory. Both occupants could feel the Blazer lurch and roll as they sped around the winding dirt roads that provided passage to that area. Beech was holding anything he could grab onto in the Blazer's cab. "Jeez Sam, aren't you gonna' put the lights on too?" Sam was too busy driving to look back at Frank, "Nope. Don't want them to know we're coming, Frank." Frank smiled, "Aah, that's my Golden Boy. Always thinking one step ahead of everybody else."

Town Farm Road was coming up fast and Sam slowed to make the ninety degree turn onto another dirt road that led into the suspected field. The road passed by a little farmhouse, went up a small rise, and passed behind some tobacco sheds. "Think I see 'em, Sam," Frank managed to blurt out despite all the bumping and rolling the Blazer was gyrating through. Sam came back quick, "Keep your eye on 'em. I can't take my eyes off this ditch I'm driving in."

Then Sam saw what Frank had been watching. About one hundred yards ahead was a black pick-up truck that had been backed into the high brush with the bed area facing out toward the field. Two men jumped down out of the bed and climbed up into the big truck's cab. The truck seemed like it was lifted extra high off the ground to clear off road obstacles. Frank yelled within the confines of the Blazer, "Man, look at the height of that truck! We're gonna' need a ladder to get up to the cab." Just then the big truck's wheels spun a curtain of mud up behind its back end and they were off across the field and headed for the wood line. "C'mon, Sammy, they're headed for that tree line over there. If we don't stop 'em before they get in, we'll lose 'em." Inside the Blazer, Sam was doing his best. The Blazer was only raised the standard height from the ground that the manufacturer provided for a four-wheel drive vehicle. With all the bouncing and rolling, they had already damaged one tail pipe and lost another. Inside the cab, maps, flashlights, snares, and coffee cups flew about like uncontrolled chaos.

"Frank! Try and reach the radio mic. We have to call in that we're in pursuit." Frank rolled his eyes and shouted over the noise, "Oh yeah, sure Sam, and would you like me to serve beverages too? I can barely stay in my seat with the way you're driving, and God knows where the mic disappeared to." Sam kept his concentration on the quickly disappearing pick-up truck in front of him. "Just do it, Frank." Frank reluctantly let go of the dashboard with one hand and unclipped his seatbelt. Just then, Sam drove over a deep pit full of muddy water that had been hidden between rows of built up earth where cornstalks had once stood. A wall of brown water covered the front of the windshield and the Blazer came to an abrupt halt. Frank was thrown under the dash where his feet would normally be positioned had he been wearing his seatbelt. The cab was instantaneously quiet. After a moment Sam said, "You okay, buddy?" A concerned corporal looked at his partner all jumbled up under the dash in front of the passenger seat. Frank opened his eyes and smiled, producing the radio mic with his left hand. Moody just shook his head, "How many times have I told you to fasten your seatbelt?"

The two wardens exited the nosed in Blazer from the rear window which now pointed to the sky. Once they were both out, Sam keyed his radio mic, "Headquarters from 419. We need the hook out here. Car 6 is temporarily out of business." As Sam spoke, both officers watched the black pick-up truck disappear into the tree line. "Well, at least they're getting a good laugh out of this," Frank mumbled.

The activity had aroused other hunters in the area. A party of four pheasant hunters walked by the warden's Blazer now looking rather pathetic. The vehicle was covered in mud from the hood to the rear seat and buried from the front grill to the windshield, in what now appeared to be a sink hole. The red and blue lights were still flashing. The older man in the party made sure he got Sam's attention and shook his head in disgust.

A worried Lieutenant Alban burst into the dispatcher's office. "What's Moody doing? Why does he need the hook?" The hook, as it was endearingly referred to, was nothing more than a tow truck. The chief dispatcher shrugged his shoulders and said, "Don't know LT. I sent him into the Southeast Territory off Town Farm Road on a hunting complaint. Next thing I know he's calling for the hook." Alban replied, "Did he call in a pursuit?" "No sir...not yet. Just the hook." Alban's face started to redden, *Damn Moody... Doing the cowboy routine again.*

Back in the cornfield, Sam and Frank watched a huge six wheeled tow truck pull Car 6 from its sunken prison. The tow truck operator smirked down at the two muddy officers, "You want I should get it started for you too, or just bring it back home for ya." "Just leave it there...Thanks, We'll take it from here," Sam replied in an embarrassed tone. The Blazer's front end was pushed in, the hood was crinkled, and both tail pipes from the dual exhaust system dangled loosely from their hangers. "Wait until the LT sees this, Sam. He's gonna' have your balls." Sam crawled back into the cab and tried the engine. The engine turned over first try. Sam yelled to Frank who was still outside the vehicle, "Okay, get in. We're out of here."

The two wardens clunked along in their disheveled Blazer and came upon the same party of four hunters that had passed by them when the Blazer was still nosed into the mud pit. Sam stopped the Blazer and looked over at Beech. "Ready for a hunter safety check?" Beech nodded, "Right behind ya' Sam." "Okay, I'm going for their paperwork. You know the procedure...stay about thirty feet back and keep an eye on things...and stay cool." Beech smiled back at Sam, "You got it, chief."

Sam stepped down from the Blazer's running board and started for the hunters. They had already stopped moving when they saw the green Blazer approach, anticipating a field check. When Sam got to within twenty feet of the party he yelled, "Okay boys, safe those guns for me." Simultaneously, all four hunters raised their guns in the air and clicked their safeties to the "on" position. Sam walked up to the group, "I'm looking for a black pick-up truck. Hunters from that vehicle were shooting too close to the houses over there." The older man in the party stepped forward and interrupted Sam. "Well, it ain't us, Sonny. What in the fuck are you botherin' us for? Me and my boys here are all legal. You fuckin' wardens come out here and disturb everybody's hunt and then start trying to blame people for stuff they had no part of." Sam just smiled at the man. It was the smile he always gave when he had got the better of the other man.

Beech saw it and thought, *Buddy, you just caused yourself to be thoroughly inconvenienced by the one and only Golden Boy.*

Sam looked the older man in the eye and then each of the other three hunters. "These your sons, sir?" "Well yeah, if you gotta' know," the older man came back. Sam stepped right in front of the four hunters. "Good. You see, sir. It wasn't you I was looking for. I only asked you for information and you decided to be a bit nasty...so since you're here and I'm here, I think I'll check you anyway. Let me see hunting licenses, hunting permits, pheasant tags...and open those breeches so I can check your ammo." Frank Beech just watched from his position on the perimeter, thirty feet away with a big grin on his face, *Yeah, go get 'em, Sammy.*

Finally, Sam and Frank left the muddy cornfield with nothing but a wounded pride. They knew the boys back at the P.D. were going to give them a real razzing when they saw the muddy Blazer, and they also knew they hadn't got the 'in pursuit' call off in time. Alban was sure to have picked up on that. Sam pulled the Blazer out of the field and back onto Town Farm Road. He picked up the radio mic and called in, "419 clear of the cornfield's north section off Town Farm. Proceeding routine patrol cornfield off Broadbrook." Suddenly, Frank noticed something at the far end of the field. He said it looked like a hunting blind with occupants. "There Sammy! At the one o'clock position," Frank pointed at the scene which was on the Blazer's left. Sam glanced through the driver side window in the direction Frank had indicated but saw nothing. Trusting in his partner's keen eyesight he turned sharply into the dirt road that led across the field. "Okay, Frank. I'm trusting you on this one. I don't see shit out there but we're going to pull up nice and slow and park well away from their position just in case they are hunting." Then he sarcastically added, "Don't want to disturb their hunt...don't ya' know?"

As the Blazer approached, a short tree line became visible that seemed to divide the field's north section from the south section. A goose blind comprised of four huge, round hay bales about five feet in diameter positioned on their sides, materialized just north of the tree line's end. Sam stopped the Blazer and looked at Frank. Frank spoke before Sam could open his mouth, "I know, stay thirty feet off the blind and watch your back. Don't you worry old buddy." Sam just nodded and the two wardens exited the Blazer and started for the blind. The hunters in the blind had seen the muddy green Blazer as soon as it started its trek across the soggy field, and had already began to prepare to meet the wardens.

Sam and Frank got within fifty feet of the blind and as if on cue, Frank started to fall back. Sam trudged on ahead until he was standing directly in front of a group of five water fowlers, guns all lying neatly on a square hay bale. The hunters stood facing Sam in two rows. Three men in the first row with two in the rear. The two men in the rear were almost completely hidden by the three men in the front. However, their grimaced faces were in plain view.

Sam looked over the group. They seemed friendly enough except for one of the men in the back row. He stared at Sam with such defiance, Sam felt it might have been someone he had arrested before. One of the men in the front row spoke first, "Something wrong, Officer?" Sam shot him a quick look, "Don't know. Let's have a look at your paperwork." Sam kept his eye on the man in the back row. He was fidgeting uncomfortably and the facial glare seemed to get worse as Sam checked everyone's permits and licenses. "Well," Sam looked at the group, "paperwork is in order but you have one man too many in the blind." The man in the front row retorted loudly, "What are you talking about? We hunt this same piece every year, with the same guys." Sam replied, "Well, you've been doing it wrong for all those years. Let me have a look at those shotguns. Open the breeches and hand them to me, slowly, one by one." At that command the man from the back row bent down, grabbed the nearest shotgun off the hay bale, and pushed through the front row of hunters, swinging the muzzle to Sam's belt buckle. Sam had just enough time to look down and see the muzzle almost touching his waist. In the clear, crisp air of the quiet cornfield the next sound was that of Frank Beech's holster unsnapping. All five hunters froze and looked over at Frank, who had been partially out of their sightline from the position of the hay bales. It was as if the metal snapping noise had caused them all to freeze in their tracks. Sam continued to watch the end of the shotgun's muzzle.

In a calm, steady tone Frank said, "Put the shotgun down nice and easy son or I promise you've had your last look at life." Frank Beech stood poised and ready. His jaw was set, and cold dark eyes stared down the stainless steel barrel of his .357 Magnum revolver. His legs were slightly bent at the knee and spread a little more than shoulder width apart. Both hands were cradled around his hand canon that pointed directly at the gunman's head. Sam looked into the man's face in front of him. The hunter's face had gone from windburn red to ashen and white. Sam softly coaxed him, "Better do it son. He never misses." The gunman lowered the shotgun and Sam quickly snatched it from his grasp.

All five hunters stood facing Frank and his .357. No one moved except Sam, who was busy collecting all the shotguns. Finally, one of the hunters broke the awkward silence, "Hey, tell your buddy to back off with that canon of his. All we've done is put an extra man in the blind." Sam was over by the hay bales that lay on their side making a temporary table for the other four shotguns. He already had two shotguns under one arm and was about to pick up the third. He stopped and looked at the complaining hunter, "Oh. Is my man making

you nervous?" The hunter glared back at Sam with an angry
snarl, "He's got no call to be pointing that thing at us. He
looks like a crazy man!" The hunter's voice was escalating
as he spoke. "Call him off!" Sam paused for a moment as he
watched the man complain, then straightened up from his
gun collecting chore, looked down at his newly acquired
bundle of steel, looked back at the man, shrugged, and
dropped all three shotguns on the ground. "Hey...our guns,"
yelled another one of the hunters. Sam looked sheepishly at
the five hunters glaring at him, "Oops. Guess he's making
me nervous too." Sam's face suddenly became rock-hard
serious. "You five, on your bellies...now!" One of the five
hunters started toward Sam, "Why you miserable...," His
action was interrupted by the sound of Beech pulling back
the hammer of his revolver in preparation for firing. Sam
drew his own .357 and pointed it at the group.

Holding his gun in the standard "cup and saucer" position,
Sam yelled, "Back off!" Everyone froze. "Hands where
I can see 'em." Five pairs of hands rose dutifully into the
air. "Officer, check each man for hidden weapons." Beech
holstered his revolver and frisked each hunter. He confiscated
hunting knives, and one .380 semi-automatic pistol from the
group. "Looks like we got us a problem, Corporal. This
guy's playing with the wrong toy," Beech held up the pistol
so Moody could see it. Moody was still holding his weapon
on the angry group and gestured toward the muddy earth,
"Okay, now everyone on the ground...and face down." The
men reluctantly lay down in the muddy field, grumbling and
cursing as they did.

"Keep your eye on 'em, Frank. I'm gonna' call for back up.
We're gonna' need a paddy wagon for all these guys." Sam
turned away from the group and started for the Blazer that
waited patiently in the distance like a noble steed awaiting
his master's return. One of the men spoke up as he lay in

the mud, "Look officer, I didn't mean to point that gun at you. I got flustered...ya' know? Forgot what I was doing." Sam stopped walking as the man spoke. All five hunters watched as Sam slowly turned to face the group. He looked the man right in the eyes and with hardly an expression replied, "Guess you'll never do it again...will you?" With that, Sam turned and walked to the waiting Blazer to call for prisoner transport.

★ ★ ★ ★

CHAPTER 22

The sun was rising across the fields from Pine Hill Farm. It was five forty-five AM. There was no movement except for the occasional pine branches that moved in the fall breeze. Darkness was subsiding and the sky was transforming in color just above the pines that bordered the farm to the south. The grey curtain that brought morning to Pine Hill was giving way to the bright and cheerful colors that came with a welcoming dawn.

Jake Farmer stood in Helen's front room and watched the sunrise. He was not a man that appreciated such natural and god given wonders. His mind was on other things. He stared down the long narrow driveway that had brought him to this place so many months ago. It was such an innocent place, acres and acres of fertile fields waiting to be used again, surrounded by as many pine forests. A beautiful place but isolated. The pines that surrounded the farm offered seclusion and acted as a natural barrier to wind and sound. No sound in, no sound out. It was a perfect place for his plan. He had chosen wisely.

Farmer raised his coffee cup to his mouth and took another sip of the hot, black liquid, *I gotta' get into town today and start roundin' up some guys. The cool weather is gonna' have the game moving soon and I want to be ready. Hope Helen isn't planning too much for me today. I gotta' break loose from these lousy chores and get some things done.* As Farmer watched the woods from Helen's front window he noticed some movement just inside the tree line. It was a huge doe. She cautiously took a step out of the thicket and stretched her neck forward but down a bit, as if to hear something. Farmer smiled to himself, *There's one of my beauties now.* Slowly, the big doe took another step into the field. Half of her body was now exposed. She stood very still and looked to be listening for the slightest of sound. Feeling safe, the doe ventured all the way out into the field and a small yearling followed her, tagging close behind.

Jake grinned approvingly. The doe was proof his plan was already beginning to work. He had intentionally let a lot of the corn fall from the "catch truck" while helping Helen with the harvest two weeks ago. He knew the sweet corn that fell on the ground would begin to ferment in the fall sun and attract animals, especially deer. If Helen noticed it, she didn't mention anything. After all, it was the first real harvest from one of her fields in several years and she wasn't about to complain. If anything, she probably just considered it as spillage. He thought about his agreement with Helen to help with the chores as part of his keep. To win her trust, he had probably overextended himself to the point where Helen now seemed to expect more and more from him. Getting into a sexual relationship with her right after the first week was probably also to blame, but he needed this woman to believe he was her white knight.

Jake took another sip from his mug of coffee and smiled at how he began to win the affections of this lonely old widow. *A little make-up and some new threads and she cleans up pretty nice*, he thought. *Not bad for a woman in her mid-fifties.* The sex was good, probably because she hadn't had it for so long. He smiled to himself again, or maybe it was because of who she thought he really was. Jake was so proud he'd been able to distract this old woman from the memories of her late husband to that of giving him all the attention and affection he could want. His face stiffened and a wicked little smile appeared at the corners of his mouth, *I'm gonna' take everything I can get. She's stupid enough to let me, so why the hell not. This property is a goldmine. She doesn't even know what she's got out there and if she wants to give herself to me every time I ask, then...*Suddenly, an unfamiliar feeling came over him. He'd never felt guilt before and he couldn't tolerate it now, *The hell with it, she's an adult. I ain't forcin' nothin' on her. As long as I play my cards right, I got a woman, a place to stay, and a farm full of wild game to poach. Just gotta' remember to get the hell out when the time is right.*

His thoughts were broken by the sound of Helen's footfalls as she padded lightly down the wooden staircase from her bedroom. *She's up*, he thought with a start. He turned from the window just in time to see Helen get to the bottom of the stairs. Quickly, she rounded the banister and walked up to him, reaching up under his arms, placing her hands on his shoulders in a very intimate embrace. Jake looked down at her and Helen smiled. Then she reached up and kissed him on the mouth. Jake surrendered himself to the sensuous assault and put his free hand around her waist. Pulling her mouth slowly from his, she smiled up at him, "What have you got planned for today, Honey?" Jake straightened up and looked away from her, "Uh, thought I'd go into town for a while...probably most of the day for that matter. Got some things I want to look into." Helen released her hold on Jake and stepped back. "Oh, okay. Should I expect you for supper?" Jake started for the kitchen, if for no other reason than to avoid Helen's gaze, "Nah, better not plan on me. I don't really know how long I'll be." Helen followed Jake into the kitchen staring at the floor, "Well, when can

I expect you then?" Jake answered, "Leave the light on... might be awhile."

Helen turned and began busying herself about the kitchen. After a silent pause and without looking up, she said, "I guess some of the chores can wait until tomorrow." Jake's blood began to boil. *She's already putting pressure on me. I'll go where and when I want.* Then he caught himself. He was letting the situation get to him. He reminded himself, Okay, *stay in control. Don't let on that you're pissed. Gotta' keep things smooth with her.* Jake turned and looked at Helen, "Hey, why so serious? I'll be back by bedtime anyway. You can look forward to snuggling up to this magnificent body once again. I know that'll get you through the day." Helen returned his gaze and smiled. "Okay, Jake. I'll leave a plate out for you in case you forget to eat supper."

Jake slowed his big Dodge pick-up as he neared the little town of Otis. It was about five miles north of Pine Hill Farm. He was looking for low key, discreet, out of the way gathering places. Hangouts where the local men would go to discuss hunting and fishing. Dark, dank places where only the most macho of the breed would take the time to pit one's male prowess over the others. Places where women of any reputation would not be found. Finally, Jake spotted an aging diner along the two lane that led into town. The area was heavily forested with no other businesses around except for a local bait shop another mile north and on the other side of the road. He pulled into the gravel drive. *Aah, here we go, and just far enough from the busy part of town not to stir any attention.* The parking lot was no more than a wide driveway with telephone poles laid on their sides to create a border for the parking area.

The diner was the stereotypical long, silver, trailer type with a gaudy sign over the entrance that spelled DINER in big, bold, neon letters. Jake stopped the truck and parked. He reached down and pulled his .22 caliber derringer from the inside of his right boot, checked his ammo, then slapped it back into his boot holster. Almost ready to leave the truck, he looked down at his watch. It was around noon. He scanned the parking lot and took inventory. Three beat up pick-up trucks and an old jeep were parked at the other end of the lot. *Perfect,* Jake thought. *The vehicles of men's men. I ought to have some promising employees in here. Just gotta' be careful on how I approach 'em.*

Jake left the truck and walked into the diner. The room was fitted with a long, narrow counter that ran the entire length with swivel stools for the patrons, and booths were positioned across a narrow aisle by the circular windows. Jake was right. All the patrons were men, and they were all seated along the counter. Jake went to one of the booths where he could observe everyone in the diner. Down at the far end, two grizzly looking characters in flannel shirts and dirty blue jeans sat talking about whose tractor could pull the most weight. They wore dirty baseball caps sporting the names of different tractor manufacturers. One man sat alone sipping his coffee and occasionally added to the conversation making his point with off color expletives which were accepted as common place. The other two men sat together but away from everyone else and appeared to know the other three but were engrossed in a much quieter conversation. Jake strained to pick up any key words that might offer a clue as to what their discussion was about. He watched their mouths and their body language. Soon he began to hear words and phrases like "rifles in the car," "eight pointer," "gut pile," and "lights." *Lights?* Jake said to himself. *Did I hear guns and lights in the same sentence? Maybe I already have a little competition.* Jake got up from his booth and walked over to the counter. He stood directly behind the two men, uncomfortably close. Close enough to make them stop talking and notice him. When they turned and looked blankly up at him, Jake gave them his Oscar winning friendship smile, "Hi boys. I'm new up here and I was wondering if anyone could tell me where all the deer are?" The men just stared at Jake without saying a word. Jake continued, "I've got a pretty successful business back in New Jersey and thought I'd come up here and get some trophy deer heads to hang around my office building...Gotta' do something to impress my clients from out west, if you know what I mean."

The diner became a quiet place. Even the two tractor guys at the end of the counter had stopped talking and were staring at Jake. Jake smiled to himself, *Ha, got their attention now.* Jake waited a few moments longer before speaking and made it obvious he was looking about the room for an answer from anyone. "I understand they're most active at night. Anybody got any suggestions?"

Without saying a word, Jake stepped up to the counter and sat at the stool between the two would be hunters, he had just addressed. "Coffee-black," he announced, without looking up at the waitress. When she put the coffee down in front of him, Jake took a long sip, aware of the two men's eyes on either side of him. The situation became more tense with each passing moment. Now timing was everything. He let a few more seconds go by and said to no one in particular, "I asked about the deer around here and so far haven't heard as much as a hello from anyone." The two men started to get up from their stools, and without looking up, Jake said in an easy, flat tone, "Sit down, boys. I have a proposition for you." The men looked blankly at one another and sat back down.

The bigger of the two men swiveled his stool to face Jake, "What do ya' want Mac? We don't want any trouble." Jake, still staring at the countertop but acutely aware of what everyone was doing, smiled and said, "I want to get some deer...and I don't want to work too hard for it." He glanced up at the big man and looked him squarely in the eye, "Get my drift?" The other man entered the conversation, "Hey buddy. We don't know you. It's pretty ballsy of you to come in here and ask a question like that." Jake saw his opportunity, "Question like what? Just lookin' for some deer." Before either man could backpedal, Jake guessed at what the two men had been talking about and gave them his interpretation. "Heard you guys talking a little while ago about hunting deer from a vehicle...with lights. Now, where I come from, that's against the law." The big man started, "You don't"...and Jake cut him off, "Look, I have all of your license plates out in the parking lot. I know you're poachers, and if you don't let me play, I'm turning you in." Of course, Jake was taking a huge risk. He had only surmised what they were from the few words and phrases he had picked up from the last fifteen minutes but thirty years in the trade told him he was right and to go for it.

The two men looked at each other with raised eyebrows. After a period of silence the smaller man asked, "Who are you and where are you from?" Jake replied, "Name is Jake. That's all you get." The bigger man leaned in closer, "Well, suppose we are...poachers. What's it to you?" Jake took another sip from his coffee, "Well, I have something to offer. We could help each other, but on my terms...I'm in charge."

★ ★ ★ ★

Chapter 23

Sam and Frank could see the brightly lit P.D. as it stood out against the jet black hills of Thompson. Autumn brought nightfall earlier these days although their shift ended at the same time no matter what season it was. They were both tired. The episode in the corn fields behind Town Farm Road had started their day off on the wrong foot and consequently taken its toll on energy usually reserved for other sorties of the same type. The two wardens still sported the mud left from the cornfield but now it was dried and caked on their skin and uniforms. The rest of the day had been routine but uneventful.

A half worried Frank Beech shot a glance over at his drowsy partner, "What do ya' think the LT is gonna' say about the Blazer, Sam?" Sam didn't seem the least bit worried, in fact, he was struggling to stay awake. "Aw, who gives a shit, Frank? We were just doing our job and ran into a ditch. Let him get as worked up as he wants...it's his blood pressure." Beech just rolled his eyes, "Don't you ever worry about those ass chewins' the LT is famous for? I mean, I'm always waitin' for the guy to ask for my badge." Sam just let his head sink into the high back seat of the Blazer and closed his eyes, "Yeah...sometimes," a drowsy, indifferent Corporal Moody replied. Frank looked at his partner and smiled, *Cocky little bastard...always knows what's worth worryin' about and what ain't.*

Sam lazily picked up the mic from its clamp on the radio, "419 and 429, twenty-two and out of service." Twenty-two was radio code letting dispatch know they had just arrived at headquarters. "Roger, 419," a curt and snappy answer came back. Frank pulled into the last bay of the P.D.'s garage and the two tired officers began to get out of the truck. "Frank, we've got to pull all the gear out of the Blazer so it can get cleaned tomorrow. Take everything out including Farmer's gear that's tucked in the way back." Frank rolled his eyes again, "C'mon Sammy. Do we have to do it now? I'm dead on my feet and you look like shit too." Sam just sighed as he walked to the Blazer's tailgate, "Come on pal, let's just get it done.

The two wardens began emptying the back of the Blazer onto the cruiser's bay floor. Frank reached up behind the back seat and grabbed a green duffel bag. There were black letters stenciled on the bag under the handle...CPL J. FARMER. "Hey, Sam. What do you want to do with Farmer's shit?" "Burn it," Sam joked as he turned to view the duffel. "Well, should we just send it to him, or what? We don't even know if he'll be back." Sam looked thoughtfully at the green duffel lying on the concrete floor. "Some of the stuff in that bag is issue along with patrol information that should be filed... and you know how conscientious Farmer was about that." Sam paused, shrugged his shoulders and said, "Open it up. It's our truck now and if we're responsible for the contents we should know what's in the bag before we just give it to someone else." Frank unzipped the green duffel. Sam knelt over it and said, "I'll go through this shit while you empty the rest of the Blazer." Frank looked disapprovingly at Sam, "Oh sure, Mr. Golden Boy gets to do the easy stuff and ole' Frankie gets to deal with the mud and other nasties in here."

Sam didn't smile, he just said, "Rank has its privileges. Don't blame me for the way Farmer kept his Blazer."

As Sam picked through the contents of Farmer's duffel he spotted a folded piece of note paper sticking out from one of the inside pockets. He pulled the paper from its place and unfolded it. The note was from Jake and was addressed to Billy Jaggs. The note read, *Billy, tell my sister I'm going to be up north for a while, at least until this thing with Fish and Game blows over. Also, I may be moving the business up there. Tell the boys to be ready if I call.* Sam couldn't take his eyes off the letter. Sam began to concentrate and put things in perspective, *He must have forgotten to deliver it. Sister? Jake has a sister...and who's Billy? If Jake's sister is mixed up in this, which would explain why he was so tied in with the cabin people and the goings on up there. I wonder if that's the known poacher Billy Jaggs, who also lives up in that area. Now it's all starting to make sense. That's why Lee told me I was in over my head. This poaching ring goes deep.*

Sam's concentration was broken by Beech's complaining, "Hey, Sammy! Now you're reading Farmer's mail while I'm bustin' my ass over here. Come on man, what gives?" Sam folded the letter up and stuffed it into his jacket, "Nothing', Frank. Just some stuff Farmer was planning on. Come on. Let's get this stuff put away and got out of here." Frank knew when not to push the point. Not another word was said between the two wardens. Quietly, they carried their gear to their lockers and left for home.

Sam drove home through the dark Thompson Hills. The unlit roads in the dark valley offered none of the usual distractions from the passing countryside so he began to think about the new information he had linked Farmer to. *So what's he doing up there in New Hampshire? If he was part of that poaching ring out in the West Territory, I'll bet he's starting all over again up there. That bastard! What an asshole!* Sam pictured

Jake's face in his mind, the wise guy sneer he was famous for, the big weathered frame that struck fear into most people he antagonized. Then he thought, *How did he ever get a badge? He's nothing but pure evil.* Sam's thoughts momentarily drifted back to his academy roommates, *What a difference in people!* He thought about Tom Stafford and Pat James. *Now those are men of substance and integrity. Those are guys you can trust with your life. Those are guys that deserve to wear the badge.* A bump in the road jarred the truck breaking Sam's concentration. He looked up into the night sky. There were no stars, obviously overcast, but subdued light from the moon appeared to fight through layers of grey clouds. He turned his eyes back to the road, *I've heard about this Billy Jaggs character. He's one of the cabin people...suspected poacher...been arrested a few times. Could he be Farmer's brother-in-law? Pretty poor people up in that area...Do anything for a chance to make a few bucks...and who's he talking about in that letter? Who are the boys? Obviously, By the way he wrote the letter they are friends of Jaggs, if not Farmer too.* Sam looked to the east seeing nothing but the dark silhouette of the hills that outlined the Eastern Territory, and his thoughts drifted back to the problem, *That sly old Lee. He knew everyone up in the West Hills was involved. That's why he didn't want me up there. That must be why he got so upset when I told him I was going there with Farmer to check things out.* Sam smiled to himself. Lee had been looking out for him after all. *I have to figure out a way to get to the bottom of this. Got to see what Farmer is up to. Shit, I don't even know where in New Hampshire he is. Well, maybe I can get that out of Alban.* Sam was intensely upset that in spite of everything else, he belonged to a Fish and Game Department where at least one of the officers was bad.

The turn off for Sam's road was coming up. The truck's headlights unveiled the Virginia Rail fence that marked the entrance to his gravel road, surrounded by tall pines. Sam turned left onto the road and put Farmer in the back of his mind for the time being. He pulled into his drive and drove up to the barn door. The cabin was lit with a warm glow that seemed to spill from all of its windows. *Aah, home at last!* Sam climbed down from the truck and walked wearily to the front porch. He could smell Peg's cooking as it emanated from the cabin. He looked up at the chimney. Smoke flowed out in a gentle stream, light against the night sky, *Peg's got a fire going,* he thought. He smiled to himself and walked up the porch stairs and into the cabin.

Sam was quiet through dinner. The boys were at their usual bantering and arguing as brothers do, but tonight Sam didn't mediate. He just let them go and sipped his coffee. This behavior got Peg's attention. She shot him a few glances but said nothing. It was obvious Sam had something on his mind.

★ ★ ★ ★

CHAPTER 24

Sam rolled out of bed early the next morning. Last night's discovery had caused him a sleepless night. He needed to get back to the P.D. to find out more about Farmer's whereabouts. He sat on the edge of the bed and thought for a minute, *that note is a few months old. What has transpired in the meantime? How far has it gone? Have the West Hills poachers made their move to New Hampshire yet?* Suddenly, "Sam?" It was Peg. "What's the matter? Why are you up so early on your day off?" Sam stood without looking back at her, "Gotta' tie up some loose ends at the P.D. I'll be back early." "But Sam," Peg reminded, "you told the boys you'd take them hiking this morning." Sam didn't answer. He just walked to the bathroom and got ready to go.

The drive to the Police Station always relaxed Sam. The scenery was always beautiful and he just loved to sit in his beloved truck, sip his coffee and listen to the tunes as the world passed by outside. He always did his best thinking when he was alone and in a relaxed atmosphere. Sam's thoughts were focused on how he was going to get any information from Alban, *I have to get Alban to give up some info on Farmer. He'd never do it willingly so I'm going to have to get it without him realizing it.* Sam began to consider how he would draw Alban into a conversation and steer it in the direction he wanted it to go. He looked at his watch, *Got about twenty minutes before I get to the P.D. C'mon let's get a plan going here ... how am I going to start this?* Sam continued his drive to the P.D without noticing his favorite scenery as it passed outside the truck and his coffee soon got cold as it sat untouched in its coffee holder.

Back in New Hampshire, Jake Farmer was on his way back to the farm with thoughts of his own. *I gotta' call Billy and find out when those guys are gonna' get up here.* Then a frightening thought hit him, *Oh man, did I ever mail Billy that letter? If not Carol is still in the dark as to my whereabouts and plans. 'Better give him a call tonight. Gotta get those boys up here and camped so we can start laying out the business*

The sun had fallen below the New Hampshire hills' outline hours ago. It was around eight pm when Jake pulled into Helen's gravel driveway. *Hmph, no truck. Where the hell could she have gone? Not like her to just take off without telling me.* Jake parked the truck by the side of the barn as usual, stepped out of the cab, and looked around before he left the vehicle. The house was dark. Jake moved away from the truck slowly and opened the barn door. *Maybe her truck's in here*, he thought. He pulled out his mag light and swept the interior of the barn...no truck–no Helen. Jake turned and headed for the house. He could feel a tension starting in the back of his neck, his heart was beating a little faster and his eyes started to dart around more than usual. It was as if he was suspecting something...but what? Then he caught himself, *What the hell am I doing? She probably just went out for something. Must be gettin' old. Every time I'm about to start a new ring, I get a little paranoid. Feels like it's been happening a lot lately.*

Jake took advantage of Helen's absence. *I'll use this time to give Carol a call.* He picked up the phone and called his sister back in Connecticut. The phone rang for a long time. Jake was getting impatient, "Come on, come on." Suddenly, "Hello, who's there?" "Hey Carol, its Jake. Did you get my letter?" "Jake? Where the hell have you been? You take off for months, don't call, and don't let anyone know where you are. The police department won't tell us anything…Where are you?" "Look, calm down woman! Did you get the letter?" "What letter?" Jake rolled his eyes, "I wrote Billy a letter telling him to let you know what is going on. Thought I mailed it before I set off for New Hampshire." There was a pause, "New Hampshire? When did you send it?" Jake was getting irritated, "Back in June when they suspended me. I told you what I was doing and I'd be calling for the boys to move up here for the hunting season." Carol's tone was more even now, "Oh no. I never got any such letter… Billy never said anything. Where are you?" Jake looked at the ceiling, *I know I wrote Billy a letter. What did I do with it*? Carol continued to ask questions but Jake didn't hear the words. His brain kept searching, *Aah, must have got lost in my gear when I packed up…I don't know.* He decided to let it go. "Jake? Jake, are you there-you're starting to piss me off." Jake came back to the moment, "What? Oh yeah. Yeah I'm here. Uh, just forget it. Look, tell Billy to get the Boys up here. I'm in a little town called Pine Hill. Billy knows where it is. Just remind him that it's the same place where I went deer hunting last year. I need them, provisions, tools, hunting equipment and ammo. Just tell him the usual, and plenty of batteries. Okay that's it, you got it?" An irritated, "Yes," came from the phone. "Carol, tell them to be here next Wednesday afternoon around five. Come to Pine Hill Farm ready to go."

There was a long pause on the phone. Jake thought she might be writing it all down. *She's been through this so many times, you'd think she'd know the drill by now.* Then Carol's voice broke the silence, "Jake you look out for my man up there. You guys are getting older ya' know. It gets scarier every year. I can't sleep sometimes. He's the only thing I have." "Yeah, Yeah, he'll be fine, Carol…believe me. Remember, it's all about the money. Now don't forget. You won't hear from me again until after this thing is over."

"Okay, Jake. Be careful." With that, Jake hung up.

Moody pulled into the P.D.'s parking lot. The morning shift's vehicles were gone and there were only a handful of officers manning the station. Alban's vehicle sat in its usual spot behind a sign that said "LIEUTENANT-FISH AND GAME. Moody slapped his steering wheel, "Yes! He's here!"

Sam parked his truck and stood just outside the cab eyeing the entrance to the station. *I may be getting in over my head. 'Could cost me my career…Nope, gotta' go through with it.* He started toward the building. It seemed like a long walk. It always did when he was going to see Alban. Sam flashed his officer I.D. card in front of the door's entry way and it unlocked. He stepped inside to see Alban standing at the end of the long hallway talking to the Chief of Police. Alban saw Sam come in and looked away, obviously immersed in the conversation with the Chief. Sam was determined, he kept his focus on the lieutenant and made directly for the two officers. The two officers ignored Sam's approach. Sam was so full of determination and nervousness he forgot himself for a moment. Without warning to himself, or anyone else, he walked right up to the two men and blurted out, "Lieutenant Alban, may I see you in private?" Sam seemed to be a little out of breath. The Chief and Alban just turned to Moody and stared in utter surprise. They were both speechless. A corporal had just rudely interrupted their conversation without so much as an 'excuse me,' for a greeting.

Alban's face began to redden. Sam noticed the color and realized what he had just done. His heart began to sink. "Corporal Moody! How dare you interrupt?! Can't you see the Chief and I are having a discussion…and no you may not have a word with me right now! Apologize to the Chief and ask me later…with some manners." Moody took a step back, his own face reddening to scarlet. "I'm sorry Chief. Sorry LT. I don't know what came over me." Sam realized he had let his own need get in the way of good judgment. He knew he couldn't ever let this happen again. Sam began to turn back toward the door. "Just a minute there, Corporal." The chief looked at Moody with a concerned grin. "Obviously, there is something so important to you that you feel you can interrupt two superior officers without so much as a hello." The Chief paused, "Must be something so important that you can't say it in front of me." He paused, "Am I reading this right, Corporal?" Moody didn't know what to say so he went with his gut, "Yes sir-sorry." The Chief stared at Moody for a painful few seconds then smiled a little. A very little. He turned toward Alban and said, "Lieutenant, see to your man. We'll continue our discussion later." Alban replied, "Yes sir-thank you." With that, the Chief headed off toward his office. Alban turned toward Moody and with a stern look, raised his right arm and pointed toward his own office.

★ ★ ★ ★

CHAPTER 25

Sam sat in Alban's office. As usual, the lieutenant ignored his presence until he was ready to start talking. Alban had followed Sam into the office and immediately walked to the window to calm down while Sam took a seat. By now, Sam was accustomed to the drill and knew his place. The room was silent except for the intermittent crackling of the police scanner that sat on Alban's desk. After a few minutes, Alban turned from the window and came over to his desk. "Okay Moody, let's have it. What's so damn important that you found it necessary to embarrass me as well as yourself in front of the Chief?" Moody sat bolt upright in the chair. He was already on Alban's bad side and hadn't had the chance to pump him for information about Farmer yet. He decided it was best to start with the plain truth. "I'm sorry about the interruption LT, but I've recently got some information about Jake Farmer that disturbs me and I had some questions." Moody looked directly into the Lieutenant's eyes. Alban looked at the desk and shook his head, "Look rookie, forget about Farmer. None of that is any of your concern. You have enough to think about with your own career. I suggest you let any of your concerns regarding Farmer, be my problem. If I need your assistance I'll ask for it." Sam kept his gaze fixed on Alban, *He's sidestepping. He doesn't even want to know what I know. He's averting the issue.* "With all due respect sir, I think you ought to at least hear me out." Sam thought, *If I piss him off enough, I may be able to get him to slip.* Alban slammed his fist down on the desktop, "Corporal Moody, how dare you tell me what I ought to do. First, you interrupt two superior officers engaged in conversation, then you come in here telling me what you think I ought to do!" *He's losing it,* Sam thought. Alban's face was getting red again. Sam decided to push just a little more, "Sir, It's one of our own guys…one of your own guys…up north, possibly making us look stupid back here. I would think that would concern you." Moody kept a stern but quizzical countenance. The statement and Moody's demeanor just set Alban's blood pressure through the roof. Moody had struck a nerve. These same thoughts haunted the lieutenant night and day, and Moody's accidental mention of them was just enough to open the floodgates, "One of my guys! You think it's my fault about Farmer? Do you? Do you think I sent him to wreak havoc in New Hampshire just to get him out of my state?" Moody got the first clue, *Okay there it is-New Hampshire.* Alban was starting to shout. He stood up and looked down at the Corporal, "You don't know anything yet. Nothing! A couple of months on the Unit and you're telling the Commander his job. The guy makes a mistake, won't talk about it, comes in here and causes me to suspend him right before our busy season. You think that makes me feel good?" Alban continued, "Goes up to the old hunting camp and gets into more trouble…I should've taken his 9mm too." Moody was listening for every little bit of information he could glean from the lieutenant's emotional outpouring, *The old hunting camp-where was that? He's also armed, at least with a nine.* Moody figured the lieutenant would soon realize he was spilling his guts, so he tried to calm Alban by interjecting some naiveté, "Sir, if he went to your old hunting camp, he's probably just spending time in a familiar place to think. You know, get his head together." Moody didn't believe this but was pushing Alban in a more gentle way. Alban sat back down, "Nah, he moved from there and got involved with some woman. He's working her farm...so to speak" Moody saw the opportunity, "Farm? Up in New Hampshire? Alban still staring at his desk, was starting to come down from the emotional outburst, "Yeah, little place called Pine Hill. It was the piece of land east of our hunting territory." Moody thought, *Okay, that's enough, Pine Hill Farm, New Hampshire. Better back off before he realizes what he just did.* Moody was too late. Alban suddenly realized he had just spilled his guts to the clever rookie and looked up from the desk, "What am I doing? You've got me so pissed off, I'm saying things that are none of your business." Alban paused, then looked back at Sam. His voice was calmer now and he talked in a quieter more even tone. "Sam, just forget about Farmer, - okay? He's my problem. You're going to be a good officer some day and I want you to concentrate on that. This stuff is for the brass to worry about. I appreciate your concerns... shows good character...but it's my problem. Now get out of here." With that the lieutenant dropped his gaze back down onto the desk and waved toward the door. Moody rose from the seat, turned, and without another word, left the room.

Sam walked down the long corridor from Alban's office. *I've got to find out what he's doing up there. I know he was up to no good in the West Hills Territory and I think Alban suspects something too. That letter he wrote to Billy telling her to have the boys be ready when he calls for them...I bet he's moving his business up there. I bet he's poaching up there too and he's gonna get some of Jaggs' cabin people to follow him up there. Deer season is just around the corner.*

Sam went into the cafeteria for a cup of hot coffee. He poured himself a cup and sat down. Sam sat back in the chair and closed his eyes. *Maybe I should just let it go. It's another state. Let their wardens worry about it.* Then Sam pictured Jake's snarling face and the attitude he generally carried with him. He hated the man…hated everything about him. Sam opened his eyes, took a sip of his coffee, and closed his eyes again. He began to remember that day last winter when he snow shoed the West Hills territory with Farmer. A lot of excuses, a lot of avoidance. He remembered he had suspicions back then and tried to talk to Alban then too. *Alban didn't want to talk then either…was he in on it? No, not the Lieutenant. He was the heart and soul of Fish & Game.* Sam couldn't accept the idea. Sam's head was pounding. *I have to find out. How? I don't have any more time off…used that on vacation. How am I going to…then an idea popped into Sam's mind, Lee! I'll get Lee to go up there and track that bastard. Lee will be able to watch his every move and Farmer will never know it. That's it, I'll get Lee. Means another trek up into High Meadow. Probably should pick up some of those cigars he likes first.*

Sam opened his eyes again and took a long swallow of his coffee. He was beginning to feel better. He stared out the cafeteria window. It was turning out to be a bright, sunny day. *Okay what if he's got a poaching ring going up there. What'll we do then? Maybe Lee will have an idea.*

★ ★ ★ ★

CHAPTER 26

"You want me to track Jake Farmer?" Lee stood by his fireplace, one foot up on the fieldstone hearth. His left arm lay across the top of the roughhewn wood mantle. He looked incredulously at Sam. "What has gotten into you boy? First of all, you don't know he's poaching up there in New Hampshire. Second, it's out of your jurisdiction."

The interior of Lee's cabin was always a friendly place for Sam. The aroma of dried wood, smoke, and stale coffee floated about the cabin's interior. It wasn't a big place but it was comfortable and sported a lot of memories the two friends had shared through the years. Because it was so far up in the hills there was no electricity except for the juice that could be supplied by a portable generator kept in a small room attached to the back of the cabin. Heat and light were mostly supplied from the fireplace and strategically placed kerosene lanterns that hung from the cabin's overhead beams. Windows in the cabin walls provided the necessary light during the day. Sam and Lee were in the kitchen and dining area. A hallway extended from that room toward a bathroom and the cabin's only bedroom. Above the dining area, a small loft extended above their heads. The way up was by a vertical ladder attached to the cabin's wall. It was a small room Lee used to tie his flies, load his empty shells with new ammo, clean his guns, and prepare for up and coming fishing or hunting tours. The cabin was functional but without frills. It was the way Lee chose to live his life.

Sam eyed his friend. The lanky, six foot two, Lee leaned against the fireplace just sipping a cup of coffee. He scuffed the fireplace hearth with his right foot as if in anticipation to Sam's reply. Sam thought, *Aw shit, he's in one of his stubborn moods. I'm going to have to let him in on the whole smack. He'll never do this without knowing what the reason is.* Lee shifted his gaze from Sam to the floor waiting for a reply. "Okay Lee, I've got information about Farmer that tells me he's poaching up north." Lee looked up at Sam, "Poaching? How would you know? He hasn't been around for months." Sam shot back, "I found a letter in Farmer's old Blazer. It was written to a Billy Jaggs, asking him to pass the information to his sister. He must have forgotten to mail it. Anyway, the letter was asking for some of the cabin people to meet him up in New Hampshire and to be ready when he calls for them." Lee knew all about Farmer and his secret life in the West Hills Territory. He knew more about it than Sam or any of the other wardens put together. Because Lee made his living in the woods, it was only natural that he could be anywhere within a fifty mile radius of his cabin every day checking his traps, hunting, tracking animals, taking photographs, or taking clients for a wilderness adventure. If you were out in the woods within a fifty mile radius of Lee's cabin on any given day there was a good possibility that you could at least cross paths with the wily tracker. Without Farmer's knowledge, he'd witnessed the old warden assist in poaching activities, watched him make deals, and seen the exchange of quiet money. He never mentioned it to Sam. Those goings on were none of his business as long as they didn't affect him.

"I told you to stay out of that area Sam…for your own good." Lee stared directly into Sam's eyes. "It goes deep up there. Deeper than you think." Sam replied, "I know you warned me, but I'm beginning to put everything together and if it's what I think it is, I can't allow it." Lee sighed and put his coffee mug on the mantle. He looked back at Sam and came over to the table and sat down. "Sam, I was going to try and keep you out of this but now you leave me no choice. That whole area…the whole West Hills Territory is heavily poached. All under the watchful eye of Jake Farmer. He runs it! That woman you mentioned…Carol? That's farmer's sister. She's married to the head of that whole ring up there. Guy by the name of Billy Jaggs. Bad dude. He's got no conscience and he's vicious. I've been watching these people for years, just to make sure they don't infringe on my hunting and tour business. They make some big bucks selling the stuff they poach and they'd kill anyone that gets in their way. They're not afraid of jail but they do have a problem with somebody taking money out of their pocket…and that's what you'd be doing as a game warden." Sam was shocked, "You knew this stuff was going on and you didn't say anything? I can't believe you!" Lee shot back quickly, "Look Sam. I was protecting you. I knew the minute you found out you'd be up there waving your shiny new badge around and probably get yourself shot." Sam stood up sharply from the table, "How dare you. Damn it, Lee, that's my job!" Lee said, "Sam, sit down." Sam turned his back and started walking away from the table, "No, I'm not going to sit down. I feel foolish. My best friend allows me to go around working with a known criminal? Hell, I've been up in the Territory with Farmer snow shoeing. By not letting me in on this, you actually put me in harm's way." That remark gave Lee a new outlook on the situation. He just stared at Sam while he digested his remark. Sam was right. He had put his friend in danger. "Okay, I realize that now Sam, but it's more than you can handle by yourself."

With that, Sam turned around, "That's why I'm here, Lee. Can you help?"

* * * *

Jake farmer stood outside his big Dodge pickup truck awaiting the arrival of Billy Jaggs and the boys from the West Hills Territory. It was a cool evening and the sun was starting to slip below the mountain line to the west. Jake had parked his truck by the side of the road, way out of sight from Helen and the farm. The old farm was out of the way and the access road hardly ever saw any traffic. Jake thought about the boys and meeting them again for the first time in six months. Could he still trust them? Hey, they were a certain breed of man. There was only so much they even thought about. Staying within the confines of the law wasn't one of them. If it affected their pocket book they'd probably go to great lengths to keep any secret. Jake reached down to feel inside his right boot leg. His new nine mm was still there. It was a comfortable feeling. He drew it from its holster and pulled the slide back to check its readiness. These men were, after-all, poachers…lawbreakers…the type that would sell their own souls for a few bucks and then blow it all on women or booze. Jake depended on their self-greed to keep the business working. If any of them sold out it would cost them big time…probably their very life. There was too much money to be made here. Jake started to pace alongside the big diesel. His thoughts now turned to the newest members of his ring. The new guys from New Hampshire, the natives. How trustworthy were they? Should he keep them if they worked out? If they stepped out of line, he could dispose of them with no strings attached. No one knew of his ties to any of them. That was part of the deal. Jake was brought back to the moment by a distant rumble. The sound of large trucks laboring up a steep incline began to fill the stillness of the night. *That's gotta' be them,* he thought. *I hope they carpooled. 'Don't want too many vehicles around. It'll attract too much attention. That big Chevy of Jaggs, all raised up higher than it needs to be is one thing. The noisy engine is another. 'Need a damn ladder just to climb up into the cab. Good for a getaway, I guess. Just cruises right over the stumps and logs layin' around. We'll use that as the main work truck.*

The first truck crested the top of the hill. The silhouette of a large vehicle with illuminated lights over the cab and below the front fender as well as the two regular headlights adorned the dark shape. Another vehicle, not as large as the first followed, and then a third that appeared to be a small car, maybe a jeep, lagged behind *What are they doing? This isn't a parade damn it! Talk about making an entrance!* Jake was counting the vehicles as they approached, *Only three trucks... good. We can hide those.* Then two more trucks crested the hill, *Aw shit, five trucks. Where am I gonna' put all these vehicles? Damn guys! They never think about anything.*

The trucks were getting close. Jake looked at his watch. It was 5:30 pm. *They're late too.* He walked to the front of his big Dodge and reached inside his coat to pull out a flashlight. It was his police issue mag-lite He held the mag ready to signal the approaching caravan. He still wasn't sure if it was Billy and the boys yet, so he kept the mag-light dark. Distinguishing features from the first truck began to present themselves. It sounded like Billy's truck, and then the big roll bar with the cab's side handles confirmed it. *Okay that's them,* Jake the flashlight on and waved it back and forth. The first truck started to slow, pulling over to the road's shoulder across from where Jake was parked. Jake shined the light right on the driver's window. The big mag light blinded the driver, "Hey Jake...that you?" It was Billy. "Yeah, you asshole. And what if it wasn't?"

The cab was quiet. Jake continued, "You guys are making so much racket, and what's with all these lights? Tryin' to tell everyone in Pine Hill that you're here?" Billy shut off the engine, "Jeez, Jake. There's no lights around here and there's no moon. Didn't really know where we were until I saw your light." Jake turned the flashlight off and stared up the road as if waiting for someone else to approach, then walked across the street to the waiting Billy Jaggs. The other four vehicles began to slow and started pulling off the road. Jake stopped in the middle of the road and motioned to the other vehicles, "Turn off those damn lights. We got a friggin' convoy here." Jake walked up to Billy's truck. He had to look up because of the extended height of the cab. Billy looked down at his boss, "Hi Jake." Jake allowed a slight smile, "Billy, what took ya?"

★ ★ ★ ★

CHAPTER 27

Billy Jaggs' caravan followed Jake's truck down an old fire road that ran alongside one of Pine Hill's empty fields. The tree line to the west was dense with pine trees and occasional scrub brush that tangled itself around the forest floor. The road was bumpy with mounds and ditches, and traces of tire ruts caused by trucks that were used to tend to the fields long ago. Eventually the corner of the field appeared and the dirt road forked in opposite directions. A turn to the right took you around the north side of the old field and to keep straight led into the dense New Hampshire woods. The forest entrance appeared as a tunnel opening into the dark night.

"I hope he knows where he's going. It's so dark out here I can't even make out the ruts in the road," Billy said as he spoke to his rider, Ricky Dee, who jostled about in the seat next to him. The truck creaked and bumped with an occasional bang. The road hadn't been used in years or taken care of either. Ricky strained to stay in the middle of his seat, "There's gotta' be another way into this place." Billy kept his eyes on the back of Jake's truck, "There is. It's the one Jake used to hunt this area but it would be in clear view of the farmhouse that Jake's living in and he doesn't want the owner to know anything about this." Ricky looked out the truck's side window. The forest was so dense not a distinguishing feature presented itself. Trunks of trees faded into the blackness and one looked like another. There was no telling how far apart the trees were or how wide. "How are we gonna' be able to shoot anything out here, Billy? It's too dark and I don't think we could get a straight shot to anywhere. Woods are too dense." Billy glanced quickly at his rider, "You don't know anything about this area, Ricky. You can look it all over in the morning." Just then the truck hit a deep hole. The front passenger side listed sharply down to the right, "Damn it, Jake. Friggin' stupid road!" Billy was beginning to worry about the beating his truck was taking. Billy stopped the truck. The cab was at such a steep angle the seat belts were the only thing that kept them in their seats. "Ricky, get out and check for damage. If I undo my seat belt, I'll fall out of my seat." Ricky rolled his eyes and unclipped his seat belt causing him to fall against the side of the truck's door panel. "Ricky groaned at the impact and said, "If I open this door I'm fallin' out, Billy." Just then the interior of Billy's cab lit up from behind. The truck behind him had come up on Billy's stopped truck too fast. The shrill squeal of brakes being applied cut the night air. The second truck's driver, Jonny, yelled out the window. "What the hell are you guys doin' in there?" Billy stuck his head out of his own window and yelled back, "Quiet down or Jake is gonna' have our asses. I got my front sneaker in a huge hole. Back up so I can get out, will ya?" The second truck complied. Billy shifted his big Chevy Z-71 into four wheel drive and started to rock the vehicle in an effort to free it from the hole.

Jake saw the two vehicles behind him stop. *What the hell are they doing now?* Jake stopped his own truck and waited. After five minutes Jake's patience hit the boiling point, *Damn guys!* He put his own truck in reverse and gunned the gas.

Billy looked up just in time to see Jake's tail lights disappear below his front hood. He closed his eyes and waited for the impact. Jake was coming on too fast and didn't judge the distance correctly in the dark night. The impact from Jake's truck pushed Billy's Z-71 out of the hole and right into the waiting truck behind. The Z-71's raised bumper slammed into Jonny's front bumper. "You asshole!" Jonny was yelling into his own windshield. The impact had forced Jonny's head against the glass. Jonny's passenger just sat in his seat cursing and holding his head. Jake appeared at Billy's window, "What in hell is goin' on here? Look at the mess we've got now." Billy climbed down out of his high perch in the Z-71, grabbed the cab's side handle and swung down onto the dirt road. "Jonny! You guys okay in there?" Jonny yelled back, "Yeah, but I think Pete cracked his head open on the dash. He's bleedin' a little but I think he'll live." Some muffled cursing could be heard coming from Pete's side of the truck. Jake just shook his head in disgust, "Billy get over there and see if his radiator is okay. If he's stuck here we're all going to be in plain view come morning." Billy looked under Jonny's truck. "Nothin' leakin' right now. We'll check it again in the morning." Jake nodded his head and said, "Okay everybody, let's move out and quite screwin' around. Got a lot of work to do before morning. Camp is another five miles from here. Watch the holes. I'd like to get some sleep tonight."

The next few miles were as hard as the first two. Visibility was only what the truck's head lights could provide. Suddenly, Jake swerved his truck hard left and drove into a small clearing. It was as if the sky suddenly turned a lighter shade of black…almost blue. Stars twinkled overhead but still no moon. Before the tired trucks lay a serene little pasture outlined by tall pine trees. Tall grass about waist high filled the field and bare, gnarly branches of fallen trees struggled toward the sky as if drowning in the sea of grass.

Jake parked his big diesel but kept the parking lights on. The rest of the caravan pulled in close to Jake and waited for instructions, "Okay, we're here boys. Keep the trucks on the northeast side. We'll pitch camp in the middle. That'll give us the most light. Tomorrow, we'll set up the business end. For tonight, just get your tents up. One of you get a fire goin' and try not to burn the place down."

★ ★ ★ ★

CHAPTER 28

The night had been a long one. Billy and the boys hadn't finished making camp until after two in the morning. As daylight descended on the little clearing, only a weak twist of smoke floated up into the New Hampshire sky. The camp was quiet and looked vacant except for the hastily constructed tents and lean-tos that had been put up the night before. The tall grass was mashed down in the more active areas of the camp especially around the tents and campfire ring. The trucks stood quiet over in a corner of the field concealed from the sky by huge pine trees and their long branches. Now and then the shriek of a hawk hunting for its breakfast interrupted the solitude of the quiet little camp. There was no wind except for an intermittent breeze that massaged the tops of the tall grass. The pasture was for the most part protected from wind and sound by the tall pines that surrounded it.

Jake had spent the night back at the farm. Helen would have asked too many questions about where he was and why, so he made the uncomfortable ride back to the farm once the boys had settled into their new campsite. He was now back in his truck headed for the pasture. He told Helen he was going to check on some fire roads that may have been blocked by fallen trees. This way he could stay in the intended area and not make further excuses about where he was. *Those guys better be up and getting' things in order. They're so slow and lazy. Better see what they brought for booze and take it away until they get things going.* Jake was so excited about finally getting the poaching ring up to New Hampshire he was beginning to get over anxious. His patience was non-existent and he caught himself feeling a little paranoid at times. He was starting to suspect everything around him was a threat to the success of his new business.

Jake turned the last corner in the old fire road. The trucks lay parked on his immediate left where they had been the night before. It was amazing to see how sloppily the trucks were arranged. In the dark, everything had appeared neat and orderly. The darkness of the pines had given a false picture of what really was there. The same was true for the camp's appearance in the middle of the field. The tents appeared to sag where they shouldn't, tent cords were loose or missing, plastic bags lay strewn on the ground, and articles of clothing hung from hastily placed poles in the soft earth

Bastards are still sleepin.' Guess I'm gonna' have to be tougher on 'em than I thought. Jake parked the truck and started sounding his horn. Long blasts from the big diesel's horn would get everyone's attention. He slammed his door closed and walked into the quiet field. "Okay everybody up! Let's go! The wood cops are right on my tail. C'mon, let's go…move!" Jake only had to shout these commands once. People were scrambling from the tent flaps. They all knew Jake's temper and didn't want to be the brunt of his early morning mood. Billy was the first out of the tent. He stumbled to his feet while trying to pull on his jeans. "Cops? How'd they find us?" Billy's eyes were still blurry from sleep. He stood outside his tent and desperately scanned the field. Jake just stood before the camp with his hands on his hips and shook his head, "Relax, nobody's here. But what if some wardens just happened to pick this area to patrol?" Billy looked confused, "What do ya' mean Jake? We haven't done anything yet…just been sleeping." Jake's face turned a little red and he turned away from Billy, "Yeah, well, you never know. What if they came in here and started checkin' around?" He knew he was being a little paranoid…again. The camp started to come alive with the movement of tired bodies and the clang of pots and pans, and tent zippers.

Jake decided to take a walk while the boys picked up the camp and prepared for breakfast. He thought he'd take this opportunity to go have a smoke and calm himself while the boys got their day going. He walked for a while through the dark pine forest without looking back at the camp. It would be interesting to see what the view would be through the trees from a passing hunter or worse, a warden. Jake came up to a little ravine that supported a shallow brook and thought this would be the place to stop. Before turning, he took a long last drag of his cigarette, blew a long audible puff into the cool mountain air, and flicked the used butt into the clear water. Jake turned and looked for Billy's camp. He saw nothing. At first he felt a little worried, then remembered his woods sense that had been drilled into him from many years in the field. He closed his eyes and listened. Blotting out all thoughts and would be distractions, Jake concentrated on only the sounds he wanted to hear. Finally his training paid off. He could hear the muffled sounds of human voices and the occasional clang of a pot and the cracking of wood. It had only been about ten minutes since he left the camp, yet a normal man would never had guessed that just a few hundred yards away lay a camp of twelve men busily working with chatter and movement. He smiled and walked back to the camp.

"Okay, here's the plan. We start getting game today." Jake was sitting on a sawhorse someone had placed near the campfire. "Billy, I want you to break this group into three man teams. One team is getting' the deer, one team's getting small game and water fowl, and the last team is goin' fishin'.' There's a small stream back in the woods there that empties into a good size lake. Looks landlocked. There's gotta' be some good game fish in there. I'm looking for salmon and trout." Jake eyed each member of the group as they sat around the fire listening. Their faces were stoic and unassuming. They all knew they would have to do their share because every animal they poached and sold meant money in their pockets. Jake and Billy would get the lion's share and what was left would be split up among the rest of the party.

One man raised his hand as if in a classroom. "Yeah, Ricky, what is it," Jake acknowledged the question. "I heard we're gonna' have some help from some guys up here. What's going on with that?" Jake looked toward the road that brought them to this place," They'll be here today…this afternoon. There's four of 'em. We're gonna' use them to get the lay of the land and where the good spots are. They'll be your guides until you get to know the place. If they work out, we'll keep 'em on. I've been out scouting the area with them…showed me some pretty good places and hideouts for stashing game." Someone else spoke up, "Can we trust them, and what's their take gonna' be?" Jake stood up, "Okay, that's enough. We can trust them. I checked 'em out pretty good…and don't worry about their take. That's my business." Jake never allowed the help too much information. He stood up from his seat on the sawhorse. "Okay, that's it. Get to it. After lunch team up with the mountain boys and get something done. I want some game in here tonight."

★ ★ ★ ★

The afternoon was sunny but cool. November was right around the corner and autumn breezes had started to make their presence known. Still, the tall pines that encircled the area kept most of the cool wind off the little group of hunters. The camp had been transformed, in the area of a few short hours, from a confused little group of sagging tents and loose ropes, into an organized village of work tents with benches and tables, encircled by a ring of tents to house the men. Several cooking fires had been constructed near some of the work tents along with the necessary metal hangers and implements for skinning, curing, and cooking. Men filtered in and out of the camp hauling one thing or another. Suddenly, as if without warning, a jeep and one pick up truck appeared at the parking area. There was no forewarning…no sound, no way to see anything coming. The camp was so well hidden from the outside it was equally well hidden from the inside as to what was outside. Billy was the first to notice the two vehicles, "Hey who's that?" He yelled into the open air as if talking to no one in particular. One of the men nearest the gun loading table placed his hand on a rifle that lay prone and loaded on the table next to him. Another reached under his left arm and held the 45 caliber revolver that sat nestled in a shoulder holster. Jake looked up from one of the work tables where he was studying a topo map, just in time to see Jerry going for the rifle. His heart suddenly felt as if it would come through his chest. Quickly, he shouted. "It's cool, it's cool. It's the mountain boys. They're here to help." The men kept their positions. No one moved. Jake eyed Jerry and slowly but firmly said, "Jerry, it's okay. They're friends. Let go of the rifle." Without looking at Jake, Jerry kept his eyes fixed on the two vehicles at the end of the clearing. Jake said again, slowly, "Jerry, it's okay." Finally, Jerry started to move his hand from the rifle. Jake let out a sigh of relief and sat back in his chair. *I'm getting' too old for this.* He rubbed his temples and stood up to greet the mountain boys from New Hampshire.

★ ★ ★ ★

CHAPTER 29

It was early afternoon. The light breeze that had visited the camp earlier had picked up. Tent poles swayed in the wind and the tall grass that surrounded the little camp rolled as if it were waves of water. The tree tops moved in unison and the looser leaves began to depart their summer homes. The mountain boys had arrived and after hasty introductions the band of hunters was broken up into teams of three plus one mountain boy to be used as a scout for each group. Billy and Jake stayed with the camp and spent their time studying topo maps and discussing the week's plan.

Ricky's team had been assigned the task of luring deer into the area. He and Jerry and the youngest member of Billy's group, Tommy, a boy of only 22 years, were led by Big Louie, the tallest and largest of the mountain boys. Louie never said much except to point out a landmark or a place where evidence of deer was present. He led the foursome through the woods at a good clip never stopping to explain anything or chat. Louie seemed to know exactly where he was going and was very intent on what he was doing. Paths were not used, even if there were any, and a sincere effort was made by all to never use the same route in or out of an area so a path could not be started. The foursome walked for close to an hour, then without warning, the scout stopped and said, "Here. Set your cameras up here." The site was near a small stream and between a pine forest and a huge area of laurel the deer used to bed down in during the day.

Ricky took off his backpack and started unpacking three night vision cameras. In the dark, the cameras were used to record any history of what moved in or out of the area during the night. Specific trees were chosen to mount the cameras on and record any deer movement in a specified area. Usually the cameras were placed in groups of three and viewed a triangular area around a specific point that was baited with grain piles or salt licks. When an investigating deer came into the area to sample the tasty treats, the cameras would be set off by the deer's movement and record the exact time, and date of the incident. Footage of the camera showed the deer, its size and its movement, and its direction of travel in or out of the area. After several recordings, the cameras provided valuable information as to their living habits, how many, and which way they approached the viewing area.

Ricky set about choosing the trees to mount the cameras on and took Tommy with him to hold things while he worked. Jerry unpacked bags of fresh grain to pile about the area that were in view of at least two cameras and started construction of a tree stand that had a clear shot to any one of the grain piles. He drew his machete and whacked a corridor through the brush that gave him a clear shot to each one of the grain piles. Any branch or piece of foliage that obstructed the shooter's view or threatened to deflect a bullet or arrow from its target was removed.

Ricky, Jerry and Tommy worked hard for three hours. They loaded the cameras with film, tested their operation, put out the grain piles, and threw down a salt lick. Construction of the tree stand took most of the time. Jerry had to climb the tree when he got the platform assembled and drive climbing spikes into the tree as he went up. The climbing spikes made it more difficult than a ladder, but the ladder would have been too easy to spot by a passing hunter or hiker…or game warden. Finally the poaching area was ready. Big Louie had watched the three toil at their duties without offering to help. He just smoked a cigarette and watched. His job was to guide them in and guide them out and make suggestions for the best baiting areas. Nothing more.

Ricky and his team were beat. He sat down on a tree stump and grabbed a canteen of water. Leaning back against a large rock he took a big gulp and closed his eyes. Big Louie noticed the work was complete and took a final drag from his cigarette. Flicking the butt into the near-by stream he said, "Okay, pack up. Let's get back to camp." Jerry looked up and flipped him off, "You go. I'm resting here." Then Jerry looked up at Louie as if making a stand. Ricky followed Jerry's lead, "You heard 'em. We're gonna' rest awhile big man." Tommy just sat down next to Ricky without a word. Louie stared at the group without emotion. He shrugged his shoulders, turned and started walking away. Ricky jumped up, "Hey! You can't leave without us! We don't know our way out a here yet." Louie just kept walking as if nothing had been said. Jerry pulled a small semi-automatic pistol from under his arm, "Hey, pal. Hold it right there or you won't be leavin' either." Jerry had the pistol; pointed right at Louie's back. Louie stopped but didn't turn around. He said nothing. He just stood there staring into the forest, then just started walking as he had been. "Shit," Jerry slammed the pistol back into his shoulder holster. "Come on you guys. This guy doesn't have the brains to know when he should be scared. We better follow him." Ricky and Tommy breathed a sigh of relief, gathered their packs and followed Big Louie. No one spoke all the way back to camp.

The other three teams had been out setting up their own poaching areas. They placed set lines in the streams that led to the land locked lake Jake had talked about. The heavy set lines were secured at opposite shores and had several shorter fishing lines attached to them. The lines were baited and left to fish on their own. The area was then marked so someone could come out after sundown and retrieve the catch. Several set lines were placed along a three mile length that led to the lake. Another team hiked out to the lake at the river's mouth and set up two duck blinds. They could see the honkers flying overhead as they worked. Each blind was placed specifically so the other blind was out of ear shot from the other. This prevented waterfowl from being scared off from the other blind's shooting noise. The blinds were mounted on a raft of logs so the blinds could be moved from time to time. The mountain boys that scouted for the other three teams behaved in the same manner as Big Louie. Billy's crew didn't like the work set up but it was Jake's agreement with the natives and without the guides the poaching effort would be futile, and they all knew it.

★ ★ ★ ★

CHAPTER 30

The fourth team had been out hunting for small game all afternoon. They came walking into camp wearing big grins and their dead trophies hanging from a long pole.

Two men shouldered the pole, one at each end, and a turkey and two rabbits hung from the middle. Everyone stopped and watched as the successful hunters paraded their take into the camp. Some smiled and shouted cat calls while others just watched with no expression. Jake heard the commotion and came out of his tent into the waning sunlight. He saw the hunters and stepped in front of them, "Is that all you got in the six hours you've been out there? Son of a bitch! What kind of hunters are you?" The men's smiles disappeared instantly. They just stood there holding the long pole with the animals, feeling foolish. Jake kicked a beer can that lay on the ground in front of him. The camp was silent. Then, someone spoke up, "Hey, fuck this." The man holding up the back end of the pole shrugged the pole from his shoulder letting the dead animals fall to the ground. Jake heard the comment and turned around to see the man walking to his tent. He flew into a rage and in a half run grabbed the man by the collar of his hunting vest, spun him around and smashed his fist into the man's mouth taking two front teeth with it. The man fell to the ground and Jake kicked him in the stomach. The man lay writhing on the ground in pain and when he rolled over, back in Jake's direction, Jake kicked him again. Ricky stood near Billy watching the bullying and started toward Jake. Billy grabbed Ricky by the arm and whispered, "Let it go. He won't kill him." Ricky turned toward Billy and stared into Billy's eyes. There was anger and desperation at the same time. Ricky started to say something but Billy cut him off, "It'll all be over in minute. Just stay put." The stricken man lay on the ground moaning and Jake stood over him waiting for him to move again. Jake's eyes were full of rage. His fists were clenched and he gritted his teeth. He could hear himself out of breath. Finally, Jake turned and looked up at the shocked crowd of men. The entire camp just stood there aghast at what had just happened. Jake looked around and saw the surprised look on everyone's face. Without saying a word he just nodded his head a few times, turned and walked back into his tent.

Finding the poacher's camp hadn't been easy. The only information Lee had was what Moody had dug up from his discussion with Lieutenant Alban back in Thompson three days ago. The farm was easy enough to locate but there was 300 hundred acres to deal with and several fire roads within the confines of the property. The other obstacle was the fact that Lee's arrival at Pine Hill Farm had to be at night under the cover of darkness. Tracking would be almost impossible. The choice to pick the fire road furthest from the farm house had been a good one. After hiding his jeep in the woods, Lee had set out on foot with a flashlight to look for fresh tire tracks in the dirt road, especially any off road or oversize tire tracks. He walked with his flashlight pointed down in a vertical position so the light beam wouldn't be detected from anyone that might be in the area. He found the deep rut that one of the poacher vehicles had fallen into and a fresh disruption in the dirt road from spinning tires and pieces of metal from what looked to be a small accident. The tracks looked to be only a few days old but there were many of the kind of tracks he was looking for. Compared to some of the other dirt roads that led into the property, this road was the only one that had been used recently. After three hours of following the same tracks, Lee smelled smoke. He continued tracking until he came upon a small field with several tents pitched in the middle. The tops of the tents showed like white triangular beacons illuminated by the moonlight. Lee wondered if they belonged to his quarry or were just regular hunters or campers, so he decided to make his own camp for the night and be up before dawn to see who was living there.

Morning came to the poacher's camp. There were no more outbreaks of any kind after last night's display of violence and anger. The camp was quiet and no one had as yet stirred. Early rays of sun struggled to peak through a partially overcast sky. A slight breeze drifted through the pines and over the field's tall grass. Lee Sparks, lay on the ground watching the silent camp from the southeast side of the poacher's field. *No guards. No one watching the camp, Hmmn. These guys are pretty sure of themselves.* The skilled tracker took in as much detail as possible as he drew his mini binoculars across the field. His movement was so slight, so slow, it appeared he hardly moved. Stealth was an extreme priority. He continued to scan every inch of the field, and forest surrounding the camp. *They sure picked a good spot but they're vulnerable from the air. Probably not expecting any search planes in this area. Woods are too dense for them to hear anyone approaching the camp though…keeps the noise they're making within the field.* Lee smiled to himself as he began to understand the poacher's thought process.

Lee was dressed in his best camos. Because of the pine forest, he wore the black and green combination that covered him from head to toe. His jungle boots protruded out from underneath and were comfortable especially when he needed to have a light foot. Hunting gloves wrapped his fingers tightly allowing the utmost in dexterity. He would leave no trace. He wore the Vietnam era slouch hat with the same camouflage. His six inch military K–Bar hunting knife hung upside down from his left shoulder and across the left side of his chest, under his left arm a shoulder holster kept his nine mm where he could reach it quickly. He wore a black garrison belt with ammo cases for his pistol and the .300 mag rifle that lay by his side. *I'm gonna' sit right here and watch this place all day. I'll move tonight after dusk. Right now I just want to see what their routine is and how many of them there are.*

Lee was in a good spot. He positioned himself on the southeast side of the field so the sun would be rising behind him, making him harder to see. He was on a little knoll that seemed to form an elevated rim above the field so he could look down on the camp just enough to give him an advantage, and all around him were dense pines which made his hiding area dark, even in the best sunlight. The terrain was thick and unsettled making it an area someone wouldn't necessarily pick to walk through.

"Oh, oh…What's this?" A lone uniformed officer exited the tree line on the northwest side of the field. Lee focused his binoculars on the lone figure. It appeared to be a game warden of the New Hampshire variety. The man wore the characteristic dark green uniform with New Hampshire Fish and Game patches on both shoulders. The brown Stetson sat atop his head with a shiny hat badge gleaming in the morning sun. No one in the poacher camp had noticed the lone figure as he approached the tented area. He walked slow at first, then seemed to pick up a little speed as if he began to feel more comfortable with the scene in front of him. *"Yup-It's a game warden all right. Wonder what he thinks*

he's got here?" Lee adjusted his binoculars and continued to watch the scenario as it began to unfold before him. *Oh, man, this guy can blow the whole thing right here. If they try to hurt him I'm gonna' have to step in…Shit! Just keep cool fella.' Just say hello and keep walkin'. Maybe he's just on patrol and decided to pass through the Pine Hill Farm property.'* The lone officer was armed with a revolver that hung from his right side. He walked as though it was just a routine meeting with campers in the woods. The warden didn't sport any kind of caution or defensive posture. He just continued right on toward the little camp as if it was normal. Suddenly, Billy Jaggs stepped out from his tent flap. He was about to answer nature's call when he caught site of the lone figure from the corner of his right eye. Billy stopped dead in his tracks. *What the fuck is this?* Billy rubbed his half open eyes, *Shit! Where did he come from?* The approaching warden had been watching the camp and noticed it was quiet. When Billy stepped out of the tent the warden noticed him immediately, "Hello, the camp." The greeting cut the quiet of the field as if an alarm had just been sounded. The warden continued as he approached the ring of tents. He was smiling and looked as if he was here to have coffee. Billy walked toward the warden, "Hey, what can I do for ya," Billy couldn't muster a smile and came on as if he had been inconvenienced. The warden's smile started to wane. He was now within twenty feet of Billy, "Good morning sir. I'm on patrol and was passing through the adjoining property when I noticed your camp. You guys all hunters or is this just a big camping party?" The tables for cutting up game and the specially constructed racks for skinning stood just the other side of the camp. Billy thought quickly, *Too much out in the open. Can't hide all this stuff. He'll start to suspect something.* "Uh, just a bunch of us got together for some hunting, is all. We're all doing our own thing. Most of us are here to drink and get away from the wives. Just a big drunk…you know?" The warden scanned the campsite, "Well, I hope you're not hunting while you're under the influence," and smiled dryly at Billy. "Oh no, no of course not. We're all about safety. I'll see to that." Billy's heart was in his throat. *I hope Jake doesn't wake up. No tellin' what he's liable to do.* The warden looked over at the far end of the field and could see the jeeps and trucks parked at the field's edge. "Do you have permission from Helen to use this land?" Billy's mind was racing, *Helen who? Must be that widow Jake's been seein.' Must be her land.* "Guess you mean that widow that lives in the farm house north of here. That's my buddy's girlfriend. He set the whole thing up with her. I'm just in charge of the guys. Make sure they stay in line, ya' know?" The warden eyed Billy a little closer now, "Where's your buddy? I'd like to talk to him."

Jake Farmer had been watching the discussion between the warden and Billy ever since the officer hailed the camp. He peered through a small hole in the side of the tent as he held his new nine mm Berretta with his right hand. Jake couldn't hear what Billy was telling the warden but knew it couldn't be anything he could feel comfortable with. *I better get out there.*

Jake came out of the tent making a little extra noise with the tent flap so as to get the two men's attention, "Who's making all this racket out here? Jake smiled at the warden. "Oh, well now. Looks like we got us some first class company." Jake walked up to the warden and stretched out his hand, "Nice to see you guys are keeping an eye on things. Gives us hunters a warm, cozy feeling knowin' you're watching the riff raff. How are ya'- I'm Jake." The warden looked at Jake, taken aback by the sudden burst of friendliness, then back at Billy, "Is this your buddy?" Billy, in a hurried tone replied, "Yeah, this is him. Hey Jake, this is a game warden." Jake looked at Billy and thought, *Stupid bastard looks too nervous. He's gonna' blow our cover.* Once again Jake went into actor mode, "Well, I can see that Billy." He looked back to the warden, "It's a pleasure sir. I always did admire what you guys do out in the woods. Can't be easy – that's for sure. Why, look how early it is and you're already out on patrol. How about a cup of coffee?" "No thanks. I just wanted to ask about your permission to hunt and camp here." Jake saw his opportunity, "Why, my girl, Helen Woodruff gave us free reign of the place. Said to get out of her hair and go have fun." The warden continued to eye Jake, *Well he did give me her full name and he wasn't out here when I mentioned it to the other guy.* Jake knew what the warden was about to ask so he called his bluff. Still smiling, Jake offered, "Hey, you want to see my permission slip?" "Nah, I guess you're alright. Knowing Helen's name and all. I guess you wouldn't offer if you didn't have one...right?" Jake pushed the point while Billy's eyes looked as if they'd pop out of his head, "Just give me a second officer, got it right here in my tent." Of course Jake had no permission slip but gambled on the warden's good nature. Jake started for the tent. "Nah, forget it." The warden was smiling again, "You're good. Now how about that cup of coffee?" Billy just shook his head and started for the campfire.

Jake and Billy entertained the wayward warden for the better part of an hour over a couple cups of coffee. Finally the warden stood up and announced he had better be on his way. The stop at the Pine Hill Farm property had not been planned and his usual patrol was falling behind schedule. Jake stood up from his camp chair and gestured toward the parked vehicles at the field's edge, "Well, let me walk you back to the main logging road." The pair of game wardens walked toward the parked trucks. As they neared the trucks, an early morning hunting team had just parked their pickup truck. Unbeknownst to Jake they had just bagged a deer and when they saw the camp had an unfamiliar visitor, hid the deer carcass under the engine hood and tucked it between the engine and engine block. The truck was an early 1970 vintage and had the extra room since there were no hoses or air pollution control equipment to get in the way. As Jake and the warden got closer to the truck, Jake spotted some fur from the hidden deer protruding from the front grill. *Those assholes! They're gonna get us caught yet. Better try to steer this guy toward the other vehicles.* Just then, as if on cue, the warden noticed the vintage pickup truck. "Hey, will you look at this!" Jake stopped dead in his tracks and felt for his nine mm. The game warden went on, "I haven't seen one of these old carriages in twenty years. These trucks were before all that friggin' air pollution control crap they put on them now." Jake stood still. The unknowing warden walked by the front grill and around the side of the truck, "She's a beauty. A little beat up but still vintage." *He missed the damn fur. I can't believe it,* Jake started to walk again. "Yeah, well, the guy that owns this truck loves it more than his wife. Surprised he even took it out on these dirt roads." The warden turned away from the truck and in a half spin, gave Jake a halfhearted salute, "See you later. Good hunting." With that the warden headed back down the logging road and then turned off into the woods to get back on the same course he had originally been following when he spotted the poacher's camp. All trace of the warden was gone in just a few minutes. Jake just stood there staring in the direction of his departure when Billy came up to him, "What was that about? You think someone reported us?" Jake just kept staring out into the woods where the warden had just slipped back into the tree line. "Nah. Just pure dumb luck. He hasn't got a clue. Thinks we're just a bunch of drunken cronies out here away from our women for a few days. It's alright." Jake put the safety back on his nine mm, reached around to his back side and stuffed it back into his pants again.

★ ★ ★ ★

CHAPTER 31

As mid-morning arrived at Pine Hill, Lee was beginning to get hungry, *Think I'll head back to my camp and get something to eat. Looks like routine camp activity for now. The early teams are in and the other teams are still sleeping or getting ready for the day. Probably won't be doing anything until tonight. Gotta' get some stuff down on paper so I can start feeding Sam some information.* Lee slowly rose from his hiding place in the dark pines. There was no noise. All his movements were gauged for silence, probably from years in the woods. Every movement was deliberate and precise. Still in a crouch, the six foot-four tracker backed away from his vantage point, stepping quietly, but keeping his eyes on the poacher's camp. From their viewpoint it would appear that the mountain man seemed to fade slowly into the shadows…like the forest was absorbing his form. Without a trace, without a sound, the tracker was gone.

Once Lee was well away from the poacher's camp, he started to straighten up and take longer strides. In keeping attention to silence, the tracker moved swiftly and easily through the dense forest. Instinctively, Lee's eyes darted about as he moved around trees, under vines, and stepping over deadfall. His movements were natural and catlike. It was a necessary skill he had acquired, first from practice and then by necessity.

Without these skills, his whole career as a hunter and guide would be of no consequence. Lee began to pick up speed as he fell into a rhythm. It was a sight to see – a man of that size, moving so quickly and quietly, through the forest.

Half an hour passed and Lee stopped to check his position. He knelt down on the bank of a small stream that passed at his feet. He removed the rifle that had been strapped to his shoulder, and leaned it against a nearby tree. Lee looked down at the water, slowly passing by, and saw his reflection. He just stared for a moment. The water was clear and painted a blurry picture of the forest canopy above. Then he reached down and pulled a canteen from his belt. Lee unscrewed the cap and let it fall loose. The cap's chain made a slight metallic sound as it fell to the side of the canister. He closed his eyes and tilted his head back, putting the canteen to his mouth. He took a long pull from the canteen and let the sun warm his face. It felt good after lying in a cool, dark, place for so long with hardly a movement. The poachers were at a safe distance and he could finally relax.

His muscles seemed to thaw and his whole body seemed to warm, and a comfortable sensation took over his entire being. *This is what you're supposed to feel in the woods,* Lee thought. Slowly, he opened his eyes and looked back down at the water. He reached into his pocket and took out his compass. Lee took a bearing on a huge rock that he had noticed this morning, *My camp should be just the other side of that ravine over there. Can't even see the tent from here. Least I'll be able to hear someone coming if they try to climb the other side.* Lee smiled to himself, put the canteen back on his belt and headed for the ravine.

Lee's camp was as he had left it. The low rig tent he used rose no higher than two feet off the ground. Just big enough for him to lie down in. The tent was nestled in among some laurel which was close to the same color as the tent. There was no fire ring. He'd be using a compact camp stove for any cooking. There was nothing else. He didn't even clear the area so as to blend in with the forest surroundings. The camp was virtually invisible to anyone who came within twenty feet.

The tracker lay inside his tent, on his stomach, with his head facing the tent flaps. He had taken out some paper and began to write some notes that he would mail Sam from town, tomorrow morning. Lee wrote; FOUND THE BOYS CAMP. IT'S OFF THE LOGGING ROAD FURTHEST WEST OF THE FARMHOUSE. FOLLOW TO THE END ABOUT THREE MILES AND TAKE THE LEFT FORK. OPENS INTO A LARGE FIELD OF TALL GRASS AND DEADFALL. THEIR VEHICLES ARE TO THE LEFT. THERE ARE 17 MEN INCLUDING FARMER AND JAGGS – HEAVILY ARMED AND HAVE THEIR VEHICLES PARKED ON SITE. HAVE SEVERAL SKINNING AND CUTTING TABLES AND BOILING STATIONS IN THE CAMP. TENTS ARE IN THE MIDDLE OF THE FIELD FORMING A CIRCLE. FIELD IS CUT OFF FROM EVERYTHING OUTSIDE. VANTAGE POINT FOR SURPRISE IS FROM THE SOUTHEAST OR FROM THE NORTHWEST. SAW A NH GAME WARDEN ENTER THE FIELD THIS AM UNNOTICED UNTIL HE WAS ABOUT THIRTY FEET FROM THE TENTS. (IT WAS NOTHING–JUST PASSING THRU.) STATE FOREST THAT SIDE. Lee put down the pen and rolled over onto his back, *Gonna' take a nap for now. Probably be up late tonight.*

It was midafternoon and Lee was up and traveling again. The late morning nap had rejuvenated him. He circled around to the south side of the poacher's camp staying about a mile from its approximate location. After an hour of slow walking, he came back to the same stream he had stopped at this morning, but further to the southwest. Kneeling down to scoop some water onto his face, Lee bent over the stream. As he opened his eyes he caught a glimpse of a wire protruding from the opposite bank, *Set Line! Damn it!* Lee's blood pressure started to rise. He stood up and began to shed his gear. Lee hung his rifle on a nearby branch from its shoulder strap and walked into the shallow stream. Looking along the shoreline across from where he spotted the wire, he found the other end of the set line, anchored securely into the bank. He grabbed the wire with his right hand and followed it out into the stream. He had been right. Just under the stream's surface he could see fish lined up, almost in a row, as if they were all swimming upstream but not making any headway. He reached down to the snout of the first trout and closed his hand around it. Sure enough. A line protruded from the fish's mouth. Lee slid his hand along the line until it came to another line that it was tied to. This line stretched across the stream and was anchored to the other bank. *Bastards! Poaching fish too.* Lee tried to calm himself. He looked up at the forest canopy and thought for a second, *Still, don't know if this is theirs but back this far in the woods? Has to be them.* Lee let go of the line reluctantly and left the captured fish to their fates. *If I let 'em all go poachers will know something's up.* He turned, slapped the water with the back of his hand, and headed back to the shore he had entered from.

Once ashore, Lee put his gear back on and grabbed his rifle hanging from the tree branch. *Better follow the stream awhile and see how many more set lines they've got.* Pulling out his map and notebook, he noted the location, turned once to look up stream, and started following the bank.

An hour had passed and Lee found two more set lines. They all had between five and seven fishing lines attached to them. *All right, that's probably it for this stretch. Stream opens into a landlocked lake up there. I'm gonna' see if I can find any tracks and follow 'em. See where they bring me.* Lee looked around for a while, starting at one of the set line anchors. The poachers had been careful- no boot prints. Lee looked at the wooden stake that anchored the set line to the bank. It was freshly cut elm. Standing up, Lee scanned the forest around him. About twenty yards away, he noticed a fresh cut on a medium sized elm tree. When he compared the size of the set line anchor stake to the stub on the tree, they matched. *Okay, we got a starting point.* Lee looked at the base of the tree. The leaves were all rustled up and lying in unnatural positions. He knelt down and scanned the forest around him. He could see disturbed leaves turned in the same manner, which showed moisture on the upturned side. Normally, the wet side would be facing the ground. Slowly and deliberately, Lee started to follow the trail of newly disturbed leaves.

Following the poacher's trail was very slow work. Sometimes the leaves were undisturbed and Lee had to use some guesswork. He looked for newly broken branches, especially at the waist level. Since the poachers wouldn't be using any paths, they would most likely be snapping twigs on the ground with their feet, or breaking or bending small branches that caught on their clothes as they passed through the underbrush. Suddenly Lee stopped. He reached down to a small sapling and grinned. Attached to the end of a small branch hung a small dark colored piece of fabric, *Hmmn, probably off one of their hunting vests.* Lee tucked the fabric into his own vest pocket.

Another hour passed and Lee was still sure of the poacher's trail. He stood up straight and looked ahead and thought he could see a break in the forest wall, a thinning of the forest that had been so dense. He closed his eyes and listened. At first he heard only the natural sounds around him, the wind passing through the branches overhead, the creaking of tree limbs as they rubbed against one another, then something else. As Lee listened through all the sounds in his immediate vicinity, noises occurring in a more distant location made their way into his senses. The metallic clang of a pot, someone sawing wood. The distant sounds seemed to drift in and out. Lee concentrated, blocking out all distractions around him. An engine noise came through but went away again… then a human voice could be heard.

Lee opened his eyes. Those distant noises were coming from the direction ahead of him. He continued walking but more cautiously now. He was nearing the camp. The people who had left this trail seemed to have gotten careless as they neared the camp. Lee bent down and found a candy bar wrapper, then a cigarette butt. He stopped and listened again. Light showed through the once dense forest wall. The woods were thinning. He continued his approach when suddenly two men appeared directly ahead of him. They were coming from the direction of the camp. Lee dropped to the ground. His rifle lay next to him on the soft forest floor. Slowly he reached down to feel for his boot knife. Still in its sheath. He heard the men coming closer. Lee tried to calm himself. *Don't think they saw me. Looked like they were looking over to the left when they came out of those pines.* He raised his head slowly and scanned the area. He was lying in a patch of ferns which seemed to close over him as he fell to the ground. *Good natural cover here. If they don't walk right to me, I'll be okay.*

"Hey, Jerry! What did Farmer say about always takin' the same way out? Ricky Dee stopped walking when he noticed they were on the same path as they had been earlier after checking the set lines. "Screw him!" Jerry shot back. "It's bad enough we have to go check our own night cameras—now they got us checking the other team's set lines too

'Takes forever to get anywhere." Ricky replied, "Yeah, I know, but I don't want to get the big guy pissed off. You know what he's like when he gets mad. Jonny's still hurtin' from Jake's beating the other night." At the ugly reminder, Jerry stopped dead in his tracks. He reached up under his arm and felt for his 380 semi-automatic pistol, "Yeah, maybe you're right. Okay let's go left here." The two poachers stepped off the trail that led to where Lee lie in the ferns. Lee heard their footfalls going off in a different direction. Slowly he took his hand off his boot knife still in its sheath, *Well, that was close. Should have known better. Following a trail in-somebody's liable to come back out.* Then he smiled to himself, *Guess we got ownership now.* Lee lay in the ferns listening to the poachers as their voices trailed off in the distance. Slowly raising his head to the top of the ferns, he watched them disappear into the forest. *Yup, that's two I remember seeing in the camp this morning. I'll let 'em get ahead and follow 'em. See what their up to.*

Jerry and Ricky continued toward their deer staging area. It was time to check the cameras and replenish the grain piles. The two young poachers walked toward the stream but farther west of the set lines, following it almost to the landlocked lake. At the mouth, they crossed the stream and started across a grassy field. Lee stayed well behind the two men, just far enough to keep them in sight. One man carried a rifle. He was the larger of the two, and the other man struggled with a large plastic bag, which contained grain for their deer lures. Soon the deer staging area was in sight. The men set about checking the night cameras and changing out old film with new. Ricky busied himself with the grain piles. "Hey Jerry, all the grain is gone. We just put new grain in last night. Must be a lot of deer on that film." Jerry nodded in compliance but never looked up. He just continued working on the cameras. Since the poachers had now stopped, Lee found a good place to watch from and just settled in. He propped his 300 mag rifle on a log, focused his rifle scope on the two men and watched the poachers work the area. Suddenly, as if out of nowhere, a large black bear came charging out of the brush to the left of where Ricky was working. Ricky turned just in time to see the bear lunging at him. Jerry turned at the same time, picked up his rifle, pulled the bolt back, aimed, and shot the bear through the chest from thirty feet away. The bear dropped at Ricky's feet. He had frozen and hadn't been able to move. "You son of a bitch!" Lee spoke aloud as he continued to watch the scene through his rifle scope. The poachers were well away and couldn't hear Lee's cursing. Once again Lee's blood pressure began to rise. Ricky stepped away from the bear, backing up, but still watching. "Thanks, Man. You saved...," Ricky was cut off by an angry growl. The bear seemed to come to life and started to rise onto his front legs. Ricky screamed in horror as the black beast began to rise, bleeding profusely from the chest. Jerry started walking toward the bear, pulled the rifle bolt back and shot the bear again. He fired three more times as he walked up to the dying animal. The last shot was at point blank range. Jerry stood over the heaving animal as it struggled with its last breaths, blood trailing from its nostrils, smiled and said, You're gonna' make a good rug for somebody," and fired once more into the back of the bear's head.

Lee almost stood up from his hiding place but continued to watch the grisly scene through the scope of his 300 mag rifle. The mere savagery of the murder was almost more than he could stand. "You bastard! You bastard!" was all Lee could say. The bear lay still and blood started to pool around the animal's side. "Nice shootin' huh?" Jerry puffed out his chest as he looked over at Ricky. "You didn't have to shoot so many times Jerry." Then Jerry held up his hand as if listening to something, "Shh, something's coming." Two bear cubs came piling out of the brush, nipping and

Dan Hayden

bumping into each other as they ran to their dead mother. "What are we gonna' do now," Ricky just looked at Jerry. The two men watched as the two cubs jumped on their mother and tried to get her to wake up. Jerry raised his rifle again and shot each cub. The cubs lay still on the ground near their mother. "Say goodnight, asshole, "Lee was talking aloud as he placed the cross hairs of his rifle scope on Jerry's chest. He started to squeeze the trigger. One shot from his 300 mag would drop Jerry where he stood and he would be dead before he hit the ground.

Don't engage. Just watch and report. Sam's words back in Thompson played over and over again in Lee's head. *No matter what you see-do not engage.* He continued peering down the rifle scope. He could see the buttons on Jerry's chest as he continued to squeeze the trigger. Then, with a lightening quick movement, he snapped his trigger finger out from behind the trigger guard and placed his whole hand against the back of his head. *Almost lost it.* Lee closed his eyes, let the rifle lay over on its side, and rested his head against the cool damp earth.

★ ★ ★ ★

CHAPTER 32

It was Saturday morning and Sam lie in bed staring out the widow, *Wonder how Lee is doing up there in Pine Hill. It's been a week. Should have heard something by now.* Peg had been up for hours making breakfast for the boys. She was hurrying them about the house and getting them ready for a trip to the dentist. Finally, Sam heard the door slam. They were gone. Sam was thinking about getting out of bed too when he heard Peg come back into the house. "Sam, you got a letter from Lee," She yelled her news into the house not knowing if Sam was awake or not. Then, as she turned and headed back out the door Peg said, "Mailman just dropped it off. I don't recognize the address though. He must be on one of his adventures again. Okay, see you later...I'm taking the boys to the dentist." With that, the cabin door slammed behind her.

Sam jumped out of bed and threw on a pair of jeans that hung on a nearby chair, *Oh Man this it!* He headed for the bedroom door and in a half run stumbled down the hallway to the kitchen where the mail lay on the table. Lying on top of the pile was Lee's letter. Sam tore it open and began to read: As he read he commented aloud on what Lee had written, "Okay, we got a location... camp complement...

armament," Sam read on, "Umm hmm – Umm hmm." Then Sam was quiet. He was reading about the set lines and dear staging area. He read on, then said, "Killing momma' bears and cubs too, huh? He turned to the window, shook his head and said, "Those Bastards!

Sam put the paper down on the table and walked across the kitchen. He was trying to digest what Lee had just reported in the letter. He turned and walked over to the coffee maker and poured himself a cup. Sam took a swallow and felt the warmth travel down his throat. He stared out the kitchen window and took another gulp. *We've got to do this right*, he thought.

Sam began to pace the floor again and continued to talk out loud in the empty cabin, "First of all, I've got to get up there and see some of this stuff myself. Can't just go charging in there on Lee's say so. He's not the one with the badge. Second, do I get the local law authorities involved? After all, I am out of my jurisdiction up there. If I don't get local help they could say I'm taking the law into my own hands – which is against the law. If I do get the locals involved they could decide to take charge and make me stay out of it completely." Sam stopped pacing at that thought and considered what that would mean. Then, he began to pace again, "or they might let me be of help. That's it. I'll ask them for Special Police powers." Sam breathed a sigh of relief at that thought. He didn't want to break the law for the likes of Jake Farmer or anyone else for that matter. He walked over to the kitchen table and sat down. Sam shook his head as if he had just had a kind of revelation then took another sip of his coffee.

Then another thought came to mind, *What if they say no – and how do I go about getting Special Police powers in New Hampshire without the New Hampshire authorities contacting Alban. He'd crush this thing in a minute.* Sam looked up from his coffee. Once again he was at a dead end. He got up from the table and resumed pacing the kitchen floor. He walked over to the mud room just outside the kitchen and pulled his day pack from the pegs in the log wall. *Got to clear my head. Go for a little hike-straighten things out-let my subconscious work on it for a while.*

Sam took one last gulp of coffee, pulled on his boots and coat, and headed for the door. He took the path that led from his back yard out into the forest that abutted his property. He walked and let his mind wander, just as he had done so many times before when he needed to find answers. Sam just let the forest take him in. The aroma of musty wood and leaves, the fresh air that filtered through the pine trees, the woodpeckers that busily pounded away on dead trees – the quiet peacefulness that had always been his sanctuary would help to bring him an answer. The woods were quiet but bright with sunshine. It was getting cooler and Thanksgiving was just around the corner. Time and again, thoughts tried to penetrate Sam's consciousness but he pushed them away. He fought to think of only what was in his immediate surroundings. Eventually, he felt himself start to relax. He was noticing more about the forest and considering less about his problem. Half an hour passed bringing him to one of his favorite spots along the path. Sam stopped and leaned against the nearest tree, looked up at the sun and closed his eyes. He blanked out all around him and let the sun warm his face. He was ready to go home now.

Sam followed the same trail back to the cabin. He was beginning to feel happy again. The little hike had been a good one. He had walked fast and worked up a sweat. Things were starting to fall into place. Then, out of nowhere, an old memory came to mind. It was early in Sam's career as a game warden. He and the family had been visiting some

Dan Hayden

friends at a lake in upstate Massachusetts when a group of college aged boys on jet skis were tormenting the younger swimmers close to the shore. One parent, knowing Sam was an officer, asked him if there was anything he could do. Sam explained that he was out of his jurisdiction and had no powers in this state. Then, as if on cue, one of the jet skiers nearly ran over one of the younger swimmers. The child screamed, and in so doing, got a mouthful of water, causing him to choke and cry. Peg looked at Sam and said, "Honey, you have to do something. Somebody is going to get hurt." Sam walked over to the family van, pulled out his badge and proceeded down to the dock where the jet skiers were recklessly riding in-between swimmers and parked boats, laughing and yelling as they did so. Sam hailed the closest jet skier and called him over to the dock. Seeing this, the other four stopped their machines to watch. Sam waited until he had all of their attention, and with his badge still behind his back said, "You guys are making a lot of people on shore pretty nervous with the way you're driving those machines." The jet skier replied, "So what's it to ya' pal?" With that, Sam produced his badge and held it out so all could see. "I'm a Connecticut game warden, that's what." The skiers' faces became very serious. "Now boys, you know as well as I do, that what you're doing this close to shore on those machines is illegal. So here's the deal. One word from me to the local constable is going to mean a hell of a lot more than a routine complaint from some irate mom." Sam waited for effect. Then he continued, "I want you guys and your machines to go play in that bay the other side of the lake. If I see you guys with those jet skis, in this area again, there will be no warning. The whole lot of you will be taking a little ride downtown. Do you understand?" Sam waited again for comments. No one said a word so Sam ended the conversation, "Alright then, beat it." The boys took their machines and quickly left the area.

"That's it," Sam said aloud but under his breath. "That's it! Same scenario. I'll get my guys up to Pine Hill, ready to go in. Then I'll call the locals and report what's going on and that we're going to need some help just before we enter the camp. By the time they arrive, it'll all be over." Sam was excited. He had a plan. *Yeah, this will work*, Sam thought. His mind started racing. Ideas started to flood his brain. *We'll surround the camp under the cover of darkness. On my command we'll light up the place, announce ourselves and say that we know what's going on – that we've been watching their activities. Tell them we don't want any trouble and that New Hampshire Fish and Game are on their way so just stay calm and don't move.* Suddenly, Sam's new found euphoria came crashing down. He stopped walking and his face suddenly serious. *It's time to get Stafford and James involved.* Shaking his head, Sam thought about the odds. *That's four of us, myself and Lee included, against 17. Not enough. Who else can I get?* He thought about the rest of the Unit. He knew the men well enough to know who could be trusted and who might be up for such an ordeal. Shaking his head, Sam realized, *there is no one else.* He started walking again. *I can't drag the entire Thompson Fish and Game Unit up there anyway...or even half of them for that matter -wouldn't be right - Even if they agreed. Nope, it's got to be the four of us. If it's planned well enough, and organized well enough, it just might work. Just need enough time until the locals get there.*

★ ★ ★ ★

CHAPTER 33

Monday morning had finally arrived. Sam couldn't wait to get to the station to tell Stafford and James about Farmer and the goings on in New Hampshire. He didn't want to talk about it at work. It just didn't seem right. He drove his truck to work and contemplated how he would present the idea to his friends. There was a lot to consider. Would they think he was taking advantage of their friendship? After all, it was going to be dangerous-people could get hurt or even killed, and how would they feel about going out of their jurisdiction? Sam putting his own career on the line was one thing, but to risk two other private careers was another. The different considerations flooded Sam's mind. Before he knew it, he was turning into the Thompson Police Station gates. Sam parked the truck and just sat for a minute. *You're thinking too much*, he thought. *Just lay it out for them. Pure and simple...see where it goes.* He knew their dislike for the old warden would help persuade them but Sam hoped it would be easier than that.

Sam was still staring through the truck's windshield when he heard Frank Beech's voice, "Are you coming in or not?" Frank was standing in the cruiser bay preparing their Blazer for morning patrol. Moody heard Frank and quickly turned his head toward him. He had been in such deep thought he was oblivious to what had been going on around him. "Morning Frank. How's it going'?" Moody opened his truck's door and stepped down from the cab. Beech grinned at his partner, "Awesome, Corporal buddy. Looks like you need a cup of coffee." Moody just grunted as he walked by Beech.

Sam walked into the warden's locker room. Everyone was busy dressing, shining boots, loading speed loaders, combing hair. There wasn't much spoken. An occasional, "Hand me this... or throw me that"..., were exchanged but not much conversation was present. Moody looked around the room. Stafford and James were at the far end getting ready for roll call. Stafford looked up and saw Sam come in, "Hey buddy-where ya' been?" Sam didn't answer. Stafford just smiled and said, "Better get a move on, Sam. roll call is in ten minutes." Sam looked at his watch, went to his locker and started getting ready.

The day passed without incident. Sam followed a stream of tired wardens back into the warden's locker room. Stafford and James eyed Moody as he came in. It wasn't like him to be so quiet. "Hey Sam," James yelled over to Moody. "How about a beer after we get out of here?" Sam saw his opportunity, "Yeah, okay. You too, Tom?" Stafford looked sarcastically back at Sam, "Well of course. You two can't go drink beer without me. Who's gonna' look after your welfare?" Sam finally let out a small chuckle, "Okay, meet you in the parking lot in twenty minutes. Gotta' get a quick shower." James shot back, "Yeah, that's right Sammy-get yourself all prettied up for us, but you're still buying the first round."

The three old friends agreed to meet at a small restaurant located at the outskirts of Thompson. The location had been

Sam's choice. All three arrived at the same time and followed Stafford into the quaint little building. The restaurant was old and rustic-like, as was most of Thompson's architecture. After all, Thompson was a wilderness paradise with hardly any industry. The building's exterior was a log cabin that sat upon a fieldstone foundation. The windows were tall and narrow divided by small glass panes to break up the sunlight. Stafford held the heavy oak door open for his two buddies. The usual pushing and shoving was present along with some good natured verbalization as the three passed through the door.

"Come on Sam pick a table...beers are waiting," James was trying to get Sam into the mood. "Yeah, okay big boy. I'll make the decision. Like I always do. You guys can't even pick out a table to sit at without me," Sam was starting to lighten up. After the waitress had brought them their drinks Sam decided to open the conversation about New Hampshire. "Guys, I need to talk with you about something." Stafford reached out and pushed Sam's shoulder, "Oh, you're gettin' serious again Sam." Sam looked directly into Stafford's eyes, "No, Tom. I mean it." Tom and Pat had seen this look before and settled into a serious mood. The table was quiet for a few seconds then Sam began with his story. He laid out the entire scenario for them starting with the tree stand he had stumbled on last winter when he snowshoed with Farmer. Stafford and James sat mesmerized not saying a word. Finally, Sam finished with the last report he had received from Lee. Tom Stafford and Pat James turned to look at one another. Sam just looked down at his beer, picked it up and took a sip. A few moments passed without anyone saying a word. Finally, Stafford said, "Wow! That's a hell of story Sam-and you kept this from us all this time?" Sam started, "Now wait a minute," but James cut him off. "Why didn't you tell us Sam? Don't you trust us? I thought it was us three-always-no matter what." Sam knew he had to talk fast. They had gotten the wrong idea. "I didn't tell anyone because I didn't know exactly what I had yet." James cut in, "You told your buddy Lee about it." Sam answered back, "Yes, I did– because he knew the area and some of the parties involved. I needed advice. You two were as green as me about the whole thing." Stafford kept silent but continued staring at Sam. James just looked down at the table. "So why are you telling us now," Stafford spoke in a more even tone. James looked up at Sam after Stafford posed the question. Sam began, "I need your help. I want to go up there and get these guys. I want Farmer put away for all the damage he's done and I want those cabin guys brought to justice for going along with the whole thing." There was a minute of complete silence at the table, then Stafford began, "You're going out of your jurisdiction and so are we if we go in with you." Sam explained his idea about notifying the New Hampshire authorities right before going in on the camp. Stafford looked up into the rafters of the old restaurant and breathed a deep sigh while James looked back down at the table shaking his head from side to side.

The atmosphere around the table was uncomfortably quiet for quite a while. Each man was keenly aware of the other two's presence but was immersed in his own thoughts at the same time. They just sipped at their beers and thought. No one said a word. Presently, a waitress came by and brought another picture of beer. Eventually, Tom Stafford opened up the table for discussion. "Well Sam, there is a hell of a lot to consider here." Tom paused, then began again. Sam just stared into his beer. Tom said, "No one would like to see that old bastard Farmer behind bars more than me. The guy doesn't even seem to like himself, let alone anyone or anything else...but I hate the thought that because of the likes of him we could have so much to lose." James looked at Stafford, "What are you saying Tom?" Tom looked back at Pat, "I'm saying that I'm in. This guy's a bad apple and has been eluding his rightful fate for a long time." Tom Stafford looked back to Sam who had not yet lifted his gaze from his beer. "Okay, Sam what's your plan?" Then James put in, "I'm in too–whatever you need Sam."

Sam looked up from his beer and smiled. "Okay guys–thanks. Just remember this is going to get real sticky and people could get hurt. Once you're in–you're in for the whole game." Stafford and James nodded their heads in agreement. Then James stuck out his arm with a clenched fist and the other two did likewise until they all bumped knuckles. Sam put both hands on the table, leaned toward his two partners and said, "Alright, let me tell you what I've got in mind."

★ ★ ★ ★

CHAPTER 34

The little restaurant was fairly quiet. After all, it was a Monday night. Sam looked around the room. A few locals were having dinner with their families, a young couple sat tucked away in the comer, oblivious to anyone else in the room, and a few men looked as if they had just come in for an end of the day drink. There was no one he recognized. It was unlikely any one from the West Hills Territory would even be able to patronize an establishment like this. Even so, Sam was cautious.

Pat James and Tom Stafford sat staring at Sam in eager anticipation. "Well Sam, we're waiting," Pat was starting to fidget in his seat. Tom nudged Pat, "Shh take it easy, Pat." Tom's gaze was also fixed on Sam. Sam looked around the room once more and cleared his throat, "Okay. I told you guys most of the story. I figure we'll go in just before midnight. It's got to be a night where there is no moon. The whole success of the mission is based on surprise. If we can overwhelm them with the element of surprise and take control of the area before they know what to do, or what hit them, the casualty factor will be greatly reduced." Stafford raised an eyebrow, "Casualty factor?" Sam looked down at the table for a moment nodding his head. Then he

275

looked up and right into Stafford's eyes, "Tom, these guys are poachers. Ruthless poachers who don't give too much consideration about any living being's life. They are in it for the money and nothing more," Sam paused, "and they will kill anyone who tries to take that away from them." Both Stafford and James remained stoic. It wasn't news to them how poachers could be but Sam's story was not yet a reality to them. It wasn't like going out on patrol and seeing it firsthand. "Look! You guys have to take this serious or I don't want you with me." Sam raised his voice a little for effect. "Lee almost blew it when he watched two of those guys murder a mother bear and her two cubs about a week ago. I have been living with all this crap for about a year now...tracking down loose ends and generally putting the whole puzzle together with names and places. You guys are hearing it for the first time so I expect you'll be a little matter of fact about it but this could end up being a real showdown in the woods. We're going to be fully armed and ready to shoot. If you're not up for it, I gotta' know now." Sam sat back in his chair, took a deep breath and slowly took a sip of his beer.

Both Stafford and James felt a little embarrassed about their behavior. They looked up to Sam as their leader and to have fallen short in his eyes was unacceptable. Stafford was first to speak, "Sorry, Sam. You're right. I have to get a handle on this thing but you know we're going to back you. We just need a little time for the whole thing to settle in." Sam looked up at Stafford, "Tom, I don't want you guys in on this merely because of how you feel about Farmer. I want you to do it because of the injustice that's being done and that has been done–right under our noses, and because he's one of ours that has gone bad and has brought it to another innocent place. It's our responsibility to bring him back." Stafford and James were beginning to get the picture. Sheepishly they each took a sip of their beers nodding in acknowledgement to what Sam was saying. James finally broke the silence, "Okay Sam, Lets hear the rest. How many of them are there and how do you plan to get the drop on them?"

Sam continued on about his sneak attack on the camp, "Okay, as I said before, We're going to need the element of surprise. There are seventeen of them against our four. We'll have to use every condition of the night to our advantage. Timing is everything." At that, Sam noticed the two wardens eyes widen a bit when he announced the number of players but realized they were holding back their comments until after the last conversation.

Sam went on, "I figure it's going to be real dark. Their camp is surrounded by pine forest. The forest canopy hasn't dropped yet so sight and sound are on our side. It's going to be hard for them to hear us, let alone see us. We'll go in on the old logging road that leads to their camp and split up about 500 yards from the camp's entrance. I'll go over the topography with you later from a map Lee sent back to me. Before we split, we'll go over check points and times, and equipment. Everyone will have their radios on low response but we'll be in complete communication the whole time we're surrounding the camp." Stafford and James sat stone faced listening intently to Sam's plan. The more he talked the more focused they became. Sam could see his friends were getting down to business, *Ahh, Finally! I've got their attention now. Thought it might be a little harder than this though.*

"Once everyone is in position, I'll have you all check in by radio. Then, I'll direct each of you in to a predetermined spot already agreed to on the map. When everyone is in position, we'll light 'em up with our spot lights and that's when I'll announce our presence." James put his hand up,

"Where's Lee gonna' be?" Sam said, "I'm going to put Lee in a tree dangerously close to the camp where he has a good shot at everything. If we lose the element of surprise and things get sticky – he'll be our ace in the hole."

★ ★ ★ ★

CHAPTER 35

The night was clear and dark but illuminated by a crescent moon. Three vehicles sat quietly along the side of Highway One East in New Hampshire's White Mountain area...two pickup trucks and a jeep. Sam Moody scanned the road ahead and behind as he raised a portable radio to his mouth. He turned the channel selector to Channel 3 which was a private talk-around frequency that couldn't be scanned by other radios. "Okay guys let's get out." Sam was first to step out of his truck. He headed toward the tree line that lay about fifty feet from the side of the road. Tom Stafford and Pat James climbed down out of James' pickup truck and followed Sam to the prescribed meeting spot. Lee had arrived before the rest of the group and stepped out of the shadows to meet Sam. Sam said, "Hey, buddy. Good to see you." "Likewise," came the reply.

When Stafford and James reached Sam and Lee, there was an uneasy and awkward moment. Sam got right to the point, "Okay, guys this is it. Everybody okay with what we are about to do?" He scanned the group of solemn faces. Then he spoke to each man, one at a time, saying his name and looking into his eyes. When he made eye contact he nodded at the man and waited for a return nod. When Sam was satisfied everyone was okay he asked the group to stand in front of him with their backs to the highway to form a barrier against any approaching traffic. Sam then reached into his vest pocket and pulled out his topographical map of the Pine Hill area. James held one end of the map and Lee the other. Sam's mag lite revealed notes of the surrounding area and every man's position. "Okay, here's the plan. We're about a mile from the old logging road that leads to the camp so we'll park our trucks over there between that tree belt and the tree line." Sam motioned to a secluded spot by the side of the highway that looked as if it was a pull off for tired truckers or romantic parkers. "We'll take Lee's jeep into the logging road and ditch it here," Sam pointed to a small depression off the side of the old logging road. "That's about four miles in. The camp is about five miles in, so we'll be on foot for the last mile. We'll check armament and weapons before we leave the jeep. That's when I'll call New Hampshire Fish and Game and announce our intentions." He looked up at the group, "Okay so far?" Everyone nodded in agreement.

He looked over at Lee first, "Lee, I want you to go directly to that big oak tree on the northeast side of the camp. It's right on the field's tree line and about fifty feet from the closest tent. Don't get too high because you may need to get down in a hurry. Just get high enough where you can provide cover fire over the entire camp." Lee just nodded. Sam looked over at Stafford, "Tom, I want you over on the northwest side of the field. Use the trail the New Hampshire game warden came in on when he stumbled onto this place last month. You'll be the furthest position out. To get there you'll split off from us just before we get to the end of the old logging road – just before the field's entrance. Another fire road breaks off to the right and goes onto state forest property. Follow that road bearing left for about a mile. Take the first fork in the road which breaks hard left back toward the field. It's about 500 yards. Your position is a depression right on the tree line with some deadfall in front of it. Don't worry, you're position is off state forest property. That ends about one hundred yards back up the trail, so you'll be back on Helen's property again." Stafford looked relieved. "Call me on channel three when you're in position." Sam looked at the group. "That's the only time anyone makes a call unless it's an emergency. I'll handle all the communication. Is that understood?" Again, everyone nodded in agreement. Sam looked over at Pat James who was anxiously awaiting his assignment "Pat – You'll be on the southeast side of the field. It's Lee's old observation spot. About a quarter mile from the field entrance you're going to start south around the field's outside perimeter. Keep a fifty foot buffer between you and the field's tree line. Watch for the moonlit sky through the trees. That will help you to gauge that distance. There is no path for you to walk on so travel as quietly as possible. Your position is on an elevated rim above the field's floor. Make sure you set your rifle scope for night vision."

"I'll be walking straight into the field." He looked over at Lee, "You're going to be the closest one to me buddy so keep me covered. When I get inside the field I'll move southeast to get that tree line behind me so I don't stick out too much. That's when I'll give the command to light 'em up with your high powered spotlights. At that point, I'll announce our presence and ask them to stand down. Remember, we are going to have to work fast because New Hampshire Fish and Game will already be on the way. I figure it'll take them about thirty minutes to round up their posse and at least another thirty minutes before they can get to the field." He looked at Stafford and James, "You guys are going to have to make good time getting to your positions." Sam handed

Stafford and James each their own topographical map. Once again, Sam looked at the group, "Any questions?" No one said a word. "Okay, park the trucks."

★ ★ ★ ★

CHAPTER 36

Everyone was silent as Lee's jeep rolled along the old logging road. Occasionally, Lee would drive into a huge rut causing the jeep to pitch and tip so bad that it felt like the vehicle would roll over and spill its contents. Lee couldn't use his headlights because the cover of darkness was one of the team's advantages. It was bad enough noise from the jeep's engine broke the stillness of the night, but it was a risk the team had to take. Time was now a major consequence. Lee had looked over the old road prior to this night and knew where some of the bad spots were but in a pine forest with only a crescent moon, little of the noted landmarks could be recognized. None of the jeep's occupants complained Everyone was silent, concentrating on the task at hand.

Finally, the jeep approached the crest of a small hill. For a moment, the jeep and its four occupants became illuminated. Then the jeep started down the road's incline and disappeared into the shadows again. Lee looked down at his odometer and said to himself, *four miles from the highway. Got to be on the left around here somewhere.* Then he noticed a small clearing at the bottom of the hill surrounded by deadfall. *There it is.* Lee started to relax a little. The small depression Sam planned to ditch the jeep in could be seen in the dim moonlight.

Sam checked his watch. It had been thirty minutes since they hid their vehicles by the highway and piled into Lee's jeep. Sam had also started to get nervous, *Gotta' be around here somewhere. There's the bottom of the hill*, Sam thought. Lee slowed the vehicle to almost a crawl and pulled the jeep over to the left, turning into a cleared area surrounded by old logs and stumps. He turned off the jeep, "We're here," Lee said in a muffled tone.

Quietly, the four men started to climb out of the jeep. Sam was first to step out. He walked away from the vehicle and checked his watch again, *12:43 AM. Right on time.* Lee remained in the jeep and let Stafford and James extract their equipment, then he got out and removed his own backpack. The rifles and Lee's bow were strapped to the jeep's roll bar and would be the last items to come out. Sam looked up at the night sky. He took a few deep breaths and listened to the quiet that filled the forest around him. There was no breeze. The tall pines shielded them from most of the environmental factors that would normally be a concern. He turned around and faced the three men, "Okay, gear up." The sound of Velcro tearing, buttons snapping, and felt lined zippers opening could be heard around the jeep as the small team began to prepare for the night ahead.

Sam walked over to the jeep and removed his own backpack. Stafford and James were busy gearing up. Lee had taken his own gear over to a nearby uprooted stump and started his preparation away from the group. Sam stood behind the jeep and reached down and felt for his boot knife. It sat inside his right boot on the outboard side. It always made him feel more comfortable just knowing it was there. He put on his combat belt that held his "high rider" holster. The high rider held his model 66/357 magnum higher than waist level and close to his arm pit. He slid two speed loaders onto the belt and checked to see if they were full. His mini mag lite hung at the back of his combat belt right next to his folding knife. Then he reached down into the right thigh pocket of his cargo pants. He felt for two boxes of shells for his service revolver. Both were there. He removed the contents of one and slipped them into the right vest pocket of his hunting vest. He checked the left side vest pocket for his compass. The topo map fit folded up right next to it. Sam couldn't help but to think about Peg and the boys back in Thompson while he prepared. Hopefully, they were all sound asleep, sleeping the sleep of innocents in preparation of a new day.

Lee walked back to the jeep carrying an empty pack. He stopped and looked at Stafford and James. They were done adjusting belts, stuffing pockets, and checking their weapons. Finally, Sam said, "Okay, check your ammo." All three men opened their ammo caches one more time in front of Sam. Sam watched them go through their checks in the dark. "Lee, are you all set with the 300 mag rifle and the bow?" "Yeah," came the reply. He looked at Stafford and James, "All set with small arms ammo?" Both nodded. "How about your rifles?" Stafford replied, "We've both got ammo pouches with extra rounds. All set, Sam." Sam nodded. "Make sure your high intensity spotlights are readily accessible. When I give the signal to turn 'em on, it has to be simultaneous. It's our biggest distraction." They all showed Sam that their lights which hung from a carrying strap were slung over their left shoulder. "Any questions?" He looked at each man. No one said a word. "Okay, sit tight. I'm calling New Hampshire Fish and Game."

Sam pulled out a cell phone from his shirt pocket. He pushed the numbers for New Hampshire's Fisheries and Game Department. That transferred him over to the state's "Turn in Poachers" line. A female voice came on the line, "Good evening. Fish and Game TIP line. What is your complaint?" Sam said, "This is Connecticut State Game Warden Sam

Moody from Thompson, Connecticut, badge number 419. I'm here in the Pine Hills area north of Highway One East near the Woodruff property, with two other officers on a tip that one of my men is running a poaching operation here. We came up here to bring him back and we'd like you to help us stop this activity. I am requesting special police powers in the event things get out of hand." There was a short pause. Then the voice said, "Standby Officer Moody. I'm transferring your request to the Shift Commander."

A new voice came over the phone, "Shift Commander Bowles. Can I help you?" Sam repeated his request. Bowles spoke rather loudly into the phone, "What do you mean have us assist you? You are out of your jurisdiction, Moody." Sam was quick, "Yes sir, I realize that but this is one of our men and we'd like to have a hand in bringing him in." Commander Bowles was taken aback, "Look, this is all very sudden. I can't just grant you special police powers. You could be anyone calling in. There is paperwork to do and phone calls to make." Moody responded with, "Sir, I understand all that but this is an emergency. It's going down tonight and we need to stop it now." Moody appealed to the understanding all police have in common with one another, "Sir, It's our guy in your territory and we want to get him out of here and bring him to justice. We are embarrassed and upset. Can you look at it from our point of view...Please?"

There was a pause, "Okay Moody, I'm not promising anything but I'll have to confirm who you are and make some calls. I've got your badge number but I'll also need your Captain's name, your social security number, and your birth date. I will also need the same for the other two officers that are with you." Sam complied, making no mention of Lee and offering Captain Fletcher's name and the rest of their personal information. Commander Bowles said after a short delay, "Moody, We ask that you wait before going any further with this. If anything, you'll be assisting us. Is that understood?" "Yes, sir," came the reply. I'll call back once your Captain clears you." Moody answered, "Yes sir." The line went dead. Sam pushed the end button on his phone and looked at his three friends who just stood there watching him. "Okay, boys, let's go. It is now one AM. Everyone on channel 3?" Every one nodded. "Let's move."

Sam walked in front and on the left side of the dirt road. Lee was on the other side of the road directly across from Sam. Stafford and James were in the rear, Stafford on the left and James on the right. Sam turned toward the group as he walked, "Keep separated boys. Just in case we're spotted you'll be a harder target." The little assault team walked briskly but quietly toward their separation point. Soon the fork in the road that led to the state forest appeared on the right. Sam looked back at Stafford, "Okay, Tom there's your road. Be quick. Call me when you get there." Tom Stafford said nothing and hurried off down the road. The group remained motionless until Tom's figure disappeared into the shadows. Sam started walking again and the others followed. The forest was dark and quiet. Occasionally the rub of one tree against another squeaked and groaned but other than that there was nothing.

The group of three continued on for ten more minutes. Suddenly a break in the tree line appeared about fifty yards ahead of them. "Everybody down," Sam motioned with his hand. "There's the entrance to the field." A small ray of light emanated from the ground into the otherwise dark sky. "That's probably from their campfire. If it's still going they probably have someone on watch, so be careful. Stay out of site as best you can." Sam turned and looked at James and Lee. He said nothing for a minute then, as he knelt crouched in the road, said, "Lee, your tree should be over there fifty feet right of the field's entrance." Lee nodded and said, "I know exactly where it is." Sam reached out and grabbed Lee's left forearm, "Lee, I'm not going to be able to get you Special Police Powers because you're a private citizen. If you continue with this tonight you are considered a volunteer. You'll be acting on your own and if you injure anyone I can't guarantee...," Lee put his hand over Sam's and patted it twice, "Sam, I've had enough. Seen enough. I'll take responsibility for my own actions." He stared into Sam's eyes for a few seconds, then he said, "See ya', pal." Before Sam could answer, Lee had disappeared into the dark night, without a sound. Sam cleared his throat. James knelt beside him with the butt of his high powered 7mm rifle in the dirt road. Finally he looked into James' eyes, "Pat, you're up. Don't get any closer to the tree line than this. It's about a twenty minute walk from here. You're going to come to a pile of four huge glacial boulders. When you see them, look directly right about 90 degrees. Head straight for the tree line and you'll come right to your position. It's elevated from the field so stay in a crouch. You can't miss it." James just nodded and started to get up. Sam grabbed James' left arm, "Pat, I gave you the harder position to find because I know you're good in the woods." Pat just smirked and said, "No problem buddy. I got it covered," and headed off.

Sam waited for Pat to put some distance between them and then rose from his kneeling position. He strained to hear any sounds coming from the field. All was quiet. He stared into the darkness ahead and looked for human shapes that might be silhouetted against the night sky. Nothing revealed itself. *Okay, let's do this*, Sam said to himself, and headed for the field's entrance. It was a lonely walk. Sam felt nervous for his friends who had disappeared into the woods and for their welfare in the next sixty minutes. *It'll all be over soon.* Sam thought. *Finally all over.*

Sam reached the field's entrance and saw the tents pitched just north of the field's center. The waning campfire threw enough light that Sam could count the tents. *Five tents for sleeping, five more for working.* Sam entered the field and moved southeast inside the field's tree line. Suddenly his cell phone vibrated inside his shirt pocket. Sam dropped to a squatting position in the tall grass and opened the phone. Sam said in a muffled tone, "Hello?" "Moody, this is Commander Bowles." "Yes, sir," Moody replied. "Okay, officer, you have six hours of Special Police Powers from this time. It's now 0130 hours," which was one thirty in the morning in laymen terms. We have our people on the way to your position. Do not engage until we arrive. Is that understood Officer Moody?" "Yes, sir," came the reply. There was a small pause, then Bowles continued, "Your Lieutenant isn't real happy right now." Sam replied, "Yes, sir. I understand." *Alban's going to have my ass*, Sam thought. Once again the line went dead. Sam closed his cell phone and put it back in his shirt pocket. Sam's radio came to life, "422 to 419. In position." It was Stafford. Sam relaxed a little, "Okay Tom, get ready. Remove your safety. I'm waiting on Lee and 421."

Lee had almost reached the halfway point in the big oak tree. He was searching for a nesting spot where he could have uninhibited use of his compound bow. One step higher would get him a position where two large limbs provided almost a natural bench for him to sit on. He hung his quiver of arrows on a smaller limb within easy reach of his nesting position. He placed the quiver so he could reach down and grab the end of the arrows from the quiver in one easy, quick movement. Then he unslung his 300 mag high powered rifle and hung it on a branch a little further away from his bench so he could have more maneuvering area for the bow. Lee settled into his position, making some adjustments and waited for Sam's call.

Pat James kept watching the tree line making sure to stay a good distance from its edge. *Walking quietly isn't easy especially if you're in a hurry,* Pat thought. The big man was better than most at this and kept watching for the glacial boulders. Finally the large dark shadow up ahead started to show some detail, *There they are,* Pat thought. *Thought I'd never find 'em.* Just then Pat's radio crackled. "Pat where are you?" It was Sam. Pat raised the radio to his mouth, "Almost there, Sam. Just found the boulders. Be in position in about five minutes. I can see the rim from here." Sam reminded him, "Keep down. You'll be exposed up there." Pat walked up to his position and began getting his equipment ready. When he was comfortable, he picked up his radio again, "421 in position." Sam replied, "Okay Pat."

Sam was looking over to the northeast side of the field where Lee's tree stood. Once again he raised his radio and said, "Lee how are you doing?" "Ready," came the reply. Sam took a deep breath. "Okay boys, get ready on your high intensity spotlights. On my signal everyone comes on at the same time."

★ ★ ★ ★

CHAPTER 37

Three green SUVs, carrying two New Hampshire game wardens each, raced toward Pine Hill, New Hampshire with their lights flashing but no siren. The vehicles bore the New Hampshire state seal with the Fish and Game crest boldly marked on the passenger doors. The first call was from the lead SUV. New Hampshire game warden Lieutenant John Sears spoke into the car's radio microphone (mic), "Car one approaching the Pine Hill area. Ready to enter the Wooddruff property. ETA is one minute." Sears hung up the mic and looked over to his driver, Corporal Dan Aldridge, "The old logging road is up on the left about a half mile. Start slowing. Comes up on you fast and it's a ninety degree turn." Sears scanned the roadside for vehicles. "No vehicles in sight yet. Must be hidden somewhere." The small caravan of SUVs approached the crest of Highway One East. "There it is! On the left." Sears pointed as he yelled over to Aldridge. "Make a left right here." Sears picked up the mic again, "All vehicles–left turn ahead fifty yards. Turn off your lights as you enter. Make it slow and careful. This is going to be a bumpy ride."

Sam sat in the field scanning channel one on his radio. He listened to Sears talk to his men, then said to himself, Okay *they're on their way in. Time to rock and roll.* He switched his radio back to channel 3, "Okay boys. New Hampshire Fish and Game are at the logging road. Get ready." Sam called each man, "422?" "Ready," came the reply. "421?" James came back, "Ready Sam." "Lee?" "Ready." Sam took a deep breath, "Okay boys, light 'em up." At that instant all four men, including Sam, trained their high intensity spot lights on the camp. The little field lit up like day time. "What the hell?" someone yelled into the night, "Who's there," another yelled, "Hey!" came another voice. The poachers had been unsuspecting and off guard. Sam's plan for surprise had worked. He had caught the poachers working late, skinning fresh carcasses, cutting up meat, and tending to other camp chores that couldn't be done during the day. Sam rose to a standing position and stood on the southeast side of the field with the tree line behind him. Still holding his spot light out and away from his body, raised his badge in front of him and said, "Thompson Fish and Game. No one move. Put down any weapons. We want to talk with you. We are out of our jurisdiction, but New Hampshire Fish and Game is on their way in. Please remain still. We don't want anyone to get hurt."

Lee watched the reaction of the camp from his nesting point in the old oak tree. He saw the poachers running to and fro as Sam spoke. Everyone was blinded by the sudden onslaught of the bright spot lights except for Lee as his high perch kept him above the illumination. Suddenly, Lee noticed one of the poachers, Jerry Taylor, who had been standing close to one of the cutting tables, reach for his bolt action carbine, *Uh oh,* Lee thought. Then, Lee remembered the man, *That's the guy that murdered that bear and her two cubs.* Carefully, Lee set his spotlight on his bench and balanced it with his left knee. Slowly, he raised his bow to shooting position while keeping his eye on Jerry. Then with one quick movement, Jerry grabbed the carbine, pulled its bolt back, and shouldered the rifle. *He's gonna' take a shot at Sam!* Lee thought. Lee pulled the arrow back to its hold position on the compound bow and waited. Just then Jerry shot at the light coming from Sam's position. "Shit!" Lee said aloud as he let his arrow fly.

Ricky Dee had been standing next to Jerry when the spotlights came on. He saw Jerry reach for the rifle, "No Jerry. You don't know where they are." Ricky no sooner finished speaking and his mouth dropped in horror as he looked at Jerry. A bright shiny arrow tip protruded from Jerry's chest with blood coating the four inches of shaft that followed. Ricky yelled, "We're under attack! We're under attack!" and ran off toward one of the tents. Jerry's eyes rolled back into his head and he fell to the ground in a heap.

The spotlight shattered in Sam's hand. He stumbled backwards and the force of the carbine's bullet spun him halfway around. Sam fell to the ground and lay on his belly in the tall grass. He pulled his radio from his belt and switched to channel one. Sam said, "New Hampshire Fish and game from Thompson 419." There was a pause then the radio came to life, "Lieutenant Sears here. Go ahead 419." Sam kept his head close to the ground as he spoke into the radio, "This is Thompson Fish and Game awaiting your arrival. We are under fire and request permission to engage." The reply came back quick, "Negative-negative, Thompson. Your orders are to wait for us." Sam came back, "I repeat we are under fire. Shots fired. We need to defend." New Hampshire came back, "Stand-by Thompson." Lieutenant Sears was having a difficult time talking on the radio because of the rough ride he was having in the SUV. He called New Hampshire Dispatch, "New Hampshire Car one to Headquarters." Dispatch replied, "Go ahead Lieutenant." Sears relayed Moody's request.

"New Hampshire Car One to Thompson Fish and Game."
Moody keyed his mic desperately, "Thompson 419 here."
"Okay 419. Permission to engage is granted but only for
defense. Hold your positions but do not take any more
steps than necessary." Sam keyed his mic, "Roger, New
Hampshire." Sam went back to channel three and called his
team, "Okay boys, you are cleared to engage if necessary.
Defense only. Only shoot if you have a sure shot."

★ ★ ★ ★

CHAPTER 38

Jake Farmer stood at his tent opening in disbelief. He stared into the spotlights and thought, *Was that Moody? How could he...? Sounded like Moody!* Billy Jaggs ran up to Jake and disrupted his thinking, "Jake!" Jake continued to stare out into the field where Sam had announced his presence. Billy said again while grabbing Jake's arm, "Jake, its Moody and his boys. They're all around us! What do we do?" Finally, at Billy's urging, both audible and physical, Jake came back to the moment and looked at Billy, "You think it's Moody too?" Billy replied, "Yeah, that's him–Seen him when his light went out." Suddenly, Farmer felt a sudden and extreme urge fueled with hatred and anger. He started walking toward the area Moody's voice had come from. He walked faster and faster while pulling his nine mm pistol from the back of his pants. He started to yell into the night, "Moody... you son of a bitch." Jake raised the nine mm into the air and began shooting wildly into the night. "Sneak up on me will ya'...You bastard." Farmer stopped and looked down at Jerry Taylor's body. He lay in a heap with an arrow protruding back to front. Another surge of anger filled Jake as he raised his pistol again and continued shooting in all directions. "Where are ya' Moody?" Jake turned and shot in another direction, "How's that feel? I get ya' yet? I'm gonna' get ya'

Moody." Billy watched Jake run around the camp shooting into the night. *He's flipped. Jake's gone nuts.*

Pat James aimed his high powered 7mm rifle on Jake Farmer's chest. He adjusted the infrared scope with night vision onto Jake Farmer as Farmer walked back and forth shooting into the air like a wildman. *Bastard's lost it*, Pat thought. Farmer stopped and was shooting in a direction to the right of where Pat lay on his elevated rim. *He's gonna' run out of ammo, then I'll focus on his range*, Pat thought as he watched Farmer through his rifle scope. Jake kept shooting and suddenly, all that could be heard were the metallic clicks from the hammer of his pistol as it closed on an empty firing chamber. Jake stood still while he pulled another clip from his pants pocket. Billy took this opportunity and ran up to Jake, "Jake, we need to think about this." Jake was wild with adrenalin. He was sweating and breathing hard. Then Billy gasped as he saw a red dot playing on Jake's forehead. "Jake. Stop moving!" Jake continued working his clip and getting the pistol ready to fire, not listening to his brother-in-law. Billy grabbed Jake at the shoulders with both hands, "Jake–Don"t move. You have a red dot on your forehead. Someone's sighted in on you."

The mountain boys had retreated to the far west of the camp. They all knelt in the high grass waiting for Big Louie to join them. One of the poachers spoke up, "Come on let's get out of here. It's over. They're gonna' be all over us in a few minutes." Another of the mountain boys, Little John, spoke in a quiet tone, "Remember the plan. If we're found out, we head to the west of the camp and split up, but we all leave together." The poachers from New Hampshire had made a secret pact that if there was trouble they would abandon their Connecticut partners and head to the west side of the forest which led even deeper into the woods. Knowing the woods better than anyone, the plan was to just leave their equipment and flee the scene. Finally, Big

Louie ran up to the little group, stumbling and tripping as he fell down in front of the rest. He looked up, "Everyone here?" Little John nodded yes. "Okay let's go." The poachers headed for the dimmest lit area of the field's perimeter, which was the area between Stafford and James.

Tom Stafford watched the four New Hampshire poachers make their way to the west perimeter of the field. He picked up his radio and keyed the mic, "Sam, from 422." Sam lay on his belly in the tall grass and answered Stafford, "Go ahead." "Sam, a bunch of these guys are heading for the west perimeter. What is your pleasure?" Sam smiled and replied, "Let 'em go. We'll let New Hampshire Fish and Game track them down. Less for us to deal with." Stafford keyed his mic, "Roger."

Sam lay on his belly in the tall grass watching Farmer. Jake stood in the field motionless with Billy Jaggs. They seemed to be talking but Sam noticed Jake was starting to move his nine mm in the air again. *I have to get to him before he starts shooting again. One of these times he liable to hit someone.* Sam waited for his opportunity and slowly raised himself to a kneeling position. Then he started creeping forward in a crouch, slowly at first, then faster, until he was in a full run. Billy still had ahold of Jake's shoulders, "Come on man! Snap out of it!" Billy watched the red dot from James' 7 mm rifle scope dance around Farmer's forehead. "You've got to put your hands up. He could let you have it anytime now." Jake just stared off into the direction of his unseen shooter. Suddenly, Billy heard something coming toward him and turned just in time to see Sam launch headlong into an airborne tackle crashing into Jake at his left shoulder. The force knocked Jake into Billy and all three men fell to the ground.

Lee watched Sam approach Jake and Billy in the field below. "No Sammy-not now," he said in a muffled tone. As Sam crashed into the two men, Lee saw Farmer's nine mm fly into the air and Jake come up swinging. *Now's my chance to get that arrow.* Lee climbed down from the tree almost in a controlled fall and hit the ground running. Sam was now returning Farmer's punches and Billy Jaggs crawled around in the grass looking for Jake's nine mm. Lee sprinted toward Jerry Taylor's lifeless body while keeping his eye on Jake and Sam. Lee reached Jerry and rolled him over onto his back. He put his boot on Jerry's chest and pulled the aluminum shaft from his body. Then he heard Jaggs yell, "I got it. I found the nine Jake." Lee stood in the tall grass only twenty feet from the other three men. No one had noticed him yet. He reached down and pulled his boot knife from its sheath. Billy turned the nine mm in the direction of Jake and Sam as they wrestled in the field, "Stay still Jake so I can get a shot." Farmer paid no attention to Billy's request. He was too busy trying to get control of Sam. The two men rolled about on the ground, punching and straining. Lee raised his knife to throwing position when suddenly a patch of clothing seem to tear loose from Jaggs' right shoulder followed by a stream of blood. Billy fell violently to the right of where he was standing and lie motionless in the tall grass. A bullet from Stafford's .3030 rifle had pierced Billy's shooting arm buying Sam more time with Farmer.

Farmer and Sam struggled in the tall grass. Both men were beginning to tire as they had been brawling for two to three minutes. Jake was holding his own against the younger Moody. Farmer let go with a hard right to Sam's jaw, knocking him onto his back and a bit dazed. Farmer fell forward after the punch and brought himself back up to his knees, "I'm gonna' kill ya' Moody." With that, Farmer mustered the rest of his waning strength and leapt forward in an attempt to land on Sam.

That last punch almost knocked Sam unconscious. He fought to keep his eyes open. *Stay conscious*, Sam thought. *Stay awake.* Just then, Sam felt the crushing weight of Jake Farmer's body as it landed on his. *"Gotta' keep fighting. Gotta' get him off of me.* Sam's vision started to clear. He struggled to raise his arms when he noticed Jake wasn't resisting any longer. *What? What's he doing?* Sam started to panic. *Where's his hands? Probably reaching for a knife.* Sam breathed deeply, then with one extreme effort, arched his back and threw Farmer's body off his. Sam quickly got to a kneeling position, reached down for his boot knife and pulled it from its sheath. Then with one fluid movement, Sam grabbed Farmer by the hair pulling his head back exposing his bare neck while holding the boot knife to it. "Give it up Farmer. You're done." Sam was breathing hard and had trouble getting the words out. Farmer just lay there with his eyes closed. "Farmer!" Sam yelled into Jake's face. Sam yelled at Jake again, "Farmer!" Jake remained motionless in the field's grass. Sam reached down and picked Jake's arm up by the wrist and let it drop. The arm fell listlessly back to the ground.

* * * *

CHAPTER 39

The field came alive with flashing lights from the New Hampshire Fish and Game SUVs. The three vehicles came bouncing through the field's entrance and split up. One went to the right, one to the left and Car One with Lieutenant Sears came straight in. Sear's voice came over the vehicle's PA system. "New Hampshire Fish and Game. Everyone stay where they are. No one moves." Lee turned from where he had been watching the scuffle between Farmer and Moody just in time to see the vehicles enter the field. *I'm outta' here.* Still holding his used and bloody arrow, Lee ran back to his tree.

Lee climbed the old oak as fast as he could, unhooked his bow from where he left it, and let it fall to the forest floor. Then he grabbed his 300 mag rifle, slung it around his back, and slid down the tree as fast as he did the first time. He picked up his bow and looked back into the field. One man lay dead, another with a bullet through his right shoulder, and Sam stood over Jake Farmer, knife in hand, facing the New Hampshire SUVs. Lee nodded his head up and down slightly and thought, *It'll be okay from here. Looks like the rest of those poachers lit out during the confusion.* Lee looked back at Sam. *He'll be okay.* Feeling as if the situation was under control, Lee turned and melted into the dark forest. As always, Lee left without a trace. No sound, no visual contact, no spent ammo. There was no sign that Lee had ever been there.

There had been so much confusion beginning with the high intensity spotlights, every man scrambled around searching for his own self-preservation. But there was nowhere to go. The foe behind the lights could have been anywhere around them. The sudden illumination without warning was blinding and caused a feeling of great vulnerability since their foe could not be pinpointed, yet each poacher knew they may have as well been under a microscope. Panic and a feeling that somehow, someone had to do something filled each man's mind but there seemed no way to make these things happen. Their leader had given in to selfish revenge and ignored the immediate needs for his men and the camp. There was no direction, no answers. They were prisoners in a ring of light that could not be interfered with. Their expensive, high powered weapons were of no use against such a force as this. No one had even witnessed Jerry Taylor's death in the confusion, except for Ricky Dee, who had been talking to him when the arrow struck. Finally, confusion and urgency turned into a feeling of helplessness and defeat. Sam's idea of using the spotlights as an element of surprise had worked and probably minimized the number of casualties. The eleven remaining poachers from Thompson's West Hills Territory remained frozen in their tracks.

Sears stepped from the SUV, "Hands where I can see them. No one moves." Sears called to his men, "Round 'em up boys." The poachers held their hands high while the New Hampshire wardens approached with guns and handcuffs. One by one, the poachers were cuffed and stuffed into the SUVs. Then from the tall grass Corporal Aldridge yelled out, "Hey LT, we're going to need an ambulance."

Lee Sparks ran through the dark woods. The light from the illuminated field had since diminished behind him. He was concentrating on getting back to his jeep, *Don't think Sammy and the boys are gonna' need a ride out now. New Hampshire will take care of that. Gotta' get back to my jeep before they spot it.* Lee hit the access road that Stafford originally took to get to his position. *Ahh, finally, dirt road!* Lee stopped to catch his breath, listened for a moment, then took off in a dead run in a direction that took him back to the old logging road. When he got to the fork that would take him back to his jeep, the field's entrance lay only a quarter mile behind him. Lee stopped and looked back. The field, still illuminated by the high intensity spots, was now full of red and blue flashing lights too. *Good luck Sam. I hope you know what you're doing.* With that, Lee Sparks turned and trotted down the dark and lonely dirt road. His job was done here.

★ ★ ★ ★

Chapter 40

Sam sat quietly in front of Lieutenant Alban's desk. It was a place he had sat in many times before and also under adverse conditions such as this...but this was the worst trouble he'd been in yet. Alban paced back and forth behind the desk, not saying a word. He went from one side of the office to the other. Once in a while he'd stop pacing, stare at the floor, and then resume his pacing again. Sam was allowed to sit at attention and not say a word. He'd been sitting like this for close to an hour. His muscles were starting to ache. Sam thought to himself, *Well, come on, Alban. Get on with it. Fire me, send me to jail, yell...do something. This is killing me.* Sam considered the situation and tried to study Alban's face when he passed in front of where he sat. *I've always had to force the situation. Hmmm, but this situation is a lot more severe than he's used to. Aah, I'm going to give it a shot.* Sam started to blurt out a formal salutation, "Sir, if I may....," Alban turned, glaring at Moody and pointed his finger at him, cutting Sam short, "Shut your mouth, Mr. Moody." Sam thought to himself, *Uh oh, He's never called me Mr. Moody before.* Sam remained quiet. Alban resumed pacing, then stopped with his back to Sam as he stared out the office window. Alban began in a quiet, almost fatherly tone, "Sam, you were one of my best officers...without a doubt. I saw you come in from the academy. Hell, I had you on the boat before you went to the academy." Alban looked at the floor nodding his head, "Very promising officer, very promising." Alban went on, "You were always in the thick of it...yet you always made the right calls...even as a rookie. Then you pull something like this. Do you realize you had just made Sergeant? Passed the test and the promotion papers were completed before you went to court. You blew it Sam...really blew it."

Alban turned quickly and faced Sam. His voice started rising as he spoke, his face reddening, "Who the hell do you think you are? You take the law into your own hands, keep vital information from your commanding officer, endanger the lives of two other officers, and go on a manhunt in another state that is out of your jurisdiction." Sam continued to sit at attention and stared straight ahead. Alban paused glaring into Sam's eyes still not expecting him to speak. Alban took the pencil he had in his hand, snapped it in two and threw it across the room. He turned to look at Sam again and yelled into Sam's face. "There is one man dead, another wounded...who may lose the use of his right arm, and a fellow officer confined to a hospital bed, because of you. You are just lucky that old bastard didn't die." Alban turned away again and kicked the other guest chair across the room, then he continued to pace again as he spoke, "I seriously don't know what I am going to do, Sam. This situation has given rise to many other concerns. It's no wonder your nickname is Cowboy. This isn't even a mistake. From what you described in court, this was all premeditated...over a long time frame. It was planned in minute detail." He raised his voice again, "Hell, you even took advantage of another state's Fish and Game department." Alban stopped, as he seemed to be getting out of breath. He walked away from Sam again muttering, "I can't believe this."

The lieutenant stood staring at the floor. Finally he looked up and out the window. In a serious tone he began, "Sam, stand up and at attention." After Sam rose and settled into position Alban began, "Fish and Game Sergeant Samuel Moody, you are hereby demoted to Marine Officer with no rank. You are taking a reduction in pay of $20,000.00 per year and will be responsible for river patrol on a forty hour work week subject to emergency calls around the clock. This new position will begin after a thirty day suspension without pay. If you decide to fore-go the offer this department in the town of Thompson, Connecticut has offered, you are obliged to hand in your badge, radio, and police I.D., immediately. All weapons and town issued clothing will be collected before the end of that week." Alban turned and looked Sam square in the eyes, "Do you understand Officer Moody?" Sam had all he could do to keep his mouth from falling to the floor. "Yes, sir. I understand." Alban didn't answer. He just kept glaring at Sam. Sam thought, *I'm not fired? Thank God!* Alban turned away to the window putting his back to Sam, "Dismissed," came the curt reply. Sam turned quietly and headed for the door.

It was dinner time at the Moody home and Sam sat with his wife and three boys. No one spoke. The boys didn't know what had happened but they could sense the tension between Sam and Peg. Sam tried to bring up the subject, "Peg. I spoke with Alban today. Looks like I still have a job. I'm busted to river patrol with a reduction in pay." Peg raised her hand as if to stop Sam, "We're not discussing that now." Joey spoke up hearing what Sam said about the river, "Oh cool! Do we get to ride in the boat too?" Peg looked at the boys, "Never mind. Finish your dinner. You all have home work." Without even granting Sam a glance, Peg got up out of her chair and started clearing the table. Sam just watched her move about the room and thought, *Got a worse problem here. Can't blame her though. This will be the worst punishment I'm going to get.*

After dinner Sam went out to the farmer's porch that wrapped around most of his cabin. He looked up at the black night sky and just let his mind wander. Then his thoughts turned back to the stifled discussion at the dinner table with Peg. '*Not discussing this now,*' reiterating Peg's words. *When are we going to discuss it then? I know I endangered our family's way of life and put myself at risk but she understood that could happen when I took the job.* Sam looked down at the snow covered ground. *Guess she's got reason to be upset because I didn't explain what I was going to do, with her. It's not that I didn't trust her to keep it quiet...it's that I know she couldn't fully understand why I had to go get Farmer. ..and she probably wouldn't have allowed it anyway.* Sam thought back to the afternoon's discussion with Alban, *I made Sergeant during this whole deal! Wow!* A smile came across Sam's face then disappeared as fast as it had arrived. *Well that is of no consequence now...really screwed that.* Sam kicked a pebble that lay on the porch floor in front of him and watched it roll out onto the gravel driveway. Sam took a deep breath and decided to go up to his office above the barn.

As Sam climbed the barn's staircase he wondered how Stafford and James had made out as a result of the court hearing and their own meeting with Lieutenant Alban. Sam opened the door to his little hideaway above the barn and headed for the phone. *Think I'll give Stafford a call.*

The phone rang and rang. Finally a distressed sounding Tom Stafford answered, "Hello?" Sam spoke into the phone, "Tom, it's me Sam. How did you make out with everything?" There was a long pause then Tom said, "I got 30 days without pay followed by another 30 days for shooting Jaggs." Sam felt a sudden sadness that everything was his fault. Sam replied, "Did you lose anything?" Tom replied, "Well, I was up for Corporal but that's gone now." Sam replied, "I'm sorry buddy. It's my fault for getting you involved. Had I known you were up for promotion, I would never have asked for the help." Stafford said, "Nonsense. I'm a big boy. I made the decision to go, not you. I knew what the risks were. No one's at fault but me." There was a long pause then Stafford said, almost in a fatherly tone, "You know, Sam. They ought to congratulate you for what you did. Yeah, some people got hurt but it could have been a whole lot worse. You stopped a poacher that was raping the forests in several states and using his authority as an officer to do it. Who knows what other crimes he was linked to as a result of what he was doing with poaching animals." Sam remained silent. Then Stafford said, "How about you? How did you make out?" Sam replied quietly, "Busted to marine patrol officer." Stafford knew it would be extreme so he expected the worst but was shocked that they demoted such a promising officer so far down the ladder. It was, however, a relief to hear Sam still had a job. Once again there was silence on the phone. Sam could sense Stafford's uneasiness so he eased his way out of the conversation. "Good to hear your voice pal. Thanks for everything you did up there in New Hampshire. Gotta' go." Sam hung up the phone.

★ ★ ★ ★

CHAPTER 41

Sam spent the night in his loft. Peg still wasn't speaking to him. He turned in early and slept on the bottom rack of the old bunk bed in the corner of his loft. The night was a restless one. Dream after dream interrupted Sam's sleep. Every dream was a variation of what happened the night he attacked the poacher's camp. Jake Farmer's face would suddenly appear from nowhere, whether it made sense to, or not. He continued to wake through the night. Finally, he just lay on his back staring at the bottom of the bunk above him. *I have got to get closure with all this*, he thought. *There are too many players-too many people that were affected. Should I have just left the whole thing alone?* Sam was beginning to second-guess himself. He was starting to feel guilty for everything that had come as a result of Farmer's arrest. His own marriage was in jeopardy. Sam thought hard, *What is it about all of this that is really bothering me, anyway? Is it Farmer's incapacitated condition…the loss of life that occurred…the punishment my best friends will have to endure because of something I started…Peg's anger?* Sam decided to consider each and every scenario. He spent the entire night weighing one matter against the other and as the sun began to rise, he came to the realization that it was because of all those things he considered last night… and probably more that he hadn't thought of yet. In the end he figured he had done what he had to do and sometimes it doesn't make sense to anyone else, but he did it for all the best reasons, and accomplished what he had set out to do. The collateral damage that befell his friends and wife were a risk he knew he had to take, but the best thing he could do now, was try to make that better. Sam also came to the conclusion that he had no remorse for Farmer's outcome, or Billy Jaggs' condition either. Jerry Taylor's death was unfortunate, as the death of any living creature would be, but the man did intend to kill him, so Sam felt comfortable in dismissing the matter. He was glad Lee had been there for him, and although his best friend's life and welfare had been endangered, it was Lee who had made the decision to continue with Sam's plan.

Feeling better about himself, Sam jumped out of bed and started the coffee on his little potbelly stove. He watched the flame in the stove's burner as it warmed the old coffee pot. He was starting to relax. Finally, the pot began to perk. Sam waited for his favorite color to show in the percolator's glass and poured himself a cup. He took a sip of the hot, black, liquid, and then, very confidently, said aloud in the confines of the loft, "I'm going down to the house and tell Peg where I'm going, give her a kiss on the cheek, and then I'm going to meet Tom and Pat, and tell them how I feel. I'm going to see how they feel too." As Sam turned with his coffee cup for the loft door, he said aloud, "I am going to get all of this out in the open...Today!"

Sam drove down the road from his cabin smiling to himself. He was thinking that the look on Peg's face was of sheer confusion and surprise when he walked into the kitchen this morning, stated his intentions, kissed her on the cheek, and walked out the door. He felt like the old Sam again. He knew what he wanted to do and he was going to do it. It was the first time he saw her smile at him since he came home from New Hampshire. Maybe things would lighten up after all. Sam reached under the truck's dashboard, pulled out his cell phone, pushed the button for Pat James and waited. After a few rings he heard. "Hello…Sam? That you?" Sam smiled, "Yeah Pat, it's me. How's it going?" Pat replied, "Good…considering." Sam said, "Look, I'm on my way to meet with you and Tom. We're going to talk. Call Tom and tell him I want the both of you to meet me over at the cliffs, just east of the West Hills Territory, you know, by Bixler's Bridge." James replied, "Yeah, I know the spot. Be there in half an hour." "Good," Sam replied, and snapped his cell phone shut.

Sam sat on his truck's tailgate. He had backed his truck up to the cliff's edge that provided him a panoramic view of Thompson's West Valley and the rolling hills of the West Hills territory in the background. The view was amazing, absolutely beautiful! In the distance he could hear the shrill screech of a hawk as it hunted its prey. Far down below he saw two people standing in the river peacefully fly fishing. Unbeknownst to them, a lone deer sipped water from the same river just a few hundred feet upstream. He felt a sudden rush of enthusiasm and thought; *this is why I did it. I'm glad I did it! These are nature's gifts and I'll be damned if I'm going to let any man take advantage of that – of this!* He looked down at his watch, *Tom and Pat should be here any minute.* He looked up at the sky, closed his eyes and let the autumn sun warm his face.

Sam leaned back against the sidewall of the truck bed and was close to dosing off when he heard the distant rumble of a truck's engine. *Here they come*, he thought. *Late as usual.* The truck was getting closer as its engine noise became louder. Sam still lay in the bed of his truck, his feet dangling from the tailgate. He began to concentrate on the sound, *James' truck sounds a little loud. Must need a tune up. Either that or he's souped it up.* The approaching truck topped the crest of the hill and rounded the corner. He could hear the truck's engine getting louder as it picked up speed. Sam began to smile to himself, *Alright then! They're going to try to scare me. Thank God …they're back to their old selves. Never thought I'd catch myself saying that.*

While Sam lay listening to what he thought was Pat's truck, another truck had just come around the bend. It was Pat James and Tom Stafford, "Holy Shit!" Pat yelled as if shouting through the windshield of his Ford F150. The men felt helpless as they both took in the action only a hundred feet in front of them. A big red Dodge pickup truck had left its own travel lane and crossed the oncoming lane heading right for Sam. The truck picked up speed as it closed the distance between itself and the unsuspecting Sam Moody. Pat could see Sam's legs dangling from the truck's tailgate. Without looking at Tom, he yelled, "Why isn't he getting out? Why isn't he moving?" Tom looked on horror stricken as the big red dodge closed in on Sam. Pat yelled, "Sam get out…get out! He's gonna' kill you!"

Sam heard nothing except the approaching truck. Feeling lazy in the sun, he decided to open one eye, *These guys,* he thought, *just like kids,* and started to raise his head. He turned his head only to see the front grill of a large truck. Then everything went black.

★ ★ ★ ★

CHAPTER 42

Sam suddenly woke up. He was still lying in his bunk, safe in his loft above the garage. His heart was pounding as it might come through his chest. He felt out of breath. Sam sat up, rubbed his eyes, and murmured out loud to himself, "Another damn nightmare."

As if repeating his nightmare, Sam got up and went through his daily regimen. He had his coffee and looked out the loft window. He looked down toward the kitchen and tried to see if Peg was in the kitchen yet. *Yup, there she is*, he thought. *Doesn't look like she's in too good a mood.* Sam took a deep breath and straightened up, *I am going forth with my plan... ready or not.* Sam opened the door to his loft and proceeded down the stairs. He walked across the gravel drive and up the stairs to the farmer's porch that surrounded the cabin. As Sam entered the kitchen, Peg turned to see him and went back to busying herself around the stove. Sam began, "Honey, I'm going to meet Tom and Pat over by the Cliffs. We've got some stuff to iron out." Then he walked up to her and kissed her on the cheek. Peg continued cleaning a skillet. She just nodded her head without looking up. Sam turned and headed for the back door. As he reached for the door knob he heard Peg say, "Sam." He stopped and looked back at her without saying a word. She was looking directly into his eyes and her face was stiff with a serious expression, "Be careful. We have some things to work out too." Then her face softened and gave way to a small smile. Sam's heart felt as if it would explode. *There is a chance!* He thought. *Yeah, alright!* Sam replied, "Okay Babe, I'll be careful. We're just going to talk about our situation…get everything out in the open. I'll be back around noon." Peg smiled back. This time a bigger smile, *He's actually telling me what time he'll be back. Okay, maybe he's learned something.* Peg just nodded her head and went back to work on the skillet.

The drive out to the cliffs was just as it had been in Sam's dream. It was a drive he had taken many times before but under different circumstances. He looked forward to meeting with his two buddies. Suddenly, Sam thought to himself, *Should I get Lee over here too? After all, he's the one who actually took a life.* Sam thought about that for a while. *Hmmm, come to think of it, I haven't heard from that boy since that night in New Hampshire. I wonder if he's having nightmares too… or feeling guilty.* Sam thought about the kind of man Lee was. He wasn't the kind to get into sharing feelings or emotions either. *'Better leave him to himself,* he thought. *Can't call him because he doesn't have a phone. Guess I'll just get some cigars and pay him a visit someday soon. He probably wants to let his role in the New Hampshire deal just fade away…especially, because of Jerry Taylor.*

Sam reached the top of the long incline and rounded the bend. He had arrived at the cliffs. He pulled his truck over to the other side of the road and carefully backed up toward the drop off. There was no guardrail to keep anyone or anything from going over the edge except a very flimsy wooden plank and post arrangement. Like something you would see at the end of an old deserted road. Sam shoved the parking brake into place, opened the door and stepped out onto the gravel shoulder. He walked over to the back of his truck and let his tailgate down. He turned and looked out over the valley. The view was breath taking. He just stared for a minute. How he loved this place. He took a few deep breaths and closed his eyes. He was beginning to feel like the old Sam again. He felt his body relax, settling into a calm that he only got from being in the outdoors. He opened his eyes and sat down on the tailgate.

In the distance a truck could be heard ascending the steep incline to the Cliffs area. Pat James' truck rounded the bend just below the crest of the hill. He sounded his horn as soon as he saw Sam's truck. Sam turned and watched Pat drive up with Tom Stafford riding shotgun. Pat parked his Ford F150 nose in and next to Sam's truck. "Hey buddy," Pat yelled from the driver's seat. "Is this the place?" Sam smiled and nodded at the two friends. Things were getting back to normal.

Sam turned back to the valley and threw a stone out into the void that covered the valley below. Pat and Tom walked up behind him. No one spoke. The three men just stood there in silence taking in the view and the peacefulness. It was humbling. Finally, Sam said, "How have you guys been? Haven't seen you in a while." Tom curtly reminded him, "Since court." Pat cleared his throat, "I'm good, Sam. Uh, it's good to see you. Glad you called." Sam turned and looked at the two men, "Either one of you could have called me too, ya' know. Do I always have to be the one?" Stafford was quick to reply, "You can stick that attitude right where the sun don't shine old buddy. We have had as much to answer for as you. We're feeling everything you are." Sam stepped away from the truck, "I don't doubt that, Tom. That's why I asked you guys to meet me here today. There is a lot that I can't get comfortable with. A lot of it is guilt." James put in, "You're not feeling bad about that old bastard, Farmer I hope. He deserves everything bad that comes his way." Stafford said, "Or that Taylor character. He was going to kill you, Sam. As for Billy Jaggs, hell, I could have snuffed him easily that night. He was about to shoot you with Farmer's gun."

Sam was looking at the ground while his two friends got it out of their systems. They deserved to be bitter. He just let them speak their minds. Finally, there was silence. Sam began to speak and looked up at his friends as he did, "It's not that kind of guilt. The guilt is about how many people were affected by something I felt I had to do. Look at your careers...both promising officers with bright careers ahead of them. That has all been compromised now." Tom put in, "Sam, we still have our jobs–you realize that?" Sam replied, "Yeah, I do, but this will be in your personnel files forever." Pat said, "We made the choice, Sam. Not you." Sam looked at Pat, "But I put you guys in a bad spot. Deep down, I knew you wouldn't let me do this on my own. I took advantage of our friendship." Stafford said with a surprised tone in his voice and a lot of sarcasm, "Do you think we did all that because of our love and admiration for the great Sam Moody? Do you think we put our lives and careers in jeopardy because of you and you alone?" Sam didn't reply. He was beginning to understand that this wasn't just about him and his guilt. Stafford continued, "We're game wardens too, Sam. Just like you. We also believe in what we're doing or we wouldn't be who we are. Yeah, some people got hurt. Some inconveniences happened, but in the end we did what we had to do...what we believed had to be done...and we did it together...and we did it well. And now it's over. We made it, we're safe, and we still have those same careers. The bad guys are all done."

Stafford had put everything into perspective. He had said it well. He also made Sam realize that he hadn't really considered everyone else. He had been looking at this whole thing without considering anyone else's point of view. No one said a word for a few minutes. They were all glad to be getting these feelings out in the open. Now, after Stafford's speech, the feeling was that that there wasn't anything that couldn't be talked about. Sam asked a general question, "Are you guys having nightmares too?" James laughed and said, "You mean all night or just every time I close my eyes?" Stafford said in a very serious tone, "Yes Sam, every night. I think it's normal." Sam looked up and Tom was staring directly into his eyes. Tom continued, "Yeah, normal. Look, there were four of us against seventeen poachers. Poachers who think nothing of taking a life, and I mean animal or human, if it means a buck in their pocket. And because of what they do, they are all very good with guns and knives. I think that most of our problem with what happened is about what could have happened if things had got out of hand." Pat added, "Sam you had that attack so well planned, even down to the timing of when to call in New Hampshire Fish and Game. Those guys never had a chance." Stafford added, "Look, we only fired two shots. It's true all of us were only seconds from unloading more than that, but it turned out we didn't have to. We had the element of surprise and the cover of darkness on our side. If not for our careful planning and special training, the seventeen against four would have proven fatal. Our belief in what we do also played a special part in the outcome. Like I said before, we chose to be there knowing what the odds were. That gave us a huge edge."

Sam looked out over the valley again, shaking his head, "Two shots. Can you believe it? Only two shots, one from a bow and one from a rifle…against an entire poaching arsenal. That's amazing!" There was a pause, then Stafford asked, "Hear anything from your buddy, Lee?" Sam was careful about how he answered, "Nope. I thought about getting him up here today but you know how he is. He probably wants to let the whole thing fade into the sunset." Then Pat asked the question, "Did anyone ever suspect whose arrow had made the hole in Taylor's body?" Sam replied, "Forensics knew the damage was done by a hunting arrow. Everyone was questioned but no one even saw it happen, except for that kid, Ricky Dee, and all he saw was an arrow that suddenly appeared in Taylor's chest. The arrow was removed during the confusion. No one knows anything."

That night the Moody's sat down to the first family dinner that they had had in weeks. The mood was different. It was comfortable, easy. Everyone was happy. Maybe it was the way Sam was behaving now that he had gotten so much off his mind. Maybe he wasn't telegraphing those inner feelings to the rest of the family that he had unknowingly done in the last few weeks. Whatever it was, the usual banter and disagreements and laughing were now present and even Peg had more to say. She even laughed a few times. The family was healing and Sam was headed to a new career on the river.

★ ★ ★ ★